I0762750

THE LAST WOMAN OF WARSAW

ALSO BY JUDY BATALION

THE LIGHT OF DAYS

WHITE WALLS

THE LAST WOMAN OF WARSAW

A NOVEL

JUDY BATALION

DUTTON

DUTTON

An imprint of Penguin Random House LLC
1745 Broadway, New York, NY 10019
penguinrandomhouse.com

Information on the photos in this book can be found on pages 323–324.

Book design by William Ruoto

Library of Congress Cataloging-in-Publication Data has been applied for.

ISBN 9798217045686 (hardcover)
ISBN 9798217045693 (ebook)

Printed in the United States of America
1st Printing

The authorized representative in the EU for product safety and compliance is Penguin Random House Ireland, Morrison Chambers, 32 Nassau Street, Dublin D02 YH68, Ireland, https://eu-contact.penguin.ie.

In loving memory of my grandmothers, Zelda and Annie,
the young women of Warsaw.

And in loving memory of my mother, Sara, whose profound passion for Yiddish literature and Hebrew folk songs, and whose wariness of anything fashionable—especially political opinions—inspired every page.

THE LAST WOMAN OF WARSAW

Geneva

August 30, 1939

WARSAW. MILAN.

Two tickets.

She sat at the mahogany desk, thumbing the slips of paper, immeasurably thin yet thick with her entire future. Out the window before her: a grand boulevard, elegant cupolas, shop fronts flaunting sophistication, balconies bedecked in floral arrangements, in ombre no less, hues leaking seamlessly into each other. Soon, at dusk, the manicured lawns and magical lakes would give way to dazzling lights and the murmurs of champagne toasts.

Picture perfect. *It's all how you frame it.*

She took it in, capturing the serenity. *Click.*

East back to Warsaw or south to Milan.

What had she learned this past year? To follow her gut.

Out the window, smartly dressed women strolled along the even sidewalks with ease. She watched one woman cross the street, her coat end flapping just so, the triangle of contrast perfect; she was hardly rattled when she arrived an instant too late for her tram.

An instant.

All of fate was determined by moments. She knew this, she'd felt this. But it was the rare time when you were consciously treading on the turning point. When you *knew* the choice mattered.

Warsaw. Milan.

Sweating. Palpitating. She could hear her own heartbeat.

She recalled: He'd come in late last night, his stubble already angling for a morning shave. He was clutching the certificate. The ticket. *Hitler is through the gate, strolling up Poland's garden path. Take the train to Milan. Then, onward.*

Her dream. Her yearning.

Or. Her responsibility. Her roots.

She'd never said goodbye.

A knock on the door. She jumped.

"Mademoiselle," a muffled voice inquired. "Would you like help with your bags?"

What had she learned? That her decisions must be motivated not by fear but by desire.

"I'm fine," she managed to answer. She turned to look at her single leather suitcase, perched upright at attention, packed with undergarments, a few shirts. Enough for forever? What did one need, really need? "Thank you."

She fingered the knob on the desk drawer. Marble. Chiseled. Perfect.

She waited for another knock.

It didn't come.

It was up to her.

Warsaw. Milan.

She stood.

She picked up her bag.

She picked up one thin ticket.

Onward.

Twenty months earlier . . .

PART 1

Warsaw, 1938

Two young Polish girls look at a beauty parlor storefront in Warsaw.

CHAPTER 1

Fanny

The *LEŚNY MECH*, or wooded moss, was usually Fanny's favorite. Today, it comprised a spectacular bright green, spotted with lush red cherries, resembling a forest floor in bloom. Next to it, a square of sweet-cheese cake was bedecked by a perfect fractal of sliced apples and thick blackberries. The *herbatniki* biscuits, crunched with chocolate, sat by a grape meringue *placek*, which looked like a layer of thick snow, still fresh, perched atop the soaked fruit, reminding Fanny of her childhood winters on the slopes. The *miodowiec*, a dainty palimpsest of biscuit and custard, sat quiet but firm, while the lemon glaze on the poppy seed *makowiec* glistened in the afternoon sun's rays.

Fanny's eyes scanned the cakes, taking them all in as the baker went on about creams and wafers, melts, and mélanges. It was a veritable visual symphony of sugar and sweetness and joy, joy, joy. And yet.

All these delicacies in front of her, but Fanny couldn't fathom swallowing a thing. This was all supposed to be happy! *Once in a lifetime*, Mamo had told her. *You only get married for the first time once!*

Mamo, of course, was divorced.

"How delicious!" her mother now said, waving an icing-streaked fork in the air.

"Nu, try . . ." The caterer stabbed tines into a burgundy gelée and offered it to Fanny. The woman, round and doughy like her food, stood on the opposite side of the counter from Mamo and her.

Fanny moistened her lips, hoping in vain that this would catalyze a hunger pang. *Action creates reaction*, she'd once read. She brought the fork to her mouth. "Tell me again what's in this?"

"Whinberries," the woman replied. Then she addressed her mother. "These cakes you've selected could have been served to Piłsudski himself. What excellent taste you have, Madame Zelshinsky. You are more Polish than the Polish!"

Mamo beamed. "Well, what am I supposed to serve . . . babka?" To Fanny, who was clearly not eating, she added, "Don't be nervous, Fan-Fan. We'll pick one type for the main wedding cake, but we'll also serve three or four desserts in addition. Of course, they'll all be decorated with pastel roses of the finest confection. There's no need to hold back." And then, to the baker, "Put it on her father's tab."

Fanny noted how each piece of silverware was perched on the side of its plate like a row of soldiers standing at attention. If only Fanny could capture the angle . . . it reminded her of Professor P's ashtray shots, where she'd positioned articles to create a mood. Even inanimate objects, her mentor had explained, could evoke feelings. Fanny looked to the side of the kitchen where she'd left her camera bag; hidden but safe. She exhaled and forced herself to take a bite. The cake was soft like a pillow, but with a tangy cream nestled inside. A surprise twist.

"Remind me, where is the wedding taking place?" the caterer asked. "At a synagogue?"

"At *the* synagogue," Mamo said. "The Great Synagogue." For someone who didn't even fast on Yom Kippur, when it came to marrying off her only child, Mamo was strangely obsessed with religion.

"And when?"

"Six months to the day!" Mamo answered.

That feeling again, in the pit of her stomach.

"Try this torte and tell me more." Fanny noted how this woman handled Mamo. She'd sniffed out her soft spots, using them instead of fighting them. She'd just met her and was better at managing her than Fanny was after twenty years. "Who's the lucky bridegroom?"

"Simon Brodasz," Mamo replied. "He's on a professional tour, traveling all over Europe and even America. His mother's family are bankers, and the father, import-export. Like Fanny's father."

"I know the name."

"You do?" Mamo looked so pleased, but Fanny could tell that the old woman didn't.

Simon Brodasz. Fanny said it to herself. She'd known him since she was a young teenager, from weeks spent at their summer house just outside Radzymin, near what had been her grandparents' sugar factory. Their families had long been friends; they used to eat dinner together on the grand porch. Simon was always attentive, making sure she had sufficient servings of meat pâté, goose neck, and entertaining repartee. ("Do I impress you with my wit?" he'd once asked. "What wit?" she'd teasingly replied. "This wit," he'd said, and flexed his arms.) She could tell he fancied her, and Fanny liked being fancied. Eventually, Simon began to take her for long walks, and then, last year, dates in Warsaw, to gourmet ice-cream parlors and new restaurants whenever he was in town. Fanny had always known she had to marry *someone*, and here was a suitor who suited her needs: financial security, kindness, and a union that would bring their families together with so much joy, even providing Mamo with relatives of a sort. Simon had proposed a few weeks earlier, in Padereweski Park where he embraced her near a sculpture of a bathing woman. He'd wanted to set the wedding date before he left on his travels; they'd settled on a week after his return, in six months. The ring was a Brodasz heirloom, the cut a little gaudy, Fanny had thought.

She tried the name on in her head: Fanny Brodasz.

She picked up the next fork from the silverware cue but couldn't even manage to bring it to her lips.

"You're so pretty," the baker told Fanny. "And you're getting married so young! Most people are marrying later these days . . . I suppose it's good to get those children out of you quickly. Those gorgeous hips of yours—well, at least you had them for twenty years!"

"Yes, well, Fan-Fan is meant for marriage," Mamo asserted. "She was trained to be a beauty. A balabusta! She was never trained to work. She can't hack independence, like you, Pani."

Fanny opened her mouth, but nothing came out.

She reminded herself: She'd said yes, and Simon was nice and handsome, and he liked her, and he was more athletic than Jerzy, the law student with the acne, and more interesting than Michael, who had more horses than books. He was gentler than almost all the men Mamo had insisted she meet at the Europejski Hotel, the spot where years earlier Mamo had taken her to a ball and the newly released *Nikodem* swing had bounded through the lush interiors as Mamo had shown her off to celebrity actors and directors. More recently, her mother had been setting her up with growing urgency while awaiting Simon's proposal, just in case it didn't come. But he'd asked, and she'd said yes. Fanny would have a good life, experience the best there would be of 1938, 1948, 1958 . . . She'd be able to continue with her passions, wouldn't she?

"Well, I suppose for your strata, you're not that young. The shtetl Jews marry later, they need to save up."

"Exactly," Mamo said. "Not for the cream for Warsaw!"

"Warsaw," the old woman repeated and winked. "You know, it was not named for war, but for love."

Fanny knew this. She shook her head and looked down to avoid any more address. That's when she noted her watch. "Oh no, I'm late."

"For what?" Mamo asked, irritated.

"For class." She didn't mention which class, certainly not now.

"What a beautiful timepiece," the baker said.

"Thank you," Fanny said, but Mamo was already explaining how it was a Cartier, a gift from the betrothed.

"What should I do with the rest of these cake samples?" the baker asked. "Do you want them? Sometimes I give them to beggars outside . . . So much poverty these days."

"Let them eat cake!" Mamo laughed as Fanny cringed. "Fanny, tonight we must discuss dance lessons, and the flowers. Time is of the essence."

Fanny grabbed her bag and her coat, thanked the baker, and headed out the door to where her bicycle was parked.

"Oh, maybe we could do a bouquet with thyme!" Mamo called after her, giddy as ever, but Fanny didn't turn back.

WARSZAWA WAS NOT NAMED FOR WAR BUT FOR LOVE, FANNY repeated as she pedaled faster. This, she knew, was despite the city's long history of siege and recovery, of endless ransack and renewal. Its motto: "defying the storms." And yet the story goes: *Sawa* was a mermaid who chanted sweet tones. *Wars* was a fisherman who fell in love with her voice. But even if he caught her in his net, he could never have her for on land she would expire. Her beauty only existed where he could not go.

Fanny took her eyes off the road and looked out at her beloved Vistula, the longest river in Poland, connecting every one of its main towns and bisecting the capital. The water reflected the sky, an ombre of orange and red, and the farther Fanny traveled down the hill toward the university, the more of the view appeared. More of the river, more leafless winter trees, more white and cream brick buildings, each moment hinting at how much there was left to see, at how much one hadn't seen before.

The few bites of cake felt heavy in her stomach.

Fanny wanted to stop, to capture the scene in this particularly bucolic part of town, but . . . she checked the Tank watch. She was terribly late for class. It may not have been the wisest idea to use a bicycle on January roads, and Fanny pedaled faster as the cold wind cuffed her cheeks the way Nanny used to spank buckwheat pancakes with thick flour. Fanny reached up to secure her silk kerchief, cream with blush pink roses that reminded her of summer.

What had Professor Wanda Petrovsky said about photographing water? Was it to capture reflected rays? To show movement? Did water ever stop?

Could we ever really feel water, or did we just feel its temperature?

She couldn't recall how Professor Petrovsky—or Wanda, as Fanny referred to the legendary photographer in the privacy of her own head—had answered these questions. But Fanny did remember one thing her teacher had declared: *Art is like water. It soaks your hand while slipping through your fingers.* Contrast, juxtaposition—these were Wanda's guiding aesthetic ideals, shown in her close-ups of ornate Jugendstil-inspired office buildings with their wailing gargoyles, Art Deco vases posed like triumphant eagles, and illegal union marches.

Fanny's own portfolio sat awkwardly in her bicycle basket, and each bump caused her heart to skip within its shell. She was proud of its contents. Of course, her fashion photography was less broody than her teacher's oeuvre, but these were some of her best shots, including eleven close-ups of a customer at the Fashion Café who wore a woven pillbox hat—or rather, Fanny thought with some derision, the hat wore her. Though straight from the pages of *La Femme Chic* and *Przegląd Mody*, this hat was perched on the woman's head so gawkily it looked like it might topple off at any moment. The rest of the outfit, too, was all work, labored and ungenuine. Fanny's photos, she hoped, captured the effort behind how this woman presented herself, how "effortlessness" did not really exist. Oh, how she wished, how she prayed Wanda would call on her to present them! She usually called on the art majors, not the French ones, but maybe, just maybe, fate would be on her side today.

Suddenly, the road turned to reveal a new element of the vista—the water reflected not only the sun's rays but the side of the hill, sky and land, light and dark, breath and constriction, the sky reiterating the water, reiterating the sky.

Fanny jerked back on her breaks, jumped off her bicycle, kicked the stand, and took out her prized Leica camera from her satchel. *Click, click, click.*

The Vistula was the country's lifeline, its spiritual aorta. Fanny had toddled around its banks as a child at their family friend's country estate in Kazimierz Dolny, where all four of her Jewish grandparents—the Yiddish side and the Polish side—met for summer picnics. Her *Dziadek* had told her the legend of Princess Wanda who became the queen of Poland after the death of her father, King Krak. When Princess Wanda refused to marry the German Prince Rudiger, he took offense and invaded Poland. The Poles fought him off, but nonetheless Wanda committed suicide by throwing herself into the Vistula, all to ensure that he and the Germans would never invade their country again. This ancient waterway, Fanny saw now, flowed with legends, connected and divided at the same time.

Fanny brushed off these deeper thoughts and wasted no time jumping back onto her bicycle. Thank goodness for her new racing green lace-ups with only the suspicion of a heel. "*Allons-y*!" she said out loud as she picked up speed for the final sprint to the lecture hall, keeping one hand on her portfolio to make sure its precious contents stayed secure. She barely noticed her new ring.

"Coincidence, contagion, or epiphenomenon?" Professor Petrovsky asked, but with her booming voice it came out more like a proclamation.

Fanny could feel her pulse beat through her whole body. At the front of the class, Wanda held up an enlarged print. It showed a political rally, young people crushed together in central Warsaw. Framing the scene were two women, both shielding their eyes with their hands in the exact same way, same angle, same form.

"Did these women catch this gesture from each other unawares, or was it happenstance?" Wanda probed. "Did a separate phenomenon cause them both to shade their faces this way? Does this mirroring reflect nature's underlying logic, or has the artist imposed her eye on the scene? Do we search for the patterns in this world, or"—here, she paused and cast her sharp eye over the crowded classroom—"do we create them?"

These lofty ideas made Fanny feel faint, as if her whole self could just buckle. Instead, she gathered herself and leaned over her fellow students to get an even better view of Wanda's masterpiece. Wanda was barely even older than Fanny, maybe in her late twenties. And yet there was a generation gap of knowledge.

"The religious do not believe in coincidence," Wanda declared. "Neither does Freud!"

Wanda's short hair sat flat along her cheeks and her sweater had a fashionable sailor-suit collar. Even if not a bohemian, she was still a true artist. Fanny imagined herself ten years in the future as an art professor, her photos hung at all the city's important cafés and galleries. "The photography queen of Warsaw," she would zip around town on high-speed metros but, in contrast to Wanda's curt functionalism, would wear long flowing gowns bedecked in shimmering floral prints, which, she was sure, would be the cutting edge of design in 1948.

"Finally," Wanda said, "are these women shading themselves from the sun, or from what it illuminates, from sniffing the dirt right under their noses? From their own class privilege?"

A few hands shot up.

"I'm not looking for answers!" the teacher cautioned. "I am only looking for questions."

Quiet, surprised murmurs ricocheted through the class. If only Fanny had a question, something clever and poetic. She promised herself she would say something, at least *one thing*, before the term was over.

"I called this photo: Shades of White."

More murmurs, this time of approval.

On Fanny's trip with her mother to Paris last year, they happened upon a Claude Cahun exhibition. Fanny had stood agape in front of one self-portrait, a version of the artist looking like a man, cropped hair, checkered collar, serious facial expression, scrutinizing her viewers—all of this in front of a mirror that reflected her image, but at a jaunty angle, so her piercing eyes seemed vulnerable, off in the clouds. How many versions of a person existed? Did Cahun control what the viewer thought of her, or did Fanny, the viewer, dominate the artist? These questions had shaken Fanny just as Wanda's did: Are we nothing more than what others see in our reflections?

After the exhibit, they'd gone shopping, straight to Galeries Lafayette. Feeling flush, Mamo had bought her a camera on a whim, mostly because Mamo enjoyed flirting with the salesman. Since then, Fanny had been taking photos of what she knew best, her first love: clothes. Fanny quickly understood the power of the click, how the whole world folded into that moment. When she looked through the lens, homing in on a perfect seam, a twist of textile, the pose of an arm, nothing else mattered—no past, no future; she was alive.

It's a cute hobby, her mother had agreed, *taking photos of clothes. Men like a woman with a hobby,* she'd said. *But keep in mind that a woman of your class does not take her hobbies too seriously.* This was before Fanny had been engaged. They had not discussed what would happen once Fanny was a Mrs., but she assumed Simon, who always seemed tickled by her passions, would let her finish her degree. Wouldn't he? She'd been too nervous to ask.

Soon after Paris, Fanny had begun visiting photo galleries here in Warsaw and had come across a Petrovsky, which had stopped her in her tracks. The image was of a storefront; two girls in thick braids and wool coats looked intently at the beauty supplies on offer, curled wigs and chic lipsticks displayed on curvy mannequins. The viewer did not see the girls' faces, only the inanimate models' dazzling smiles, as if these dolls were the reflections of the aspirational young women trying on new versions of themselves. *What might I become?* Then she found out that Wanda Petrovsky taught at the university; Fanny enrolled in her class right away, even though it didn't count toward her major. She was immediately taken by her no-nonsense tone. Wanda had gravitas, a self-seriousness that Fanny only dreamed of.

Fanny hadn't told anyone she was at this seminar. Not Professor Nowak, who would scold her for wasting time by taking art classes, and certainly not Mamo. Months earlier, when she'd mentioned that she was considering auditing an art class, Mamo had panicked, accusing her of becoming another Tamara de Łempicka, *a girl from one of Warsaw's finest families who became the finest floozy in Paris!*

Mamo, she's a famous painter! Fanny had tried.

Oh please, Mamo said. *She paints titties. Warsaw's crème de la crème must stick to the top.*

"White," Wanda now went on. "Some say it's cold and stark. But it's also aggrandizing. White makes everything look bigger. White gives us breathing room. White is the presence of all color, yet it lacks a hue. It lets us choose. White is *agency*! Speaking of which, whose homework will we look at today?"

"Mine!" The word slipped off Fanny's lips before she even thought of it. Suddenly, all eyes were on her. The wood-paneled room felt enormous.

The professor was silent. Waiting.

Oh boy oh boy oh boy, she had really done it. "Okay, then." Fanny fumbled with her portfolio. With trembling fingers, she flipped past the hat images and instead picked out a close-up of a wool skirt with striped folds, draped down her own leg. Here was a peasant pattern, which she was recasting in a new light. Literally.

Fanny had taken this shot a few weeks earlier when Wanda's homework assignment had been to "defamiliarize." The students were supposed to present an expected view in a new way, or as Wanda had instructed, "force us to *see* something we're already looking at." That day, Wanda had shown the class one of her close-ups of a glass vase that showed her own reflection, camera and all, as if the artist and the object were in direct conversation. Wanda had won awards for that image in her early career. That evening, at home, Fanny suddenly *saw* Mamo's vases, not just as flower receptacles but as objects that surrounded her, that knew her. Sitting in her drawing room, imagining a conversation with Wanda (*What is familiarity, really?*), Fanny had looked down and noted her own skirt, which was embroidered with elements of a folk pattern that she'd barely noticed earlier. It had struck her how in that mix of high and low, a Polish fashion could emerge, one genuine to her country, not copying the French or trying to be something it was not. She looked at the image now: juxtaposition, contrast, all of it. It was one of her best.

Professor Petrovsky examined the print, then held it up for the whole class to see. "The light is interesting. But what does this photo *mean*?"

"Mean?" Fanny was being critiqued, challenged, taken seriously. She was delighted.

"What in the world *is* this?" Professor Petrovsky bellowed.

Fanny felt her cheeks go hot. "A skirt."

"A skirt?"

"Yes, a peasant skirt, with traditional striping, but—"

"Are you interested in the proletariat?"

"I'm interested in our folk traditions and how we can incorporate them into—"

"Do you know what 'skirt' means?" Wanda interrupted.

"A garment that fastens on the—" Fanny tried.

"'To skirt' is to avoid danger. To avoid discovery. I need you to be *inside* the danger. I need you to be where every cell of yours tells you not to be. Not all art is overtly political, but politics are always implied. In your work, I want to see your perspective, and truth. You and the universe, wrapped in one."

No pressure. Fanny nodded.

"Bring me a picture that is both from your unique point of view and authentic to others. Something relative, yet absolute. This is a complicated and ambivalent notion, but in every photograph, we must see the mark of the photographer and yet the photographer cannot exist at all!"

"Is she losing her mind?" a student in front of Fanny whispered.

"Remember," Wanda went on as she handed back Fanny's photo, sliding it directly into the portfolio—on the bottom. "The meaning of a work is not always immediately clear, even to the artist. Sometimes it's emotional. You feel it, a shiver. *That's* the artist in you."

The artist in her. Fanny flushed, thrill and mortification all wrapped in one.

"Now, I have an important announcement. *Very* important. It's about your exhibition." Wanda cleared her throat. "As those of you enrolled in the arts program know, you will be putting your best work on display at the end of the term. The exhibition will take place in the university hall, and this year, in attendance will be not merely your peers and teachers but gallerists. From Paris."

Paris! The room buzzed.

"I can't promise anyone will show interest in your photographs, but this is a unique opportunity to share your talents and demonstrate what you've got—vision, grit, potential. This show could be the beginning of your independent career, launching you as a bona fide artist. You have five months to prepare."

Independent career. The words rang in Fanny's ears.

Five months. Just before the wedding . . .

And then she knew: This here was her answer! She could show Mamo that she was independent, that she could pursue her ambitions and lead a life of her own.

Reality flashed in front of her. Life with Simon would be like life with Mamo: dinner parties, hotel waltzes, skiing in Zakopane, keeping up with the Curies. It would be a life where Fanny disappeared, her outlines dissipating into her surrounds, her identity vanishing into her role and position, into children and society functions. It would never be a life with a Leica. It would never be a life in which she could have her own vision.

She understood her stomach: She did not want to marry Simon.

This. Fanny wanted *this.*

"But remember," Wanda went on. "This is only for art majors. The show is not open to students from other departments, even those enrolled in this class. I want to see ten possible photographs from each of you eligible students next week."

The class erupted into excited chatter as the bells chimed.

Fanny couldn't breathe.

"Professor Petrovsky?" Fanny approached the lectern. She had nothing to lose, everything to gain. "Is there any universe in which I can convince you to include my pictures?"

"It's not up to me, Miss Zelshinsky," Wanda said.

"Why not? It should be!"

"Well, that's true." Wanda almost smiled.

Perhaps Fanny knew how to handle people more than she'd thought. "Please, Professor, I'll do anything." Fanny immediately began to tidy Wanda's papers.

"I'd like to help you, I would," Wanda said. "Your work today, though imperfect, was better than ever before. I see that you're growing in this class, Zelshinsky. I see a future. Besides, the exhibition needs more female artists. Why *aren't* you an art major?"

Fanny was embarrassed. "My mother thought that French was more ladylike."

Wanda shuffled through her open briefcase and retrieved a light pink page. She showed it to Fanny: It was a petition form to switch majors.

"Why don't you come to my office tomorrow at five p.m. Bring your best shots. If you can convince me that they belong in the show, if you can show me the shiver, I'll petition for you to change to the art major at the last minute. I believe the committee will meet one final time this term."

In a swoop, Fanny straightened Wanda's piles, wrapped her rosy kerchief around her head, and headed for the door. "You won't regret this. I'll be there tomorrow."

CHAPTER 2

Zosia

Cracked hands running through flour; wrinkled fingers swatting flies. *You are the child I trust. You will take over.* Who was speaking to her? Someone who was both there and not there. Someone who was missing. *You.* She sensed the body behind the voice, recognized the tone, the energy, and yet. There was something she couldn't remember, a finger missing from a hand. *You.*

Corn and peas. Salt and pepper. Caraway, all bittersweet, striped like an insect. She poured them into canvas bags, careful not to mix, not to spill. *Every grain counts.*

Then, suddenly—search lights. Searing, sinister illumination. A light so bright it hurt, so bright it turned all to blaze, to blank, occluding that which it elucidated. The gleam was directed at her, at them, at her home, hearth, heart. *Close your eyes and pray.*

Come! *You!* They were running, running, knocking on a door, hard wood, jammed tight. *Please, please, let us in, please*—

And then, as if emerging from under the earth, a shriek. A scream curling off her like the smoke off a burning onion, louder and louder and—

"Hey!" Someone was shaking her, waking her.

For a long moment, she had absolutely no idea where she was.

"It's your stop," the conductor said.

"My stop?" She nodded her head back and forth, trying to jiggle her disorientation into reality.

"It's time!"

She stared out the window as the train came to a halt. She read the sign: "Chełm."

Chełm? Legendary town of fools. Locus of misunderstandings and mistakes.

"This isn't my stop." Zosia had a way to go. She forced herself awake. *Come on, Zosia, get it together.* She was on the move.

As the train approached Warsaw, Zosia stared out the window at the cold afternoon, already dark around the edges. She took a deep breath, gathered herself, and watched as shiny cars and braying horses fought for their right of way on streets that catered to different centuries at the same time. Mongers, neons—opposing worlds shared the same space, coexisting among the cream-colored buildings with their slouching cupolas and slanted roofs. *Little Paris*, it was called.

Zosia put out her cigarette and alternated the grip of her hands, right over left, left over right. The first position was so instinctive, she barely noticed, yet the second was so odd, it felt as if you were holding the hand of a stranger. A simple twist, and everything changed. *For we were once strangers in a strange land*, her father used to quote from the Torah, shaking his finger, reminding them of the importance of compassion.

Zosia wasn't a stranger here, not quite. This wasn't her first time in Warsaw, but it was her first time *moving* here, though this was just a temporary stop on her journey. At least, she desperately hoped so. She was here for Dror, or "Freedom," her youth movement. *Home is where you stop running*, they said. And for Zosia, that would be in the ancient Jewish homeland, the ancestral Eretz Israel.

To be in charge of our own destiny. To be agent and self-sufficient. To live our fullest lives.

Zosia had been given a new leadership position and was in the city to pursue her goals: to help those in need, to better the world, and to get on the visa list so she could acquire the coveted papers, move to British Palestine, and work to create an autonomous and socialist Jewish state. Today was her inaugural lecture at the national headquarters; though not a formal audition, today's speech could decide her direction. If all went well, they might make her the new head of education, which she hoped would mean she'd be prioritized for a visa. A full year of work in the movement, and it boiled down to right now. She took a deep breath.

The train slowed to a halt, a tinny screech all the way to the stop. Announcements passed in a city Polish that was quicker than the country lilt she was used to. The conductor declared: "Warsaw Central!"

"Can I help you with your bag?" a man asked, and she jumped, startled.

"No, thank you." Zosia reached above for her luggage. If she couldn't lift her bag by herself, it meant she had brought too much. One needed to hold one's own burdens. Self-sufficiency above all. *She* was the carrier, the savior.

She grabbed her satchel. As she had packed it the night before, folding each of her belongings into thin squares, she recalled how her mother used to stay up all night laundering her daughters' shabby rags. She'd made it a priority for them to have crisp clothes, to appear as well-off as the others in town, though no one in Byten, with its one gaslit main road, was all that well-off.

As Zosia glanced out the window at the bustling platform, she recalled that today was *Rosh Chodesh*, the beginning of a new month on the Jewish calendar. She remembered her childhood: Tateh reciting extra prayers, her little sister Bella parading around in a semi-sewn dress, and Mameh busy in the kitchen. On Rosh Chodesh, Jews were supposed to add an additional dish to their usual meal, a beautiful tradition but one that, Zosia knew, caused financial strain, even for a small tray of noodle kugel. After all, since she'd been nine years old, Zosia had been the one to help her father with the books; each week, they'd stood over the counter in the back room, Zosia adding and subtracting as Tateh read expenses. Zosia suddenly recalled their very last hug, gripping shoulders, breathing in sweat, spices, soaps. In hindsight, she'd been memorizing her parents' smells.

Now, Zosia shook off all these memories. She had made her choice. She was leaving—for Warsaw, and then for the Levant. Her family had never understood, and would not join her. Bella, after all, was engaged to be married—but Zosia had to leave.

As the movement had taught her: no distractions.

Zosia disembarked the train. She fastened her long wool coat, inherited from a widower neighbor, that was lined with fur at the neck and wrists. It had seemed like a needless extravagance until she felt the damp cold. The station was a sea of bowler hats and peddlers hawking soda water; Zosia stumbled her way through the crowd. It dawned on her to take a tram to headquarters. But no, she would not waste złotys.

Outside, she got her bearings and, following directions, darted along the streets toward the Jewish Quarter, past chicken liver sellers and jugglers, careful not to slip on the snow-dusted sidewalks and right into the cucumber vendor or the local schlepper who was balancing a particularly oddly shaped load.

"What's wrong with you?"

"Sorry!"

Stupid, she scolded herself. She wasn't used to the way people were in your face, too close.

"Pssst," she heard from behind her.

Zosia pivoted. A man looked at her with crazed eyes and laughed.

"Never make eye contact, dear," a passing woman advised.

"Oh, thank you." She pivoted to face a newsstand. There was an overwhelming selection and, among them, dozens and dozens of the city's Jewish publications, which were socialist, religious, anti-religious, Zionist, anti-Zionist, and every permutation thereof, printed in Yiddish, Polish, and Hebrew. In Byten, several families shared one sole paper: You had to be careful not to spill your buttermilk, sour cream, or herring on it, or the next household would be mad! Here, she glanced at the copious headlines: The association of Polish trade unions had been founded; The Camp of National Unity, with their platform based on Nuremberg laws, was being recognized as an official Polish party; the Polish Council of Physicians was planning to exclude Jewish and Slavic members. Zosia felt herself tense; the Jews may have been emancipated, but they were not equal citizens. Not even close. She'd seen firsthand what lurked under the surface, what could erupt at any second.

"You read, you buy!" the salesman hollered above the traffic, shaking her from her thoughts.

"Sorry." She turned away, acclimatizing to Warsaw's ways. "Not what I'm looking for."

Well, at least her Hebrew was good enough to read headlines. She'd come from a working-class family, from a religious shtetl where Yiddish was the main language. She was a public-school girl and had not had Hebrew tutors like many of the other comrades who were preparing to make aliyah; she was teaching herself the *ima*-tongue whenever she had a rare moment of free time. She should probably use some Hebrew words in her lecture today.

Zosia picked up her pace, passing busking fiddlers and fruit stalls loud with bargaining over afternoon produce.

"Fresh bagels, three groszy!" a vendor called. Her stomach rumbled—but no excesses. Instead she rehearsed her opening lines in her head. *To be in charge of our own destiny. To be agent and self-reliant. To live our fullest lives.*

"Groszy, please, groszy . . ." Zosia turned to see two children holding hands, an eight-year-old boy and his little sister, maybe two or three. Their limbs were thin like the legs of chickens and barely covered by jackets that were too small. Dirt was streaked across the little one's cheek. "Please . . ."

A woman in an enormous fur coat, as if the entire Warsaw Zoo were on top of her, ignored them. Zosia watched as the toddler pulled at the hem. "Don't touch me!" she scolded and stormed off. The kids flinched in surprise, then sat down in the gutter.

Zosia returned to the bagel seller and handed over six coins, warm from her pocket. "I'll take two. Hey, *chapt dem*!" she called to the kids, and threw over the twisted round doughs as if she was pitching horseshoes.

They scuttled over and caught them. "*A dank, a dank.*"

"My pleasure," Zosia said as she hurried off. Like most of the population outside the big cities, her family too had struggled since the Great Depression. New department stores and large factories meant that Jewish artisans and small shopkeepers suffered. People in her town had been known to use eggs as currency. Jews were shut out from so many trades, from jobs in national and municipal governments to public transport and railroad work. The Dror family also struggled. Austere measures were the norm; hers was a life of beets and cabbage, borsht and sauerkraut. For every fox fur, there were a thousand Poles going hungry.

Zosia had no future here.

And then, there she was, at the Dzielna address. Zosia entered the courtyard, passing the wealthier apartments that faced the street and were graced by sunlight, to the back of the building where the country's Labor Zionist youth headquarters was housed. Her new home. For now.

Zosia schlepped her suitcase up several flights of stairs to reach her assigned room, where a young woman was piling clothes on a cot. "Are you Rachel?" Zosia asked. "I heard we'd be roommates."

"And you must be Zosia," the brunette responded. She had a freckled face and round features. "I'm afraid I'm heading out of town for a few days. Just packing now."

"Where to?" Zosia couldn't help but be disappointed. She knew no one in Warsaw well and had been hoping that her new roommate might at least show her the ropes.

"I'm off to the provinces to lecture on the history of Jewish poetry," Rachel said as she examined a sweater. Zosia detected her literary Vilna accent. "At least you'll have the room to yourself."

"I don't need much space," Zosia replied as she took in two small cots and a gas lamp. The "shelving unit" was comprised of a series of milk crates. On the floor were piles of worn notebooks and novels. *The Count of Montecristo*, she noted. "I think we've seen each other at conferences from afar," Zosia said when Rachel didn't respond. She was sure they'd danced the hora together at an Oneg Shabbat celebration last summer, stepping the vine and flowing in a circle as they chanted the new song "*Mayim, Mayim*," celebrating the recent find of a new water source in Palestine's Kibbutz Na'an. "How long have you been in the movement?"

"Five years," Rachel replied. "I am passionate about Jewish literature. It's poetry that brought me to Dror. A sequence of words can evoke feeling; there is truth in rhythm. That's what I'll be teaching. What about you? What brought you to Dror?"

Zosia placed her bag on the spare bed, now hers. Her case looked shabby in comparison to Rachel's. "I'm a shtetl girl," she said. She was certainly not the only small-town girl in the group, even though it sometimes felt that way. "About a year ago, a blond girl, Dvora, who used to come to our family's grocery to buy dill, told me about the movement. *We will better the world*, she'd said. *We help the poor, we care for the weak, we develop ourselves for the good of the group. We prize Jewish dignity*. She invited me a few times, and finally I went to a meeting at a nearby Peretz library."

Zosia thought back to that first Dror meeting. It was mere weeks after that fateful night, back when she had not known what to do with her anger and fear. Zosia had cowered at the back of the room, barely able to mumble hello, nervously examining everyone in their neat blouses and ties and confident smiles. But once the lecture began—she could still remember it, given by a tall woman who commanded attention without even talking, about the importance of Jewish self-determination—Zosia's self-consciousness dissolved, and she became fully ensconced in Dror's mantras. Here were solutions, not complaints. Here was promise: of a Jewish land, of autonomy. Here was hope: for peace. Her life had become so heavy and panicked, but at that meeting, she understood that she'd been experiencing the pain of a people. No wonder these groups were the cornerstones of the Jewish youth; they focused on the future, a future that was not about turning inward while stocking spices and kasha, as she would be doing in the grocery, but about fighting for justice, equality, and dignity. Here were people who saw the dangers, but instead of grumbling, they were active, optimistic, and smart. And they were all friends. All these people who knew each other, who liked each other, coming together for the good of the Jewish people—it was dizzying.

Zosia walked out that night with a new life purpose. She walked out, feeling better.

In the short time since, Zosia had rocketed from rank-and-file comrade to regional leader. Not that rank mattered: equality above all! She'd started an initiative to send poor young Jewish children from her area to summer camps, offering them weeks of fresh air and hot meals. She'd worked on a local farm and delivered food to orphanages where she also taught Jewish children about holiday traditions. She attended all the symposia and conferences she could afford, and she read, read, read. The leaders said they'd never seen anyone work as hard and as fast as she did. Zosia took care of sick comrades, cooling their fevered brows. She began to find her feet as a teacher and started to lecture, in particular about class consciousness. Dror had even asked her to participate in the national kosher-law-appeal campaign; her role was to sit in on planning meetings and report back. She was meant to learn how to act.

Zosia had given up everything, including her role in the family business and her religious observance, for this secular movement that had taken up almost every second of her life, and indeed that saw itself as "the primary family." This busyness she appreciated, as it kept her out of her head and in her skin. *No distractions, move forward, go, go, go!* . . . Plus, it was all for the greater good, for the future of the Jewish people, and for the dream of embarking rocky ships across the rushing sea. For the dream of leaving Poland.

"So you've been with Dror for only one year?" Rachel repeated, oozing condescension. "Things have changed. We need to work harder than ever now. The British are offering fewer and fewer visas for Jews to go to Palestine." Rachel closed her packed bag and sighed. Zosia understood: Visas had spiked in availability after the Balfour Declaration and the British commitment to creating a Jewish homeland, but since the swell of German Jewish emigration from 1935, and the Arab Revolts that began in 1936, the allotted number had decreased and they'd become much, much harder to obtain. "We're losing steam. They're calling us 'romantic dreamers,' and not in a nice way. The chances of aliyah are going down by the minute."

"I know." Zosia's heart began to race. With increasing anti-Jewish laws, hooligans, and political parties here in Poland, tensions were on the rise. Sure, Jews had lived in the country continuously for over one thousand years, and had dealt with their share of threats during that time, but life felt more frightening now, unstable and hopeless. Zosia realized these fears might reflect her own take, emphasized by her personal situation, but there were so few chances to get out and make a better life. She needed to get a visa before there were none left at all and the gates closed for good.

She took a deep breath and reminded herself that she was a comrade, a leader in the movement. It was her duty and her calling to uphold her ideals, strengthen Dror's bonds, and create a place where Jews felt safe. Zosia sometimes told people that her last name was "Dror."

"Okay, well, I'm heading out to meet someone," Rachel said. "Good luck today with your lecture. Hopefully, I'll catch it before I need to leave for the train. Everyone's talking about it. Oh, and welcome!"

"*Todah rabah*," Zosia said, thanking her in Hebrew. "Good luck to you too."

"THE REAL BEAUTY OF THE PROMISED LAND, ERETZ ISRAEL"—Zosia stressed the Hebrew and neared her conclusion—"is that we can be in control without apology. We can ride at the front of the train. And the middle of the train. And the back of the train. Our own train. Driven by our own drivers." She paused. "I too am just a Jewish girl finding her way, but it is through our collective goals that we will become realized and fulfilled."

The forty faces in front of her, including Mira, the national leader, were rapt. Zosia considered for a moment going off-script. As a child, her parents used to make her climb up on a kitchen stool and speak every time they had guests over. They wanted their painfully shy daughter to learn to express herself. Back then she'd utter a few words, jump off the stool, and flee. Look at her now.

"We need to focus our energy on the work that matters: self-actualization, the pursuit of truth, and caring for the members of our community—and our world—who are disadvantaged and cannot care for themselves."

The eager faces nodded.

"*Chazak v'amatz!*" she called out in Hebrew. Be strong and brave.

The group broke into applause.

Zosia breathed relief. She tugged the edges of her jacket and remained tall at the front of the room as the crowd began to mill.

"Your earnestness is compelling," a leader from Bialystok told her. "You speak from the heart."

"What a wonderful Yiddish accent," someone else said. "So folksy."

"Thank you," Zosia muttered. People crowded around her. She felt wobbly. And then, she heard it start up again: the sound that had come and gone, usually emerging at the worst time, haunting her for the past year. It was faint, but pungent, and then louder—

"I just need a moment," Zosia blurted to drown out the timbre of the scream. She made her way to the window. She struggled to open the pane, but at last it lifted and she stuck her head out. She lit a cigarette and peered into the courtyard. The headquarters were located in the interior of this labyrinthine tenement. The less light, the lesser view, the cheaper the apartment. She looked onto other windows that reflected back her own poverty and commonplace. Finally, stillness in her head.

"Zosia, we'd like to talk to you." Mira was now behind her. "Do you have a minute?"

"Of course." Zosia collected herself and followed Mira to a corner of the room where several leaders congregated. A man Zosia recognized for his impassioned seminars on the importance of working the land and reaping spiritual nourishment from Jewish pastures was smoking. Yossi, who directed youth theater and ran music programs, leaned against the wall holding his guitar. Malka, a Warsaw comrade who, Zosia heard, had forfeited a scholarship to Haifa University to stay in Poland and lead a musical performance workshop for the city's impoverished Jewish youth, pulled over a rickety chair. Zosia knew that Malka's family had also experienced a trauma when their butcher shop had been ransacked in a Jewish boycott rally. All of them, principled and dedicated. The cream of the self-grown crop.

Then, by the door. There he was.

Abram.

Had he been here all along?

Handsome, tall, with intelligent eyes, he had a soft way of moving. His burly torso, his thick head of hair. He was a rising leader as well. They had been in the same study group for a couple of weeks last spring, and he'd also participated on the kosher law-appeal campaign. Her crush had been instant, but she could barely look him in the eyes.

Now she glanced at his broad shoulders, long legs, biceps like challahs. She imagined him folding himself over her again and again like origami; she'd lose herself in his peppery warmth. Her heart fluttered.

She needed to pull herself together. *Attraction is distraction.* That's why the movement did not allow it. Or at least, strongly discouraged it. Passion was messy.

Besides, she reminded herself: She was leaving. Warsaw was just a temporary stop. There was no time for feelings. For silly, wasteful feelings.

"As you know," Mira began, her green eyes darting back and forth across the room before settling on Zosia, "we have all been impressed by your work and are very excited that you are joining leadership here in Warsaw."

"Thank you so much." Zosia was sweating. "I am fully committed to the movement," she said, then quietly added, "and I'd love to lead education."

"You have many talents to share," Mira went on. "Leadership will have a meeting tomorrow, and we'll let you know in the next few days which section you'll head up." The next few days? So long to wait. "We'll also let you know who your teaching partner will be." Every study group had a male and female leader, the "parents."

"Thank you."

"In the meantime," Mira added, "you have a message. Wanda. She wants to meet with you. I assume you know her?"

"Of course." Wanda Petrovsky was a senior movement figure, audacious and bold, at the center of most new initiatives and old fracases. She was also a working-class girl who grew up in the town next to Byten. In fact, she was the very woman who'd been delivering the lecture she'd recalled with Rachel earlier. Once, Zosia remembered, she'd been nervous before a talk, struggling to find her voice at the microphone. *You must rise to the occasion,* Wanda had told her, then literally picked her up right on the stage. But, other than that, Wanda, who was also an artist, had never paid Zosia much attention at all. In fact, Zosia had found her to be rather standoffish, which had surprised her given their common roots.

"Go to her office at the university tomorrow. She said she had to tell you something right away."

Really? Zosia lit a new cigarette and exhaled, with some relief and a thrill of pleasure. These were all good signs that she was being taken seriously. Wanda was finally noticing her. "I'll be there, of course," Zosia replied, nearly saluting, as Mira walked off.

"Wanda," Zosia thought, *meant "wanderer" in Polish, but "healer" in Hebrew.*

"Hey." Rachel pulled on Zosia's sleeve. "Is it true Wanda wants to meet you at her office?"

Zosia nodded.

"Wow," Rachel winked at her. "Lucky."

"What do you mean?"

"Her last two protégées both got visas," Rachel said. "Pesia just left for Eretz last week! And now that I think about it, I believe they were both country girls like you."

"Interesting." Zosia tried to keep her cool. But could it be that Wanda had cherry-picked her to be her next mentee and that she was on a direct path to aliyah? "Thank you for letting me know."

Rachel grabbed her luggage and said farewell. Zosia, flustered and energized, looked over to see if Abram was still by the door. He wasn't.

She felt her heart droop, just a little. Then she told herself it was for the best.

No distractions.

Zosia had a mission. To work hard and get out of Poland.

CHAPTER 3

Fanny

FANNY RUSHED, RUNNING HOT IN THE MORNING'S COLD. Silence, except for boots squeaking through the snow. She clutched her bag and pulled it into her side, as was her habit, only this time her hands shook. She breathed in, then slowly exhaled, the smoky condensation curling up around her cheeks. She felt like a spy, a grand secret tucked under the layers of her fabrics.

Fanny felt wide awake even though she'd been up the entire night looking through her photographs and negatives. She'd selected her seven best prints from that shoot of the pillbox hat at the Fashion Café. Then there were three more negatives from a series she'd done of a wool blazer that her father had accidentally left hanging in their apartment, a dark blue trace of her childhood. She hadn't developed them yet, but she felt—she hoped—they might be her best work to date. It was always hard to tell from a negative, where everything was reversed, the world turned inside out, light as dark and hefty as feathery, but Fanny recalled that when she'd taken these shots it had caused something like shivers.

At around four a.m., her hands had begun to actually shiver and shake, perhaps from the evening caffeine (Nanny Lena had made her three cups of coarse coffee before midnight) or perhaps from the anxiety . . . but she reminded herself that Wanda *wanted* to get her into the program. The cards were stacked in her favor, and Fanny just had to live up to the opportunity. Besides, she'd still have several months during which she could take even better pictures to display. Tomorrow, all she had to do was prove herself:

her raw talent, her grit. She had to give Wanda a reason to fill out the pink petition form.

The other thing she'd been doing during the night was thinking about what she hadn't been thinking about. She wasn't imagining her home with Simon, their bedspread, the morning meal, their decisions about where to vacation with their "French family" of two children. She certainly hadn't been planning wedding bouquets or debating who to invite from her girls' gymnasium class. None of that held real estate in her imagination, which was filled instead with pictures of dresses and jewels, angles and exposures. She may have even fantasized a university lecturing job when they opened them up to more women.

No, Fanny had barely considered married life at all. It's not that she didn't like Simon; she actually did. He was an honest man who'd confided in her about his envy toward his older brother Joshua who was always securing more trade accounts than he ever could and who was the pearl of every party. Fanny didn't have siblings, but she understood. As she and Simon had walked across Warsaw's Royal Castle grounds, she'd regaled him with tales of her days at gymnasium where one Karolina Zubrzycki somehow aced every exam while also starring in the soccer club and managing to attract the attention of all the older boys at the neighboring academy. How enervating she'd been! *Don't worry,* Fanny had consoled her beau as they'd promenaded. *No one likes a person who everyone likes!* Simon had laughed. He found her charming. She'd told him about her French studies and she'd even mentioned her photography hobby, though she'd never brought a camera on their dates. She did once show him a photo of her hair in a barrette—a defamiliarizing close-up, or so she hoped—and though he hadn't quite understood it, he'd asked her questions about her intentions.

Simon was a few years older than she was, and accordingly, he seemed more experienced, in the world and physically. She liked that too. They had kissed many times and even gone a little farther than that, especially that one night in the back of his father's car, but he always stopped, told her they should wait until the big day. He respected her. Of course, he didn't know how she'd almost gone all the way with Antoni back in high school—*almost*—but she imagined he'd had several lovers, proper ones. Maybe he even had one now? What did she know?

Simon was attractive and witty. She enjoyed how she felt when she was around him. She felt wanted, desired, and even taken care of. But was it love?

Love . . . When Fanny thought of flutters, she thought of her work. She loved photographing Mamo's crystal candy dish at noon sharp, when the rays that warmed the drawing room seared through the cuts in the glass to create concentric shadows of blue and purple haze that jetted across the marble coffee table, conceiving a whole world of pattern and symmetry that hadn't existed minutes before. Fanny loved going to Jabłkowski Brothers Department Store at dusk. The windows, showing off mannequins in wool coats, scarves, and gloves, would darken in the receding light, and a cascade of shadows would fall across their faces, as if they carried great secrets. Fanny would click and click, angles of limbs, hands, visages, her own reflection in the way, an obstruction to the beauty, to the hidden messages. She loved how her pictures shared that idea: we all get in the way of ourselves, in the way of our own knowledge.

She wasn't ready for her "hobby" to be buried by wifely duties. She had things she needed to do in place of marriage. Or, at least, first.

Now, in the frosty morning, Fanny picked up her pace and checked her Tank watch. It was later than she'd hoped. Fanny had wanted to arrive first thing at Pan M's but had been delayed by Mamo, who had—unusually for her—stirred before noon. Fanny had been tiptoeing around the house; she hadn't even asked Lena to make her another filter coffee for fear that the aroma would arouse her mother. And yet, as soon as she was ready to slip out, Mamo had called to her from her bedroom. "Don't forget, dear," her mother said, still donning last night's eye shadow, her glistening green frock spread out on the floor as if marking out the victim's body at a murder scene. "We're meeting the chef tonight."

"Tonight?" Fanny asked. "But we have so much time."

"We need to lock everything down, Fanny. Lock down and throw away the key!"

Fanny wasn't sure what had gotten into Mamo, but this marrying-her-off urgency was only growing. She was engaged, for crying out loud! Was it that Fanny had turned twenty? Was it that Rachel Unterbacher had recently had a baby boy? (And yes, she'd left her sociology program for it.) Was it that her options really were running out? But surely that was ludicrous. Warsaw had well over one million residents, and more than a third of them were Jewish, which was something Mamo still insisted upon for some reason.

"Half past five," her mother had said, shuffling on her silk pillows so she sat straight up on her canopy bed and faced Fanny directly. "We want to seal the deal, make sure no one changes any minds. You are running out of time."

Fanny didn't know what to say. She was going to see Wanda. She would never make it there for half past five but figured she would deal with Mamo's wrath later on. Hopefully Mamo herself would be fashionably late. *It was going to be alright,* Fanny told herself. She would cultivate Parisian interest, show her mother that she was competent and independent, and ultimately stall the wedding, at least until she had signed with a gallerist and had plans for her first solo show.

Fanny walked quickly along the icy pavement, slipping back a little with each step. Cool air stung her teeth, bringing out the taste of an Italian mint she'd sucked on earlier. Small trees, bald and decapitated, lined the streets of her upscale neighborhood. Fanny passed the city's newest modern apartment building to be influenced by the Bauhaus style, its corners rounded like in her own home. For a second, she stopped to wonder as she had a thousand times: Would Wanda like that picture?

Her mother's words rang in her ears: *You are running out of time.*

FANNY WAS PANTING BY THE TIME SHE REACHED PAN MADjeter, Warsaw's finest photograph developer and, as she feared, he was already busy. She opened the front door, stirring the chimes, but no one heard. The shop was full of street photographers, catering to the new explosive fad for street portraits. These men roved around Warsaw taking photos of strangers on their way to lunch or to the theater; then they handed them a card with an address and told them if they wanted the photo, they had to pick it up the next day for a hefty fee. How was it possible that so many people bought their photos? Sure, many Varsovians had never been casually photographed, but why were people so easily swayed by someone who told them to smile? They hadn't even asked for the print and had to make the effort to go pick it up, and yet, it seemed these men (all men, she noted) made a living because they were endlessly developing pictures.

The small space was cramped, and reels of film as well as paper-wrapped packets of photos oily like fish were being flung around overhead. A *bousculade.* Fanny muscled her way to the counter, opened her camera, and gingerly took out the roll, careful to wrap the end around so nothing was exposed. "Pan M," she called. "Please, I have this for you."

Busy dodging angry photographers, handing out pictures, and going through lists, he thoroughly ignored her.

"Pan M!" She let her vowels elongate to sound particularly feminine, and needy. Finally, he looked her way. "I'm sorry, I'm full up for today. No more films."

"What do you mean full? I'm here."

"Full."

"But I'll pay you."

"I have all these men to look after, Fanny. Come back on Monday."

"But I have the money. I always do."

"I can't."

"I'll pay you more," Fanny pleaded. "This is an emergency. Life or, well, not-life! I need them by four thirty."

"Fanny, look around you. I'm busy today."

Fanny wanted to tear her neatly clipped hair out. "But—"

"Okay, okay, I'll try to do one or two."

"Try? One or two?" She shoved her films his way, then turned and stomped to the front door. *This film is my future!* she wanted to cry.

"Next time, do it yourself," a man said as she passed him.

"Pardon?"

"Make your own darkroom."

"Excuse me?"

"Use a closet. A toilet. Buy some chemicals and make your own pictures. It's easy. What do you think this is, 1880?"

Her own darkroom. She'd never considered it before, but imagine that! Her own little space of utter blackness from which she could create authenticity. From darkness comes illumination.

"Just do it yourself," the man repeated. Then he chivalrously opened the door for her.

The Fashion Café was one of Fanny's favorite places in all of Warsaw, and if she had to spend a few hours waiting, she'd prefer to spend it here. She ran straight to the café after her morning lecture, where, today, she had a date.

Clutching her portfolio, praying that whatever shots she ended up showing Wanda—with or without the ones at Pan M's—were good enough, Fanny took a seat at her usual table, hung her camera bag off her chair, and, in an attempt to distract herself, scanned the room, taking in the surroundings. The café was established in a former orangery; the proprietress had covered the glassed-in ceiling with yellow fabric so that it always seemed sunny inside. The three dining rooms, two large and one small, were adorned with lush cacti and huge porcelain lamps, as well as sofas and armchairs draped in yellow, orange, and blue linen; the waitresses' uniforms, trays, and even coffee cups matched the colors. The smoky interior was rich with the scent of java and the sounds of impassioned chatter; a rounded window overlooked the seasonally lush garden where the runway shows took place, and an arched doorway led to a hall with a small gallery, studio, and office. As soon as her rendezvous with Natalia was over, Fanny would head that way and have a look at their current exhibition for inspiration. Hopefully, she would have the chance to take even better shots for the university exhibit. Shiver shots.

Mamo was going to have a fit when she didn't show up at the chef's on time. But didn't Mamo see the irony? She was obsessing over a marriage for Fanny, when she had bolted from her own, leaving a trail of shredded hearts in her Chanel-scented wake. At first, back then, Fanny hadn't even known what to say to her father. He wore his devastation like a new beard—utterly visible, shocking, a great discomfort to others who weren't sure if or how to respond. She'd been just twelve, and though they'd always been close, they had never talked seriously of matters of the heart. Sure, they'd taken Sunday walks together in Łazienki Park and shared strudel at Cukiernia Rzymska while playing their favorite game: They'd guess at the relationships of the people around them and make up elaborate life stories for each. Were that elderly man and woman sitting together and drinking coffee in silence because they were meeting for the first time and shy, or because they'd been married for fifty years and had run out of things to say? Papa taught Fanny to examine the nuances: how closely people stood near each other, whether they gesticulated freely or if their arms were constrained by the weight of falsehoods. *Never judge a book by its font,* he once told her. *The design is not just on the outside of a book, but it's spread throughout the text, shaping every word, every thought.* Fanny and Papa had also enjoyed skiing, and they'd gone a couple of times without Mamo, just the two of them. Only now did it dawn on Fanny that perhaps Mamo hadn't come because of her "side business."

Back then, when their union was faltering and after weeks of his morosity, during which time Mamo was extra chipper like a cuckoo on coffee, her parents had called her into the living room—

the formal one—and sat her down on an embroidered armchair. They explained that their marriage was no longer going to work and that Papa would be moving to Łódź, where the heart of his business was based. *But what about the heart of his soul*, Fanny had thought, but said nothing as the tears streamed down her face like a car wash.

That night, Mamo had gone out and Papa had tucked Fanny in, in place of Nanny. The whole day had been so unusual that Fanny couldn't resist and blurted out how sorry she was for her father, afraid that the moment she acknowledged it he would crumble into pieces like one of his favorite "nothing" cookies, those twists of dough with curled edges that seemed thick but the smallest crack tore them apart. Instead, he smiled and caressed Fanny's cheek. "Darling, you are young, but you must understand that relationships involve two people. Both people's actions and desires determine the course of their dynamics. Couplehood is always about the couple. Even one affair is about two spouses."

Fanny hadn't understood, but somehow her father's sense of control, his knowledge, made her feel better. He hadn't been left totally unloved. She, after all, loved him desperately. And the thought that he would be in Łódź, two hours away by train, and she would only see him one weekend every couple of months, was unbearable.

Now, Papa had a new wife, four new children, and a textile business that expanded to meet the increasing demands of the growing industrial city. He sent Polish-made fabrics to England for a British stamp and then reimported them to Poland where he sold them for more money. "The English stamp doubles the value," he'd once explained, though Fanny had always been skeptical of what seemed like fraud. Papa had longed for the opposite of Mamo in this latest round of marriage: He'd connected with a homemaker with wide hips, a matronly high-collared and shapeless-skirt style, and a penchant for producing children and meals. Fanny barely knew her stepsiblings. In the early years, she'd gone to stay with Papa and Ruth over the Christmas holidays, their house filled with the smell of baking bread and the rumble-tumble sounds of little children, the cacophony that had no rhyme or reason—pitter-patter punctuated by loud shrieks. Fanny had tried to connect with these toddler-relatives of hers, people who apparently had as intense a connection with Papa as she did—or once did—but her mere presence had made the children hyperactive, and Ruth became apoplectic by their running laps around the kitchen. Ruth, who acted as if she alone held the answer to the fundamental equation of the universe, but no one would listen, also hadn't been thrilled when, on her last visit, Fanny had accidentally spilled jam all over the sleeve of her silk dressing gown. Now her father rarely invited her to stay, and he rarely found time to come up to Warsaw, though Fanny found it hard to believe that he didn't make the one-and-a-half-hour train ride on the MtE diesel express for business many times a year. True, they met once in a while at an Old Town café, but with an increasing list of things they could *not* talk about (mainly, anything to do with Mamo or Ruth), their conversations had grown awkward. Fanny had never shown him her camera. Papa had yet to call her to congratulate her on her engagement. Over the years, the thread between them had begun to fray, becoming thinner and thinner and in risk of snapping.

Would Simon be like that, on the road, away, absent?

"Fanny Zelshinsky!" Natalia had arrived at the entrance and broke her thoughts. Fanny waved at her friend and her gorgeous blue, cape-like bolero. Fanny had never seen anything like it. Nat's father was an industrialist from a landowning family, and she reminded Fanny of the "glam girls" with whom she'd gone to gymnasium: "hussies," as they affectionately called themselves, who dressed chic and sporty, loved skiing, and counted boyfriends by fives.

Natalia said hello to at least a dozen people on the way to their table. She was a fixture here and seemed to know everyone—customers, staff, artists, managers.

"That's a beautiful blouse." Natalia gestured at Fanny's white top as she picked up Fanny's water glass and took a long, deliberate sip. "How did it go?"

"How did what go?" Fanny's heart skipped a beat. She was sure she hadn't told Natalia anything about Wanda and the exhibit because she hadn't told anyone, but had Natalia found out somehow? She was the kind who would.

"The date!" Natalia replied. "With your beloved, the other week. Did you romance the night away, smooching all along the Vistula. Did he take you to the Adria? I wish my parents were as into love as yours!"

"Love," Fanny repeated. And to herself, she mumbled, "In tennis, it means nothing." Indeed, earlier that month, before departing on his business trip, Simon *had* taken her to the Adria where they'd tangoed to the tunes of the Argentinian house orchestra, swishing by the club's glass-encased winter garden filled with blooming flowers and exotic birds. Fanny had worn a chiffon and tuille short-sleeved gown, with layers of floral pattern and geometric striping held together by a row of gold buttons down the front. He'd told her she looked like an angel.

"Why are you avoiding my question? Did he kiss you good night or was it more?" Natalia's eyes lit up.

"Natalia!" Natalia's Catholic guilt couldn't handle her hussy lifestyle, and she often ended up confessing to Fanny all about her affairs, partly to absolve herself, partly to regale. At least Jewish guilt was more about mothers than sex, Fanny always thought.

"I like the sound of Simon, but I'm not sure he can compete with the Gdansk shipping heir or comrade Antek, the 'fauxilist,'" Natalia joked and made a salute.

Fanny chuckled. Several months earlier, before Simon's proposal, the son of a brewery magnate (and friend of Mamo) had taken her to a new nightclub with a shiny mahogany bar, colorful highballs, American jazz, and a rotating dance floor. But instead of jiving, he spent the evening spewing socialist propaganda, going on about peasants and the importance of the workers. *The last time I checked, your father owned half the Grand Theatre*, Fanny had offered. *We can't change where we come from*, he'd replied, *but we can move it forward.* Then he'd told her it was unbecoming for a lady like her to smoke a cigarette. Men . . . they could recite every revolutionary syllable that Lenin ever scribbled, but when it came to women, they were still in 1850. When she had told Mamo afterwards that he was a bit of a socialist, Mamo didn't seem to mind. *Oh, they all are these days,* she'd said. *It will pass.*

"Listen, Fanny." Natalia now changed the subject. "I have a proposition for you. I just found out that I am going to curate my own fashion show here at the café. I want to show a line of women's work clothes. And I want you to model. That is, assuming you have time with the wedding and all. I know that planning a party can easily take up one's whole life."

"I have time!" Fanny blurted. "But me to model?"

"Yes, you're perfect. Gorgeous, but with an air of the student about you."

"Thank you." Fanny felt a streak of envy. Natalia had talked her way into her very own show. Then it dawned on Fanny. She pulled her Leica from the bag. "Maybe I can take some pictures?"

"Of me? I'd love that!"

"Not quite," Fanny said. "Pictures of the show, of preparations, rehearsals."

"What show?"

"Your fashion show, the work show."

"You want to work at the work show?" Natalia's lipstick was dark, a deep purplish red, which made her lips appear bruised and her teeth a sharp white. "You want to be a model *and* a photographer?"

"Well, no. What I mean is I understand how to frame shots, how to create texture in an image by using different perspectives." *Truth and perspective.* "This is the newest model," Fanny continued, offering her camera. "It's entirely handheld and can even capture movement."

"Oooh, fancy," Natalia said. "Speaking of which, have you decided on a thesis topic?"

Of all the changes of subject, this was the one Fanny was least interested in. She did not have a thesis topic and was busy trying to avoid Professor Nowak. Inspired by her own skirt photo, she had considered writing about Warsaw's fashion scene, or its core problem, as she saw it. The city was known as the Paris of the North, but when it tried to live up to that, it failed. Polish clothes needed to celebrate Poland, highlighting the unique sophistication of a Central European metropolis, one that housed significant minority populations. Here, women had the vote in 1918, before most Western countries; women participated in sports with vigor. If Fanny had more inclination, she would propose writing on the question of truth in costume. But . . . who would read such a thesis?

If she switched majors, she wouldn't have to do one at all.

"Do you know Wanda Petrovsky?" Fanny asked, changing the subject again. She didn't mean to talk about her but couldn't help it. Wanda, like water, had slipped through her fingers yet seeped under her skin.

Natalia eyed the menu offering teas and appetizers, hot savory pastries, toasts and sweet cakes, as if she didn't know it by heart. "Of course," she replied. "In fact, have you seen her old pictures of the city? 'Golden Warsaw,' she calls the series."

"I don't think so," Fanny said.

Natalia sprang to her feet. "A few of them are hanging by the back office."

Natalia snapped over the waitress, whose yellow uniform matched the upholstery, ordered for them both (borsht, pork pierogies, and hot bread rolls with butter, stat!), and then led Fanny down the hall. Four square photos hung along one wall. In one: a statuesque woman in a velvet dress, fur muff and scarf, wrapped like a present, staid yet undulating, distant yet sensual.

In another: two workers on a break. Women peddlers, wearing intricately patterned kerchiefs, selling oranges on Smocza Street. They were perched on a step, one smoking a cigarette, the other absentmindedly peeling fruit.

Finally, in another: a puddle on a street corner, and in it, splattered on the ground, was Wanda's reflection merged with the reflection of the city. It appeared that her dark eyes stared right at Fanny, yet also into the void, as if Wanda looked right through her.

Fanny's breath was taken away. The elegance, the confidence. She had never thought of seeing Warsaw and capturing bodies from those viewpoints. She was reminded of sheer possibility; one could look at life from a thousand new angles! Plus, the photos showed fashion . . . Fanny wasn't wrong after all; she could photograph clothes, as long as through them she could demonstrate herself and the universe, wrapped in one.

Fanny felt it: If Natalia could get her own show, then Fanny could succeed too. She was meant to be a photographer. She *had* to get into that student exhibit! She felt the engagement ring on her finger tightening like a noose. Her stomach felt taut, the air around her heavy. "So will you consider me taking photos?" she spouted to Natalia to stop herself from choking on her potential future.

"I will definitely consider it," Natalia said. "But now, I'm starving. Please, let's see if our food has arrived."

Fanny looked at her watch. It was almost four: She had to get to Pan M and then to the meeting. "I actually have to run, dear."

"Where to?"

Fanny opened her mouth, but the truth wouldn't emerge. It made her feel vulnerable. What if Wanda rejected her? What if her last chance at freedom was quashed? She looked up at the photo of peddlers on Smocza Street. "The Jewish Quarter."

"Why there?" Natalia scrunched her face. "By yourself?"

"I have an appointment," Fanny lied. "A tailor fitting."

"The wedding dress? I want to hear all about it!"

"It's a secret," Fanny mumbled.

"So full of secrets today," Natalia said, speed-walking toward their table where their food waited. "You really should model. You're so very pretty."

Fanny nodded but thought of Wanda's face staring up at her from the bowels of the city, knowing her through and through; an illusion, yet piercing.

"So you're not eating?" Natalia sat and cut into a pierogi. Meat juice bled onto the porcelain white plate.

Fanny picked up her camera bag. "I'm afraid I don't have time."

"I've never seen you so concerned about someone else's schedule," Natalia teased. Her fork was raised, as if stabbing the air. "Don't worry so much. Time is just a construct."

CHAPTER 4

Zosia

It was just before five and already dark outside, black like burnt toast. Zosia, in a leather jacket, which functioned as both her socialist sartorial badge and her comfort blanket, headed along the campus path lined with university buildings, taking in the evening buzz of students with no worries in the world except for if mathematics was a human invention or a natural phenomenon. Years earlier, she too had wanted to go to college, dreamed of becoming a professor. She'd worked so hard at school, studying for hours after toiling at the grocery. She'd been top of her class, and her teachers constantly compared her to Rosa Fishman, a Jewish girl from her same town who a few years earlier had won an academic scholarship to a nearby secondary school. And of course, there was Wanda, but she was a rare exception: a Jewish woman who'd managed an education, an art career, an academic post, *and* stayed involved in the movement. Imagine Zosia had stayed that course—now she'd be walking to a seminar, or an exam . . . But, alas. Her life had demanded different things of her. She couldn't afford *not* to work in the family store, and then, well, a sudden hairpin twist. It had taught her: Dror, and only Dror, was her true calling.

Now, she wondered, what was Wanda going to tell her? Rachel, who seemed to know everything, had implied that she'd offer to guide Zosia and get her a visa, sooner rather than later. But why had Wanda suggested they meet, not at Dzielna, but here, at a Polish university?

In the past few years, though there were no official national quotas like there were in Russia, many Polish schools had been severely limiting admission to Jewish students, especially in medicine and engineering. But the quotas had not hit Jewish women, who made up the majority of women in Poland's universities, quite as hard since most studied the humanities.

The bourgeois subjects, Zosia thought as she looked around her at the foyer with its high ceiling, elaborate cornices, and grand staircase. A swanky chandelier, a collection of white globes encircling brimming lights, hung in the center of the hall. Where was Wanda's office? And, even more of a question: *This* is where comrade Wanda had an office? It seemed wrong, anachronistic.

As if on cue, a woman draped in silk kerchiefs waved at her from down the hall. "Yoohoo!" she called.

"Excuse me?" Zosia said. "Are you talking to me?"

The woman ran toward her, stumbling like a bird in her high heels. Was she wearing a cape? A belt the size of her head? Was this woman here to study or play cricket with the queen of England? "Your look is so intriguing," she said.

"*My* look?" Zosia replied.

"I love the jacket, the way it folds around your face, as if you were a coach driver. Can I snap you?" The girl began to assemble an apparatus.

"Snap me?"

"Well, your collar, really," she said. "It's not necessary, is it, the collar? It's just expected. It's both worn and hard, angled and soft. A smattering of the universal yet coming from deeply within. I need to keep taking pictures . . . hopefully I'll have the chance to create something better for the show."

"You want to photograph my collar?" What was this world coming to? No wonder it was her duty to knock some sense into her generation, to save them all from the dilettantes whose dainty handprints were all over culture. "Believe it or not, I'm not a model," Zosia said. "And I don't have time for games. Do you have any idea where I can find the office of Wanda Petrovsky?"

"Oh yes, I'm headed there myself," the woman said. "I'll tell you what. Let's strike a deal."

"A deal?" Was this girl for real?

"Two collar photos and I'll show you the way."

Collar photos? Zosia had potentially life-altering business to discuss with Wanda, not whatever this was about. "Are you serious?"

"Dead."

"*Gatenyu*, fi—" But before she could even finish agreeing to this preposterous arrangement, the woman was at it. *Click. Click.*

"Thanks," the woman said. "No one has ever said 'no' before." Then, smiling, she ran up the stairs. "Follow me! I'm Fanny, by the way. Sorry if I'm being a bit funny. I'm just nervous. This meeting means everything to me. Everything!"

Zosia rolled her eyes and began to climb.

It was nearly six o'clock, and still: no Wanda. Zosia, who was as loath to waste time as money, chastised herself for not having brought with her work or at least a book, so she paced the hall's marble tiles, quizzing herself on Hebrew vocabulary.

Land, *adamah*. Respect, *kavod*. Intention, *kavanah*.

Her companion, meanwhile, was taking photographs of the wall.

"Excuse me," Zosia muttered as she stepped over her, their paths colliding yet again.

"The walls tell stories," Fanny said. "Don't you think?"

"Not really."

"Walls aren't just dividers," she went on. "They have their own layers; they have depth within."

Patience, *savlanut*.

"My Yiddish grandmother used to always say that I was someone who *shlogt meyn kop in vant* when I wanted something. I smash my head into the wall. I do everything possible—and even impossible—to get what I desire."

So she's Jewish, Zosia thought.

"Professor Petrovsky's not coming, is she?" Fanny looked at her with puppy-dog eyes.

"She's late," Zosia said.

"Artists are often late, though, right?"

"Maybe," Zosia said. "But Dror comrades usually are not." Respect for someone else's time was important, a value of the movement. We all share the same clock.

For the umpteenth time, she reread the schedule that was posted on Wanda's door. Lectures, studios, office hours. How did Wanda have the time for all that? How did she work at the university, maintain an artistic career, and run programs for Dror? No wonder she was late. She was clearly overly committed. Comrades had to be focused. "Maybe she forgot," Zosia said.

Now Fanny began pointing and re-pointing her camera at the locked office door, the knob, the keyhole. "I really need to speak to her."

She needed to speak to her? "So you've said."

"She was going to get me into the exhibition. It's a matter of life and not-life." Fanny looked like she was going to cry.

"I'm sure she just forgot. Why don't you go to her class tomorrow?" Zosia gestured at the schedule on the door. She had no *savlanut* for this girl's tears. "It looks like she's teaching at three."

"Oh?"

"*B'sha-ah shalosh*," Zosia practiced . . . it was important to know practical words too. Maybe Zosia herself would come back at that time, if her schedule allowed, and she didn't receive a message via Mira first.

"I'm guessing you're in the Hebrew scouts like Professor Petrovsky?" Fanny asked. "One of those clubs?"

"Clubs? They're spiritual, social, and intellectual learning circles," Zosia explained. "Jews make up a tenth of the new republic's population. Our Jewish parties are trying to find a solution to Poland's growing anti-Jewish sentiment, to the question of whether we belong here or not, in a place that barely wants us."

"I do love a good party," Fanny quipped.

"That's good, because there are many. The Bundists, the religious, the Folkists, the assimilationists, the illegal communists, and the Zionists, from the religious right to the left-wing labor socialists. Each of these parties has their own youth movement," Zosia said. She couldn't help herself: Her duty was to educate. "One hundred thousand young Polish Jews are members of these *clubs,* as you call them. Each movement has its own vision for the future of Polish Jewry—is it a religion, a secular culture, or a nation? Should we speak Hebrew, Yiddish, or Polish? What type of government will best serve our community? We Labor Zionists are fighting for the dignity, equality, and freedom of our people!" It struck Zosia that she was explaining the need to eradicate class to the very reason for this need. Wealth bred ignorance. *If you want to know what God thinks of money, just look at the people he gave it to,* the English writer had quipped.

Just then, footsteps came down the hall, accompanied by a jangling of keys. Finally! Fanny jumped up as Zosia turned toward the noise.

Alas, it was a cleaner, mop and bucket in hand. The short older woman, lips in a sour pucker, headed toward Wanda's office. Zosia sighed. People should clean up after themselves.

The cleaner pushed past the two waiting women and put her key into the keyhole.

Fanny piped up. "Can we go in with you?"

"Huh?" the cleaner replied, gruff. "You talking to me?" Zosia bristled at her curtness. Her Polish accent spoke volumes, reminding Zosia that they were not friends.

"Yes, dear," Fanny said, now turning her posh Polish accent down a thousand degrees. "We need access to Professor's office. She asked us to get supplies for her."

The cleaner raised an eyebrow. She wasn't buying it. Zosia was relieved by the woman's suspiciousness. She scolded herself for being so jumpy around every Christian . . . The cleaner had done nothing wrong; Zosia needed to be kind, calm.

"Please, it's very important."

The cleaner shook her head.

"Come, Fanny, let's go," Zosia said. "Let's leave this woman to do her job in peace."

That's when Fanny began rummaging in her purse and pulled out a full chocolate tablet—from Wedel, no less!

The cleaner shrugged. Then, she grabbed the deluxe cocoa bar, shoved it in her apron pocket, unlocked the door, and, as if nothing had transpired, walked calmly back down the hall.

"You go home, we'll clean up," Fanny called after her. "Have a restful evening."

Zosia sighed loudly to cover her nerves. "What will we do in her office?" It's not like Wanda would have an extra visa just lying on her desk. Or would she?

"I don't know, but maybe we'll find some answers. Or a pink form. Come on!"

Zosia watched without moving as Fanny pushed open the heavy wood door. The room was strewn with papers. Photographs were scattered across a coffee table. Books were piled on the desk, chair, rug. No visa spotted.

"I know artists are messy," Fanny said, "but it looks like she left in a hurry." Fanny pointed to where a half-eaten slice of bread with cheese lay in waiting. "Maybe she ran to go photograph something big, something wild, something happening right now?"

"Maybe . . . Don't touch," Zosia warned as Fanny stepped nearer to the piles. Suddenly, her head felt tight, her forehead squeezed, and she began to hear it, shrill, a caterwaul. She wasn't welcome in this room; she sensed it. "I think we should get out of here."

But Fanny had already taken out her camera. *Click.*

First, papers on the desk. The sandwich. A hair barrette.

"Don't touch anything," Zosia repeated. She'd barely stepped inside.

Now Fanny was all the way on the ground, lying on her side, clicking away, panting. What was she even photographing? Dust?

Zosia strode back. "Come on, we need to leave. Truly."

Fanny sprung up, "Okay." But instead of following Zosia to the door, she lunged to the window and gasped. In a frenzy, Fanny started shooting out into the blackness of night.

"What are you doing? It's dark outside," Zosia said. "There's *nothing* there." If she was going to risk their reputations, at least she could photograph something worth capturing.

"The picture is everywhere," Fanny replied. "This is my self-portrait."

Zosia was sure she heard footsteps down the hall. None of this felt good. Why was she even waiting for this airhead? Zosia pivoted on her heels and headed out the door.

Fanny caught up to her in the hallway. "I am sweating!" she squealed. "I don't know what any of it meant, but it was all heart. Shivers, I *feel* it. Now I'll need to develop these too . . . Pan M better have time."

Zosia shook her head and walked quickly toward the staircase.

Fanny kept up. "Want some chocolate?" Like a magician pulling a rabbit out of a top hat, the girl pulled yet another tablet out of her velvet handbag.

"No, thank you, I—"

"You cleaned so fast?" The cleaner was standing on the bottom stair, looking up at them.

"We did!" Fanny said.

"Well, we—" Zosia started. The last thing she wanted was for this innocent woman to get in trouble because of the dilettante's sense of privilege. Then again, there was something about her accent, her tone, that bothered Zosia, that reminded her of—

"Actually, Pani," Fanny interrupted. "The truth is, we did not. I am not able to clean like you do; I do not have the experience that you have. We appreciate all your work. We could not function without you." Fanny smiled and handed the woman the second cocoa tablet. Then she pulled Zosia toward the front door.

Outside, Zosia breathed in the crisp night air. She looked up, but only a few stars were visible. In the countryside, the stars were so dense that Zosia could make out the shape of the sky. The stars showed her the contours of the world. In the countryside, she felt protected by a canopy of light.

The city was different. Evasive and unpredictable.

She would have to find Wanda another time.

"I need to go see a chef," Fanny said. "Tout de suite."

"A chef?"

"What's your name, by the way?" Fanny asked.

"Zosia," she answered. "Zosia Dror," she said as she speed-walked away from the university building. Zosia needed to start new leadership role by leaving a good impression, and she had heaps of work to do back at Dzielna. Besides, she reminded herself, Wanda wasn't her only ticket. She could also be put on the education track, demonstrate her value, and rise on the visa list through hard work, as she had planned. She would soon have an answer from Dror leadership about her role. *Education, education, education*, she prayed. "Goodbye and good luck becoming an artist. Have a nice life."

"I will!"

Zosia sighed and lit a cigarette. Smoke exited the side of her mouth, like a dragon.

What an end to the first full day of her life in Warsaw.

Her *temporary* life in Warsaw.

CHAPTER 5

Fanny

THE NEXT DAY AT THREE P.M. SHARP FANNY ENTERED THE cavernous classroom. Her mind churned over what to do: Approach Wanda after the lecture to remind her of her offer to help Fanny switch to the art major? Or impress her during the class and volunteer to share her photos again?

Pan M had managed to develop one of the images and she'd been right: It was good. The sleeve of her father's blazer was shaped like his arm, tracing his bent elbow, as if holding his glass of cognac, the angle just so. His limb was absent, yet entirely present; Papa emanated off the glossy page. The sight of her father's nonbody had shocked Fanny at first, and as she'd stared at the print she was consumed by desire for that arm, for it to reach up out of the paper into the third dimension and wrap itself around her, firm, reassuring, clasping and pulling her into the picture with him. It had been years since she'd allowed herself to long for her father's embrace. Her mouth had gone dry.

Alongside the ten prints, Fanny had brought her camera, filled with last night's film. The scenes had included the dark outside and reflections in the window, bits of the office, and even of her own face. It was all mashed together, a cubist collage, reflection and reflex, the outside, the inside, and the artist stamped on top of it all; flat and layered, dark and light. *Nothing*. And everything.

At last, the door opened!

In walked a man. He was short, with brown hair combed over his scalp and a moustache.

"Good afternoon, class," he said, before even reaching the podium. "Today we will look at landscape."

Landscape?

"Sorry," Fanny whispered to a thin boy who sat next to her. "Is this not Petrovsky's class?"

He shrugged.

The mystery teacher put on a pair of thick-rimmed glasses and opened a book from which he began to read. "When we talk about land, we also mean sky."

"Excuse me." Fanny could not sit still. "Sir? Professor?"

The man cleared his throat, then looked at her from above his lenses.

"Where is Wanda Petrovsky?"

"Do I bore you, Mademoiselle?"

"Certainly not, Professor—"

"Dean," he said. "Dean of economics."

"I'm sorry, I thought this was Professor Petrovsky's class."

"Professor Petrovsky is on leave."

"Leave?"

"Yes, I will be teaching for the rest of the semester," he said. "Unless that doesn't suit you?"

"Thank you, Dean," Fanny said and fell back in her chair, dizzy.

How could Wanda be on leave? She had just been here yesterday and had given them homework assignments for next week. She'd asked Fanny to meet her last night. She'd never mentioned anything about a leave . . .

Fanny had no time for a leave.

She'd been unpunctual for the chef appointment last night, to say the least, arriving even after her fashionably late mother who'd been furious; but all was forgiven when Chef Piotr brought out his finest sturgeon caviar. *Delicious!*, Mamo had cooed, scooping it into her mouth as if it were ladles of country borsht. Fanny's nausea had prevented her from tasting anything; even a small pearl could barely slide past the lumps in her throat. *Do you like it?* Piotr had asked her and she nodded along, wondering whether Simon would?

Not that she wanted to impress him per se, but it struck her that she had no idea of his true tastes. Sure, they'd shared many meals over the years, from sardines and vodka to French food at the Oaza, but had they had caviar? She couldn't extrapolate. She didn't know enough. Soon she'd be meeting with the florist . . . what were his favorite colors, smells, shapes? The pang in her gut got worse.

The second the bells chimed, Fanny bolted from her desk and across the yard to the lecture hall that also housed the administration offices.

"Excuse me," Fanny called to a rake-thin woman who was hunched over a desk. "Can you please tell me where Professor Wanda Petrovsky is?"

The woman slowly looked up from her papers. "Who are you to know?"

"I'm her student, we had a meeting set up, about the possibility of switching majors . . . It was a special—" Fanny could hear herself blathering.

"She's sick." The woman cut her off. "Petrovsky is sick."

"Sick? But the dean just said she was on leave."

"Jesus Mother Mary! Why are you bothering me if you already talked to the dean?"

"I just wanted to double-check," Fanny said. She fumbled through her purse looking for chocolates, but she stupidly hadn't brought any. For a second, she debated throwing out her family name. Her father's donations to the faculty club . . . but when had he last given? "I thought maybe you could share some information on where she took her leave. And for how long."

The secretary shook her head and looked back down at her papers. "She's on sabbatical. For a while. I don't know anything else."

Sabbatical? Who had ever heard of a sudden sabbatical? A minute earlier, she'd been "sick"!

Besides, hadn't that Zosia Dror studied Wanda's schedule? There was no sabbatical indicated, was there?

Rattled, Fanny backed out of the office and right into Professor Nowak. How stupid! She had completely forgotten to avoid the building where her French lecture took place, also at three p.m. Fortunately, Nowak was with Natalia, whom she hoped would read behind the lines and help rescue her.

"Fanny, are you alright?" both Nowak and Natalia asked.

"Yes, I'm—," she started to say. "I mean, no, I'm not very well. My apologies for missing class."

Without skipping a beat, Natalia put her fingertips to Fanny's forehead. "You look pale. Fever?"

"Yes, fever," Fanny said.

"Then what are you doing here?" Nowak asked.

Fanny drew a blank. She coughed to buy time.

"She must be collecting the special medical forms from the office," Natalia smoothly answered. Lord, she was good. She wore a yellow-and-green-checked knit dress, like that of a Hollywood starlet.

"What medical forms?" Nowak asked.

"The new ones," Natalia simply said. "Fanny, it's already four thirty. You need to get to the doctor quickly. Get out of here!"

"Please do rest and get well," Nowak said. "But I must talk to you about your thesis topic, next week at the latest."

The topic she still didn't have. She must have gone paler because Natalia immediately said, "I've been thinking about your request for my project at the Fashion Café. I'm happy for you to do it."

Fanny nodded. "Thank you." This was good news, but she'd have to register it later. Nothing was making any sense. And it was four thirty . . . Fanny sighed: There was a place she knew she needed to be.

An epidemic of lunacy. That's what the papers had called the city's nightlife. Fanny looked out the tram's window at the dazzling neons announcing bars, cafés, cigarettes. In one gleaming red-and-white advertisement, lights converged to form the image of a rotund chef carrying a platter of steaming roast. All promise, all grandeur. Jewels in the dusk.

Posters for American movies—*The Prince and the Pauper, The Grand Illusion, Double Wedding*—lined the streets. Everyone was talking about Shaw's *Candida* and a new adaptation of *Merrily We Roll Along*. There had never been so many shows in production, local and foreign too; 1938 was the year of spectacle.

The cable car screeched to a halt. Fanny clutched the strap. Her camera bag jerked to one side and she secured it with her arm.

"*Dybbuk!*" the driver called out her stop in the Jewish Quarter, naming it after the popular Yiddish play that was being performed in a theater down the street. Fanny disembarked and checked the address she had scribbled on a scrap of envelope. Four blocks to go.

Despite the winter cold, the busy jumble of streets that comprised one-fifth of Warsaw was where most of the city's Jewish restaurants could be found alongside Jewish schools, libraries, cafés, theaters, markets, wholesale showrooms, and more than four hundred houses of worship, and it buzzed with after-work activity. On Nalewki, vendors packed up stalls, horses brayed, beggars pleaded, roving carpenters angled for a final odd job for the day, for a few more groszy so they could bring home a chicken. The air was infused with the smells of baking bagels, pickle juice, garbage. Street musicians strummed their fiddles; evening headlines were blared out. There were so many long dark coats, thick black boots. Though Jews lived all over Warsaw, the ultra-popular Polish picture, *The Girls from Nowolipki Street*, about the lives and loves of five Jewish girls, was set in this very neighborhood. Fanny felt as if she was walking through a staged movie set, this rambunctious locale another land entirely from the Warsaw of her day-to-day.

Fanny hadn't been to this area for a long time and suddenly remembered an afternoon when Nanny had taken her to buy new shoes. The salesman had x-rayed her feet, seeing right to her core, analyzing each joint and bone to find her exact size, her essence. Fanny passed the building where Isaac Bashevis Singer had worked as an editor before moving to America. She remembered Mamo hosting him for lunch; Fanny had curtsied, thinking how she preferred both his brother's and especially his sister's novels, filled with family strife. She passed an open door with people spilling out onto the street; Fanny peeked in and through the smoke, saw that it was a working-class cinema where they used a bedsheet as a screen. The audience laughed and heckled, even from the sidewalk. Someone threw an onion.

The wind picked up and snow began to swirl around her, as if Warsaw were a snow globe that, just seconds earlier, had been turned right side up. Through the flurries, Fanny saw the Montbel Marteau Cognac neon, the way the bottle tipped over and added pointillist lights to the glass. Half empty. Half full. All excitement.

At last, here was the address! But Fanny saw no entrance way, no awning. Then, on her left, she noticed a courtyard, which led to a doorway.

Fanny took a breath before pushing open the door to Dror's headquarters.

CHAPTER 6

Zosia

KNOCKING, HARDER AND HARDER, FIST SMARTING. *PLEASE, LET us in. Please!* Heat on her back, her neck, and then, an opening, slowly, creaking, a slender gap. Zosia slithered through . . . And there she was, in another dark space. Another door. Locked. A palimpsest of blockades. The door was burning hot. *Please, open up. Please!* Now she turned back, but the gap had disintegrated; the first door was locked too. She was trapped, between in and out, entrance and exit, and she began to fall, fast, and then the scream, shrill, familiar—

Zosia awoke in a sweat, her moist nightgown clinging to her bony frame.

She raced to the window. Shaking, she fiddled with the wooden pane, shimmying it as high as it would go, lapping in the night air. She was overwhelmed by all these changes, she told herself. If Wanda was going to take her under her wing, maybe she'd ask her for advice about how to manage the transition from town to city, from local leader to national guide. Maybe she should try to find her today at that three p.m. lecture. Then again, she didn't want to get her hopes up or interfere with the movement's plans.

Once her rhythms returned to normal, Zosia lay back down, shut her eyes tight, and prayed for sleep. She pleaded to be taken away, far away, to a dream, to a promised land.

She went nowhere.

Zosia checked her old watch. It was four thirty. She needed to get up. Though it was only a few days into her life in Warsaw, she had already been assigned the duty to procure bread for the group with comrade Yossi. And they had to get it before Dror's breakfast of toast, butter, and black tea was served, beginning at dawn.

She rubbed the sleep from her eyes.

ZOSIA SUPPRESSED A YAWN AS SHE ENTERED THE DINING ROOM. *Be alert! Be actively conscious!* Everything felt complicated here in her new life. Despite the city's pace being faster than the countryside's, it all took so much time in Warsaw. It had taken them nearly an hour to get to and from the baker's this morning. It was not just the size of the apartment complex but the time it took for Yossi to wave good morning to the tailor, the teacher, the children, then hear about Pan Grosky's drunk husband and Mr. Fleishman's opinion on the new proposed requirements for artisans to join the crafts guild in order to practice their trade, which further disadvantaged Jews since the guilds did not accept non-Christians.

Zosia had spent the following twelve hours mostly alone, writing lectures, preparing seminars, and setting up her side of the bedroom; she hadn't had time to return to the university. Not to mention, she'd feared straying too far from Dzielna as she waited for word from leadership. Would she be put on education? Or maybe Wanda would stop by, or at least leave her another message . . . Zosia had never actually seen a visa. She imagined it: a small piece of card stock, bright yellow, with her name scrawled in black ink, thick like sweet prune juice.

Finally, the rumbling in her stomach had grown louder than her inner thoughts. For communal consideration during these poverty-stricken times, Zosia ate only two meals a day. At nearly five p.m., it was time for her second. She'd made her way downstairs to the "dining hall," a small room with tables and benches also used as the meeting room, social room, and workroom. Thick slices of the brown rye she'd procured earlier were laid out next to cuts of farmer's cheese, tomatoes, cucumbers, and a pot of bean stew. Near that was the leftover oatmeal from this morning, and Zosia decided that it would be most responsible to use that up first.

Zosia ladled her oats from the pot. Gooey, they clung to the wooden spoon, and she had to shake hard for the grains to fall into her small bowl. She looked around the room, where comrades had begun to gather for the evening meal, and noticed a few leaders scattered about, deeply engaged in conversations. She needed to impress them somehow . . . *No!* She caught herself. "Impress" was the wrong approach, all egotistical, anathema to the movement. She needed to make sure the leaders saw her true dedication, her unique commitment, her seriousness to the cause. She stood ramrod tall. *Posture is not posturing*, she thought.

Then she shook her spoon with vigor, dropping clumps of mush *back* into the communal pot. She didn't need much to go on. Hunger made one focus on what was necessary. She had long ago learned to love it. *Don't fear hunger. Don't feed it, but feel it. Understand from it.*

She grabbed one thin slice of bread.

As she thought about where to sit, she wished she recognized somebody, anybody; it would not look good if she ate alone. Zosia noticed an empty seat at the table closest to the stove—the sole heating source for the building. A group of young members—they looked to be about sixteen or seventeen—sat around eating and talking. She took a breath and nodded hello to the youths as she sat down; thankfully they welcomed her. For a second, she was tempted to utter the blessing over the food. She may have rejected her religious upbringing, but it was always there, nestled right under the surface; it was the standard around which everything else was compared. Sabbath and Tu Bishvat soon approached, and Zosia was overtaken by reminiscence, one memory leaking into the next: Mameh preparing *cholent*, a hefty burgundy potage of beans packed in with tears of meat, a rich, fatty dish that her family couldn't afford yet her mother made happen. She pictured her mother clutching the heavy pot, walking to the baker's oven, where she left the stew overnight to slow-cook. Zosia imagined Mameh sweeping the floor and washing the table; Mameh combing Tateh's hair, making sure the oily strands were perfectly parallel. A daily act of utter commitment.

Earlier that morning, when Zosia had returned from the bread run, she'd been told that a letter had come for her. Hands shaking, she opened it to find it was from her mother. When had she sent it? Weeks ago? At first, she'd crumpled it and thrown it across the room, but after calming herself, she'd picked it up, smoothed it out. The pages were now folded in her pocket and Zosia touched their contours.

Have you had enough of Warsaw yet? Mamenyu had written in wobbly Polish script. Though they spoke to each other in Yiddish, her mother had only learned to write in the national language in her few years of schooling. *It's not safe in the big city, and it's certainly not safe in Palestine. What kind of mishiggeneh movement have you joined that asks you to run across the world? We need to stay here, together, and observe Jewish laws. Are you lighting Shabbos candles? Come home, Zosheleh, we need you in the grocery. We've hardly seen you all year, we barely recognize you. We need you. Light the candles.*

Her family had always supported the religious party that cared mainly about Orthodox observance and believed in the Diaspora. To them, Judaism was a practice of devotion to God, not a secular, nationalist movement; the ancient holy land could only be reestablished with the arrival of the Messiah. Her mother had been worried about it not being safe in the big city, which seemed ridiculous to Zosia when it was really *Poland* that was unsafe. Why couldn't her mother understand that she had to fight, to defend? Why couldn't she—

Zosia took a breath. No distractions.

Zosia brought her food to her lips, and tuned into the conversation around her. One male comrade at the table was going on. "Freud locates truth in the unconscious," he said. "The whole point of psychoanalysis is to bring the unconscious forward, to make it conscious through language."

Zosia was startled by this topic. Freud irritated her. The eighty-two-year-old spoke publicly of the Germans' tyrannical rule yet he wouldn't leave Austria. He famously joked, "They used to burn me, now they just burn my books . . . It's progress!" Sure, he had some interesting theories, but you can't separate a person from their actions. They *were* their actions.

"True desires are unconscious," the comrade went on. "Our identity is based on desire."

"We can only access ten percent of our minds," another said. "Ninety percent of our own brains aren't available to us. Freud thinks we don't know ourselves at all."

"Then who are we?" Zosia intercepted. Interrupting wasn't the friendliest tactic, but she was, after all, the "elder" here. "There is no greater foundation to running a collaborative society than knowing ourselves. We cannot fully cooperate until we are aware of our own limitations and possibilities. Let's go around the table and share what you perceive your strengths and weaknesses to be." She turned to a young woman who smiled warmly. A potential friend? "Why don't you start, comrade—?"

"Leah," the young woman said and contemplated for a moment. Zosia liked it that she took time to think. Plus, her voice sounded like she might be from a shtetl. "For my strength, I am very capable of expressing myself. For my weakness, well, I am very capable of expressing myself!" The group laughed. Zosia was impressed by her confidence.

"What about you?" Zosia asked the young man to her left. Next to his bowl sat a worn copy of Rabindranath Tagore's *Gitanjali.* She scanned the room again: Leaders were still speckled about.

"I suppose my strength is that I analyze every situation," he answered after a long moment. "And my weakness is that, well . . ." He paused again and clutched his Tagore. "I hesitate." More chuckling.

"Do you hesitate to analyze, or do you hesitate because you analyze?" Leah asked him.

He paused, for comedic effect. "Both?"

"'Both' is correct," Zosia said. Mira had entered the room. "For most of us, our strengths and weaknesses are the same. Our best traits, taken to their extreme, become our worst ones. It's a matter of degree."

This was when Zosia heard a loud voice. "What magnificent lighting in here," the perfect Polish crooned. "How wonderfully rare for this time of day."

Zosia froze. She couldn't believe her ears, then her eyes.

The girl from the night before was wearing a fur shawl and pumps. An enormous button hung loose from her dress's white collar that looked like it belonged on a clown or priest. *Oh no* . . . the girl approached Mira. She was talking to Mira. She was babbling to Mira about—oh lord—the high ceilings. She was threatening to take out her camera and "capture the cracks."

Zosia nearly fainted.

What was she doing here?

Zosia had to stop this. She jumped up from her chair. "Fanny!"

"Oh, there you are, darling!" Fanny said. "So glad I found you."

The whole room was staring. Zosia turned red.

"Excuse me, *chevrah*," she said to the group at her table. "This is for a community service project I'm working on." She got up, approached Fanny, grabbed the arm that was reaching for the camera, and pulled it straight into the hallway, out of Mira's earshot.

"What are you doing here?" Zosia asked quietly once they were outside the room.

"I've never seen the lighting at the back of a building like this," Fanny said, fumbling with her bag. She seemed nervous.

"Why are you here?" Zosia repeated.

Fanny lowered her voice. "Something strange is going on with Wanda. Remember you told me to go to her lecture today? Well, she wasn't there."

"So?" Zosia said. "She's probably busy. She's wildly overcommitted."

"But it's her job!" Fanny said. "And the dean of economics was substituting. He said she was on leave. I went to the office, and they said she was sick, and then they said she was on a sabbatical for the rest of the term."

"So maybe she is," Zosia said. Maybe that's why she hadn't heard from her either. She sighed. At this rate, she might never learn what Wanda had wanted to tell her or become her apprentice. "Why would they lie to you?"

"I don't know," Fanny said. "Everyone was being so vague. *She* never mentioned that she was leaving. It wasn't on her schedule, as you saw. It makes no sense."

"Your teacher is on leave. It is a little odd, sure, and I know she means a lot to you," Zosia said. She meant a lot to Zosia too. "But you need to accept it and move on." Zosia gestured toward the door—take a hint!—but fashion girl wouldn't budge.

"But why would she disappear with no warning?" Fanny went on. "And why is the university being so strange about it?"

"Well," Zosia said. There were reasonable explanations. From the corner of her eye she could see into the dining room, where Mira was talking with some of the leaders at a table. "She's Jewish."

"Jewish?"

"Yes. Jewish."

"So?"

"So?" How naïve could one be? "So . . . there are quotas on Jewish students and professors. Even when it's not outright law, the universities still limit us. They're allowed to make their own rules, even though they don't always admit them out loud."

"You think they kicked her out because she's Jewish?"

"Haven't you heard of the ghetto benches around the country? Professional limitations on doctors and lawyers?" What world was this woman living in?

"Of course, I've heard of all that," Fanny said. "But those are provincial affairs, countryside politics. This is *Warsaw*."

"So, Warsaw, with your fancy chocolates, is so much smarter than the countryside?"

"No, I didn't mean that. I'm sorry," Fanny said. "Look, Zosia, something is going on here and we need to find Wanda. Can't you ask around about her?"

We? "No. Wanda is probably sick. Or busy. Or on a sudden sabbatical." Yes, *of course* Zosia wanted Wanda's guidance and to find out what exactly Wanda had meant to offer her, but not like this. If Dror leadership saw her in cahoots with bourgeois fashion girl, they'd think she was ridiculous; they'd take her straight off education . . .

"Zosia," Fanny said and tugged her sleeve. "My whole life depends on this. My identity, my future. I need to find her. What can we do?"

"Your future? Your identity? What can *we* do?" Zosia spat back. The gall of the privileged. "*I* worked on a campaign to repeal the country's kosher laws."

"The kosher laws?"

"I learned how government worked, the lobbying, the connections, the bribes. And I learned how little power Jews really hold," Zosia said. The year before, the Polish government had proclaimed that kosher ritual slaughter would no longer be legal, disingenuously citing animal rights violations. In an unprecedented move, all the Jewish political parties had come together to protest, even the secular ones. The law that was eventually passed thankfully allowed ritual slaughter but severely limited the number of animals permitted for kosher killing, based on some cockamamie calculation of Jew-to-cow ratio, limiting the supply, raising prices, and driving kosher butchers out of business. "It took six months, dozens of activists, thousands of złotys, and ten thousand conversations navigating power, back channels, paybacks, bribes, favors, and pure racial hatred. So, what can we do to change Poland's ways? To find Wanda? There's *nothing* you can do. Nothing. Go back to the fashion magazines. That's where you should be putting your effort."

"Okay, then," Fanny said abruptly. "Forget it."

Zosia watched as she walked back into the dining hall—and began taking photos of comrades eating dinner. Then of their cups. And their napkins.

Zosia rushed in. Everyone stared. "Please, go," she whispered.

Fanny straightened up and glared at her.

"Look, the movement is family, and Wanda is part of it. She's our family. If she is missing, then this is more serious than you can handle. Go back to school. Move on."

Just then, Mira, who was looking at them strangely, motioned for Zosia to follow her out.

Zosia took a deep breath and followed Mira down the hall into a small room. She felt thirsty, so thirsty. Her heart raced.

She'd expected that her verdict would arrive in a room filled with leaders, but the space was empty except for Mira and her.

"How have your first days in Warsaw been?" Mira asked. She didn't even sit.

"Intense," Zosia answered. "In a good way," she quickly added. "Exciting. Interesting. I'm learning the ropes." In case Mira had been suspicious of her relationship with Fanny, Zosia riskily added: "I'm doing outreach in the community. I have plans to bring together diverse elements of Polish Jewish youth to help foster a sense of responsibility."

"That's interesting," Mira said. She made no eye contact. "Very interesting for our education curriculum. I've often said we do too much within our own group, and fostering cross-movement connections is a smart move, especially in times of adversity when we need to band together. The left-right divide can be so complicated."

Zosia nodded, surprised that her lie had gone down so smoothly.

"I know you worked on the kosher campaign, with other movements too," Mira said, looking out the window.

"Of course," Zosia answered. "All of these issues are important to me. I am dedicated to education in all its forms. I have tunnel vision. But," she threw in, "sometimes a tunnel has two lanes."

"We'd love to advance you in leadership with a new role."

"You would?" Zosia went hot, cold. This was it!

"But something's come up," Mira said. She rarely smiled, but now she was particularly not-smiling. Finally, she looked at Zosia and sighed. "That's why I wanted to talk to you."

"Oh?"

"When you saw Wanda yesterday, did she say anything about leaving town?"

Zosia gulped. "I didn't see her," she answered truthfully. "She was late, so I left."

Mira shook her head. "She didn't show up last night at the Grochów branch."

"Oh? She does seem to be very busy."

"So, we'll need you to do it."

"Do what?"

"Her job."

"What job?"

"She was supposed to start weeding out imposters."

"Imposters? You mean people who join the movement just to meet a match?" Zosia blushed. "Or just for the sports league? Diluting the idealist heart . . ."

"We need you to get rid of the comrades who want to go to Eretz Israel for all the wrong reasons. When these imposters arrive, they don't even settle on the kibbutz but immediately run to Tel Aviv."

Zosia took a deep breath. A few years back, when more visas were available, the movement had been inundated with imposters; she hadn't realized that this was still a pressing issue. Imposter weeding was a notoriously difficult and undesirable job.

"It's extremely challenging work," Mira went on, as if she'd read Zosia's mind. "Sometimes even dangerous. But we trust you to take Wanda's place."

Zosia tried to keep a straight face. Was it a good thing that she was considered to be Wanda's replacement, suggesting that the movement respected her, or would this task take her completely off track? Had Wanda pawned this job off on her and hadn't shown up last night because it was easier not to tell her firsthand? Or, maybe in exchange for taking on this work, Wanda would help her get a visa even faster?

"I will do whatever is needed of me," Zosia said. She had to show the movement that she was open to anything! Frankly, she would take a visa, no matter how it came. She had no idea how to get rid of imposters, but she would worry about that later. "I will weed, cull, and extract—until Wanda returns." Focus. In Hebrew: *Lehitmaked.*

"Thank you, Zosia. And one more thing," Mira said as she headed to the door. "Abram will be your teaching partner. He'll be the 'husband' to your 'wife.' Your group will have eleven 'children.'"

Abram? Zosia wasn't sure whether to laugh or cry. "Right," she said.

"By the way," Zosia asked as Mira crossed the threshold. "Where do you think Wanda is?"

"We're not sure," Mira answered. Then she whispered, "But probably jail."

CHAPTER 7

Fanny

THE CAR INCHED ALONG THE TRAFFIC ON TŁOMACKIE STREET, Mamo tsking as it stop-started. *Had you expected the entire city to make way for you?* Fanny had not asked. She had been surprised earlier when her mother rang for the car driver; she'd assumed Mamo would have preferred to make her grand entrance classically, by upscale *droshky*, an over-the-top adorned horse and carriage like nostalgic nobility. But alas, she should have predicted her mother's whims. The racing green Packard Six, with its bulbous lights and beetle-like crawl, came straight from America. Though money was never discussed with Fanny, she knew that Mamo had spent nearly nine hundred US dollars on it from a special auto importer who claimed it was next to impossible to procure—Mamo's favorite type of object. It always amazed Fanny how her mother, all sass and self-worth, could be so easily seduced by the claim of rarity; she had watched as antique dealers, travel agents, even mushroom sellers, played to this time and time again. Why did her mother need to feel special so desperately?

Tonight, they were heading to synagogue—a rare occurrence. Fanny was from a Polish Jewish family, emphasis on the Polish. But her mother had heard that the Brodaszes, her in-laws to be, were hoping to attend Friday night services. She felt this would be an opportunity to re-impress them and to examine the space for wedding-planning purposes. *Plus,* Mamo had told her, exaggeratedly batting her eyelashes, *it never hurts to say hello to the rabbi.* At least she still retained some sense of humor. Fanny sighed.

Now, through her window, Fanny could make out the temple from down the street, solid gray and splendidly grand, appropriately so for the largest synagogue in the world. Mamo's parents had been members since it first opened on Rosh Hashanah in 1878. Tonight, Mamo had firmly prohibited her from bringing her camera. "For religious reasons?" Fanny had asked, smirking. "For sartorial ones!" Mamo had replied, gesturing to the battered leather satchel where it lived. Grand buildings were not Fanny's main interest, but she had to admit that the angle, especially from the car, was intriguing: the columned portico, the balustrade, the grandiose dome in the shape of a crown, itself topped by a flagpole upon which was perched a firm Star of David, the symbol of the Jewish people. Fanny felt no particular passion for it, was the truth, but she heard Zosia Dror's words in her mind: *the dignity, equality, and freedom of our people!*

The activist was right, Fanny had realized. Who was she, Fanny Zelshinsky, to look for a missing person? She didn't want to make trouble or to get involved in something so terribly over her head. Could Wanda really have been fired for being Jewish? It irked her when everything was turned into a drama of the persecuted, especially when she, Fanny, was on the persecuted side. She felt no persecution; she'd been able to go to university and, frankly, to go wherever she wanted—and driven by a chauffeur.

Besides, Natalia had agreed to let her photograph the making of her fashion show; Fanny had already named the series "Behind the Seams." *That* was what Fanny should be focusing on. That, or on finding another teacher to sign the pink slip and let her into the exhibit. The café, the university—those were her spheres. Yes, Zosia Dror was right. Fanny, with her "fancy chocolates," was in no position to track down an MIA professor!

"Do you remember that time we had the architect Leandro Marconi over for a luncheon?" her mother asked as if to prove her point.

"No," Fanny said. "Because I was two years old." Marconi had been Warsaw's most expensive designer and Fanny had heard this story before. Many times.

"Of course, you were a toddler, Fan-Fan." Mamo smiled. "The cutest thing. Nanny brought you down to show you off. Always beautiful." She squeezed Fanny's arm. They wore matching fur stoles and the hides brushed each other. "Leandro had been lambasted for this design. What did he care? Anything avant-garde is worth fighting for."

Fanny had never thought of the synagogue as avant-garde. Which reminded her: "Aren't we *not* supposed to drive on Shabbos? Do you really want to pull up in front?"

"Of course we are pulling up in front. Do you expect me to walk in these heels?" Mamo retorted. "Besides, it's still light out!"

"Aren't you quite the *rebbetzin*," Fanny jibed.

"Talmudic reasoning is all about finding the loopholes." Mamo laughed. As usual, mother and daughter best connected over clothes and self-aggrandizing jokes, which held some truth.

Now it appeared that the entire line of cars and carriages in front of them was headed for the shul's looping driveway. The Great Synagogue's members were from Warsaw's elite—lawyers, bankers, captains of industry. Papa had himself joined when his textile business began to flourish. Now Fanny wondered if this was where her parents had first met. She considered asking but feared bringing up her father or any link to the subject of marriage, especially after the letter she'd received that morning.

But she had no time to think about that now. The car came to a full stop in front of the Doric columns. The driver opened the door for her, holding out his hand. Fanny, wearing an off-white maxi-length frock printed with large black flowers, a black belt that cinched her waist, and shiny black high heels, took it. She stepped gingerly down onto the car's step and then the pavement, getting ready to ascend into the holy building. So many steps. As her mother had taught her, when climbing up, you must never look down but straight ahead, visualizing a direct line to your end point. Then you must put all your weight on the ball of your foot. Launching yourself straight was the only way to propel, to progress without falling.

And dear, one must never fall.

"Tu Bishvat is the new year of the trees, one of four Jewish new years," the rabbi's voice boomed in Polish. "Fruit trees were awarded special status in the Torah because of their importance in sustaining life."

From her vantage point, a bird's-eye view over the men, Fanny could make out a resplendent men's choir. Chandeliers burned along both levels of the sanctuary, their wax dripping down them like tears, even though the synagogue had modern central heating and gas lighting systems.

"What do you think of the chandeliers?" Mamo whispered. "For the ceremony, we'll light all the candelabras but we must find more elegant candles. Don't forget, we need to go to Bierański's this week to look at fabrics."

Fanny shrugged.

"We are not permitted to eat the fruit of a tree that is less than three years old on Tu Bishvat," the rabbi went on.

Mamo craned her neck, looking for the *machatunim*-to-be in every direction, to no avail. She fidgeted with her scarf. "Look at him," Mamo whispered and pointed at a young man in the third row. "Son of a judge. Oh, and him, the Bregman boy; his grandfather is the head of neurology at The Jewish Hospital, Warsaw's best. Eight separate pavilions. Eleven hundred beds!"

"So what?" Fanny whispered back. Mamo's pushing men on her was absurd, not to mention déclassé.

"Or look at him," her mother said, indicating a young man who wore a bright red kerchief in his suit pocket. "Very handsome. And quirky, like you."

It was Samuel, from her French class. "I know him," Fanny

whispered. "He's nothing like me. And I'm engaged." The one good thing about getting married would be that Mamo would finally leave her alone!

Fanny looked back down over the men's section, but instead of seeing it as a sea of bobbing kippahs to which she was not permitted, she recalled having been down there herself. On the High Holidays, years earlier, she'd sat on Papa's lap taking in his minty aftershave and the toasty scent of old books. From the men's section, close to the action, she had a different perspective: she looked up at the bimah instead of down. Papa hadn't cared that she was a girl. He wanted to show her what life was like right at the front and center.

Fanny recalled her last time in Łódź, three years earlier. Papa had come to meet her at the train; she'd lunged toward him and nestled her cheek into his dark collar, which smelled of sweet tobacco. He'd shown her around, pointing out the city's new museums, schools, and libraries; Łódź, with its second-largest Jewish community in Poland, had become not merely a factory capital but an entertainment capital, with thirty-four cinemas. He'd taken her to the cavernous dining room at the Hotel Grand. The walls were golden, the tablecloths thick and cream, and the live piano music light and airy in the style of famed Łódźer Arthur Rubinstein who, Papa had told her, was off in America, playing at Carnegie Hall. Despite the early dinner hour, patrons trickled in, mainly men in suits swirling glasses of brandy. The maître d' greeted Papa by name, which sent a wave of relief through Fanny, assuring her that Papa was established and secure. Papa had ordered her a liqueur of her own, as if she too were a captain of industry. A friend of her father's had popped by their table to complain about his latest business venture that had gone south. Afterwards, Papa had whispered: Remember what your grandmother used to say: *It's easier to get a drunkard off the ground than a business.* They'd clinked glasses. The point was Papa had always believed in, just like her grandmother did: Fanny was someone who climbed the smooth walls.

Of course, that was before she'd spilled the jam on Ruth's robe. Now, Fanny thought again of the letter that had arrived for her that morning. The Łódź stamp had made her tremble. It was a note, short and formal, congratulating her on her engagement. *With love*, it said, *Papa and Ruth*. It was written in her handwriting.

No mention of attending the wedding.

Wanda was not the first person to disappear from her life.

Finally, the cantor chanted the customary blessings, and the congregation was invited for kiddush in the hall below where a long table boasted a giant challah and a Tu Bishvat "seder" of dried fruits, figs and dates, raisins, and almonds. Mamo, holding Fanny's hand, beelined to the center.

"Ms. Zelshinsky," a man greeted them. He was balding on his head, but well-moustashioed on his face. He was at least sixty and wore a top hat and black coat. Mamo beamed. "Ms." meant he knew Mamo was divorced. Fanny found it strange that she continued to use Papa's last name, as if she still belonged to him. Papa's presence lingered on her like perfume, or perhaps cologne, for other men to sniff, to arouse their jealousy.

"It's been ages," Mamo said, leaning over to kiss the man on the cheek. "I haven't been to synagogue since the Vivaldi festival. Avigdor Radetsky, please meet my daughter, Fanny. She's a French student at Warsaw University."

"Enchanté." Avigdor kissed her hand. His facial hair tickled her knuckles.

Was *he* Mamo's target? He seemed old-fashioned, and old, even for Mamo. A vague sadness overcame Fanny, but its murkiness was uncomfortable, and Fanny pushed it into a mental pocket.

"I forgot how beautiful this building is," Mamo said.

"There is much beauty here," Avigdor said, gesturing at both Mamo and Fanny.

"I was just reminding Fanny of our times with Marconi," Mamo boasted.

"Oh yes, I knew him as well," Avigdor boasted back. Fanny cringed. Perhaps they were well suited. "I have two of his drawings in my collection."

"You collect?"

"Of course. I am very interested in art of all sorts."

"Oh, so am I," Mamo flirted. "And even little Fanny loves making pictures."

Little Fanny? Making pictures? She'd never heard her mother so giddy.

"Do you paint?" he asked her.

"Oh, no," Fanny replied. "I take photographs."

"Just a hobby," Mamo quickly interjected. "Photos of fashionable ladies. It's a wonderful way to enrich her French studies while she prepares to become a lady of the home, a lady who loves a fine collection."

Fanny could feel her face redden with heat. How could her mother speak about her this way, and as if she wasn't even there?

Avigdor chuckled. "Oh, photographs can be so fun."

Fanny noted that his moustache was overly firm, moving as one whole.

"For *collecting*," Mamo reiterated.

Just then, another man called to Mamo from across the table. "Lenora!"

"I must go say hello to Samuel Lizistky," Mamo said, and left Fanny stranded. Had she meant to leave them alone, or to make Moustache jealous? In the awkwardness of the sudden energy vacuum, Fanny grabbed a handful of almonds from a glass bowl.

"What do you photograph?" Avigdor asked, breaking the silence.

"People, in the city. People of Warsaw." She knew better than to say fashion. "I study with the great Wanda Petrovsky," she decided to add, even if Mamo could hear.

"Petrovsky!" Avigdor exclaimed. "I own four of her prints. They're magnificent."

"You do?"

"I buy the works of very few living artists, but Wanda's photos are an exception."

Fanny stayed quiet, eager to see if he would offer any more.

"You should come over and have a look," he said, leaning in close. The nuts grew clammy in her fist.

"I should." Yes, she'd agreed with Zosia, sworn off the search . . . But maybe he knew where Wanda was. Maybe he had information. Maybe he could help.

"Tomorrow?"

Then again, what did he want from her? "Perhaps."

Fanny scanned the room for Mamo and finally spotted her—with Mrs. Brodasz.

"Mr. Radetsky, please excuse me," she said.

"I'm on Fryderyka Chopina, just west of the park—you'll see the house. I'll be home all weekend." He winked. "Call me Avigdor."

Fanny scurried over to the two women, as if she could ever distract them from planning a wedding.

"Don't you look resplendent," Rosa cooed. The woman smiled as she looked Fanny up and down. It dawned on her: This woman was supposed to be her new mother. Fanny had enough mother already . . .

Mamo beamed. "Rosa, I assure you, she takes very good care of herself."

"I can only imagine." Rosa was buxom, even handsome, with blond locks and hefty hips. "You know, you've left quite an impression on our cousin, Samuel. Apparently, he spotted you at the Fashion Café, talking away, looking at art—"

"Oh yes, she always leaves a wonderful impression." Mamo nudged her.

"I love taking in the cultural offerings of the capital," Fanny said on cue. How could such a big city feel like such a small town? There was no escaping.

Her stomach, again.

This was not just a kiss in a park or a date at a horse race, but her entire life sealed.

"I'd love it if you two came over for Shabbat dinner at ours in a couple of months when we're back from our winter travels in Italy," Rosa said. "We can talk about the honeymoon, and about finding you two a home. Simon mentioned you might like to set up your main house in the countryside, away from the bustle of the city. He said you'd like a large, airy home that you could furnish with antiques."

Had she ever said that?

"That sounds perfect and peaceful," Mamo jumped in. "And thank you for the gracious invitation. Without question, we'd be delighted to join you for dinner."

"We're even hoping our Simon will be back then from his business tour for a quick hello," Rosa added, winking.

Back already? Fanny had not been expecting that, not at all. Her understanding, even from his last letter, was that he was traveling throughout Europe and then heading to America, and he would not be back until just before the wedding, in just under half a year.

"He's coming home before heading to the ship to take him abroad," Rosa added, as if reading her thoughts.

"That would be wonderful!" Mamo said. "We are both so excited to see him." Fanny forced a smile.

"Until then," Rosa said, "gut Shabbos."

"Good Sabbath," Mamo replied in a Polish that sounded formal and ridiculous.

Fanny didn't know where to even begin: the country home, the collecting, the pandering, the early return. Her eyes smarted. "Shabbat at theirs?" she hissed. "Since when are we so religious?"

"What does she mean by 'quite an impression'?" Mamo replied, stern. "Were you flirting with strangers, giggling like a schoolgirl? You need to understand that your fruit is ripe and ready to eat—now. You will not be fresh forever. Do not endanger this wedding."

Just then Avigdor passed and winked at Mamo. Then at Fanny. Two winks in a row.

Mamo winked back. She picked up a prune, wrinkled and sagging. "Not fresh forever," she repeated through clenched lips. "Besides," she added, "you'd better get used to Shabbat at their house."

Fanny took a deep breath.

She may have been a fashion girl, but she was a determined fashion girl, a girl who would crawl up smooth walls to get what she wanted. A girl who knew how to be at the center of the action. She was meant to be a photographer. She had to get into that exhibit. She had to find Wanda.

As the car rolled off, Fanny took one last look behind her at the grand synagogue. Enormous, entrenched, elite. Just like her impending marriage.

She waved goodbye.

CHAPTER 8

Zosia

A country girl, Zosia slid through the gates at Grochów as if she'd been there a thousand times. The tall grass, brown from the brittle winter air, napped under a mound of tired snow. The sky looked like it had been coated by paint rollers: Streaks of cloud zigzagged above in matching angles. Nature, Zosia reminded herself, was more meticulous than wild, more cyclic than spontaneous. It made sense.

She was here to find imposters.

Though Grochów was officially considered to be the "outskirts" of Warsaw, where workers' flats were metastasizing by the minute, it still had areas that were more country than suburban. This sub-suburban piece of land was a Dror farm, a "kibbutz," as they called it, a gathering, where youth came for weeks, sometimes even months, to prepare for aliyah, learn about the movement, read, study, build deep bonds, and work the land. Self-sufficiency was one of their supreme values and agriculture was at the heart of this belief system—a community needed to be able to feed itself. Man and land were inextricably connected; farm work led to harmony with the soil and the soul, and the physical labor of sustaining oneself led to true fulfillment. The poorer comrades, like herself, were particularly keen on these *hachsharah*, "preparation farms," which had sprung up all around Poland, where they could learn to be *chalutzim*, pioneers: It was better to live here, despite the meager food and even more meager heat supply, than in smoggy urban poverty.

Zosia headed down the stone path to the house and fields. Now, even in late winter, the trees that surrounded her felt fresh and alive. Green Grochów, arboreous and verdant, was known as "the lungs of Warsaw." Zosia thought about how lungs worked counterintuitively: They did not inflate because we breathed in air; instead, our brains instructed them to expand, causing negative pressure, into which air rushed.

Zosia took an enormous breath, pushing her lungs past their edges, taking as active and positive a breath as she possibly could. She was going to find those imposters. Whether she was sent here by leadership or by Wanda, she would help Dror and show her commitment and diligence. Zosia had faced plenty of troubles in the past few years. How hard could this be?

"Morning!" Zosia waved at a few comrades who stood around a table shucking corn. Zosia smiled to herself at the sight of two women wearing baggy brown pants. This was how work got done: with two legs that could move unrestricted, with a brain that could move them, each on their own, but, working together. Left-wing legs. "I'm Zosia Dror."

"*Dzień dobry*," a pants-wearing woman replied. "*Boker tov.* I'm Sarah."

And here, her sleuth work began. Polish first, Hebrew second . . . Interesting, but did it mean anything? Zosia went straight to the shucking table. Manual labor provided purpose and calm, she thought as she tucked her dark hair behind her ears. Work was the great equalizer.

Zosia shucked, examining the young comrades at her table. She nodded and knew she should make some sort of conversation, but what? *Hi. Are you lying about your values just to get an extremely scarce and coveted visa?* Small talk was not her forte. As a comrade once told her: Your heart doesn't beat to the rhythm of minutiae. For a moment, her thoughts strayed to Abram. They'd planned to meet today to discuss the curriculum for their seminar, but of course, she'd had to postpone. She'd barely been able to tell him without flubbing her words. It was so embarrassing, all this minutiae.

Finally, Zosia introduced herself as a leader from the city (for the first time!). "How are you finding the work?"

"Good," was mumbled from around the table.

"My hands still smart from last week's laundry duty," Sarah said. "To think Grochów is the site of the first steam-powered laundry in all of central and eastern Europe."

"It's also a capital of champagne wines," another comrade replied, "and you don't see us downing that!" A smattering of laughter.

"Mine still blister from the harvest, like a bee had a buffet of my knuckles," another member said. "Zosia, did you know we're selling a percent of our crops at the local market to help plant trees in the *Yishuv*?"

Zosia shook her head and shucked. Was complaining a sign of imposing? Or would a real imposter be too savvy to kvetch?

Dror was supposed to be her primary family, yet Zosia wasn't sure how to read these kids, many of whom were from cities, with their urban ways of speaking.

Now she wished Wanda had talked to her, maybe given her tips, told her who to watch, even shared names. Zosia recalled the fashion's girl's plea, how Wanda hadn't shown up for her lecture, how the university made excuses. Where in the world was the woman?

Probably jail.

Zosia looked around her—everyone was quiet. Too quiet?

"I'm going inside to find pants," Zosia said. "See you all for a meeting in twenty minutes."

Twenty minutes. That's what she had to re-strategize.

"FREEDOM ONLY FOR THE SUPPORTERS OF THE GOVERNMENT, only for members of a party—however numerous they may be—is not freedom." Zosia stood at the head of the room and read to the group from a pamphlet. "Freedom is always the freedom of dissenters. Not because of the fanaticism of 'justice,' but because all the invigorating, healing, and purifying aspects of political freedom depend on this essence and fail to have an effect when 'freedom' becomes a privilege."

She looked up and put her sheet down. The young pioneers seemed to be listening.

Alas, twenty minutes had not been enough for her to figure out how to fish for secrets. Lecturing, at least, bought her some time.

"These are the words of Rosa Luxemburg, Marxist philosopher, anti-war activist, member of the Proletariat Party, the Social Democracy of the Kingdom of Poland and Lithuania, and the Communist Party of Germany. She was not a Zionist, left or right, but a communist, who advocated for a stateless and classless society. Rosa's father was assimilated, political," Zosia continued. "Her mother was religious. Both were well-read: one on liberal politics, one in Yiddish. Rosa was one of the only Jews, and Poles, admitted to an all-girls all-Russian gymnasium. Here, Rosa joined secret circles, studied Polish poets, and connected with the underground Proletariat Party. Her first political act was organizing a strike. That strike led to four party leaders being killed. But she kept working. In this pamphlet, Rosa is referring to the political suppression that happened after the Russian Revolution. The fight for freedom ended in repression."

Zosia had been speaking for too long. She dragged a chair to the front of the room and sat. She was now wearing pants, and was able to straddle her seat in a way that felt powerful, despite the conditions. A small fire provided heat for the entire building and the comrades shivered. The only food available for lunch was bread and tea. True, no one in the movement would dare complain about physical conditions—such were the noises of the fragile!—but still, what imposter would be willing to sit in such austere environs? Their desire to leave Poland must have been enormous. "There are so many definitions of freedom, but I pose: What does freedom mean to you? I'd like to hear each of your thoughts. Let's go around the room."

She'd purposefully left her question open. The comrade could talk about the movement or the term "freedom." Either way, she would see how they answered, assess their commitment and education, evaluate the evidence. This was the best she could do.

"There's freedom to and freedom from," Sarah said. "Positive and negative liberty. We can be free *from* obstacles that constrain our actions, and we can be free *to* act, to speak and think as we wish."

Well, that didn't sound imposterish.

"But going back to Luxemburg," someone else offered. "Can we be free to dissent ad infinitum? Where is the line? Can we refute the very system that allows refutation?"

Imposterish? Or clever?

"And then there's internal freedom, confined to an individual," another said. "This is the ability to act as you truly would like to act without any outside influences. This comes from self-control and the acceptance of personal responsibility."

"Is there such a thing as personal freedom without the group? How can we ever divorce our desires from external pressures and imprints?"

These answers, and questions, were good, too good. Zosia's heart raced. *Only a year*, Rachel had mumbled. What if she was right? What if Zosia had scaled the ranks too quickly and wasn't prepared to lead or to make aliyah? She tried a new tact. "What does Eretz mean to you?"

The answers came even quicker.

"Next year in Jerusalem! Eretz is the place we've been praying to return to for over a thousand years."

"Our people were scattered, exiled by empires and by violence, and we need to return to be free."

"Eretz is the only place we can truly fulfill our socialism."

"Despite exiles, some Jews have lived there continuously for over a millennium. Eretz is our home!"

Zosia felt dizzy. She started to hear it, building, louder, and then, a shrill peal. "What's a home?" Zosia blurted to stop the sound.

"Home is where you're free."

"Home is where you can be yourself, inhabit all the elements of your identity."

"Home," Sarah said, "is the place where you stop trying to escape."

Home. The volume rose. *What happens when the place where you feel safe is not actually safe at all?* Zosia took a deep breath. She needed to stay cool and think rationally. *Ratziolnali.*

What was she even looking for? This "investigation" was an idiotic idea, she scolded herself. She couldn't just wade in here and wing it.

"What is *your* definition of freedom, Zosia?" someone asked her.

"I believe in—" Her mouth went dry. She was supposed to lead a Warsaw seminar with Abram; she was supposed to get on a visa list and escape the continent, yet she felt like the girl on the kitchen stool. But no! She'd overcome that. The movement had helped her gain confidence, purpose.

She recrossed her legs and looked around her at a group of young, expectant faces. Truth was, she didn't see misfits or liars. She saw seventeen-year-olds who slung their limbs over furniture with a lack of self-consciousness, with total comfort. These teenagers knew each other, and the closer they were, the better for the movement. They would be building community together for decades to come. That trust, these bonds, were all-important. Zosia felt a smidgen of envy. *Walking with a friend in the dark,* she remembered her father quoting from the Talmud, *is better than walking alone in the light.*

Before she could answer, Sarah suddenly asked: "So where is Wanda?"

"What?"

"Where's Petrovsky?"

"She's away," Zosia stumbled.

"Where?" Sarah probed. "We heard she fled the country with criminals."

"What?" Criminals? Zosia's hands shook. "That seems unlikely."

"Maybe she just wanted to quit the movement," someone else offered.

"Wanda will be back shortly, and she's very pleased that you are continuing to work and study in her absence," Zosia lied.

An hour later, Zosia put her dress back on and headed to the train station. She had no idea how to read such a room. She had no idea how to find an imposter. She was never going to impress Dror this way and show them she deserved the coveted papers, and now she wasn't even on education so she could not try to climb that ladder either. But Zosia needed to show the movement she was worthy; she needed to know Wanda's plans for her. She needed Wanda to get her that visa, to get herself out of danger and into "home." Zosia needed to find Petrovsky.

It was dark by the time Zosia meandered the streets to Dzielna, and a snow had started to curl around the edges of the wind. How could it be that no two flakes were alike, considering all the snows, everywhere, forever. Such difference seemed impossible, Zosia pondered, yet it was reality. Nature's way: meticulous. Once inside, Zosia stopped to warm her hands by the fire in the main room, but she had to be quick. She needed to go to bed before Mira found her and asked her how it went.

"How did it go?"

But it wasn't Mira.

She turned around. Abram.

"It was alright," she said quietly, aware of her awkward, singsongy tone. How was she ever going to be able to teach a class with him? She had to calm down. "Hard."

"Hard?" he chuckled. "Imposter work is nearly impossible."

She nodded. Better not to speak at all.

"Here's my advice," he said, and caught her gaze. His brown eyes were dark like ground chicory. She quickly looked away. "Work them to the bone. Those who fall off are soft meat. Let the *flanken* drip from the rib. The water dribbles out and you are left with the *lokshen*. Make the holes even wider, and only the sturdiest, thickest noodles will remain. I call it 'the sieve technique.'"

"The sieve technique," she repeated. "Make it so hard that the imposters leave on their own accord."

"Exactly."

No psychological guessing, just work, work, and more work. Why hadn't she thought of that? He was smart, so smart, which of course only made him more attractive. A dog-eared copy of *La Condition Humaine* dangled from his hand.

"What are you doing tonight?" he asked.

Zosia's mouth went bone dry. She swallowed. "I was going to, well, sleep."

"Come with me to a show," Abram said.

A show? At this hour? City people were never satisfied with their days, wringing out each minute like a washcloth. She would never get used to it. And hopefully, she reminded herself, she wouldn't have to. "Oh, I don't think—"

"To see what?" a voice echoed.

Zosia spun around.

The fashion girl?

"Who are you?" Abram asked.

"A friend of Zosia Dror's," Fanny said. Her claret cheeks matched the velour of her dress. She turned to Zosia. "I came looking for you earlier, but you weren't here. I need to—"

"We're working on a community program together." Zosia interrupted her, looked at Abram, and smiled.

"I'll come," Fanny said.

"Come where?" Zosia said.

"To the show. I love the theater. And I really need to talk to my community worker, over here. I have important information for her."

Was Abram looking at Fanny's dress? Her figure? Was he smiling?

"Zosia said she might not come," Abram said. "She's tired and needs to sleep."

"Oh, I'm coming," Zosia replied. "Let's go."

CHAPTER 9

Fanny

"So, WHAT ARE WE GOING TO SEE?" FANNY ASKED AGAIN, swaying as she stepped. She was by now familiar with Dzielna Street, avoiding the uneven bits of pavement and the piles of dirty snow, blackened on top like over-roasted marshmallows. Now, she found herself squeezed between these two on the sidewalk, like the filling inside an American sandwich. If only they were a Polish sandwich, an open-faced *kanapki* . . . How would she get Zosia alone? She had something to tell her, something big. But The Boy was so . . . there.

"It's a surprise," said the boy, whose burly build was not unattractive, and who she learned went by Abram. *Abram Dror?*, she'd asked him, but he just smiled. Zosia had coughed. Now she racked her brains for what might be playing in this Jewish, working-class part of town—her new hangout, it seemed. Had she heard that a new iteration of Ida Kaminska's production of the radical feminist play, *Mir Froyen*, based on Maria Morowicz-Szczpkowska's Polish script, was showing here? She would actually love to see that, but, as they walked along Krochmala past signs for gramophone, umbrella, and underwear shops, she reminded herself: She was here on a mission.

"Isn't it amazing that each and every snowflake is unique?" Zosia posed.

Fanny appreciated her attempt to melt the awkward silence.

Snow continued to fall. Flakes blew in all directions, even up. "It's because—"

"How do you two know each other?" Abram interrupted. "What community project are you working on?"

"Fanny is at the university," Zosia said. "She's a photographer. She does . . ."

"I have my own Leica," Fanny said, patting her satchel bag. "I take photos of clothes."

Zosia sighed and shook her head. Oops.

"*Shmatehs?*" Abram asked.

"All kinds of clothes. It's not easy making clothes look good. One needs to think about presenting stark lines and frills, light and shadow, juxtaposing shapes and forms. Beauty brings me pleasure."

"Pleasure," Abram said, "is fleeing. It's happiness we must seek, and happiness comes from a pursuit. Achieving a socially beneficial goal is what leads to genuine satisfaction. Pleasure is present tense, but happiness is tied only to the future."

"Some might say a focus on the present is most important."

"She's helping us reach students," Zosia threw in, "and—"

"We're here!" Abram interrupted and urged the women to the left, into a courtyard, then toward a doorway, where the last stragglers like them trickled in.

Fanny noted the poster. Dzigan and Schumacher. "You brought us to Yiddish vaudeville?"

"Yiddish comedy cabaret. Entertainment of the people, for the people."

Which people? She hadn't uttered a word of Yiddish since her Bubbe had died in 1931.

"You'll love it."

Zosia didn't say a word.

The three of them descended a creaky stairwell into a musty cabaret theater. If this was of the people, it was of lots of people. They were touching her, crowding her like kippers in a can. Truth was, Fanny loved it. The city was life! Still, she pulled her bag in tight.

"Mademoiselle," said a man who winked at her, then tipped his hat.

Abram urged them toward a table, his arm wrapping around her back. The warmth surprised her; the limb felt heavy, like the weight of a wool blanket that's been folded over. "The show is starting."

"It's burning! It's burning!"

Dzigan played a bubbling, hyperactive beggar, darting across the stage, complaining about life in his thick and unliterary Łódź accent, and now about his burning home. A bright red handkerchief hung from his pocket, then flung from his pocket. His gesticulations were wild.

Schumacher, in glasses, was his stolid and calm opposite. "What's burning?" he asked laconically, subtly gesturing with his left hand. "Who's burning?"

How the audience laughed. Except for Zosia, who smiled awkwardly. Fanny impressed herself by understanding bits of dialogue.

While the majority of Warsaw's songwriters and sketch-scribes were Jewish, most worked behind the scenes. As her grandmother used to say, backstage was a giant clump of gefilte fish while the stage itself was thinly sliced light pink ham—which belted out the carp's lyrics. While some Jews, like Dzigan and Schumacher, were also the face of the show, these were usually all-Jewish troupes, performing for all-Jewish and working-class audiences. All to say, Fanny didn't know them well. But at least this wasn't a *szmonces* . . . Fanny could hardly believe there was a whole genre that mocked assimilated Jews, i.e., her.

Fanny scanned the room, taking in old men, young women, and everything in between. A corpulent male at a nearby table laughed with such might, it looked like he might have a heart attack. The double-chinned female next to him matched his joy; she placed her hand on the inside of his elbow, puzzle pieces locking together. And then the man to his side—oh! Fanny recognized that hairstyle, the slick side part, the cocked neck, the cheekbones high like stone arches.

It was Simon. Her betrothed. He must have returned from his trip.

Fanny's heart stopped.

Should she run? Talk to him? No, she couldn't, she—

He turned.

She froze.

It wasn't him.

The man caught her stare and grinned.

She averted her gaze.

What was she thinking? Why in the world would Simon be in a working-class theater? He would never take her to a show like this, not in a million years. He planned to take her to the countryside to raise chickens and children and chintz.

Fanny took a breath, shook it off.

At intermission, Fanny hoped to catch her friend's ear with increased urgency, but Abram lit a cigarette and started conversing. "What do you think?"

"I don't do much comedy," Zosia said.

"It's not quite to my tastes," Fanny agreed.

"Not to your tastes?" Abram asked. "This is the art of the people, of the Jewish masses. Which *we* are part of. We are part of the great Jewish population."

"It seems a little passé." Fanny needed to get Zosia alone and now was her chance. Did this man ever use the toilet?

"Passé? Au contraire. It's a new world, Fanny," Abram went on. "This"—he gestured around him—"is not our parents' Poland. We have a new republic, with political parties and elections and the hope of true democracy, even if it hasn't come to fruition just yet. Airwaves connect people across the globe. We can fly! The future is ours to write."

"Doesn't every generation think that?" Fanny asked. "Don't we all believe that we are suddenly so different?"

As she spoke, she noticed that the woman next to her was wearing a skirt with stripes that wrapped right around. It reminded Fanny of the photo she'd shown in Wanda's class, but the material was thicker, more working class. What if she took a picture that highlighted just the stripes, a fragment of material as it draped quietly around the wooden stool leg instead of a human leg? Fanny began to fiddle with her bag, but then, what was the point? Would Wanda even see it? Would anyone? Fanny realized: She hadn't taken a photo in days. She didn't know what to capture. She'd lost her vision.

Fanny had tried schmoozing at the university—could she find someone else to sign the pink form? Professor Hermann Glouberman had recently moved to America like so many others, and the only photographer left on the faculty was the modernist Bolesław Bugaj, who was notorious for refusing to work with women. She had tried to book an appointment with him this morning, and his secretary told her his schedule was full—until the end of the year.

She needed to talk to Zosia and find Wanda.

"We are different," Abram answered. "*Now* is a different time."

"Monsieur Abram Dror." Fanny changed her tone. She reached across the table for his cigarette case, slipped out a cigarette, placed it between her lips using two freshly manicured fingers, and lit it herself. She inhaled deeply, then, batting her eyelashes in a way that was both exaggerated and flirtatious, she blew out, emanating a single curl of smoke like a genie sliding out of one of Mamo's antique bottles. "I am parched. I hate to trouble you, but perhaps you may be able find us refreshments?"

He smiled at her. "I think I can manage that."

"Just water for me," Zosia barked. But right as he got up, the lights dimmed. Ugh! Fanny had lost her chance. She'd have to wait until the next intermission.

Act Two began with what was apparently, according to Abram, who whispered insider notes, a new routine. In this sketch, which mocked the current idea that there were too many Jews in Poland, all the Jews were encouraged to leave. And what happened? Poland was left with a decimated economy and no culture. There was one last Jew, "The Last Jew in Poland," who was so slow to pack, he'd missed the exile. But now, the Poles had realized they needed their Jews and were begging him not to go, even honoring him at a banquet with Yiddish songs and a government award. *"Please, please stay!"* The audience erupted in laughter.

Fanny's ear was getting used to the grating, guttural Yiddish, to the twisty vowels that went on and on . . .

She looked around at the audience. They were eating up the schmaltz. Hungry for this. Starving.

"We'll give you free rent! Food! Anything!"

A burst of applause, guffaws. People clapped and banged, heckled in agreement. In the moment of laughter, Fanny mused, people could experience no emotion except joy. The air was thick with cathartic pleasure. Which is why Fanny hadn't noticed. She hadn't heard the gasps, the confused murmurs, and then, suddenly, right behind her—screams, crashes, flinging bayonets.

"Halt!"

Pandemonium. Lights on bright. Blue uniforms pushed over a table, then another, making their way to the stage. Glasses and ashtrays flew into the air, then shattered loud on the ground. A confetti of shards lay across the floor. A woman yelped, another wept.

Zosia leapt up; Fanny followed. Abram had seated them on the side of the theater, near the front, and they needed to get back, all the way back to the stairwell—but so did everyone. Too many people headed for one exit. She followed Zosia and felt Abram's breath on her neck. He may have been saying something but she couldn't make it out over the barking orders, expletives, chaos. Her own words wouldn't form. Fanny clutched her bag, tucking it into the curve of her side. She tried to stay calm, to focus on the space immediately in front of her, the air that was available for her to breathe. But it was smoky air. Too smoky. Her lungs were deflating. She needed air. More air.

Suddenly, a surge. Fanny was pushed to the floor. Her bag flung open, the Leica tumbled out. *No, no, no.* She reached for it, slithering under the table where it landed, brushing against that beautiful striped skirt, now splattered—with, could it be, droplets of blood? "Fanny!" Abram yelped. He managed to blockade their area, to help her up, but how would they get out? She grabbed her bag with both hands. *Fanny, don't faint don't faint don't faint.*

Then, just near them, a stage door opened. Zosia was in front. "Move!" Abram pushed her that way.

Finally, they were outside.

In the back alley, people gulped the cool air. "Are you alright?" Abram asked her. His chest heaved. "Do you need a doctor?"

"I'm fine." Fanny brushed herself off, fixed her hair barrettes, patted her bag. She'd heard about these working-class brawls, about gang members and collection monies and police raids . . . Her ears buzzed hot. Fanny felt strangely alive.

"And you, Zosia?" he asked.

Zosia was composed. "I'm fine."

"They're stunt actors. This is a stunt!" someone in the crowd called out. "It's fiction, a *meiseh*."

"The only fiction is that we Jews are safe here," another responded. "The sketch was prescient!"

"Shutting this performance down is a new degree of antisemitism," someone else said. "It's getting worse."

Murmurs spread through the audience. They were now watching a new show—each other:

"Did you hear the latest news?"

"You mean the news that the Camp of National Unity was formally founded as an official Polish party? As if all the other parties calling for Jews to leave Poland weren't bad enough."

"Their whole platform is to introduce Nuremberg laws to Poland. What's next? Will they make all Jews wear dunce caps?"

"Have you heard about the attacks on Jewish students at admissions offices, with razors?"

"Ever since Piłsudski's death, the country keeps bending farther to the right. To think, we had so much hope for Poland's new iteration, and where does it all head? To fascism."

"The Church promotes it!"

"No, it doesn't . . . but, in many towns, it tolerates the antisemitic libels."

"What an outrage," someone called. *"Police shutting down a Yiddish show. This has never happened."*

Fanny wasn't so sure about any of it. Working-class bars were raided all the time, and Jews had been dealing with these aggressions in Poland for over a thousand years; it was part of living here. Rural peasants may have disliked Jews, but that was due to ignorance stemming from a lack of education. The intellectual and artistic classes adored the country's Jews. Provincial affairs had nothing to do with Warsaw. Besides, this was 1938, year of the bounce: The economy was finally recovering, and, in fact, there had been *fewer* attacks on the Jewish community.

"Jews do not have power in Poland," Zosia said as she added her voice to the mix. "We may be legally emancipated, but we do not have true citizenship. We're not equal. We're second-class citizens. We don't have political sway and are at the mercy of hosts who don't necessarily like us. We need our own country, where we can do our own silly comedy whenever we please."

"Or . . . we need to defend ourselves," Abram said out loud, pacing in the little space he had, clearly unsure what to do with his body, with his growing energy, inflating feelings. "If we Jews had our own army, then we wouldn't have to rely on Poland's forces for our safety. We could live here in calm."

"So, we're supposed to stay in a country that doesn't want us and have our own police to defend us against the government of said country?" Zosia was indignant. "We need Eretz, as Dror says!"

"But how realistic is aliyah these days?" Abram asked her. "We need a backup plan."

"Alright," Fanny joked, "break it up, you two comrades!"

Suddenly, policemen streamed out of the venue. Four of them dragged Dzigan and Schumacher by the arms. Abram grabbed Fanny's elbow and pulled her to the front of the crowd. "Quick," he urged. "Use your camera and capture this!"

"Me?"

"Yes, you!"

Fanny fast-fumbled with her bag, unlacing the ties. She scanned the crowd: Surely someone more experienced was there to capture all this. But she saw only a panicking mob, and no one stepping out with a camera.

Fanny pulled out the Leica and flash, assembled them, and held the apparatus firmly. She peered through the lens and saw police barking and the two comedians talking as quickly as they did onstage. She began to click the button, but it felt mechanical. What was she capturing? For whom?

The crowd was closing in; in the chaos, she grabbed Zosia's arm. "Come with me!" She dragged Zosia out of the melee, into the alleyway behind.

"What is it?" Zosia asked. "Where are you taking me?"

"I decided, we need to find Wanda no matter what. And we need Dror's help."

"Listen to me. I thought about it, I really did, all morning in fact. But the truth is, Wanda could be in jail. I'm afraid this is beyond you, beyond both of us. Beyond even Dror."

"Jail? Why?"

"I don't know."

Fanny fumbled in her pocket and took out a crumpled piece of paper. She shoved it into Zosia's hand. "This is her address."

"Whose address?"

"Wanda's house," Fanny said. Zosia looked at her as if she were crazy. Or a genius? "I found it in the office at the Fashion Café. No one even noticed me looking through their address book."

Zosia stared at her. The women could hear shouting in the background, police calls, and Dzigan replies. "Why are you so keen to find her?"

"I need a teacher. You of all people should understand that," Fanny said. "Come with me, tomorrow. Please. We can try to find more information."

"I really don't—"

"Something funny is going on here," Fanny kept pressing. "Something is not right. Besides, she lives close by. It will just take a few minutes. Think of your entire life, Zosia. What's a few hundred seconds? I need something from Wanda and, I have a feeling, so do you."

Zosia looked at the address and closed her fist around it. "Fine," she said, cutting her off. "I'll go with you to her house in the morning. But after that, promise, you'll leave me alone."

"Thank you," Fanny said, without promising anything. Wanda lived in the Jewish Quarter and was part of Zosia's world; she was going to need her insider's help. She wanted to hug Zosia, but Zosia did not seem like the hugging type.

"What are you doing over here?" The girls turned to find Abram walking toward them in the alley. "You need to document the police antagonizing Jews!"

"Just finding a different angle," Fanny said and put her camera away, even though she'd taken no shots. "In any case, I have to go." She whispered to Zosia, "Nine a.m."

The snow swirled heavier than before, the flakes sticking to her lashes. "The reason the flakes are all different," Fanny called back to the comrades as she left them, "is because of what they've been through. Each flake has its own path, traveling through different atmospheres, and this journey transforms them. They change during their fall. They change. And change. And change."

THE NEXT MORNING, AS FANNY WALKED DOWN THE BUSY streets with their blaring headlines and bicycle repair shops and approached the building whose crumpled address she'd passed on, it suddenly struck her that she might be on her own. What did Zosia owe her, after all? And what did Zosia even want from Wanda? Perhaps it was nothing significant, nothing that would push her to come. Fanny thought of Nowak's lecture on Descartes and his method of doubt. One was required to be skeptical: We were supposed to tear down all our belief foundations in order to build up a new set with more justifiable fundamentals. It was important, even necessary, to be suspicious. But what would she do if solo—

There was Zosia, waiting across the street.

"Good morning." Fanny waved. "You made it!"

"How should we approach this?" Zosia asked after she'd crossed.

"Come with me."

The women entered the building and located the apartment on the third floor of the fourth stairwell, tucked away from the world. Until that moment, Fanny had never considered where Wanda may have lived or what her personal life entailed. Fanny knocked on the door. They waited. She knocked again.

"Who is it?" A voice came from inside.

"Wanda's cousins," Fanny answered. "Is she there?"

A moment later, the front door was opened by an older woman with graying hair and wire-rimmed glasses. "You're her cousins?" she asked, looking them up and down. "Both of you?"

Fanny took in her own beaded scarf and hem and realized she probably should have dressed down. "Yes, city and country girls," she replied quickly. "We haven't seen Wanda for a few days, so we just came to make sure she wasn't sick."

"I don't know where she is."

"You don't?" Fanny probed. "Do you have any ideas?"

"She sometimes travels but usually lets me know," the landlady said.

"And she said nothing? Nothing about a sabbatical? Or a trip?"

"Nothing," the landlady said. "And rent is due today. She always pays in the morning."

"When was she last here?" Fanny asked.

"A few days ago, I think. I don't keep tabs."

"Of course. Did anyone unusual come here?" Fanny probed.

"Not that I know of. She had visitors, from time to time, but I don't know."

"What kind of visitors?" Fanny asked.

"How should I know? You're her cousins!"

"We haven't seen her in a few months," Fanny said.

"Then how did you know she was gone?" the older woman asked. "I thought you said you hadn't seen her in a few days. Who are you really, and what do you want?"

Fanny was being an idiot. She rummaged in her bag for a bar of chocolate, but Zosia pushed her hand down.

Then Zosia addressed the woman, in Yiddish. "We're Wanda's extended family, and like all family, we just know. Something is awry. Do you have family?"

The woman nodded. "Of course."

"And sometimes, you just have a sense that something is going horribly wrong?"

She nodded again.

"We'd like to check for any suggestions of where she might be. And," Zosia lowered her voice to a whisper, "we need to confirm that—God forbid—she's not in there, very sick, or worse."

"*Oy gatenyu*, you think so?"

"We don't know."

The landlady reached for a set of keys that had been hanging on the wall and handed them to Zosia. "Here, go in."

Spurred on by Zosia's success, Fanny was tempted to take out her Leica and snap Zosia placing the key in the lock but she waited until they were inside, with the door shut.

"Don't touch anything," Zosia whispered. "And be quiet with that." Zosia gestured at her camera.

"I know." Sheesh, this woman was acting like her mother. Then again, Fanny wasn't sure what to capture. What constituted a clue? Wanda's desk, her dresser, her bed, books, plants, pens, negatives, and camera equipment all seemed so personal, small and normal. And though this space was much neater than her office had been, there was something similar to it, a comparable energy. It reminded Fanny of how every room she inhabited, even the temporary ones, always ended up looking the same. Her jewelry on one side of her bed, her novels on the other; sweaters in a pile, cosmetics on a dresser. *We always place ourselves into space in the same way*, Fanny considered as she tried to find an angle that showed as much of the room as possible. *We orient ourselves and our things in architecture in a way that makes us feel safe. Where did that fundamental design sense come from? Our infanthood, our parents, something more ancestral? The womb?*

"Home is an extension of self," Fanny said, "filled with the traces of you. You make it but it also makes you. It's an endless reflection."

"Home," Zosia said, and looked her in the eyes, "is where you stop running away."

What was Zosia implying? Could one run and not even know it? *Maybe*, Fanny thought, *if the world was running alongside you at the same pace, then you didn't see your own motion.*

"I wonder if this is her home, or rather, *a* home," Zosia said while scanning documents on the desk. "Not all comrades live with the movement, especially here in the city, but it's strange that she lives in a rented-out room. I hadn't considered it before, but why wouldn't she live with the Dror family?"

"Stop," Fanny suddenly blurted.

"I'm not allowed to talk about Dror? I thought you were desperate for our help."

"No, stop moving," Fanny said. "Keep your feet where they are."

"Huh?"

"You're standing straight, at right angles to the desk, which means," Fanny pointed, "the rug is crooked."

She kicked over its side with her shoe. "Look!" The floorboards had a gap between them.

Fanny used the pole from her flash to pry up a board. Underneath: a dug-out area, with a contraption. Fanny took off her beaded scarf and used it to pick up the little machine, which she placed on the rug.

Zosia bent down to look at it. "I think it's a small printing press."

Click. Fanny even said it out loud: "Click!" Her first photo in days. She'd found a clue.

They looked back in the hole. No papers, nothing else. A press in a void.

Then they heard footsteps, creaking floors.

"Quick, Fanny," Zosia said. "And stop touching everything."

"Jesus, I'm not touching anything." Using her scarf, she put the press back.

Zosia kicked over the floorboard with her shoe, and it made a bang.

"You alright?" the landlady called.

Zosia looked at Fanny in panic.

Then the older lady was standing at the threshold, staring at them, suspicious. "I never asked—what are your names?"

"Zosia," Fanny answered right away. "Zosia Dror."

"Zosia Dror," the landlady repeated, slowly, as if putting it to memory.

"Thank you so much for your troubles. We found nothing unusual. We should leave you," Fanny said. "But we'll let you know if anything comes up."

"And what of her rent?" the woman asked.

"I'll take care of it," Fanny offered and took out her checkbook.

Outside, Zosia turned to her. "Why did you give her my name?"

"Oh please, it's not even your real name," Fanny replied. "What do we do now?"

"We do nothing. I'm done."

"Meet me tomorrow night," Fanny insisted. "We'll figure it out."

"No."

"Hey," Fanny asked as they came to the street. "Why didn't you let me give her the chocolate?"

"Candy is not a currency," Zosia said. "There's a fine line between sweet and saccharine. And the second you cross it, it's too late. Your teeth already sting."

Later that day, Fanny arrived at the Nowosci Theater breathless and took her seat—a box seat, no less. "I can't believe you've taken me to see Josephine Baker!" she said to Mamo, who donned a brand-new twisted green crepe snood in her hair. Fanny had been sure the meeting would be wedding related—a tailor, a butcher—but instead, "*the* Josephine Baker."

The theater buzzed with excitement. The American-born French movie star was here to sing in Warsaw for the first time. Fanny had loved *Siren of the Tropics* when her parents had taken her to see it at the Regal Cinema all those years ago. Baker's smile dazzled as if her mouth were filled with gemstones in place of teeth.

Fanny could feel the throb of the room in her body; she nearly burst.

"Why are you all red?" Mamo probed. "Where have you been?" She pointed at Fanny's bag. "Taking photos?"

"Yes," Fanny said with more than a hint of defiance, but she certainly couldn't tell her mother the truth of where she'd actually been. Fanny thought of Wanda's photo at the Fashion Café. "I was taking photos of orange sellers, hawking fruit from their carts on Smocza Street."

"Peddlers? And in *that* neighborhood." Mamo sighed for the

ages. "Fanny, enough with this idiocy. By the way, did you look at the design ideas I left for the veil and the—"

Mamo's attention was drawn to the other side of the theater. A man waved to her from the opposite box. Mamo waved back enthusiastically.

It was Avigdor, the older man from the synagogue.

Mamo smiled. "He's handsome, isn't he?" He *was* her mother's plan.

When Mamo turned away, attempting (unsuccessfully) to appear coquettish, the man looked at Fanny, raised his eyebrows, and shrugged with exaggeration. She knew it meant: Why didn't you come to my house to see the photos?

Fanny shrugged back.

And then the lights dimmed. The curtains rose.

The stage appeared like a jungle, strewn with enormous casts of branches and patches of artificial grass. The music began: a propulsive banging, animal-like. Josephine emerged from one of the branches wearing only a string of pearls and a banana skirt! The audience gasped.

Fanny watched aghast as the singer proceeded to the center of the stage where, in time with the pulsating drumbeats, she gyrated her hips, swooping like a hula dance, a Charleston gone wild! It was mesmerizing, impossible to look away. Baker owned the stage, the world, them.

Shivers ran through Fanny, up and down her entire body. Josephine Baker put herself on the line. Totally, utterly on the line. She listened to no one, and literally danced to her own tune and in doing so, captured hearts. The banana-dance skirt, the artist's complete vulnerability yet mesmerizing power—it was like nothing Fanny had ever seen. The personal and the universal all wrapped in one. This was art, genuine art, like Wanda's photos. Fanny had to become a *real* artist, a truth teller, someone who took risks—real risks.

The curtains closed. "A handheld microphone . . . wow! Warsaw's never seen such a thing!" Mamo went on and on to their seat neighbors. Then she turned to Fanny. "Let's get out of here quickly. You look like you were tumbling in the mud. A good girl doesn't roll in the streets."

"I'm not a good girl," Fanny whispered to herself, taking a final look back at the stage. And for the first time, she said it: "I'm a photographer."

CHAPTER 10

Zosia

"So what did you think of the show?" Abram asked as they sat down at the café table afterwards. Like all of Warsaw in the evening, the restaurant that Abram suggested they try was busy, and they had to sit close to each other in order to hear.

Zosia gulped down a full glass of water.

They were meant to be working on their seminar plans; that was the reason she agreed to join him for dinner. She didn't know they'd go to a restaurant. *We don't have the money*, she'd told him as they walked in. *Don't worry*, Abram had said, *the owner is my friend.*

That evening, Abram had taken a few of the Dror leaders to see another performance. Even though Dzigan and Schumacher had ultimately not been imprisoned, they were harshly reprimanded for their satire of the Polish political situation, and the incident had moved him. Abram was even more determined to support Jewish theater. The play they'd just seen, apparently one of the most popular pieces in Warsaw, was about a woman who fell in love with a man (played by a particularly handsome actor with a particularly stark jawline). Only, when she found out he was a communist, she murdered him.

Zosia had spent most of the production clutching the sides of her seat, catching her breath, and making sure that none of her—not her clothes, not her shoes, certainly not her fingers—touched Abram. She kept a nice crack of space between them, though she could feel the heat emanating from his side. Did she also emanate?

Was he leaning closer to her than to Yossi on his right? Did she want him to? The darkness of the theater had spawned revelations.

Abram took a sip of vodka from a small glass. A waiter placed two paper placemats on the marble-topped table, and Abram ordered: bread, pickles, and gefilte fish. A few sardines too. "Is that alright?"

"We can't afford it," she reiterated. The movement's money was their money and vice versa. "And even if we could, there are better ways to spend it," she mumbled. She had to admit: She was relieved he hadn't ordered meat. Though she had abandoned strict kashrut, she still couldn't imagine eating treif.

"It's no herring in olive oil . . . Sometimes you have to live. You never know what's coming." He smiled, but was it a sly grin? Her heart raced.

"Are you predicting another stock market crash?"

"If only the capitalists could keep their money in their pants," he said. "Anyway, my friend owns this place and he owes me a favor. So even if we were paying, we'd be supporting a Jewish business."

Zosia said nothing. She took out her notebook.

"So, what did you think?" Abram asked again. He was back to the show. "Are you on the side of love or politics?"

Zosia felt herself blush. "Of course she chose to sacrifice him," she said quickly. "Ideals always trump love. Especially when they are communist ideals! His politics were not only illegal but anti-Zionist."

"Romantic love is a capitalist construct," Abram teased. "Then again, how can feelings—deep guttural feelings, lurching of hearts, blushing of bodies—be created by economic systems?"

"*Everything* is molded by economic systems," Zosia said, firm. This conversation was too much for her. "Romance is distraction," she added, "capitalist or not. That's why in the movement we discourage"— she got quiet—"relations. And alcohol."

"Well, there are exceptions." He took another sip. Then he looked at her, right at her. His eyes were dark and deep, and reminded her of how, as a child, she felt mesmerized on Shabbat when she gazed into the family's goblet of kiddush wine. "L'chaim!" he said, as if he knew just what she'd been thinking.

Zosia's mouth was a desert. She drank more water, but the sips were only an oasis, and nothing helped. "It's important to stay focused, to stay in your own skin," she eked out. Then, like an idiot, she blurted, "Fanny would have loved the play."

"You think? She didn't seem to like the Dzigan show."

"You're right." Why did she bring Fanny up?

"Then again, I think she secretly did like it." He smiled. "I'm always happy to introduce Jews to their own culture. Even if it means being raided by police." He paused. "Tell me more about how you met her?"

Just then, the restaurant owner, a large and balding man, waved at Abram from behind the counter. Zosia was thankful for the intrusion.

"He's an active Bundist," Abram gestured at the owner and told her, "He's in their self-defense group. You know, they're a true working-class group. And maybe, they're a touch more realistic than we are. To them, Jewishness is a nationality that should thrive within a multiethnic state; Jews are a nation of culture. Their vision doesn't rely on visas: It's about defending Jewish equality and cultural autonomy—and particularly working-class life—here in Europe. It's why they're growing so fast."

"Good luck to them," Zosia said, and for a moment she thought of her family. "I can only hope there will be a Jewish future here in Poland." She recalled that he'd said something about Jewish self-defense the other night at Dzigan. What did this mean? He certainly wouldn't be able to stay in Dror if he was joining the Bund's street gang. Was he?

They were interrupted as the fish arrived. A very small portion, but it was oily and rich. Abram took a bite, and she followed him. The food jolted her awake, smart textures folding around her tongue.

"Take more," he said. "Don't get too skinny."

"Thank you, *Mamaleh*." It came out rude.

Awkward silence.

"So, what should our first lecture be about?" Zosia asked, getting back to the purpose of this meal.

"Well, this! Love or ideals? Let's do a seminar on the nature of romance."

Romance? No no, no . . .

"I meant emotions," he said. Her discomfort must have been apparent. "Maybe we can discuss how feelings are based in class. Are passions only egotistical? Are sensations bourgeois?"

"How did you become so interested in class?" She changed the subject.

"Is your father a grocer?" he asked.

"How did you know?"

"I saw your inventory list for the Dror seminar the other day, and it reminded me of my father's lists for his grocery store," he said. "I'm also from a small town, Zosia. I also taught myself Hebrew."

He'd noticed all this about her? She felt herself turn redder.

"My family and I moved to Warsaw six years ago."

She was so thirsty again. Where was that water?

"Are you alright?"

She nodded. No words. She had so many questions: What did his family do now? What were they like? Who *was* he? But nothing came out. She was afraid if she tried, she'd make yelping sounds like an animal. She focused on her notebook. "I need to head out but let me write up some lecture ideas and I'll leave them in your postbox." She stood up to go.

"Listen!" Abram said. "Listen to the song."

A record played. A woman crooned: *"You can be what you want, a Zionist, a Bundist, who cares? But Leibke, the time will come when even the most religious Jews will have to learn the Tango and the Charleston!"*

Now that's romantic dreaming, Zosia thought as she thanked him for the food and walked out. Their religion was famous for "two Jews, three opinions" after all.

❧

ABRAM, THE SARDINES, THE CAMERA, THE CHOCOLATES, THE police raids, the sneaking around . . . not to mention Fanny's beaded scarf! It was all so much. The next day, Zosia ate her dinner of cold beet soup and hard cheese slices, their holes created by fermenting gasses that festered within. Zosia had been avoiding Mira ever since her failed day at Grochów, but now she had to set things straight. Honesty was a core principle of the movement. Zosia needed to lay it all bare, confess what she'd done and, in doing so, obtain accurate information. Truth begot truth.

So, after dinner, instead of avoiding Mira, Zosia beelined to her room. She reminded herself: As a child, when she'd been afraid of dogs, she'd forced herself to pet them. She paused at the door before knocking. Yes, a part of her hoped Mira wasn't there, but only a small part. She had to know.

"Zosia, what brings you here?"

As Mira opened the door, Zosia peeked in. Mira had been reading a well-thumbed book by candlelight, likely so as not to waste electricity. This woman truly lived her principles. "Wanda Petrovsky," Zosia said, point-blank. As she'd learned in the movement, the truth was best served as a cold appetizer, quick and small. A piece of whitefish. A pickle. It served a finite purpose, to line the empty stomach, and then be cleared from the table to make room.

"Oh?"

Zosia followed Mira into her room, which was cold, so cold. For a second Zosia let herself dream of Eretz, of warm winds brushing her cheeks and sand trickling between her toes—experiences she'd only ever read about. "Is Wanda really in jail, like you said?" Zosia blurted, thinking of Warsaw's political prison for women. "Is she in Serbia Prison?"

"Forget about her," Mira said.

"Forget?"

"Forgetting is an important skill. I know here at Dror, we emphasize memory, remembering Jewish history, recalling our goals.

But to forget is not necessarily to repress truth. Sometimes forgetting is a method of pruning. Forgetting leads to concentration."

There were many benefits to forgetting: Zosia knew this only too well.

Still, she wasn't going to do well on the imposter task without her, which only meant she needed Wanda to help her get a visa even more. Plus, Abram was distracting her, which would mean her lectures would devolve and all her plans were going to fall apart! "But," Zosia kept trying, "where is she? Why forget about her?"

"Because you have other things to concentrate on, Zosia."

"I know."

"You are in Warsaw, on a leadership team." Mira was stern.

"I know."

"How did it go in Grochów?"

Zosia felt herself turn red again. "I'm working on it."

"Remember," Mira said. "Don't get distracted. Stay focused."

"I know," Zosia said. As she headed for the door, she asked, "What are you reading?"

"Lu Xun's satiric critical essays," she said. "I don't purchase books. I borrow them from the library."

"I know," Zosia said again.

I know, I know, I know, she kept saying. Yet it felt like the exact opposite.

That night, Zosia lay in her slim bed, eyes wide open, trying to forget; and while she managed to push away thoughts of Abram's tender smile, they were replaced exclusively by thoughts of Wanda. What had she been printing? Why hide it? Was it the list of imposter names she meant to give to Zosia? Was it a letter about a visa? It was all so unclear, so frustrating.

She reminded herself: Optimism was an obligation. It was a Dror duty to stay hopeful, not to wallow in selfish glum.

Breathe. Linshom.

And then she remembered that Wanda's landlady had her name. Zosia had heard about lists of names in Berlin . . . Jews were accused, then they disappeared, to who knows where . . . You never wanted your name out, and never ever on any list. And now, thanks to fashion girl, hers was associated with what was potentially a crime. *Zosia Dror, Zosia Dror, Zosia Dror* she saw, written in blood. Her heart raced.

If only she could sleep. She tossed, turned, and tossed again. A person could control even their wildest urges, their deepest thoughts, their most basic moods and reactions to events in this world, but they could not control their own slumber.

"Zosia, are you here?" Rachel said as she pushed open the door. "I'm back."

Zosia jolted up in her bed, unprepared for interaction with another human. She covered herself with her itchy wool blanket. "How did it go?" she fumbled.

"It was good," Rachel said, as she hastily unpacked her leather bag. "I ran seminars at four kibbutzim. I decided to focus mainly on "*Yam Lid*." I saw so many performances."

Zosia recited Bialik's Sea Song lyrics in her head, trying to calm herself. *I've forgotten my loved ones / I've forsaken my own home / I've given myself to the sea / Take me, sea, to mother's lap. / And you, loyal western winds / Carry my ship to the shore / As my heart, with eagle's wings / Has so longed for.*

She knew the longing.

"So," she began, a little unsure. She wanted to ask Rachel if she knew anything about Wanda but wasn't certain how to proceed. "When you—"

"I'm exhausted." Rachel cut her off and began to change into nightclothes.

Zosia looked away as her roommate undressed. "Me too."

"Are you?" Rachel asked. "How was Grochów?"

"Good," Zosia lied before she could catch herself. Rachel put her on the defensive.

"Was it?"

"Are you being sarcastic?" Zosia looked back at her.

"Yeah, I guess," Rachel replied. "I heard it went badly," she added.

"What did you hear?" Zosia's stomach turned.

"I heard you weren't that popular. Sorry to say it, but it's very important that we be honest. Only truth will get the job done."

"Yes, of course." Who had been talking about her? She felt the air whistle from her lungs, felt them go heavy. *Come on, brain, tell my lungs to expand,* but they wouldn't. And then . . . it began faintly, just a hum, but it quickly ballooned louder and louder to a shrieking holler.

"What's wrong?" Rachel asked. "You look white."

Zosia shot out of bed, grabbed a coat and her boots, and ran out of the room. Air, air, she needed air. Outside, on streets dotted with city people who never seemed to rest, she began to run.

She needed to move, to calm down, to feel herself. Foot after foot after foot.

"Hey, are you alright?"

Zosia had run right into Abram rounding the corner. Her body felt warm from the impact, tingling, hot. But what could she say?

So, she kept running.

"Zosia!" she heard from behind her. "Where are you going? Please, let me help you!"

For a second, she slowed down. But then she kept running.

Blocks later, Zosia still sprinted, her shame pushing her forward. She was fueled by the energy of embarrassment. Now tears streaked her cheeks. She could barely talk to Abram in normal situations, so what would she tell him when he asked why she had bolted down the street away from him? *Wanda is gone, I'm an accomplice to a crime, I can't manage the imposters, everyone knows I'll never get a visa, I don't even know how to breathe anymore, and Po-*

land's antisemitism is growing by the day? Why was she so reliant on other people? And how come she was getting ready to lead a political revolution but had so much trouble talking to a boy?

Her pace finally slowed and she began to breathe more evenly; the sound in her head quieted. As she walked around the blocks of the neighborhood, still relatively busy with comers-and-goers into the oversized tenements that surrounded her on each side, Zosia recalled her mother's letter, crumpled and then straightened, still in her coat pocket, but she couldn't think about it, not now, and instead she waded into a memory of her sister Bella, her junior by eighteen months. "Bella" meant beautiful and, with her large eyes, long lashes, and rosy, radiant cheeks, she was a natural. Her beauty made her confident, effusive, a flirt. The sisters had shared a small bed, and though they were not always close, they were certainly never far. They knew the ins and outs of each other's lives and days. Bella made jokes where Zosia took notes; Bella was June blond where Zosia was a February afternoon. Bella was her antithesis, and Zosia, despite their mere year and a half apart, and despite Bella seeming to be just fine—better than Zosia, certainly socially—instinctively knew that she needed to take care of her. That's who Zosia was: She took care of things.

One night, Zosia had been fretting, her ambivalent feelings about her presumed place in the family business thundering inside her. But it was Bella who had come to bed agitated. She was not her usual swanlike calm, easing into her sheets as if she belonged nowhere else at that moment, and so Zosia, herself accustomed to tossing and turning, had noted that something was askew. "What?" she simply asked, because they were sisters, and that was all that was needed.

"He likes me."

"Who?"

"Berl Lipschitz."

"Do you like him?"

"Berl Lipschitz?" she repeated, as if Zosia were crazy. Berl had a reputation for being charming, though how that charm manifested in their tiny religious community was to Zosia a mystery. "Of course I like him."

Zosia understood: Bella was scared. For the first time, her beauty had real impact.

Zosia could have been jealous, but that's not who she was. She took care of people. She held her sister's hand under the blanket. "How do you know?"

"He wrote me a note. Can I read it to you?"

"Of course!"

The note had not been particularly passionate, but had complemented Bella's smile and her hair. He'd compared her grace to wheat waving in the fields. "I don't know what to write back," Bella had panicked into her pillow. "What do I say?"

Zosia got up from their bed, found a candle, and lit it. "I'll write it!" Bella laughed in relief as Zosia composed a love letter. It was subtle but smart; flirtatious but only a hint; affectionate but with an air of mystery. She was taken by his words, Zosia wrote, which reminded her of a song that her mother used to sing about the beauty of our interconnectedness, about how the wheat danced thanks to the wind, which blew due to the swaying of the earth. *And the earth only swayed thanks to our spirits.*

Bella had been delighted. "Remember to wait at least a day before sending it to him," Zosia had instructed. "Actually, wait two days."

The question that ran through her mind now was: How, years back, a mere naïve youth, had she known how to respond to a wooing, to flirt, to share a connection? Where had that instinctive knowledge come from, and where had her wisdom gone? It sometimes felt like her whole life was the project of recovering that which she already understood.

How would they pay for Bella's wedding without her? How would—but no . . . no distractions.

She was being ridiculous, Zosia scolded herself, snapping back to the present. She, the country girl, was in Warsaw, for crying out loud. She had made it far, almost to Palestine. Almost. Self-sufficiency was Dror's motto. She could do things on her own.

She didn't need conventions or rules, or people—except maybe for one.

Zosia opened the door to Warsaw's police headquarters with its famous white clocktower. Despite the late hour, or because of it, the precinct was busy with people, anxious, shouting, or dozing. This was not a surprise considering the recent spike in crime, largely due to the city's increasing levels of poverty. Crime, she supposed, was also a resident who did not sleep.

Zosia quelled any fear and feelings of mistrust and walked straight to the main desk. "Excuse me, sir, madame," she said to the receptionist and officer who sat behind the counter.

No reply.

"Excuse me, sir, madam," she said louder.

"Here to report a crime?" the receptionist asked without looking up from her books.

"I'm looking for someone."

"You?"

"No, I'm looking for someone else."

The receptionist laughed; the policeman snorted.

"I need another coffee," the officer said. The woman got up to get it for him.

"I'm looking for Wanda Petrovsky," Zosia said. "She's missing. I'm seeking information."

The policeman glanced up at her. "So?"

"Do you know where she is?" She was afraid to ask if Wanda was arrested or in Serbia. Why even suggest she may be a criminal or political prisoner? "Do you have any information?"

The officer dropped his papers onto his desk. "Why would I tell you anything?" He shook his head and cackled. "Why would I have time for you?" And then he quietly added: "What do you have to give me?"

Zosia dropped her head. What had she been thinking? She was no one, she had nothing.

She slunk back out of the building. The watchtower struck. Zosia noted: It was the eleventh hour.

CHAPTER 11

Fanny

FANNY DABBED THE PIGMENTS IN HER BEJEWELED GOLDEN SWISS compact, then carefully painted the final touches of rouge onto her cheeks. Then, her favorite part: twisting the matching lipstick cylinder so that the blaring red slowly rose to the surface and then above, like a siren. She creamed her lips and pinched her cheeks, flushing them with an extra dollop of color until they were crisp and shiny like a pomegranate, pert and ready—though, for whom or what, she had no idea. It was the middle of the night. Fanny studied her profile in her small, gilded mirror, an antique gift from Mamo for her eighteenth birthday. Was it possible that the reflection that stared back at her resembled one Miss Josephine Baker with her flush lips and hair curled just so? Then, Fanny turned to examine her other cheek. Lo and behold: With her sharp features, it was possible she looked less like Baker and more like Dzigan!

Fanny suddenly recalled her grandmother's saying: People who straddle two worlds end up with split pants.

Well, she supposed, so did people who scaled walls to get what they needed.

Some rips were worth it.

Fanny closed her eyes for a moment to take in the past few weeks. The shows, the police, the comrades—what was she doing? She, the future Fanny Brodasz née Zelshinsky, a textile and sugar heiress, had a husband waiting for her; she was about to inherit tablecloths and candlesticks and saltshakers too. She was well aware that her desperation to find Wanda seemed bizarre but . . . she simply had to follow her gut, twisted and tense as it was. She had to get that pink paper signed; she needed the exhibition.

Not to mention, a hidden printing press?

Where could Wanda possibly be?

Now, in the same mirror, Fanny witnessed a curious reflection. The wave of her bangs framed her ear with the same shaped curve as her thick velvet window drapes. It dawned on her: It was just like a picture of Wanda's. She'd lied to Mamo and said she was copying Wanda's shots, but why not actually do so? Maybe if she placed herself in the exact same position vis-à-vis the lens, it would help her get inside the woman's head and provide clues. Fanny grabbed her camera while staying as still as possible and tried to find a way in. Should the apparatus's reflection be visible in the shot, alluding to the very act of seeing? Or could she somehow twist herself into an angle so that the image became more abstract, the reflection of a curve, rather than of a self?

Click, click, click.

Fanny breathed. Finally, she was shooting again . . .

It had been more than a week since their trip to Wanda's flat, and Fanny kept trying to figure out what the best next steps might be. Yesterday, she'd gone to the university library and looked up Petrovsky in the card catalog under subject but had found nothing. Then, by chance, she'd tried the author catalog and behold! There on a dusty yellow card was her full name. Fanny scribbled the call number and rushed it to the collections desk. An hour later, she picked up the book, which was an anthology of essays about and photos of Warsaw's architectural and natural landscape that Wanda and several other photographers from the Warsaw Photo Club had selected. *The Beauty of Warsaw* was filled with black-and-white shots, many of the Old Town, its pastel-colored buildings running an ombre of gray, its bright orange castle a hazy white, and pigeons. So many pigeons. Fanny tore through the pages looking for an image created by Wanda, but there were none. Her stamp was there, but she wasn't. Fanny didn't know what to make of any of it.

Think, Fanny, think.

And then, as she watched herself contemplate in the mirror, she had an idea.

"WE'RE FASHIONABLY EARLY," FANNY DECLARED AS THEY ENtered the lecture room.

"No such thing," Nat said. "Imagine, a princess arriving twenty minutes before her court. What would she busy herself with? A crossword puzzle? Her taxes? What kind of person is early?"

Zosia, Fanny thought. "Thank you for coming with me," she told Nat. "I know it's not even nine a.m., but I'd like to speak to Nowak before class, so I wanted to get here in plenty of time." Nowak, Fanny had realized the night before, might have information. Answers usually emerged from the simplest places.

They seated themselves front and center of the hall and Nat pulled out a broadsheet so they could engage in one of their favorite pastimes: reading this week's personal ads. The ads were always ridiculous, and Fanny felt relieved to engage in something so silly and normal.

"*I'm a butcher. I'm asking for kind support*," Nat read out loud. Then, in a deep voice, as if she were the gentleman, "*I'm seeking a wife with one hundred thousand in cash, undergarments and furniture. I sell tripe.*"

"Tripe!" Fanny chortled.

"Oh my," Nat said as she read ahead, suddenly serious. "Listen to this one: *I will marry the ugliest woman so as not to feel jealous.*" She melted into laughter.

"*I am seeking a woman with unusual proclivities. Priority will be given to those of an exceptionally despotic character.*"

"Gosh, these are all so stupid," Fanny said. "How does anyone ever meet their soul mate? How's it even possible that people fall in love?"

"You tell us, Zelshinsky!" Nat said. "Or is something wrong with Simon the smoocher?"

"Oh gosh, no," Fanny stammered. Telling Natalia of her stomachaches, of any of her worries or dreams, was unthinkable, she realized in that moment. It would make them so very real. "I meant in general, for the common folk," she said, attempting a joking tone.

Nat took it seriously. "True," she said, then added, "It's often the people you least expect to be with that you end up with. My mother told me, it's always best to date against type. Real love doesn't feel like you imagine it will feel. It's more like beef than butterflies. Or more like butter, with flies."

Beef? Flies? "What about you?" Fanny asked to change the subject. "Any paramours of note?"

"I actually have four men on the docket," Nat said.

"One in every port," Fanny said.

"One in every ski town!" Nat said. "But I'm mostly interested in Jan, from Kraków."

"Pray tell."

"He's well-built and has soft eyes, but"—Nat said, a devilish look in her eye—"he works at the Main Market Square, setting up tables. I met him when I was shopping for fabrics. He's deeply working class."

Fanny jolted in surprise. Not at Nat's scandalous news, but because her own thoughts went straight away to Abram, to that night at Dzigan. Well-built, his cap covering a head of chocolate brown hair, he was cute, even for a comrade. He made her smile and he took her seriously. He'd told her to take pictures.

Just then, Nowak entered the room. Fanny waited for him to lay down his briefcase before approaching the lectern. "Professor, can we speak for a moment?"

Nowak nodded. "About your thesis, I hope?"

"Yes," Fanny said. "I want to write about women and photography in France," tumbled from her mouth. "And I would like to interview Wanda Petrovsky."

"Petrovsky? What does she have to do with France?"

"She was influenced by French masters."

"Petrovsky was influenced by French masters? What are you talking about?"

"The problem is"—Fanny couldn't help but bat her eyelashes, less flirtation, more subordination, as if she was a little girl—"she hasn't been to any of her classes. Do you by any chance know where she is?"

"She hasn't been to class?" Nowak sighed. "That figures. Miss Zelshinsky, I told you on numerous occasions to stay away from art classes. Artists are messy and difficult. Daguerreotypes, on the other hand, could be a smart subject for your thesis."

Daguerreotypes were as exciting as they sounded. Why was Nowak so dull?

"So you don't know where she could be?" Fanny tried again. "On Sabbatical?"

"I truly have no idea where Petrovsky is hiding," he said, "nor do I care. But I do care about your academic career, so please, confirm your final subject with me by next week."

Next week? She didn't even want to stay in this major!

What would she do now?

Fanny's peers began to trickle into the room, and she took her seat next to Nat.

"Time for some Cartesian free will," she mumbled to herself. "To hear about how it was God Himself who gave me the freedom to sit through this." Then she opened her notebook and noticed how, despite months of scribbling, it still contained so many blank pages.

She needed to find her mentor.

AND SO, FANNY FOUND HERSELF IN FRONT OF THE GRAND stand-alone house, with its Gothic black gates and manicured lawn. Her only option, her final hope. A butler opened the door even before she rang and led her to a drawing room brimming with oil paintings and fresh flowers. There was no question behind the nature of Mamo's interest.

"So glad you made it." Avigdor rose from his chair. This time, Fanny had her hand out, ready and agent. Two teas were already poured. A plate of wafer-thin mun cookies was perched between them. "I had a hunch you'd stop by eventually," he said.

"I thank you for your very kind invitation," she replied. "I already had my tea and must decline refreshments. I am keen to see the photographs."

"Of course you are." He stood up from his armchair. "I've already taken them out of my storage room." He came toward her, and his hand grazed her back. Fanny noticed that the door was closed. She eyed the doorknob. Was it locked? "Come," he said and pulled her to the corner where a black portfolio lay spread open on a long wooden side table.

"I never hang photographs," he said. "Do you know why?"

"Paintings are more classical?" His questioning was patronizing, but she played to it.

"Photographs become ruined by light," he said. "The image fades, it disappears."

"Darkness is important," Fanny agreed. Light illuminated truth, but also, made it grow faint.

He offered nothing about Wanda's whereabouts, nothing about any disappearance. Fanny decided to stay quiet for now and wait to see if he would bring it up.

Standing close to her, Avigdor lifted the cover and revealed the first print. The photo was similar to the one she'd seen at the Fashion Café. Here, Wanda had taken a picture of herself reflected in a different puddle, right outside a butcher shop. The meat store's signage was mirrored in the water. The meaning was anchored in echoes; the context was entirely within the form.

"Huh," Fanny said, guttural. "Interesting, I mean."

He lifted the puddle photograph and showed the next. Warsaw's courthouse was shot from the perspective of the ground, as if

Wanda had been stationed under a carriage, flat on the road. The shadows were a rainbow of grays; the building had never looked so tall. How had she achieved such an angle? Was it possible she'd taken the photo from inside a manhole, literally, from within the earth?

"Wow."

The third photo felt more intimate. Wanda was looking into a mirror, not unlike Claude Cahun's portrait, but closer up. This was a picture, not of a face, but of skin, streaked with lines and blemishes, scars and sunspots. Skin, it announced, was a barrier yet porous, easily ripped but easily repaired. In the corner, the suggestion of a lip lined with thick artificial color. The image a cascade of reflections, dress-up leaking into dress-up. *This*, of course, is what she should have done the other night.

"Tell me, is your mother a fan of Wanda's?" he asked as he reached for the final photo.

"I'm not sure," Fanny said. "But I'm sure she'd love this picture. It's so powerful."

"What art does your mother like?"

"Expensive art."

"I suppose we share the same aesthetic tastes, then."

Then, with a dramatic swing of the arm, he showed her the fourth. A long line of men in a cue and, at the tail end, the focal point of the shot: one woman, waiting patiently, quiet. Fanny's heart lurched in recognition. Wanda had drawn out the feeling she'd felt at the print shop: surrounded but alone, same but different, as if she were waiting for something that other women were not waiting for, or, were not supposed to be waiting for. The woman in the picture looked meek, yet she had a rebellious tint in her eye, that of a schemer.

"What's this one called?" Fanny asked.

Avigdor read the inscription on the back. "The Last Woman."

The last woman.

Fanny took a breath. Again, Wanda's work had knocked her out. That's what Fanny wanted to make: art that touched you, that physically touched you, deep in your gut.

"You like that one?"

"I do," Fanny whispered. "Very much." *Relative and absolute . . . You and the universe, wrapped in one.*

"It's quite something."

Avigdor said nothing more. Did he not know? Fanny couldn't take it any longer. "Wanda is missing," she blurted.

"Missing?"

"She's gone," Fanny said. "No one has seen her for several weeks."

"That's probably not a first." He chuckled.

"What do you mean?"

"She's an artist," Avigdor said. "She experiences her life at full volume. Essentially, that's what we pay artists to do. We reward them for living, for exiting the box in the ways we are not brave enough to even imagine. So what if she took a few days off to frolic in the countryside? I would pay for those shots! Maybe even a self-portrait of her swimming in a lake."

Fanny's spine shot up straight. She didn't like which side of the artist-nonartist equation he was putting her on. And, like Nowak, he wasn't taking Wanda's disappearance seriously, not at all. "Sir, we think she might be in jail."

"Jail?"

"Yes, jail." As she repeated the term, something shook her. When said aloud, the word was laden with gravitas. It was one thing to think Wanda had skipped town for an exciting project or been fired from the university or was jokingly kidnapped by a jealous lover, an idea which had crossed her mind. It was another to think she'd been arrested and was being held against her will in a Polish prison. What if Dror was right, and no one cared? Fanny realized in that moment: Wanda, her wise, strong-willed, artistic genius of a professor, could really be in trouble. "You're a lawyer. Please, can you help?"

He shook his head no.

"I'm coming to you as her fellow artist."

He outright laughed. "Lenora's little lamb?"

Little lamb? So now she was a piece of meat? Fanny cleared her throat. Why did it have to be this way? Especially when women *were* successful in Poland. The country was the first to promote policewomen to the highest rank, for crying out loud! "Please, we need your guidance to help find her. We need to help her."

"Would you like a drink?" Avigdor headed toward a bar cart at the other end of the room and picked up a crystal flask of thick brown liquid.

"It's ten a.m.," Fanny said.

"The perfect time for a kiddush," Avigdor answered, lifting a heavy cut glass. Rays danced in the slits, beams of violet poked into the air. "L'chaim."

"No, thank you," Fanny said. "So, will you help?"

"Wanda is in jail like I'm in the rabbinate," Avigdor said and chortled. "And even if she were in prison . . . *You* are going to rescue her?"

"Yes," Fanny said to his peals of laughter, "I am." And she walked right out the door.

CHAPTER 12

Zosia

"Tu Bishvat is a critical celebration of nature," Zosia praised and gestured at the expanse of the park around her. "It's often relegated to second-class status among Jewish holidays, but in fact, the birthday of the trees is one of the movement's most important observances, even if in this country it comes in the dead of winter." True, the holiday had already passed, but she'd suggested a belated seminar in the curriculum notes she'd left for Abram; trees trumped romance!

The best education was hands-on, so instead of teaching today's seminar about nature in the cramped rooms at Dzielna, she'd brought the group to the Saxon Gardens, the nearly forty-acre and oldest park in Warsaw, founded in the late seventeenth century, and perhaps, with some of its original plants. She'd shepherded the young members past the classicist white water tower, the enormous round wooden summer theater that seated over a thousand people, the marble sundial, and a series of manicured lawns to this tree-lined area where they could feel enmeshed with nature.

Also, she knew that if she shook up the day's plan, it would be easier for her to deflect any questions her co-teacher may have about her mortifying scampering the other night. She'd managed to avoid him at Oneg Shabbat, Zosia's favorite Dror tradition, when weekly, the whole group—clad all white and, with all their hearts and energy—sang and danced through the night celebrating the Sabbath. Now she looked over to Abram, who had happily agreed to the outing. He smiled.

She could do this; she could do anything for Dror. She forced an awkward smile.

She had to let go of Wanda, printing presses, police, secrets and all. Even if Wanda were able to get her a visa, she was missing and Mira was right that she could not take on the search. Dror was her purpose. Its appeal rested in its devotion. Duty. No distractions. She needed to move forward. *Go, go, go.*

"Nature is at the heart of our belief system," Zosia continued. "Man and land are linked."

"Saxon Gardens was opened to the public in 1727," Abram added. "It was one of the first publicly accessible parks in the entire world. Poland understood the importance of allowing its citizens, and all its folk, to experience the environment."

Championing Poland again? "Here in Poland, there are so many trees." Zosia stepped in. "The forests are so dense, one could get lost in them, hide in them for years. But in Eretz, we have to create the desert's trees. It is up to us to cultivate our land, to feed ourselves, to produce our own oxygen. Nothing is taken for granted. Let's go!"

Zosia led the group past the Blue Palace, with its cerulean roof that floated in the background like a lingering fairy tale, all the way to the grand Palm House.

As they walked, she avoided her co-teacher, until Abram caught up. "So, the other night—"

"We're here." Zosia cut him off and addressed the group as they approached the all-glass structure.

Inside, the air was soupy, and Abram's cheeks flushed red like September apples. She turned away.

"It's like we're in another world," one of the comrades said. "There are so many types of vegetation."

"This glass house was built in 1894 for the exotic palm trees being introduced to Europe," Abram read off a panel. "The high ceilings leave enough room for the trees to spread their crowns."

They all looked up at the giant fronds and breathed in the lush aroma. Through the glass walls, their backdrop was a late winter sun, bleeding orange and red. It was magical.

"Come outside," Zosia said after they'd walked through. "Let's sing!"

The group found a clearing, formed a circle, sat down, and began "*The Almond Tree Is Blooming*," written by the poet Yisrael Dushman, who, Zosia reminded them, had made aliyah, co-founded the first modern Hebrew theater company, translated dozens of plays into Hebrew, and had dedicated his life to teaching children the language.

They blared: "The almond tree is blooming / And the golden sun is shining / Birds atop each roof / Announcing the arrival of the festival—"

Suddenly, they were surrounded. "Are you *zhiden*?" a group of teenage boys probed. They cackled. The singing stopped.

"Who are you?" Zosia asked, and her heart galloped.

"Who are you?" a boy retorted and mocked her. "What are you doing here?"

"It's a public park," Abram said calmly. "It's open to anyone."

"Not to people who sing in a foreign language."

"Actually, it is," Zosia said.

One of the boys started kicking cold dirt toward the comrades. "Get off our land."

"It's not your land," Abram said calmly. Zosia noted that her young students were frozen.

"This is our country"—one of the men was clearly drunk—"and our land."

His friend took out a knife.

Zosia's head spun. Bootsteps, hollers, the horsepower of a group drunk on the false narrative of not-getting-what-I-deserve. *We're coming for you.* Now, the timber of the scream, a whelp in her ears, louder and louder . . .

"Hey!" Zosia sprang to her feet. Suddenly she was holding a large stick. "Get your drunk asses out of our faces. You give us problems, I'll go to my friend, the park superintendent. I'll tell him everything, including how you're messing up the ground with your stupid donkey kicks." She was about to strike the stick to the ground, but it didn't budge. Abram was holding it back.

"Relax, girl," the guy with the knife said. He slipped it back into his pocket.

"I'll relax when you're gone."

"Enjoy your singing," a drunk one said. The men burst into laughter but then sauntered off.

"Zosia, you were amazing!" the comrades all agreed.

"They were just bullies," Zosia said. "All talk." Though she was shaking, she made them finish the Almond Tree song. They could not cower.

As they left the park, Abram stepped into pace next to her.

"I wasn't actually going to hit him," Zosia said.

"You need to be careful." He used a low voice. "Look what happened at Dzigan. And," he paused, "Mordechai Fuchrer from the kibbutz in Bialystok was beaten up recently. It's not all talk."

"Believe me, I know."

"Were you okay the other night?" Abram probed. "Where were you running to so late?"

"Were *you* okay the other night?" she retorted. "And can you please explain your adoration of Poland, this beautiful country where teenagers harass us for singing songs about saplings?" For her entire year in Dror, she'd seen him, above all, as a confident socialist–Zionist leader. He'd been to so many seminars, workshops, lectures . . . he really understood the movement's ideals.

"Visas to Palestine are becoming more and more restricted. You know that, Zosia," Abram said. "The establishment of a Jewish homeland in Eretz Israel was always a pipe dream, and now, well, it's bordering on delusion. We need to be realistic. There's a good chance we'll have to stay here and then we'll have to fight for ourselves. Besides, I feel responsible for the Jews here," he said. "I don't want to feel I've been forced to leave. I know it's unusual for a Dror leader, but I actually *want* to stay in Poland and help my community. And to help my family. I have four younger sisters, and I can't bear the thought of leaving them to fend for themselves."

Zosia put her hands to her ears. She'd worked so hard to lead alongside someone smart and strong like Abram, and his doubt felt like a dagger, piercing her, deflating her dreams; this betrayal was the last thing she wanted to hear right now. "I want to leave," Zosia said, "as soon as humanly possible."

"Okay, I hear you but—"

"Enjoying Lovers Park?" The voice emerged from the splash of the grand fountain as if a mirage: Fanny. "I was amused when Dror told me you two were here, in this classic date spot."

Zosia went beet red like her lunch soup.

"Hello, Fanny," Abram said, a little too excitedly. "It's nice to see you again. I never got to say a proper goodbye after the comedy show. You alright?"

"I need to talk to Fanny, now." Zosia was firm. Anything to stop the flirting. "Abram, walk the chevrah home. I'll see you later at Dzielna."

"Where have you brought me?" Fanny dragged Zosia over to—as she read from the sign—"The Warsaw Rowing Club." There really were two different ways of experiencing Warsaw: as an unwanted guest and as someone who *owned* it.

"Wait here," Fanny told her at the entrance.

It was an unseasonably warm and dry afternoon and the waterfront was busy. Large prams accompanied promenading ladies and a bagel vendor flogged hot wares. The rowing club consisted of a wooden barge with a steepled roof and several docks along the pier. It looked rustic, but Zosia imagined there must have been a first-class lounge inside.

Zosia took quick breaths and put her hands by her ears to push away any unwanted shrieks. She shook, thinking of the menacing hooligans. And, on another uncomfortable note, why was Abram constantly going on about the beauty of Poland and the hopelessness of the Zionist dream? He was supposed to be her teaching partner. Zosia had not returned to Grochów even once to work on the imposter situation and now her seminars would surely fall apart too. She wondered if Abram knew he was *not* on the visa list, like, for certain? Is that what was pushing him away?

"I got one," Fanny said, returning.

"You got what?"

"A canoe, silly! My lesson is in thirty minutes, but we can go out on the water first."

"A canoe? I don't know how to paddle." How was it that Zosia was spending time with someone so frivolous? "I barely know how to swim. In fact, I don't know how to swim. Wait . . . are you trying to kill me?"

"You can't swim?" Fanny asked. "You don't boat? How were you planning on getting to the Levant? It takes weeks on a vessel to make it to Palestine. Besides, isn't swimming part of youth movement education?"

"Strength is part of our training," Zosia said, "not water sports."

Fanny dragged her down the dock to the bank where the canoes were anchored. Was Zosia Tarnovsky really going to be swept off land? "I'm not going. I can't." She could rebuff ruffians, but not this.

"Come on!" From the water's edge, Fanny held out a tattered life vest. Somehow, she could be dressed for a nightclub and still be reeling out a boat. "I've taken classes forever. You know, Warsaw has had a women's rowing club since 1913, one of the first women's clubs in all of Europe!"

Before she knew it, Zosia found herself wearing a puffy yellow vest over her leather socialist badge. "I can't." Her heart palpated in her throat.

"These are life vests," Fanny said. "They're meant to save lives. There are always backups."

"I can't."

"You said you needed to talk to me . . . You can trust me. Not everyone is out to get you." Fanny held her hand and guided her into the boat, its sides rocking in a way she did not like at all. Her heart lurched. "Just take it one step at a time, literally."

Then, in one fell swoop, Fanny hopped in, turned around, and used the paddle to push them off into the floating nothing. Zosia could barely breathe.

"Don't look so worried," Fanny said. "You need to take risks. That's how you grow into an artist."

"I don't want to be an artist," she eked out as Fanny handed her a paddle.

"Wanda is an artist," Fanny said.

"And she's likely in prison, possibly forever," Zosia replied.

"Follow what I'm doing," Fanny said. "Focus all your fear on the action of moving; moving forward, moving deliberately."

Zosia had no choice but to listen to her and after a few minutes began to get a hang of the movement. She focused on the umph she felt as the boat pushed forward. As long as she didn't actually look at the water, at this liquid mass that had no discernable end, she felt alright. It was one thing to stare out at the Vistula, but another to be right inside it, inside its myths and legends of loss. Zosia grounded herself by staring at the Kierbedz Bridge, a steel structure comprised of diamond latticework that formed a square-shaped enclosed tunnel; its strong angles were solid and affirming.

"I went to the police headquarters," Zosia blurted. Out here, at least they weren't in anyone's earshot. "I tried to get information, and they laughed at me."

"Laughed at you?"

"They asked who I was, and what I had to give them. It was like I was performing a comedy sketch. They don't care. It's over, our search is really over."

"They asked what you have, what you are? Well, then we have to go back." Fanny began to row more quickly, and the boat rocked.

"We do?" Zosia asked.

"Yes."

"When?"

"Now."

This time, Zosia could not say it was her inaugural step up the police stairs. Now the familiarity bred a sense of empowerment, or maybe it was Fanny who did.

"Wait a second," Fanny said before opening the door. She fished through her bag—for what? The chocolate? No, a lipstick. Zosia rolled her eyes. Was she simply going to flirt her way through this?

"Excuse me, Pan, Pani," Fanny said at the front desk, pouting and pushing out her chest. Zosia sighed: This looked ridiculous and was never going to work. "Excuse me," Fanny repeated in her crispest Polish.

"Yes, Mademoiselle," the officer said.

Zosia was ready to walk out.

"I need to speak to Chief Broz."

"Do you, lady?"

"Yes, I am here under the auspices of general council Avigdor Radetsky. He sent me to meet with Broz immediately."

The officer and receptionist both looked up. "Radetsky?" the man asked.

"*Tak*," Fanny answered in pristine Polish, and pulled out an envelope from her bag. "A delivery from Avigdor. He asked me to pass this on personally. I don't think *anyone* would like it if this was left unattended, or if this got into the wrong fingers."

It was impossible that Fanny had planned this advance, and yet she seemed utterly prepared, even knowing his name. Such savvy and grace, Zosia thought, was only possible in the rich.

The policeman looked Fanny up and down.

She went on: "I'm sure your boss would appreciate it if this was handed to him directly."

"Down the hall, to the right," the policeman said. The receptionist nodded.

Zosia couldn't believe it. No one had even asked who they were.

She stepped into pace with Fanny as they headed down a long hallway with dark wood walls but light linoleum flooring; it was disorienting, the sides heavier than the ground. Fanny's heels clicked; Zosia's boots sloshed and stomped. Fanny said nothing, so Zosia said nothing. They arrived at a door inscribed with "Captain Marek Broz."

Fanny knocked.

No answer.

She knocked again.

Still no answer.

So, she turned the knob and opened it. Zosia was stunned, frozen.

Captain Broz was there, fast asleep, hunched over his desk, snoring like a donkey with consumption. The room was thick with old smoke and the yolky scent of old coffee.

Fanny frantically rummaged through her bag and took out her camera. *Click.*

"What the hell?" Broz woke up, startled. "Who are you?"

Fanny put the camera back in her bag with an assured slowness that drove Zosia mad. "Sir," Zosia said, because she felt she had to. "We are so very sorry." She was ready to head for the door.

"So sorry to wake you," Fanny said, with more pouting and more chest. Only rich people could be so comfortable around the police, Zosia thought again in disbelief.

"How did you get in here? What do you want?"

"We're here for Avigdor Radetsky."

"What does that mean?"

Zosia watched as Fanny didn't miss a beat. "He wants to know the whereabouts of Professor Wanda Petrovsky."

"Avigdor does?"

"Yes, he collects her work and has heard that she is missing."

"So, he sent you here?"

Fanny nodded, but instead of making eye contact with him, she was busy scanning the papers on his desk. It was too obvious, Zosia worried. They were going to get arrested.

"What's your name?" the officer asked Fanny. "Your *real* name."

Zosia's heart skipped a beat. She'd better not say Zosia Dror again; Zosia would murder her right then and there.

"Fanny Zelshinsky," she said after a pause, still eyeing his desk's surface.

"Zelshinsky from the sugar factory," he repeated. "How sweet. I heard you were a looker. You have your mother's hips."

Fanny blatantly examined the police captain's hands. "Please help us," she said, now shifting her gaze to look him in the eye. "Please."

"I don't know anything about this Wanda," Broz said, "and even if I did, I would not tell you. And if you ever show up at this office again, I will tell Avigdor and your mother."

Zosia felt the color drain from her own face, but when she looked over to Fanny, she was all composed. "Thank you, Captain," Fanny said. "Sorry to trouble you."

The two women walked shoulder to shoulder down the hall. Neither said a word. They passed a room filled with police uniforms, and Fanny stopped. Zosia watched in disbelief as she headed straight to a shelf lined with boots and began to click away. "Worn, yet polished. It's like they each have a personality. Look how the pairs fit together: Some snuggle close, while with others, the distance between left and right is enormous. The cracks embossed into the leather trace the experience of having been worn. The shoes have temperament."

"Let's go," Zosia said, pulling at Fanny.

"And look at these caps," Fanny said as she walked to a table strewn with police hats. "Together, they're an abstract lump of shape. Each one traces an individual head yet deprives the wearer of individuality. In a uniform, you lose yourself and become an idea. Perspective and truth, Zosia!" *Click, click, click.* "When viewed over and over, the object becomes a set of lines and shades, just as how a word repeated becomes merely a collection of sounds. But in their deconstructed forms, we can find new meaning."

"Are you crazy?" Zosia finally hissed. "We're going to be in serious trouble. Stop!"

Outside, Zosia felt overwhelmed. "We have nothing," she said, the disappointment hitting her. She was trying so hard, taking risks on all fronts, yet nothing moved forward. She was going to be trapped in the dangerous rut that was Poland for the rest of her life.

Just then they were nearly trampled by photographers jetting up the stairs to snap whomever was coming out of the building right behind the women. "Ouch!" she said as she stumbled. Enough with photographers! There was a new fad to print photographs next to news stories—as if grainy pictures had any answers—and the photographers must have been chasing some story here at the police station.

But then it dawned on her.

"Fanny," she stopped. "Did you ever develop those pictures you took of Wanda's office?"

CHAPTER 13

Fanny

WHEN FANNY ARRIVED AT KAMINSKY'S HARDWARE SHOP AT eleven, it was busy. Workmen and laypeople roamed the crowded aisles, hauling planks of wood and buckets of nails, locks and keys. Now, as the door chimes rang, Fanny recalled that she'd been inside the store before, with Papa, for their dollhouse, maybe twelve years ago. She still recalled the deep smell of wood chips, of nature in a place so unnatural—it was as if no time had passed at all instead of nearly a decade of familial severance and rearrangement, of hearts stretched thin like elastics, walls nearly snapping. But, she reminded herself, always bouncing back. Heart walls were stronger than we expected, regenerating even without tape, including the large selection of masking she was looking at now.

"Fanny, over here!" Zosia called to her. Zosia's arms were full of supplies: rope, planks of wood, metal dishes, lights, and lamps.

"I have hanging lines, red light, special paper, trays, towels, tape. You'll need to grab two vats of chemical solutions," Zosia told her. "I'll show you what to get."

"Solutions," Fanny repeated as she followed the comrade. How did Zosia know how to make a darkroom? She didn't ask. "I like how it implies answers, ones we can reveal ourselves."

"Don't jinx it," Zosia said. "Ah, I have to get back to Dzielna for a lecture."

"Come to mine at two p.m.," Fanny told her and gave her the address. "Mamo will be out for her weekly charity sisterhood meeting."

"Fine," Zosia said, "but how will you get this all home?"

"I already told my driver to meet me here; he's coming in ten minutes."

Zosia sighed and walked off.

Fanny remained silent until, in line to pay, it came over her. She was the last woman! Like in the print shop, like in Avigdor's photo.

"Excuse me," she said to the men around her as she began to move items. She grabbed the wooden planks from Zosia's pile, set them next to each other, balanced a tray on top, and created a makeshift tripod. Breathless, she placed her Leica on top of that, found the correct view, and motioned for a confused and annoyed-looking customer to come over. "Please click it for me," she asked and ran back to her spot in line before anyone else joined.

"What?"

"You're right!" It dawned on her. It was not the presence but the absence that called to her. She was last in line but could mark her spot by not being there at all. She started to shoot, fast-fire, the empty area where she should have been standing. The trace of her.

Someone walked right into her shot. "Hey! Move!"

"Who the hell are you?"

"Wanda!" she replied. It just happened.

"Wanda?" the shop owner asked from behind the cashier. "Wanda who?"

"I mean, Zelshinky." Fanny realized she had to give the correct name for the tab.

The cashier grunted. The men in line all grumbled. "She's crazy."

She felt elated. She cleared her tripod and got back in line.

At the cash register, she managed to haul her stash right up onto the counter all by herself. "Zelshinky," she repeated, proud.

The cashier checked his books. "The credit is cut."

"Pardon?"

"The tab is closed."

"There must be some misunderstanding." Fanny fished in her bag for her wallet and took out a bunch of złotys. "I'll pay you in cash, no worries. And I'll check with my mother."

"Okay." The man grabbed her money, with some haste.

"Good afternoon," Fanny said and walked out of the shop, pleasantly burdened with wood, rope, lights, metal, and many solutions.

"We need to start right away," Fanny said. They were still in the foyer, and Mamo wasn't due home until eight p.m. when they were meant to go meet the music director for the wedding, but still, they needed time. "Would you like a coffee?"

"No, thank you," Zosia whispered. Her eyes were wide like Mamo's Edwardian tea saucers. She seemed nervous.

"How about water?" Fanny offered, trying to make her feel at ease. "I know you like water. Nanny! Water!"

"Nanny?"

Fanny blushed. It dawned on her how silly that name was. She was a grown woman.

Zosia's eyes scanned the apartment as if she were watching a fast-pacing ghost.

"Are you irked by all the rounded edges?" Fanny asked. "I know, it's unusual. This is a Szymon and Helena Syrkus building, not a le Corbusier. As they would have you know!"

"Of course."

Fanny matched Zosia's stare to the shiny hallway credenza, all oak and chrome. "I know the matching rounded furniture can be a lot. I told Mamo as much. But she insisted. Personally, I do like the modernist doorknobs." Fanny placed her hand down on the front closet knob, right behind her, also round like a thick silver bracelet. "Mamo wanted *everything* avant-garde."

Zosia edged her way closer to the hallway, continuing to scan, her mouth agape.

Fanny opened the door using the knob she'd been holding. "Can I take your coat?"

Zosia awkwardly disrobed and handed Fanny her thinning jacket, the fur at the wrists matted with age. Fanny wondered where she'd gotten it, and then whether she'd better hang it in the back of the closet, just in case Mamo came home early. Smelling its mustiness, she decided to. She pushed through a selection of fitted Schiaparellis and stopped for a moment when she found her father's old work blazer, the one she'd hid in the back of the closet so that Mamo wouldn't find and discard it; the one she'd photographed but had not yet shared with Wanda. For a second, Fanny recalled when he used to live here, in this very house. How long it had been since he'd come from work and hung up his hat, and she'd come running to say hello, to urge him into the dining room. How long it had been since he'd sat up late in the lounge working on his accounts, sipping cognac while she spied on him from the door. How long it had been since the words behind closed doors, the dark truths seeping out of quiet bedrooms, his departure. So many years later, this blazer still hung in the closet, left as if an excuse, as if one day he would come back to retrieve this forgotten item and her life would be pieced back together.

"We have to build the darkroom in my bedroom," Fanny blurted. "Inside my closet. Otherwise, Mamo will find out fast. She doesn't know about my photography classes, and she can't. Follow me."

Zosia followed her down the hallway. "How many rooms are there?"

"I guess eight. Or ten, maybe. Come!"

Once they were both inside her chamber, Fanny shut the door.

"What's that?" Zosia pointed. "I've never seen such a fancy one."

"My radio? It's an Atwater Kent, from America," Fanny said. "Mamo wanted it for its rounded edges, obviously." Fanny chuckled and turned it on. "Just the boring news." She shut it off. "My favorite serial is *The Daily Life of the Kowalskis* by Maria Kuncewiczowa. It's Poland's first produced serial. Do you know Maria?" Fanny asked, and now she felt strangely nervous. "She's a Skamander-style writer, and her stories probe their characters' psychologies—and her characters are women! I love this new type of Polish writing; it's so naturalistic, apolitical, poetic, and Maria's stories are all about marriage, maternity, unrequited love, women learning to take control of their lives. She's been winning national awards. Have you read her newest book, *The Stranger*? It was inspired by her own mother, who'd given up her career as a violinist to raise a family. The main character grapples with her foreigner status while her marriage is loveless, her son dies, and she descends into a depressive rage."

"Sounds interest—" Zosia was startled by an aggressive knock on the door.

"That's just Nanny."

Nanny entered in her crisp black frock and white apron. Fanny watched as Zosia eyed the octagonal glass delivered to her and then took a sip. "Yes, even Mamo's glassware is modern. Only glasses she doesn't like round."

Zosia made a face like she was going to vomit.

"Even I didn't think the look was that bad!"

"No, it's the taste—what is this?" Zosia wiped the corner of her mouth with her sleeve. "It's so bubbly, and salty."

"It's mineral water," Fanny said. "Mamo only drinks Stefanin, from the Stefanin spring in the Polish Carpathians. She says it's good for your skin," she tried to justify. For the first time Fanny saw her most intimate surroundings—the items she touched and tasted and looked at every single day—from the perspective of a left-wing shtetl Jew. Her radio *was* fancy. Her drinks *were* salty. "But I guess it is quite ridiculous."

"Huh." Zosia put her glass down. "Let's get to work."

"Exactly." Fanny opened her closet.

Zosia had a look around. "This space will do. But what about all this?" She gestured at Fanny's heaps of clothing.

"I guess I'll have to find another place for it all. Maybe I can store some pieces at the Fashion Café. But for now, let's get it all out." Fanny had already found several suitcases and boxes to fill.

For the next thirty minutes, the women worked on quickly evacuating blouses, sweaters, and scarves: the ski suit with the fur collar, the cashmere jumper from Berlin, from when they used to visit. Fanny was quite enjoying clearing out the space. She came across the pink chiffon dress that Mamo had selected for Fanny's audition for the Jewish Beauties of Poland pageant a few years back. Papa had forbidden her from competing, feeling that it was vulgar and Fanny should be appreciated for more than her looks, and ultimately Mamo had accepted that auditioning to be "Miss Judea" was crass. "Oh, this is the gold lamé Lanvin Mamo was looking for," Fanny said and held up a shimmering blouse with short-ruffled sleeves.

"It looks just like mine," Zosia said as she worked.

Did it? Fanny was about to ask how she came to have a Lanvin, then realized that was probably offensive and then realized that Zosia was joking. She had a sense of humor! Fanny laughed.

"And this one—are you sure it isn't mine?" Zosia held up a salmon-toned shirt with enormous balloon sleeves.

"It's so you," Fanny replied.

The women cleaned for a while until Fanny suddenly spoke. "What do you want from Wanda anyway?"

Zosia seemed to be caught off guard. "She was supposed to tell me something. I think she was going to help me get a visa to Palestine. In fact, I'm quite sure of it. She comes from a town near mine. What about you?"

Fanny didn't say anything for a long moment. How strange to think that her mentor, and her key to Parisian independence, came from the same place as this awkward comrade. "Well, I guess there's no harm in telling you. You don't know my circle."

"I certainly don't know your circle . . . nor your octagon!"

"I need her to sign a pink paper so I can change to be an art major and get into the final show. Parisian gallerists will be there. I need to become independent."

"Independent," Zosia repeated and nodded.

Fanny said no more, and Zosia didn't pry. The women kept working in silence.

Once the cupboard was cleared, Zosia took a small library book out of her bag—a darkroom guidebook. She pushed Fanny away and began moving, building, laying out tubs and chemicals and wires and tongs and fabrics to block any light. Zosia's carpenter-style know-how amazed Fanny, and she watched quietly as, in less than two hours, a whole laboratory was installed in Fanny's room. Soon, this little space could produce enormous knowledge.

"Ta-da," Zosia said as she stepped out.

Fanny closed the door to the closet. It was all hidden perfectly.

"Are you hungry?" Fanny asked.

"Hungry for answers," Zosia said. "Let's start developing."

THE PICTURES DID NOT COME OUT AS EASILY OR QUICKLY AS in the darkroom. Neither woman had experience in this endeavor. Together, they dunked and mixed and waited and looked and knocked things over and messed up timing. They hung whatever images they had hope for on lines, but most ended up looking like rounded blurs of light, which illuminated nothing at all.

But then—but then! One image did begin to emerge: a close-up of Wanda's desk, a corner, with three books strewn about and even a piece of her sandwich.

"Look!" Fanny cried when another piece of shiny paper began to transform into a picture of a window frame.

"Fanny, I'm home!" The women were jerked out of their mesmerized state. Mamo was back already? Fanny checked her watch: It was almost eight. "I'm calling the car. The meeting with the music director is set for eight thirty."

"Okay, give me ten minutes," Fanny called back as she and Zosia began piling everything into the closet.

That is, until Fanny looked back at the desk photo and gasped. "An M cuff link," she said.

"So?"

"That's the same M that was on the police chief's letterhead! On his desk!"

Zosia whistled, impressed. Captain Broz had been in Wanda's office.

The other thing Fanny had noticed on his desk: a pile of receipts from Fat Josek's.

"Fat Josek's?" Zosia asked.

"The trashy dive bar that caters to Warsaw's underworld, its government, and its most wealthy. It has the cache of being for the poor—the most exclusive vibe of all."

"Destitution is chic?"

"Forget the wedding singer," Fanny said. "We need to find Marek."

CHAPTER 14

Zosia

"And how are we going to do that?" Zosia asked.

Fanny thought for a moment. "Stay here while I talk to Mamo." Then she added, "Please don't make a noise. It will be complicated for me to explain who you are, and I don't want you to have to lie about the darkroom."

Zosia was left alone in the room she had just transformed. What kind of people paid to drink salt water like at a seder? And this radio—in what universe was such size and adornment necessary? And the clothes! Piles and piles of them. Not to mention a bed covered in satin, window drapes thicker than her own blankets, and a servant. Fanny's room alone had more light fixtures than half of Dzielna, and she was referring to the entire street. Even the boxes Fanny brought out to pack them in were thick and luxurious; they could have furnished whole Dror summer camps! The list of charities to which Zosia would donate all this grew in her mind.

To think that Wanda Petrovsky, comrade extraordinaire, had brought these two Poles together. What would Mira say if she found her here now? This hunt was taking her away from her imposter work, from all her Dror duties. Zosia placed herself cross-legged on the floor in the middle of the room. She was afraid to touch anything, even the shaggy carpet she sat on. She raised her knees.

The walls in the apartment may have been bedecked in papers covered in stylized shells, but they were still thin, and Zosia could hear the conversation from the next room.

"Something's come up tonight," Mamo told her. "A charity

meeting with Avigdor. He said he needed to talk to me right away about this luncheon we'll be hosting together. Help me, Fanny, with this corset."

"That's fine, we can cancel, Mamo," Fanny said and Zosia could hear the relief in her voice.

"No, dear, you must go. I told the music director you'd be there at the temple."

Fanny paused. "Fine, Mamo. But please, we must change the rendezvous spot to Fat Josek's."

"Fat Joe's? In the Jewish Quarter? Have you actually lost your mind?" Zosia had never met Mamo but could picture the shocked look on her face. Even Zosia was shocked by the suggestion.

"Oh Mamo, you know it's *the* place to be these days. I heard that the Balinskys and the Schwabs will be there this evening."

"At Gruby Jozek's? With the pimps?"

"Yes, Mamo, Jozek's is terribly de rigeur. I'll be inspired in my music choices, and he'll be impressed by our connections with Warsaw's inner circle. He'll work even harder."

"Really, you think?"

"Mamo! This bar is *the* secret signifier of one's status. It's the most fashionable spot in town. It's Warsaw's Les Halles. Grabowski and Jaracz both drink there after hours. Please, Mamo, it will make me so happy, which will make the meeting go so much better. Please, please, please, please, please."

"Stefan Jaracz from Ateneum Theatre?" Mamo asked. "Fine, I'll change the meeting spot. But promise me, you must participate, Fan-Fan. Not like at the chef's, where I had to do all the eating."

"So, you'll tell the car to take me to Rynkowa Street?"

"Fine."

"We're going!" Fanny said to Zosia as she burst back in the bedroom carrying Mamo's scent in with her, a waft of air thick like breakfast oats, spicy and hot. "Let's get your coat and get in the car, Zosh." Zosh? Only someone from a wealthy background would get so familiar so quickly. As if Zosia's name was Fanny's domain, as if she could just reach over and run her manicured fingers through it.

Zosia said nothing and watched as Fanny tied on a sparkling scarf and spritzed herself with Chanel. She picked up a purse, grabbed the photo, and dragged a stack of magazines to block her closet door like a barricade. *Vogue*, Zosia read the English title of the magazine, and the issue title: "The New 'American Look.'" On the cover was an illustration of a woman in a garden in a pink wool skirt suit with dark pink trim. The woman looked away.

MOST THINGS IN LIFE CAME WITH GREAT DIFFICULTY, AND certainly anything worthwhile. This was a truism in which Zosia firmly believed; it formed her essential architectural blueprint, justifying her struggles. Work is self. Work is worth. There were no politics of ease.

But sometimes, things came easy. So easy that Zosia stopped to question whether they were really happening. "Come on." Fanny tugged on her arm.

The restaurant was crowded, the air thick with smoke and breath, but at the end of the bar: Marek.

"Hi, Captain Broz." Fanny, unsurprisingly, started the conversation.

He looked up from his glass. Then he rolled his eyes. "Oh no, not you two." He drunkenly slurred his words.

"We have to discuss a few things." Fanny sat down on the barstool right next to him. Zosia stayed standing behind her. She handed Fanny an envelope. Fanny dramatically pulled out the photo. It was as if they had rehearsed.

"It was you," Fanny said, calm and collected. Zosia noted that she asked no questions, she only made statements. "That's your cuff link in the photo."

"M for man," Marek joked, flexing his arm muscles.

Then he slammed his fist down on the bar, and Fanny jumped. "So what?" he said to her, spitting. "I owe you nothing."

Fanny paused.

"You're right," Zosia quickly agreed. "You owe us nothing." She was about to plead. She would appeal to his moral side. She would explain that Wanda was their teacher, and they needed to find her for the benefit of her many, many students.

"But," Fanny said instead, "I'll bet you'd rather I didn't circulate a photo of you napping at your desk. Especially to the newspapers."

Had she just blackmailed him?

His face constricted in anger but, staring into his drink, he suddenly softened. He even let out a little guffaw. "Fine, I'll tell you. But only because you are so very pretty, little Lenora." He leaned into her, and Zosia stiffened, on alert. "I arrested her, I did, but it wasn't just her."

"Who else?" Zosia couldn't help but ask.

He flexed his biceps again, then laughed drunkenly. "There were sixteen of them. All women." Sixteen?

"We need to see her," Fanny demanded.

Marek took a long sip. "She's not in Warsaw."

"Where is she?" Zosia asked.

"I told you what I told you. Now go away. For good."

Zosia felt a tap on her shoulder. She looked up to see a tall man trying to gain Fanny's attention. "Miss Zelshinsky?" he asked Zosia, as if she were her personal secretary.

"Yes, that's she," Zosia said, as Fanny straightened up and edged away from Marek.

"Wonderful," the tall man said, sporting a Polish accent as crisp as Fanny's. "I'm Joshua Reitman, the synagogue's musical director."

Was he staring at Zosia's tattered coat? "I'll wait over there so you two can discuss music in private," Zosia offered.

"Are you sure?" Fanny asked.

No, but what could she do?

FORTUNATELY, FAT JOSEK'S WAS DARK AND FILLED WITH CREVices in which Zosia could hide. She found a small table behind a bend in the wall and, after wiping down both the surface and the chair, she sat and let questions roll like ticker tape through her mind.

Who were these sixteen women? Why were they arrested? What crime had they allegedly committed and where were they?

Did Mira even know? Should Zosia tell her?

And why in the world, Zosia thought as she swatted a fly, did wealthy people find this dirty hovel exciting?

Zosia needed to calm down and focus. She checked on Fanny and the music director. They sat at the bar, chatting away. Fanny seemed fine and, as always, confident, knowing exactly where to place her limbs so they looked natural, a balletic choreography, while Zosia's arms felt like they dangled from her body like a wet rat's tail. Next to Fanny and the music director sat a man who weighed at least three hundred pounds and smoked a fat cigar. His pants barely made their way up his legs, let alone to his waist, yet he too sat confidently, as if he owned the world. Zosia wondered if he was a famed criminal or a member of the Sejm.

Imagine, Zosia fantasized, she was here on a date herself. Abram would order sardines, vodka, and pickled fish; they'd talk about their fathers and their birth towns, they'd continue to debate whether romantic love was a capitalist construct while staring longingly into each other's eyes . . . Oh, what was the point! She was leaving, he was staying. They wanted different things. And besides, he would never like her, not like that.

And another besides: They may both have been working class, but he'd never understand what had happened to her family. Few could.

"Good evening, miss." Zosia jumped, startled. A middle-aged man stood right in front of her table. "Are you a regular here? I don't believe I've seen you before. Then again, I'm not usually here until much later. You know this place only really gets kicking after three a.m."

"Not a regular," Zosia said quietly. He was standing very close, and she worried he was about to pull up a chair and sit down. Then what would she do?

"Can I get you a drink?"

"No," Zosia said. She would accept nothing from him. Besides, she did not drink alcohol. Sure, she knew many comrades indulged in cheap vodka or wine when they could get it, but the movement discouraged superfluous distractions like alcohol, sex, and smoking—and she already enjoyed a cigarette here and there.

"Then you must try the goose *pipek*. Jozek is famous for it. It's like his French onion soup. As the old Polish proverb goes, 'A good appetite needs no sauce.'"

"Oh Tomasz, leave the poor girl alone," a woman's voice uttered as a bare arm slinked its way around the man's neck. Zosia was relieved for the help but did not love being called a girl. Nor poor. "Is this man bothering you?" the woman teased. Zosia had never seen so much makeup on one face. "Tomasz, I'll have a drink," she said as her hand massaged his chest. "Get me an American one."

"Sure thing, Anna," the man said, imitating an American accent and gait as he walked off looking like a horse.

The woman pulled over a seat. "*Choleria*," she said. "Josek steps out for one minute and all hell breaks loose. You know, he runs this place with an iron fist. The president of Poland himself used to drink here. Josek judges disputes that the rabbinic court can't handle. And he keeps pimps like Tomasz at bay . . ."

Had Zosia been propositioned by an actual pimp?

"Now I have to work for the likes of him," the woman said.

"You're a—" Zosia couldn't bring herself to say it.

"A woman's gotta pay her bills," Anna said. "You know?"

"I do know." Zosia knew Dror would not approve of prostitution, the emblem of capitalist failure. She knew the Polish police force, influenced by many police-women campaigners, was obsessively against female trafficking. Then again, Zosia thought, Anna here *was* an independent person, taking charge of her life. Not to mention, Zosia was relieved by her presence; so grateful, she didn't want her to move.

"I even love the song about Gruby Jozek," Anna said and began to sing: "A sleepless, restless night / Its trace still on my lips / At Fatty Josek's on the Dung Street . . ."

"Come on, Z.D.!" Zosia looked up. Fanny was approaching the table. "Let's get out of here."

"It was nice to meet you, Anna," Zosia said, and bolted from her chair.

"The meeting's over already?" Zosia asked as they stepped onto the pavement outside, shaking herself back into reality after the past surreal hour in the tavern.

"I don't care much about music," Fanny said. "If Marek's telling the truth and she's not in Warsaw, then where is she? What if this is bigger than visas and majors?" Fanny stopped and looked around. "Do you see my car?"

Zosia shrugged. Car models could lead the list of things Zosia knew nothing about. "Sixteen women," Zosia repeated. "Sixteen! Who are they? Regular women like us? Could we be in trouble now too?"

"We're not regular women," Fanny said.

Just then a car pulled up in front of them at the entrance to the club. "Is this your car?" Zosia asked.

Fanny gasped. "No," she stammered. "But I know whose car it is."

"Fanny?" asked a tall man with cacao eyes as he emerged from the automobile. "Is that you?"

"Yes, yes, it is," Fanny said. "Hello, Simon."

CHAPTER 15

Fanny

THEY WERE BACK AT THE ADRIA, AND THIS TIME THEIR TABLE was right next to the rotating dance floor (made of rubber, lest someone slip), which was currently stopped and cleared for a show. It was hard to describe but Fanny could best explain that a comedian of sorts was conducting tricks with a chimpanzee, who was on a leash held by a woman in a tight leopard-skin minidress and golden high heels.

The audience ate it up.

"Do you like this show?" Simon asked. His left hand sat on her right hand, which in turn sat on the thick cream tablecloth catching her thick gold bangle bracelets. Fanny wore a black evening gown with lace cutouts above her bosom and along her sleeves. Mamo had insisted she don the family pearls, and six strands fell heavy on her neck. "Usually they have international stars, and even film shoots."

"It's entertaining," Fanny said. She'd been here for several press balls; she'd been here only a few months ago with him. Did he not recall? She sipped from her crystal flute. She couldn't believe he was back already; she was still shaking from the shock. And she'd run into him at Fat Josek's of all places! "And you? Do you prefer glossy nightclubs or, well, more intimate bars?"

"Oh, Fanny." He squeezed her hand and chuckled. "I had just returned from international travel. It was so late. One always goes to Jozek's for a late drink! I'm so thrilled you happened to be there, talking to our musical director of all things! I hope he took care of you."

"He did." Imagine if she told him about Marek. About Zosia, who'd scampered off as soon as she'd greeted him. About Wanda. About sixteen women! What would he say? She didn't even tell him about the contents of her bag, which lay tucked under her seat.

"Well, I'm so happy I got to see you even sooner than I'd hoped. It was a surprise to me too that I'd be back in Poland before heading to New York. And now, here we are, together."

"We are." Just over four months until their wedding date, Fanny thought.

Just then the female assistant lay down on the ground and the chimpanzee jumped into the comedian's arms. The whole scene was absurd. Fanny withdrew her hand from her fiancé's clasp, reached for her bag, opened it, and began to assemble the flash.

"What is that?" Simon asked.

"My camera."

"I know that's a camera," he said. "But why here, in public?"

"Why not?"

"You're not a professional photographer," he said. "You can't just take photos at the Adria." He wasn't angry as he gingerly took the apparatus from her hands as if prying away an extra dessert, and placed it back in the bag, which he put under his own seat. "You, my darling, are quite something."

"Quite," she repeated. Even Avigdor had been more interested in her "hobby." As for Abram, he'd pushed her to take photos of the police!

"Your zest is very attractive." Simon moved his hand to a spot just above her knee. "More wine? I heard they now serve Manhattans, and even Coca-Cola. When I return from America, I'll let you know how authentic they are!"

"I'm not thirsty," Fanny said. "Besides, I'd better not get used to living it up like this if we're moving to the countryside." She couldn't help herself.

"You'll be too tired taking care of our children to go to nightclubs!" He nuzzled closer to her. "I want a boy and a girl."

She pulled back and shivered.

"Are you cold?" he asked. "We're not used to this air-conditioning in Poland." He took his jacket off his own body and placed it over her shoulders. It weighed one thousand pounds.

THE NEXT MORNING, FANNY WAS SWEATING. SHE'D SPENT hours in the Fashion Cafe's studio, taking her first pictures for "Behind the Seams." Fanny was enthralled by the vibe, which distracted her from her worries: Wrapped canvases were stacked by one wall; nude mannequins were spotted around the space. It smelled like paint, cigarettes, coffee—like being an artist. Fanny clicked on designers and seamstresses as they created, grabbing close-ups of their hands in action, threading, sewing, sketching, tracing their working minds. Then, the real interstitial spaces: the coffee break, the cigarette. She wasn't sure if any of the photos were good (à la *truth and perspective*), but now that she had her very own darkroom, she would know soon enough.

One last shot, Fanny told herself. *Make it a good one.* How would Wanda capture the moment? She approached one designer who was particularly entranced in her creation, her hand jetting back and forth across the page leaving a trail of black charcoal like smoke.

"Wait a second. I have an idea!" Fanny said.

"Sorry?"

Fanny ran to the other end of the room and picked up a woman's fox fur scarf. Why wait to run into accidental situations that resembled Wanda's world when she could actively construct them and add her own spin? "Put it on!" she told the designer.

"Huh?"

"Please! And stand too."

Reluctant at first, the woman draped the garment exactly as it was in Wanda's photo. Only here the subject was a worker, surrounded by her equipment. "Just bend down a little, yes, that way . . ." It was perfect. *Click.*

Fanny chose not to notice that the rest of the women in the room looked at her as if she were insane. She also chose not to notice them rolling their eyes at each other. What did it matter? This is what being an artist meant!

"Don't worry," she announced to the room with a chuckle. "I'm all done now. You can go back to being your wild selves." A few women, at least, laughed.

Fanny began to disassemble the tripod she'd been using that day, as well as her various flashes. Her lecture began in twenty-five minutes and she was sure to be tardy; she'd told Natalia to head out without her. Plus, she still had no thesis topic. Nowak was not going to be happy. She'd better get—

And that's when she heard it. One of the women. "*Your* cousin was arrested? A young woman, our age?"

"Apparently, she was locked up with a whole group of women. Fifteen or sixteen, we heard. In Przemyśl."

"All the way east?"

"It makes no sense."

Fanny had goosebumps as she turned to the seamstress. "Did she by any chance have a printing press? And when was she taken? Who arrested her? Why—"

"We have no information," the seamstress said. "We're waiting to hear from the police. Or at least read about it in the papers."

Now Fanny was truly late for Nowak's lecture. She ran up the university stairwell and opened the door to the hall, embarrassed that the creak drew attention. Fanny quietly slinked her way to an empty seat right behind Natalia.

Nowak was going on about how things would be different from now: new plans, new ideals. *New plans in French daguerreotypes?* she mused. *New ideals in French—*

"Zelshinsky!" he suddenly called out.

Did he mean her? Usually, she was Ms. "I'm so sorry, Professor. Pardon my tardiness."

"Your tardiness?"

Oh, perhaps this was about her thesis . . . She hadn't submitted a topic. Had Nowak found out that she still had no idea what to write about?

"I mean, I've given it some thought, and—"

"You've given it some thought?" She'd never seen him so stern. Why was he overreacting? It was possible she even had a subject. She didn't, but it was possible she did . . .

"Yes, and I believe—"

"You believe?"

"Yes, well . . ."

"I don't care what you believe, Zelshinsky. Stand up."

Fanny was shocked, confused. What was going on? She rose, trying to stay composed, confident.

"Now move."

"Move?" She felt sweat pool under her arms.

"Yes, move."

"In what way? To where?"

The whole room was silent.

"Move like a Jew. And move to the left, to the Jew bench."

Fanny's face burned hot. "The Jew bench?"

Fanny had no idea what to do. Standing there, all eyes on her.

"If you had arrived to my class on time like a civilized student, you would have been aware."

Silence.

"There are new rules, Zelshinsky. Now, move."

Fanny looked over at the Jew bench, at a line of her fellow peers who sat quietly, hunched over, staring at the floor.

She bent down and slowly picked up her bag. Though every fiber of skin trembled, she managed to compose herself and, with grace, she walked to the left and joined.

PART 2

Fashion show at the Fashion Café at 11 Królewska Street in Warsaw.

CHAPTER 16

Zosia

A MACHINE WHIRRING, SPEWING, SPOUTING—WORDS, HEADLINES, round and round, stacking one upon another like layers of icing. Her hands—her own fingers—wound the side, rolling out sentences, a page and another page, a whole blanket, covering her, growing bigger, the machine, larger and louder and—

"Zosia!"

Someone was shaking her.

She had no idea where she was. Warsaw? Grochów? Byten?

The smell—mop water, cold tea, damp wood. She was in the dining hall, slumped in a chair; she'd fallen asleep reading a Hebrew novel. Lectures, laundry duty, late nights at Fat Josek's, rubbing sides with Warsaw's top prostitutes—everything was getting the better of her.

"Zosia!" Mira hissed. "Wake up. It's an emergency."

"What?" Zosia snapped upright.

"Ghetto benches have been instituted in Warsaw. It's horrible, shaming, unacceptable. All the youth movements are getting together to fight it," Mira went on. "With your experience from the kosher campaign we need you on it. You must go to the meeting."

"Of course." Zosia jumped to standing on unsteady legs. "When?"

"Now!"

The meeting was taking place at the Bund's Lokal, where many of the kosher campaign meetings had been held. The activists would have to figure out what the lawmakers wanted and what they would settle for. They needed to understand who was behind this, what their motivation was, and how they could offer a better motivation for something else. Zosia needed to remain positive.

In the meeting room, Zosia scanned the crowd for familiar faces. Here was a mix of youth movement representatives. The Bundists were all from their youth group—*Tzukunft*, or Yiddish for "future." Some senior Bundists were known to be gruff, in cahoots with the Polish Socialist Party, and were rumored to have staged attacks on the country's leading fascists, but they weren't in attendance. Zosia saw Sofia and Gershon and Eliezer and Abram and—

Fanny?

Why was Fanny here . . . and with Abram? And why were they standing so close?

"Thank you all for coming." Gershon the Bundist took the floor. "Despite being outlawed until now, the government has changed their mind about the Jewish ghetto benches under pressure from the right-wing groups. The government claims this measure will help stop campus violence. This is capitulation, not protection. We need a national strategy."

"We need to get ahead of the green ribbons," Abram interjected, referring to students who wore a green ribbon to show allegiance to the Nazi Party, often staging violent acts and protests. How intellectual students—young people who were in universities, those with brains and opportunities—could be so taken by an idiot like Hitler made zero sense to Zosia. The man was a buffoon. How had Nazi ideology infiltrated so deeply?

"Many professors, Jewish and Christian, are against this, of course," Gershon continued. "They are writing a letter. There's talk of a letter from international academics, from Britain and America. Professors are petitioning the Polish government."

"Have any professors in Warsaw actually implemented the bench?" someone asked.

"Yes," Abram replied. He gestured to Fanny. "A few hours ago. I found Fanny here outside her classroom, shaking in shock. She'd been shamed by her French teacher, told to get up and move to the left of the room. Until today, he'd been her mentor."

Zosia watched Fanny nod silently and blush as comrades shared their condolences. Abram touched Fanny's shoulder and Zosia felt a sharp twist of jealousy she tried to push away.

"Fanny's a photographer," Abram announced. "She can take pictures for our campaign."

Pictures? Why in the world would they need a photographer?

It was hard not to feel like Fanny was encroaching on all aspects of her life, pulling her into apartments and nightclubs and police blackmail and away from her goals. As Dror advocated, we are social, we live with and for each other. But with Fanny, Zosia felt as if her boundaries were porous, as if she were beginning to leak.

Zosia took a deep breath. "Listen, everyone!" she blurted. "Here's what we need to do."

"We're listening," Gershon said. "That is, as long as you're really committed to Poland, a country you want to leave . . . We who plan to stay here need to deal with this issue head-on."

"Well, yes, our future *should* be in a Jewish land," Zosia started, acknowledging that some truth lined his words. "But that's not the point."

"You're overly land oriented," Gershon accused. "It's all a construct."

"And you're not?" Zosia shot back. "Poland, Poland, Poland. Poland is a land too. A territory. Also, a construct." Zosia took a fast breath to collect herself. This was all part of the never-ending

Bundist–Zionist fight; the Diaspora wars. The Yiddish versus the Hebrew, the home versus the home. The constant need to defend. It would lead nowhere. Now was the time to *act.* "Warsaw's Jews cannot go to school."

"Boycott school?" someone said. "That's easy for you to say; you don't go to school."

Fanny piped in. "I'm not going back to school."

Zosia appreciated her support. Less so, how Abram looked admiringly at her.

"A boycott plan," Abram said, turning the idea over. "Jewish students stop going. Even after all the quotas, this is still a large number of students. It will be chaos."

"But isn't that just what they want?" Fanny asked. "A university with no Jews?"

"No," Abram said. "They want to shame us, not get rid of us. They couldn't manage without us. We saw it in the Dzigan sketch."

"We must maintain Jewish pride," Zosia said. "A flyer campaign to start. We'll tell students to boycott class. Then we can discuss collaborating with the letter, and a strike."

"Are you willing to collaborate?" Gershon prodded. "For real?"

"I'm here, aren't I?" Zosia retorted. She looked to Abram, but he was quiet.

"The Bund is exploding," Gershon went on. "You should see the projections for the upcoming elections. We used to be split evenly: thirty percent Zionist, thirty percent religious, thirty percent Bund. Now, the majority of Polish Jewry is realizing that the way forward is the socialist, Diasporic way. Poland has been our home for over one thousand years; we are different, but also the same. Once we end capitalism, the Poles will come to their senses and realize that anti-Jewish messages are just a distraction from their real problems."

"Or, we leave and create our own home."

"They offered you Uganda."

"You go live in Uganda!" Zosia snapped. "Palestine is our ancestral home."

"*Doikayt!* Our home is where we *are.* Our language is what we speak: Yiddish. The only people who agree with your escapist mission are the antisemitic Poles themselves. Did you see today's editorial: 'Get the Jews out and give them their own country, Madagascar if Palestine won't do.' *They're* your Zionist allies!" Gershon went on. "We Bundists are not focused on some ideological dreamworld where all the world's Jews are concentrated into a promised land where we haven't experienced our recent past. Building a Jewish homeland in the Middle East that's already inhabited by an Arab population that doesn't want us there is a recipe for conflict."

Jews have been living in Palestine for centuries, she wanted to say. *Jews and Arabs can live together side by side and in peace.* But Zosia couldn't take this . . . any of this. And why should she? This was supposed to be an urgent meeting about ghetto benches, not rehashed philosophy. She headed right to the door.

"Zosia," Abram called after her, but she kept walking. *They wanted different things.* "Please, come back."

Fanny was suddenly by her side. "Come with me to Café Ziemiańska. We need to discuss Wanda. It's very important."

"No," Zosia said. "I'm too busy."

"You can't be," Fanny said. Zosia saw in her eyes something urgent, something hurt. "I have new information."

THE CAFÉ WAS PACKED, BRIMMING WITH ACTIVITY AS IF NO other world existed. Zosia stared wide-eyed at her novel surrounds. Against the bright yellow walls, tables overflowed with coffee cups, glasses of spritz, and so many people. Five, six men and women pulled up chairs to each four-top, even two-top. Meetings took place, side conversations, readings of poems, sporadic applause. Not to mention noses upturned every which way. Only in Poland did people stand in line at the local library because a magazine had recommended a certain novel. But did anyone actually *read* the book? No! It was all artifice; they were a nation of snobs. Zosia scanned the fashionable crowd, but of course it was impossible to tell who was a socialist or a fascist or an antisemite. It was hard to tell who was a friend.

"Come," Fanny said, taking her hand. "We can find a seat upstairs." Through the smoky air they passed the long burgundy newspaper racks and glossy counters with pastries covered in glass domes as if they were rare jewels. "The mezzanine is for the upper echelon of the literary world," Fanny explained as they ascended the stairs, confirming Zosia's take that Poland was obsessed with status. "I'm meeting the wedding calligrapher here in an hour. Best invitations in town, Mamo said." Fanny was hyper. She grabbed a table. "Right now Ziemiańska is really the most important of the cafés, the 'office building' of Warsaw's artistic groups, the meeting place of painters, cabaret artists, and, oh wait—is that Paulina Appenszlak, the editor of *Ewa*? It's a weekly all about gender equality, motherhood, and birth control. I think she was even involved in the Warsaw abortion clinic!"

"Fanny." Zosia stopped the woman's frenzied tirade. "How are you feeling? What happened in class? It must have been so difficult."

"I'm fine."

"Thank you for coming to the meeting at the Bund," Zosia forced herself to say. If she spoke this reality, perhaps it would change her inner attitude. "It always helps to turn your anger to action. Not that we settled on any action, but it's a process."

"I can't believe you fight so much," Fanny said. "Everything about you is the same."

"We're nothing alike—"

"Listen," Fanny cut in. "I think I know where she is."

"Where?"

"Przemyśl. I heard women in the Fashion Café talking about it. Sixteen women, all arrested."

"What? Why?"

"I don't know. But we're going."

Zosia took a sip of water and at the same time ingested this news. Wanda, the one person who might actually be able to get her out of this country, had been arrested and was being held in a countryside prison, and this was now Zosia's responsibility. Zosia wasn't sure how much more she wanted to know.

Suddenly, a commotion began to brew below. As the volume reached a pitch, everyone on the mezzanine stood and looked over the balcony to the ground floor. The whole café became silent—a never-before occurrence. Zosia stared at the skirmish at the door: two men, wearing *payes*, *tefillin*, and black hats and coats wanted to sit down but they were being refused. "We're full." The patron was firm. "Can't you see?"

"You have tables!" one of the men shouted in a Yiddish accent. "Why can't we sit?"

"I recommend you try a café in the Jewish neighborhood," the patron said. "You will feel more comfortable."

Two waiters approached the men to escort them out, with force. Zosia was frozen. All the preparation in the world, but the moment of attack was its own thing, emotion disconnected from action, all ice in your veins and eyes gone dry.

Fanny, on the other hand, grabbed her bag. *Click.*

Then a collective gasp. One of the religious men flung off his hat. The other ripped off his beard.

It was Dzigan and Schumacher.

"You see?" Dzigan called out. "You call yourself literary and avant-garde, but Jews walk in here and you refuse them."

"Nonsense," the patron argued. "This whole café is filled with Jews."

"We were testing your basic courtesy and you failed," Schumacher called out. "You're the most progressive café in Central Europe, but someone wears their black jacket a bit longer and they're kicked out? Shame on you!"

"But you see, you *were* tricksters, liars!" the patron called. "I was right to refuse you."

"And as for all you Jews who bowed your heads and said nothing"—Dzigan waved his finger around the entire café—"what a disappointment." The comedians threw their costumes on the floor and made for the door.

"I tried to say something, I really did," Zosia mumbled among the café's hubbub, so ashamed. She'd been able to scare off adolescent hoodlums in a park but not here, in front of others, where it really counted.

She'd failed—again.

"Listen, we need to focus." Fanny was undeterred by the scene around them. "I asked you here to discuss Wanda."

"I've told you a thousand times," Zosia said. She hadn't even had the chance to go back to Grochów, to try the sieve; she'd made zero progress. "I am overwhelmed. Did you know for Dror I have to weed out imposters who are still lying to get visas that barely exist? That's how bad the situation here is. And the ghetto bench. I need to run this campaign too. You of all people should understand."

"But more important—Wanda. They've arrested women; we're women. Have you heard about some of the political prisons and camps they are setting up in Germany, and even here? Abram told me all about them." She gestured around them, wired, gulping the air as she spoke. "Look how crazy this country is becoming. Zosia"—she paused to breathe—"I was sent to the bench, to the corner. *Me.* If I could be sidelined, well, then, what's happening here? If we don't look for Wanda, no one will. Wanda told me, on that very day that she went missing, that we must be inside the peril. We must run toward danger. This *is* bigger than my exhibit or your visa."

"Toward danger?" Zosia said. What else had Abram told her? Zosia didn't want to go to the countryside, she did not want to go east, to go backward.

"I'll see you at the station at eight a.m. tomorrow."

Zosia was silent. She needed to get out of here, to get out for good. She began to hear it, echoes of that shriek, reverberating louder, like a reflection of a reflection of a yowl. She put her hands to her ears.

"You can't just freeze, Zosia. You cannot."

CHAPTER 17

Fanny

THE NEXT MORNING, CAMERA BAG BY HER SIDE, FANNY bounded down her building's front stairs and was about to pivot onto the street when a tall man nearly knocked right into her. He was thirtysomething, she'd say, and wore a pin-striped suit under his coat, as well as a bowler hat. His briefcase was brown and particularly shiny. "Please excuse me, Miss," he stammered. "I'm sorry."

"You're excused," Fanny said.

"You must be Miss Zelshinsky," he said. "Is your mother home? I need to see her."

This man was a little young for Mamo . . . or was he another one of Mamo's backup plans for Fanny? At seven o'clock in the morning?

He shifted his weight side to side. His briefcase bumped on his knee.

Definitely not for her.

"Unfortunately, you just missed her," Fanny said. "She went shopping."

"Shopping? At this hour?" The man sighed. "I came early, before work, because I was sure I would find her."

"She's an early riser. Bird gets the worm, you know."

"Is that her in the window?" he asked, gesturing up at their apartment.

Fanny looked. Why was she up? Then again, Mamo had probably just gotten home from her night out . . . But Fanny did not have time for a setup. Wanda was waiting for her, only hours away! "No, that's my grandmother," she lied. Ha, Mamo would hate that.

The man took a thin envelope out of his inner blazer pocket. Why didn't women have inner pockets? "Please give this to her as soon as she returns. Tell her it's from Pan Prosterman. This is urgent, so make sure she has it directly in hand."

"Sure, I'll pass it on," Fanny said.

"Very well," he said and tipped his hat to her. "Perhaps we will meet again. Good day."

"Good day," she said and waited politely as he turned the corner. She checked her Tank watch: She was going to miss the train! She stuffed the letter into her camera bag and galloped off.

THE TRAIN CLICKED INTO PRZEMYŚL AS THE SPRINGTIME AFternoon sun bruised the sky oranges and yellows. From the window, Fanny saw row after row of colorful medieval buildings with bright red and blue roofs, all dotted with majestic church towers.

The conductor appeared at their box, parting the oxblood curtains like a Red Sea. "May I assist with your baggage, Mademoiselles? Can I help you disembark?"

"No, thank you," Zosia said quickly. "We can do it ourselves."

Fanny rolled her eyes behind Zosia's back, and the conductor smiled. Zosia had spent the bulk of the five-hour journey explaining to Fanny how this was her first time traveling in first class, and how she disapproved of such extravagance. She could have gotten a lift with someone from Dror . . . *So why didn't you?* Fanny finally retorted. *Because I couldn't lie,* Zosia said and at last hushed up.

Fanny had told her to calm down and focus on the end result: Wanda. Besides, this was just first class regional. This train was no Luxtorpeda train-bus, nor the Polish Orient Express, the Ski-Dancing-Bridge train she and Mamo used to take between resorts with extravagant restaurants, bridge cars, and the occasional cinema. If she remembered correctly, it's where she'd seen her first glimpse of Greta Garbo.

Here on the train, Fanny reflected, she could sit wherever she liked, the left, the right, the roof for all they cared, but not in her own school? The numerus clausus had barely affected her, a woman in the humanities whose parents knew university administrators. Sure, a few friends who wanted to study science had had to enroll in schools in France or Czechoslovakia, but not Fanny. The ruling had not touched her directly. Provincial threats weren't relevant, not to a Zelshinsky. The Zelshinskys didn't even go to synagogue on Yom Kippur! *Zelshinsky!* She burned up, shuddering at the memory of Nowak uttering her name. Why had he done this to her? Fanny racked her mind, trying to recall if he'd ever seemed prejudiced before, but she couldn't think of any particular examples. Then again, had he disallowed her from accruing art credits out of bigotry? Was it because both she and Wanda were Jewish? Suddenly she had to rethink everything; most Polish intellectuals were great supporters of the Jewish community. Was that changing?

She wished she'd taken out her camera and captured the moment, taking charge of it. Regret burned her insides like a drink taken too hot, scorching her from tongue to tummy.

Should she go back to school, sit in a Jew bench? Tell Mamo? Tell Simon?

Then again, she was on a cross-country train with a socialist comrade riding to a prison. What would she possibly tell them? The truth was, a part of her still wanted to get the pink paper signed, to get into the exhibition, to show her autonomy and maturity—that is, assuming Wanda's name still held any weight. But more than all that, she needed to help her teacher.

The Przemyśl train station, with its colorful columns and landscape frescoes, resembled an ornate classical castle, but outside, the roads were unpaved and traffic lights still hadn't made their way to this part of the country despite their recent proliferation across the capital.

"Where's the prison?" Fanny asked a woman hunched over a peddler's cart. The woman looked at her as if she were crazy.

"Prison?" Zosia repeated in a working-class accent, and directions were given. Back in her element, Zosia seemed more relaxed.

"I've never been to a jail before," Fanny said.

"Me neither," Zosia replied. "Finally, we're both out of place." Their feet slid a little backward in the slush. Forward and backward, past the town square and daily market. It hit her: They were really doing this. Fanny's heart raced.

"Listen." Zosia broke the silence. "Do what you can. Flirt, bribe, I won't stop you."

The jail, a drab beige building that sprawled across a whole block, was surrounded by a guard tower and a thick cement wall. They found the single street-level door, and before opening it, Fanny made up her lips and made sure her chocolate was readily available. (If only she'd had an inner pocket . . .) To the guards, they declared themselves "visitors." Their bags were searched, and they were shown to a hallway. "No photos."

Fanny nodded.

"We did it, we're going to see Wanda soon," Zosia whispered as they walked, and Fanny couldn't help but squeeze her arm. "Don't take pictures. Seriously. We don't need the attention."

The hallways were dark and somehow colder than the streets, their stale air thick with the smell of sewage. The walls were stained yellow. *This is where Wanda was being held?* Fanny knew they were both thinking. It struck her: She hadn't really thought it through, seeing Wanda. What would they say? What if Wanda *had* been doing something terrible? What if *they* were now implicated? What if she'd been hurt, tortured? She looked to Zosia, who was stone-faced. She'd dragged this woman into this mess; she needed to act big.

A door clicked shut behind them.

"What?" an officer asked from behind a desk that sat on a raised platform. "What do you want?"

Fanny hesitated for just a second but then declared with confidence: "We are visitors here to see Wanda Petrovsky."

"Who?"

"Wanda Petrovsky, from Warsaw. Professor Petrovsky."

"I don't know who you're talking about. Who sent you here?"

"She's one of the sixteen women," Zosia piped in.

"Sixteen?"

Fanny noticed he had a gun. She also noticed that his fingers were fat, and one phalange was choked by his bronze wedding band. She felt her own engagement ring gnawing at her hand.

"The sixteen women who were arrested," Zosia tried.

"Do you have loose screws?" he bellowed. "Why would sixteen women be arrested?"

Fanny stepped forward and batted her eyelashes. "We were sent by Avigdor Radetsky."

"Who?"

"A top prosecutor from Warsaw."

"I don't know who you are talking about. Or why he would send you."

Fanny reached into her bag, but before she could even take out the chocolate, he stopped her. "Are you trying to bribe a police officer? Is that what *zhiden* think they can do?"

"No, I—I was just hungry."

"Honorable sir," Zosia tried in a particularly country-girl lilt. *Country to country,* Fanny thought. Class meant everything, more than language or even religion. That's where real ties lie, in expectations and understandings: Either life had been fair to you or it hadn't, it had given or it had taken, and that attitude rested above all else. "We are Wanda's cousins, we have traveled from far, and we would very much like to see her, even just briefly. Prisoners are allowed visitors, aren't they? We will comply with all your rules."

"Prisoners can be allowed clown buffets for all I care," he said. "Your cousin is not here."

"But—" Zosia said.

"There's no but. There's reality." He pointed at the door.

Fanny had been wrong. Either she'd misheard, or she'd made it all up, wanting to hear, wanting so badly to know, to feel there was a way forward. "I'm so sorry," she whispered to Zosia as they left the building. "I feel like I've taken us on a wild-goose chase."

"Wanda is loud and loyal," Zosia finally said. "A real wild goose."

For a while they were silent, and one could hear the crunch of the snow.

Finally, Fanny stopped. "I don't believe him."

"Me neither."

"I have an idea!" Mamo had taught her that everyone could be bought, you just needed to find their price, or rather, their weakness. She patted the Leica in its bag. What was on her roll? It was a small town, but surely she could find a developer. "Meet me back at the prison in two hours."

"You again?" the chief said. Zosia hadn't been at the door, so in the interest of time, and in the desire to prove she had not been wrong, she'd entered alone.

Fanny placed her portfolio on his desk. "Check it out," she said. "Portraits."

"So?"

"They're good. I'm a great photographer."

"So?"

"So, are you married?" She knew from his ring.

"Of course. Beautiful wife, beautiful children."

"How would she like a portrait?" Fanny said. "I'll make her look like the most beautiful woman in the entire town."

He stopped and considered. "A portrait by a Warsaw photographer?"

"A fine portrait by an up-and-coming Warsaw photographer."

"And your price is—"

"A visit."

"So . . . let's go."

"Yeah?"

"The *most* beautiful," he said. He plopped off his seat to find a replacement and a *droshky*. Fanny followed him down the hall. She hadn't expected this to happen so fast. Where was Zosia?

Just as he took her hand to help her into the old cart, she saw her friend running toward them. Fanny breathed a sigh of relief and offered her own hand to help Zosia up. Zosia hopped onto the cart.

"Call me Jarek," the chief said as he made himself comfortable, taking up too much room. He smiled and Fanny saw he had a missing tooth, right in front.

Thirty minutes later, the carriage delivered them to Jarek's family home, a wooden shack set in a snowy yard peppered with skinny yet robust chickens. Fanny and Zosia waited in the *droshky* with its whinnying horses while Jarek went to announce the visit to his wife and ask her to dress up for the occasion. Suddenly, the yard was crowded with relatives and townspeople, all buzzing with excitement.

"They've never seen a camera," Jarek explained as he helped Fanny down. "My father was shocked a few months ago to see himself in a mirror. Before that, he'd only ever seen his reflection in water. Maybe in a pot!"

An elderly lady came out of the house with a tray of tea and Sernik cheesecake topped with so much white sugar powder it formed a halo above the plate. It was sickeningly sweet. So this would be her life in the countryside. "Jarek," she said, aware the day was nearly over, "we need a clear space with good light, and quick."

Inside, Jarek's wife appeared pale, a thin version of her ethereal name, Angelika. Her lips were straight, like the edges of paper. She wore a thick red-and-green-striped skirt that draped down to her toes and a shiny pink top embroidered with designs along the front and across its balloon sleeves. Her beads hung in long layers long around her neck and a dark kerchief was wrapped around her head. Underneath all that, she seemed brittle, like a branch that could easily snap in half, yet just as easily poke you in the eye. The woman ogled Jarek as if he were a king from a fairy tale. Fanny knew: That was the look she wanted for the portrait. Blind devotion.

Had her parents ever looked at each other that way? Would she ever have that with Simon? With anyone?

People crowded behind Fanny as she set up a tripod. Neighbors peeked in from the windows. "Shh!" Fanny instructed them; she enjoyed her power as they all silenced. Fanny pulled up a wicker chair and asked the woman to sit on it. Then she asked her to stand behind it. Then, next to it. All the while, she looked through her lens to assess angle, form, light.

"Hurry up," Zosia mouthed from the threshold.

"Has it begun? What's happening?" The wife looked at Jarek, panicked.

He smiled, fat and proud. "Do not worry, my love. This woman is the best of the best."

"Just warming up, Pani Angelika," Fanny said. Then to Jarek, "Go stand next to her."

He obliged, strutting to the spotlight. Fanny instructed Angelika to sit facing sideways, look up at her husband, and pose with her hands folded in her lap. *Click.*

"What was that?" Angelika held her beads between her fingers and recited a prayer.

"Just the flash," Fanny said. "A bit of light. Hold still, I'm taking another."

Angelika looked up at her husband as if she were about to undergo kidney surgery and this might be their last shared glance. Her quavering vulnerability, her all-encompassing neediness, was perfect. For a second, Fanny flashed to Abram, to how she'd walked out of Nowak's class, shocked and confused, and he'd been there, as if he were waiting, and he'd come over, pulled her to the side, and let her cry. *Click.*

Zosia tapped on her watch. "Nu!" she mouthed.

"All done," Fanny declared to her subject. "You can breathe now."

A tear slalomed down Angelika's cheek. "I've only ever seen myself in Babcia's mirror, and it's cracked."

"I promise, you will look stunning. Your beauty will surprise you."

Jarek helped Fanny and Zosia back to the droshky, which was not easy to reach as by now nearly the whole town had gathered in front of the small home. "They all want portraits," Jarek said, proud, as if all this were his doing.

"You're a real tastemaker," Fanny lied, but her voice was drowned out by the crowd's requests. "Can you do me? How much?" Fanny stared at the long line of people.

"Look at all these potential *clients*," Zosia whispered.

"Self-sufficiency," Fanny jibed as they sat down in the carriage. Here she was, fancy little Fanny, photographing the masses. She'd come up with the idea and was making it happen.

"The camera stuns people," Zosia said, sounding not a little impressed. "It changes them. The photographer has real influence."

The driver whipped the horse. "Hey, wait for Jarek," Fanny called.

"He's not coming."

"What?" Fanny began to panic. "Jarek!" she screamed, leaning halfway outside the droshky. He was still in the yard, soaking in his pride, his faux-rich man status. "You said you'd let me see her. You need to come back and let me in."

"Sure, I'll let you see her," he laughed. "When I see the proof. Show me the picture. Show me my wife looking beautiful, more beautiful than any other woman in town. Then I'll let you in. That was the deal, *zhyd*."

The carriage began to pull out and Fanny nearly spat at him, but Zosia pulled her back. "Be calm," she said this time. "I have a plan."

Back at the prison, Zosia told Fanny to follow her around to the other side of the building. "I noticed something earlier when I walked around. There's a yard in the back, and a little break in the fence. It's just after dinner now, so I think we may be in luck. I hope you have that chocolate with you."

"Of course I do."

They heard chatter—the prisoners were out.

Zosia waved until the guard noticed. He approached the fence, and Fanny handed him the tablet. He nodded and stood aside so they could slink through the opening. He gave them three minutes.

Fanny squeezed Zosia's hand as they crept through. They'd done it!

It was that easy. In front of them: a small concrete area filled with women, roaming in pairs.

And right there, in the middle, sitting alone on a stone bench, was Wanda Petrovsky. She was smoking.

Fanny had been looking for her for so long, she'd almost forgotten that she was, well, a mere person. Skinny, petite, she was so much smaller than the giant figure in her head. Fanny was suddenly overcome with nerves. Here was Professor P, the Wanda in her brain, the holder of all artistic secrets, of her potential future, the one she couldn't even ask questions of in class—

"What happened?" Zosia blurted. "Are you alright?"

Up close, Fanny could see how gaunt she really was. Her skirt was saggy, nearly falling off of her. Yet Wanda's expression was rock hard, her eyes like nails screwed tight into her visage. She shook her head yes, then no, then took a long drag of her cigarette and put it out with her beaten-up boot. She didn't seem at all surprised to see them, here, together; it was as if she'd expected it.

"They claim there will be a trial at the end of summer, but they sent me a fake lawyer," she whispered. "He's one of them . . . who knows if they'll even try us—the justice system is a sham. The country has barely been alive for twenty years and it's falling apart. A teenager, really, committing suicide before knowing the value of life."

"A trial for what?" Fanny asked.

The guard blew his whistle, looked at them, and gestured that they had one minute left.

"What can we do to help?" Zosia asked, quick. "What are the next steps?"

"Go to Vlad," Wanda said.

"At Dror?" Zosia asked. "I don't know a Vlad."

"No, at the Jewish Writers' Union. Tell him where I am. Tell him sixteen women. Tell him they're using us as some political prop, a way to flex their right-wing muscles. Tell him they're fucking fascists."

The whistle blew.

"Tell him—*privately*."

Fanny and Zosia nodded.

Their time was up.

It may have been the longest day of her life, but Fanny felt wired. "What does she mean by a sham trial? What did she even do? They're going to keep her in jail until the end of summer? Then again, it means we have time to get her legal help."

They'd made the last train to Warsaw by seconds.

As they settled in, she looked over at her friend, who was frowning. "What's wrong?"

"Nothing," Zosia mumbled and sighed.

"Tell me," Fanny insisted.

"I didn't even ask her what she meant to tell me on that first night, and whether she had a way for me to get a visa," Zosia said. "I came all this way and forgot about my personal goal. I know it sounds selfish, but I still need those papers."

"I certainly didn't ask her to sign any pink forms," Fanny said. Her desire felt so very flimsy compared to the real threat Wanda faced. "I guess that's not what's important anymore," she added over the din of the locomotive. "We'll go find Vlad tomorrow?"

"Let's go after the flyering campaign, in a couple of days," Zosia said. "You'll be taking pictures?"

"I guess." Fanny shrugged. The truth was, she didn't particularly want to arrive on campus as a campaigner. Seeing Wanda, she realized, had unexpectedly made her pine for school, for a time when her greatest threat was a history exam. Then she mumbled, "Maybe I should go to my lecture."

"What?" Zosia nearly choked. The train reached full speed. "You're not serious! You're part of the campaign. You' re on the committee. We'll need you there, especially if the Bundists don't show."

"But why should I let them win? Why should I sacrifice my own graduation?"

"For the greater good." Clearly exasperated by Fanny, Zosia picked up an abandoned newspaper and flipped through it aggressively.

The conductor asked for their tickets.

As Fanny fumbled in her camera bag, she came across the letter from the man with the shiny briefcase. After showing the ticket, she opened the note and began reading. She gasped.

The paper dropped from her shaking hands, soaring for a moment as if it could avoid its inevitable crash to the sleet-streaked floor.

Mamo was broke.

CHAPTER 18

Zosia

Zosia waved a placard and noted that Abram held a banner nearby. no benches. They'd been the first to arrive for the boycott campaign, lugging with them dozens of "protest documents"—flyers, small leaflets, large banners. They'd spent the past twenty-four hours together and awake, creating these signs. "You two are like a well-oiled machine," a young comrade had told them. "Have you been working together for a long time?"

"Only a few weeks," Abram answered and smiled at Zosia, a thick, warm smile. Fortunately, the time pressure meant they hadn't had time to stray into uncomfortable conversations about family backgrounds, late-night loping, and Bundist affinities, and so their side-by-side labor had felt easy and natural. They might have had different life goals, Zosia thought, but they sure knew how to make things together.

Now they aimed to paper every inch of the campus. It was important to make their message loud and clear, and everywhere.

"Boycott!" Zosia rang out again and again. "We will not tolerate a Jew bench! No segregated seating for Jews!"

But, to her dismay and great surprise, she was largely ignored. "I don't want to get served disciplinary action from the school like they did in Vilna," one young Jewish student told her.

"If I skip class, I'll fail my exams," another woman said. "I've worked too hard."

"But you're Jewish," Zosia retorted and stuffed a flyer into her book bag. Zosia had never considered this, that the students would be afraid of the school. "You need to be proud."

"I'm proud to attend university."

Zosia wanted to pull her hair out but took a deep breath. There was a time when she too would have liked to debate classical literature in a stained glass–encrusted hall. Besides: optimism. She didn't always see the direct results of her work, she consoled herself. Her messaging had indirect impact: getting someone to think, discuss, share the idea with others, to change *eventually*. She was planting seeds—of pride, resistance, transformation.

Her hand touched her pocket. Inside, another letter from her mother.

She had been startled to find it on her bed that morning.

Zosia still hadn't replied to the first missive, yet once again, with her poor spelling and barely legible script, Mameh urged her to return to Byten, for her safety, for the grocery, and for Bella, who would soon get married. Would Zosia come for the engagement schnapps?

No, Zosia had thought, *she would not*. Her family was Dror. She could not leave, certainly not now. She could not be there to hold Bella's hand as the groom gave a toast, to stand by Mameh's side, one arm around her waist, as the *machatunim* offered a mazel tov, to help Tateh—no, no, she could not think about it.

She couldn't believe she'd broken into a prison yard. She banished the thought lest anyone here could read her mind.

Now Zosia noticed a group of policemen on the other side of the campus green. Had she seen police the last time she'd been here, on that night she came to meet Wanda? *They're here to keep the peace*, she assured herself. *They're always on campus, keeping order at the university*.

"Hello, Zosia, chevrah." It was Mira. "Good work." Zosia knew "good" wasn't "great." Zosia took a long breath and walked over to a few campaigners. "It's so hard," one of them said. "They don't believe the situation is that bad. They say this is Poland as usual, country of medieval Jewish ghettos, of fringe group pogroms. They don't want to be penalized."

"They feel lucky because they got in despite the quotas," another comrade said. "They don't want to give up the idea that they're 'special,' that they defied the odds."

"Students in Łódź were penalized for skipping class," another added. "The school threatened them. No one wants that."

Abram approached her, and she almost felt a fluttering in her stomach, but she extinguished it by lighting a fresh cigarette.

"We really could have used some Bundists here," he said.

Now Zosia's stomach felt heavy, like a bowling ball. She inhaled deeply, filling herself with tobacco, trying to suppress the feeling that she was so very alone. She shook her head.

"Listen, I've been meaning to apologize. I'm sorry Gershon treated you that way," Abram went on. "I tried to talk to you that day, but you ran off. I told him afterwards not to be like that." He was leaning closer; she could see the flecks of yellow in his brown eyes. "The Bund has connections with the Polish Socialists. We could use the extra bodies in our next action. It would be good to have some Christian students on our side. We need allies. It would help our cause if non-Jews protested with us. We would do it for the Polish Socialists, and our neighbors should do it for us."

He put a hand on her arm.

"I disagree," Zosia barked and her voice cracked. She shook off his arm with some force. She smoked quickly, inhaling in spurts. "It's important we do this ourselves. Otherwise, it will seem like we *need* outside help. It will seem like that to the government, to the Poles, and, worse, to us. We need to know that we, as Jews, can independently resist. We don't need others."

A pained look came over his face. "I'm sorry I suggested it." He was taken aback, literally stepping backward.

She hadn't meant to rebuff him so harshly, it's just he'd gotten so close and—

A young woman passed right in front of her. "Are you Jewish?" Zosia asked.

"Yes." The woman was startled.

"I implore you not to attend your lecture today." Zosia handed her a flyer.

"I appreciate your efforts," this young woman said, "but none of my friends got into university with the quotas; not my sister either. I can't *not* go. My parents will lose their minds."

"But you *can* not go. If you go, it will show them they can continue to squeeze and limit. Before you know it, they'll say Jews can't go to school at all. But if you stand up to this small step now, it will show them that we will not stand for it."

The girl thought about it.

Zosia looked up and saw the building that housed Wanda's office. The secret of Zosia's escape had lain inside. If Wanda was there, she'd be telling them to fight for justice and dignity above all—not only telling them but forcing them!

"We have to take care of ourselves." Zosia grabbed the book that the girl held in her right hand and put a banner in its place. "Walk out now, protest now—or it will be too late. Even if you stay, they won't let you graduate." Yes, this was exaggerated . . . but was it?

Then the girl noticed one of her classmates in the campaign circle, nodded at Zosia, and went to join her. Success!

She turned around to see if Mira had noticed but instead saw Fanny—talking to Abram. So, she *had* come, Zosia thought. Then again, she was neither papering nor handing out flyers. Abram kept touching her arm and she kept patting it back.

It's fine if he likes her. Abram and Zosia had to lead a group and run a campaign together. They were colleagues. Besides, Zosia was leaving Poland, so what was the point? *It's better than fine.*

Zosia turned away. Again, looming in front of her: Wanda's building.

Wanda was absent, Zosia thought, because Wanda was in prison. She was being held in that awful place in Przemyśl. Why was the movement not helping? Why had no one said anything?

"Mira, can I please talk to you privately?" Zosia pulled her to the side. Dror was on one side of her, Wanda's wall on the other. "Wanda is still missing. We need to help her. She might be—"

"We can't," Mira replied.

"Why not?"

"Wanda is a communist," Mira whispered. "We've tried before, and it never works."

"A communist?" Zosia didn't understand. She was a leader of Dror, not of the illegal communists. "Was that why she was arrested?"

"Yes. We don't agree with the communists, and we've had to expel her. It all happened very quickly. Stalin is insane, not to mention antisemitic. We are socialists to our core, but we're not *that* left-wing. Both the extreme right and left are against Jewish self-determination, and at Dror, above anything else, we are Jews to our core. Wanda can't be part of them and of us."

Zosia trembled and tried to swallow all this information. Wanda was a communist? No longer in Dror? She too had given up on the Labor Zionist dream? Had she been on the outs with the movement for some time?

"Wanda made her decision," Mira said. "Not everything can be your responsibility. You don't need to feel bad for Wanda Petrovsky. And you certainly should not get involved. *They* will help her."

"WE'RE LOOKING FOR VLAD," ZOSIA SAID TO A GROUP OF MEN at a table near the entrance to the Jewish Writers' Union.

"The journalist?"

Zosia nodded, though what did she know? The guy pointed across the room, across layers of cigarette smoke, debate, laughter, and—Zosia thought but wasn't sure—Emanuel Ringelblum. A portrait of Peretz hung on the wall. As she'd learned at a movement lecture, Peretz had made Warsaw the hub of Jewish literature, fathering numerous creative schools that fought bitterly with one another. So, nothing new.

Vlad was hunched over a card game. He was tall and dark in complexion, handsome in a brooding sort of way, suggesting an inner landscape of attractiveness. Abram, on the other hand, was light and muscular, handsome on the outside, like a sculpture. She shook her superficial thoughts away as she and Fanny approached the table. "Vlad?"

He raised an eyebrow. It must be the right guy.

"Gin rummy?" Zosia asked. How would they get him alone?

"Mizerka."

"Luck or skill?"

"Both," he replied. "To what do I owe the honor, ladies?"

From behind his opponents, she mouthed, "Wanda."

"Come with me," he said right away, as if expecting them. "Let me show you where we host our Friday night dance parties."

Zosia noted that Fanny was unusually quiet. "You alright?" she mouthed. Fanny nodded.

They followed him through three other rooms, a large event space, and a kitchen, all the way through to a small storage room, filled with paper, pens, and old newspapers. He shut the door behind them. There was not much air, and Zosia felt woozy. Her chest was moist with sweat. What was she even doing here?

"Where is she?" he asked.

"If we tell you, will you help?" Fanny said, finally speaking up.

"It depends where she is."

"She's in Przemyśl, in the jail, with fifteen women."

"Oh fuck. Not again."

"Again?"

He rolled his eyes. "She's always in trouble, that one. Can't keep her hands to herself."

"Is it true she's a communist?" Zosia asked. She had so many questions and started with this one.

Fanny's eyes widened and Vlad's face got serious. "What do you know?"

"She said there's going to be a trial, and it's a sham. They're trying to give her a lawyer, but she doesn't want a fake."

"What's the charge? When is the trial?"

"I don't know. She said, summer."

Vlad gripped his temples. "Fuck. Fuck, fuck. This is the end of justice in Poland. The right-wing fascists are taking over; Poland will completely fall apart if they win the next election and take charge of the courts; it will be even worse than what we have now. If we don't have truth, we have nothing."

"So, write about it," Zosia pleaded.

"Oh God, I've been arrested enough times for writing about communists . . . what was she doing? Organizing more factory strikes? Printing pamphlets? I told her to be careful . . . She's going to need help." He tried to pace but there was nowhere to step.

Zosia recalled the printing press they'd found in her room.

"So, write an article," Fanny urged.

"We don't have enough to go on. There's no proof it's a sham. Besides, 'Government Bites Communists' is not a story. 'Government Bites a Sandwich Stuffed with Fat Fascists'—maybe . . . Trust me, even Wolf Shenkman at *The Workers' Paper* won't run it."

"Please," Zosia begged. "She told us." She heard herself plead—against Mira's instructions—and understood that this quest was no longer about a visa. Fanny had been right: This was bigger than their personal desires. Wanda needed them.

"If I'm going to be arrested again, it has to be for something good. With evidence."

"Helping Wanda is good—"

"Is there someone else who could write about this?" Fanny asked and gestured at the rooms around them, filled with writers. "Should we go to the university?"

Vlad laughed. "Oh sure, they love helping Jewish women. Dror kicked her out, and the college probably did too. Or they will. She's only an associate professor, you know, like most women."

Both Fanny and Zosia were silent.

"Look, she needs a lawyer. Someone with a huge mouth and even bigger balls."

Zosia's eyes went wide. "How do we get that?"

"Money."

Zosia's eyes cut to Fanny.

"Don't look at me," Fanny blurted, and looked down at her feet.

"Relax, Rothschild," he said. "Find Chlebook. He's your guy."

"Who?"

"A guy. He knows lawyers. He helps the communists. He's not Jewish. But it won't be cheap; none of this will be cheap."

"Where is he?"

Vlad scribbled an address on a piece of paper from the shelf.

"A bar?" Zosia asked. "Why can't you go?"

"Me? Oh God, I've done this kind of thing enough times for Wanda. You two are a much better bet." Vlad sighed. He looked worried. "Take it from me," he said. "It's best to be wild in your art, but safe in love. Do you have a gun?"

"What? No!" Zosia said.

"Oh, well. You're girls, so I'm sure it'll be fine."

CHAPTER 19

Fanny

FANNY SAT NEXT TO MAMO IN THE BACK SEAT OF THE PACKard as they drove to the Brodaszes' Shabbat dinner. Mamo was flustered about Fanny's hair, which she felt was messy in a chignon with a cloche hat, and her pink dress, which she declared was too festive. Fanny, on the other hand, was trying to imagine what they might be able to get for the car, what they might save without a staff, how much her dress might be worth at resale . . . a shudder ran through her: *Who was she?* Life had always been lined with pillows; now there was just a hard floor. And what if the bank took their home, as the letter had implied. Would she even have a hard floor? Twice on the ride, she turned to her mother, about to say something, but no words came out. All she managed were a few coughs. "Are you sick?" Mamo panicked. "You must hold it in. We are guests."

Fanny had debated telling Zosia about Mamo's lack of money but had decided against it: Zosia wouldn't understand. Once people clocked you as wealthy, they couldn't help but always expect you to pay for lunch.

Now, she replayed their conversation with Vlad in her mind. At least for this, she had an idea.

Simon greeted them at the door. She hadn't seen him since their night at the Adria a few weeks earlier, as apparently he'd been traveling again within Poland. "Enchantée," he said, and kissed Mamo's hand first. "I hope you know you will not be losing a daughter but gaining a son." Mamo melted into giggles and he winked at Fanny. "You, my darling, are a vision in rose."

In the living room, which hosted at least a dozen guests, Mamo begun the evening's chitchat by boasting about Fanny's academic record, how well she was progressing in school, how engaged she was with her studies, and how seriously she took her commitments, *all* her commitments, personal too. Domestic, especially. Of course, Fanny had not told Mamo about Nowak, the benches, the campaign, nor the fact that she was no longer attending class.

"Were you affected by the benches?" a guest asked as if reading her mind.

"Benches?" Mamo repeated.

"Surely you've heard about the ghetto benches, Lenore."

"I've read about them in the papers, but certainly they have nothing to do with my Fan-Fan." Mamo turned to Fanny for explanation. So did Simon.

"The ghetto benches are silly, placating politics," a cousin pooh-poohed before Fanny could speak. "Those imbecile German Nazis are influencing Polish student groups with their eugenics and racial politics and causing riots. The right-wing student groups wanted the Jews to voluntarily segregate. The Jewish students wouldn't do it, so the fascist Poles rioted for weeks on end, shutting down schools across the country. The government is just trying to stop the fighting—"

"They shouldn't negotiate with bigots! There are many ways to stop riots that don't involve caging Jews."

Thankfully, they all seemed to forget about Fanny in the conversation about her, and she used the moment to cross to the other side of the room where the glossy walnut bar cabinet held cut-glass tumblers of sherry. She took a large sip. At last, she was seeing it all for what it really was: Mamo wasn't showing off—she was fighting for their lives. Mamo hadn't been pressuring Fanny into a status-marriage, she'd been pressuring her into a money-marriage. Without this wedding, Fanny would have no home; she would have nothing. She felt surges of both fear and anger, and took another long sip, finishing the drink.

"That was meant for the kiddush," her mother-in-law-to-be told her quietly, and handed her a fresh glass as she blushed. "You'll learn."

At the long and beautifully laid table, shimmering with crystal, Simon was seated directly across from Fanny and Mamo, and he smiled at them both, the perfect gentleman. There were no deductions for his behavior tonight: He was a record ten out of ten. Fanny smiled back, and Mamo nearly swallowed the table with her grin.

After the customary blessings, Fanny ladled her silver spoon through her matzo ball soup waiting for the right moment. Mamo pinched her thigh. Fanny knew that pinch: Act up, be more charming. But now she knew it was a lifesaving pinch. Tuition, clothes, food, shelter—it was a pinch for all that.

"I suppose now is a good time to let you know I'll finally be leaving for New York on Monday," Simon said. "Selling linens across state lines."

"New York!" Mamo cooed. "What's your itinerary?"

"I'll be sailing on the MS *Batory* from Gdynia," he replied and took a giant slurp of soup. "The journey will last about ten days, and then I'll spend several weeks in the Big Apple before taking the Twentieth Century Limited to Chicago. Then I'm off to Detroit and Philadelphia before heading back for our big day."

"Mazel tov," came from around the table, and several glasses were raised.

"I'll bring you as many gifts as I can carry," he told Fanny. "And I'll send you a postcard from the Statue of Liberty."

"Thank you," Fanny said, relieved that his trip was going forward and waiting for the right moment to change the subject.

"Next time, my darling," Simon went on, "I promise to take you with me. Herald Square, the Empire State Building, the Frick Collection—I'll show you all of it. A new branch of the Metropolitan is about to open, displaying only medieval art. I'll even take you to a nightclub in Harlem. I can hardly wait. Here's hoping the 1940 trip will go as planned!"

"You'd better make sure the linens get sold and all the contracts get signed," Mr. Brodasz said, and Simon bristled. "We have yet to recover American business since the Depression and the tariffs."

"Speaking of which," Fanny finally launched in, "I have a legal question. Is anyone here a lawyer?" Mamo cleared her throat in confusion.

"Everyone here is a lawyer!" a guest replied. "It's hard for us these days. They're threatening to throw us out of the union."

"Doctors too might be expelled from the union," Simon added. "They've already limited them from working in public and university posts. Jewish medical students are not allowed to dissect Christian cadavers. Not to mention this potential citizenship law everyone's talking about."

"What's that?" Mrs. Brodasz asked.

"The government wants to have the right to revoke citizenship if you've lived outside the country for five years," a cousin explained. "They're scared that too many Jewish refugees will come running from Germany. Too many Jews."

"Poor German Jews." Mrs. Brodasz shook her head. "Fanny, are you alright?" she asked as the housekeeper began collecting the soup bowls. "You've barely had a spoonful."

Mamo pinched. Hard.

"I'm wonderful," Fanny said. "The soup is outstanding." Then she turned back to the table. "Would any of you lawyers consider a communist client? Someone wrongfully arrested. Or, arrested for being a communist, but—"

Mamo pinched and glared, and pinched again.

"It's for school," Fanny said, which was somewhat true. "There's a professor who's been arrested. The trial looks to be a sham. She needs help."

"What are you talking about?" Mamo hissed, then tried to cover it up with a smile.

"No one will want to end their careers by defending communists right now," Mr. Brodasz said. "Besides, communism *is* illegal."

"So, no one will help?" Fanny asked, quietly, but by then the conversation had moved back to Hitler. A cousin was arrested in Germany . . . but Germany and Poland were antithetical countries . . . but they were always at war . . . but WWI already happened . . . and they wouldn't put themselves through that again . . . besides, war wouldn't affect *their* class . . . And what was one to do—uproot a family and go where? With the Salzmans on a tiny ship to Uruguay?

"Hitler is an idiot."

"An idiot who just took over Austria."

"Well, they're idiots too."

"And now he has his eye on Czechoslovakia . . ."

"Who knows how all these anti-Jewish laws will be enforced here in Poland. Jews will have to keep their jobs. What are they going to do, lose half the country's professionals?"

"Warsaw was built by Jews. It can't exist without us," Simon said, and took a bite of the meat stew that had been placed in front of him by their maid. "Half the doctors and a third of the lawyers in this country are Jewish."

"What do you think of the elections later this year?" Mr. Brodasz asked the guests. "Will the Camp of National Unity actually win over the right-wing moderates?"

"Better them than the National Radical Camp and all outfascist groups, Simon replied.

"Who knows? Central elections have been rigged and chaotic for so long," a cousin said. "Piłsudski did a lot for us but paved the way for authoritarianism and one-party politics, which never really help the Jews. Since he died in 'thirty-five, the right-wing nationalist group has been growing and growing; it's been a disaster for us."

"Jews have been left out of this and that for a thousand years," another guest said. "They had ghettos here in Poland. Up until recently, Jews were allowed to live only in certain parts of Warsaw."

"Not the most well-off ones," Mr. Brodasz said.

"We might not be well-off much longer," the cousin piped in. "The boycotts of Jewish businesses are spreading. Not to mention,

Jews pay thirty percent of Poland's taxes, and almost no funding goes to our organizations. The minority protection system never had any material consequences. Civil service jobs never opened to Jews, despite endless promises. The tobacco monopolies cut us out. The government and army never buy from Jewish businesses."

"Oh, please . . . enough!," Mamo cut in. "It's been the same for generations. We've always managed. We're strong. We find ways to survive, and even to thrive. Let's not be so dour; let's think happy thoughts, maintain morale, welcome the romantic Shabbat spirit. Our Sabbath is a bride, just as Fanny will soon be." She looked at her daughter, who forced a smile for the table. "Remember, we are resourceful and very creative people. The Poles will come to remember how tolerant they used to be."

"Speaking of which," Fanny interjected. She didn't know what had come over her, but enough was enough. Tuitions and outfits she could live without, but it struck her: She needed to be able to afford film, paper, chemicals . . . Every shot had a cost. "Would anyone be interested in a photographer to take their portraits?"

"Who—you?" a bemused cousin asked.

"Yes," Fanny said and took her Leica out of her bag. "For you, good price!" she added in a peddler's Yiddish accent.

"Fanny!" Simon gasped.

"Sounds fun," someone said.

"Sure, maybe this weekend."

"Great," Fanny replied. "See me after dinner and we'll set up a time."

"I'm just going to take Fanny outside to get some air between courses," Mamo said. The pinch was so hard that Fanny let out a yelp. "Please, just give us a minute."

Fanny followed Mamo out onto the balcony.

"What in the world has gotten into you?" Mamo nearly exploded. "Do you want them to call off the engagement? The Brodaszes can give you everything we want, and here you are, offering services, prostituting yourself!"

"*This* is not prostituting," Fanny said. "Selling me to a man for money is!" Fanny couldn't take it any longer. "I know, Mamo, I *know*."

"What? What do you, a twenty-year-old girl obsessed with dresses, know?"

"I know that you have no more money. That they'll take the house, the car, everything."

Mamo was silent for a long moment. "What did you think, Fanny? Did you think the money would last forever? Babcia and Dziadek sold the factory years ago, and they're both dead now. What did you think would happen?"

"I—I—I don't know," Fanny stammered. "I didn't think—"

"Exactly."

"What about Papa? Alimony?"

"Papa? Alimony? Oh Fanny. I am the one who left . . . and you are an adult."

Of course, Mamo had broken the marriage vow. She'd been the one in the wrong and the one who came from wealth.

"We need to count our lucky stars for surviving the crash, for surviving this long." Mamo paused. "Listen, Fanny, I've done the best I could, and now—"

The best she could? "But all the expensive things you've bought, the luxury items . . ."

"An investment, for you. For your future. So that I could marry you off well."

"But why is that necessary? Why can't I just make it on my own?"

"Oh darling." Mamo laughed. "Look at you in your silks, your Hollywood costume. I'm sorry, dear, but you will never make it on your own. You are a woman. What will you do? Sell fruit from a truck?"

"Mamo, I go to university."

"Oh, sorry," Mamo added. "Sell French fruit?"

Fanny was silent. Then she declared: "I'm a photographer."

Mamo looked at her, and then took Fanny's flushed face in her unusually soft hands. "Oh Fan-Fan." She sighed.

Now Fanny saw the real truth, an even deeper layer: Mamo didn't believe in her.

"Fanny, face reality. Get in there, sidle up to your successful Jewish man, charm the parents, and have a good life."

Just then, Mrs. Brodasz called her in. "Someone is here to pick you up, dear. A bit early, I must say . . . A Mr. Cuckierman?"

There in the foyer stood Abram in a Shabbat white shirt under his long coat. While Fanny wouldn't say he looked dashing, he did look, well—cleaned up.

"Fanny, dear," Mamo said through clenched teeth, turning beet red. "*Who* is this man and why is he at the Brodaszes' Shabbat dinner?"

"Don't worry, Mamo, we're not getting married," Fanny blurted, all her suppressed rage leaking out of her in one gentle swoop. "We're just planning a hunger strike—at the university where I'm no longer attending class."

"So this is the important political meeting?" Simon asked. He'd insisted on coming, of course. After the fracas, she certainly couldn't say no.

The waiter brought over three vodkas in small glass tumblers. Simon laughed. "My fiancée will have a white wine spritzer, Vienna style, please." He squeezed Fanny's knee.

She didn't have to look at Abram to know how he eyed her from across the small wooden table. Fanny was too embarrassed to say anything. Simon drank her vodka, as if it were his, as if he owned her. Then again, if she had no home, no lifestyle, and no photography without him, maybe he did.

"I'm waiting on my friends," Abram said.

"Where's Zosia?" Fanny asked.

"She's not coming this evening."

"Why not?"

"She's enjoying Oneg Shabbat at Dzielna. Besides, she doesn't love these friends."

"Who are they?" Simon asked, gesturing at the cramped and seedy bar around them. "Who's Zosia? And by the way, how long have you two known each other?"

"My friends are Bundists," Abram said. "I want to ask them to be security guards at our next protest."

"Who's we? And what protest?"

Abram looked at him like he was crazy.

Fanny finally spoke. "Zosia is my friend. We're all involved in the movement, together." As the words came out, she realized it was true. "We're protesting the ghetto benches, which drove me from school. We're planning our next endeavor."

"So," Simon said and took his hand off her knee. "You're not going to school, and you have all these new friends from the movement. We have so much to discuss, so much to learn about each other." Now he inched closer to her. "I look forward to it."

She could feel Abram's stare like daggers.

"Listen, it's my favorite song," she said to change the subject. The radio played "Love Forgives You Everything" sung by the famous Hanka Ordonowna. The tune was from the movie *Spy in a Mask* in which she played a mole involved in a web of love and lies. "Love forgives you everything / Turns sadness into smiles," Fanny sang along.

"Love is great at explaining / Unfaithfulness, sins, and lies," Abram went on.

"So you know the song?" Fanny cut him off.

"Love is a capitalist construct," Abram said.

Simon laughed. "You mean, along with wealth, pleasure, and joy?"

"Yes, exactly."

"There are worse constructs, no?"

The waiter brought Fanny's new drink. They all took sips.

"So you think all the world's problems can be solved by redistributing money?" Simon prodded. "Will all evil turn to good if we shift around a few rubles?"

"Simon!" Fanny hissed. Abram just shook his head.

Simon checked his watch, stretching out his arm as if he were marking territory. "It's getting late, and your friends still haven't arrived. I'd better take Fanny home."

"I'm not tired," Fanny said.

"Well, I am, and I'm leaving for America in just over forty-eight hours."

Fanny looked over to Abram. Would he offer to take her home? She realized: She wanted him to.

He said nothing.

"Well, then, I supposed we should go," Fanny said.

As she left, she may have turned back just for one tiny second, to find Abram staring at her.

CHAPTER 20

Zosia

A FEW HOURS INTO THE PLANNED FORTY-EIGHT, AND THE ENergy was starting to build. It was palpable. Zosia could feel it, thick like thunder clapping through the growing crowd. A group of them had been there since eight a.m., but with time and mass, exponentially more joined. The throng was like a giant magnet, pulling in people who passed, who may not have stuck on their own but were drawn in by the weight of the crowd. The power of the horde was immense, Zosia thought. It was often said that gathered people became *less* than the sum of their parts, as they formed into a single entity with one opinion. But here, in their sway, volume, certainty, assembled people became *more* than their sum. They were huge.

Zosia and her comrades had planned this hunger strike quickly, without even holding a formal meeting. Though he avoided telling Zosia many details, Abram had met with the Bund and convinced a few of them to join too, along with various socialist–Zionist groups, a handful of non-affiliated Jews, Christian students, and members of the faculty. The slapdash planning had several benefits: No one could overthink things or get into philosophical disagreements. Plus, this would make it harder for anyone to organize a counterprotest.

Hunger made one focus, Zosia thought, her stomach already rumbling, and now she had to focus on her secondary mission: finding a journalist who, unlike lazy Vlad and his supposed gun-toting contact, would write a genuine article about Wanda and the sham trial. Poland's ultra-right-wing party was gaining more and more traction, and if they won the next election, who knew what they would do to Wanda and the women? It had dawned on Zosia that an article that led to awareness could be powerful and helpful, and besides, no one had to know she was involved. She would be a background player in the greater goal of truth, which was what mattered to Dror in the end.

From the corner of her eye, Zosia noted Abram with two men who she assumed were Bundist guards. They tapped each other's arms as they spoke, like old cronies. Was he really considering moving movements? He laughed extra loud, as if to impress them. He was human, Zosia told herself, with foibles and unmet desires. His broad shoulders weren't really that firm, were they? Besides, she very well knew from the way he'd been ogling Fanny that he did not love Zosia like that, and this knowledge, like most, was both hard and also freeing. There was nothing left for her to do, which was a feeling an activist disdained but at times welcomed. Energy would have to be placed elsewhere. She would bottle it, use this to inspire at Grochów, and then weed imposters. She would go back tomorrow!

Then again, she thought to how well they'd made the posters together, how they'd divvied up roles, set objectives, perfected fonts; how he had leaned over her as they worked on the dining room table, his side warm and firm as it touched her back—

"No benches," Zosia chanted loudly. "Freedom to sit where I choose."

"Hey." A woman sat down beside her.

Zosia was pleased that her roommate had joined. Finally, Rachel would see her succeed rather than witness her stream of failures and spills. "Thanks for coming."

"Clearly you need me," Rachel said. "Not many people showed up. A shame."

"Not many?" Zosia was startled. "We planned it quickly so—"

"Nowhere near as many as I saw in Vilna at their protest. There, the group leaders really managed to connect and come together. The Bundists and even the right-wing Zionists joined in."

"Vilna and Warsaw are different," Zosia replied, keeping calm. "But I'm sure we will grow."

She scanned the area. She spotted a man scribbling into small notepads at the edge of the crowd. "Excuse me," she said and approached him. "Are you a reporter?"

"Did you organize this strike? What do you have to say about it? I'd love a quote."

"The Jewish community will not tolerate anti-Jewish legislation in the classroom," Zosia said. "Speaking of strikes," she added in a whisper, making sure Mira was nowhere nearby, "I have a tip for you."

The man raised an eyebrow.

"Some communists—women—organized factory strikes and were arrested, but the trial is not legit—"

"Miss"—the man cut her off—"thank you, but I need a quote for this, here, today." He walked off.

Zosia gritted her teeth. When Mira was busy again, she'd try someone else.

Zosia was thirsty.

Her mother's last letter was still in her pocket. She thumbed the edges of the page. Would the schnapps go ahead without her? Would they bring her father in his current condition? Who would walk Bella down the aisle? . . .

The hunger was making her thoughts stray. She needed to stay directed. "No benches!"

Time passed. More young Jews arrived. The volume increased; the passion too. Emotions are contagious, Zosia thought, and they spread easily, regardless of the external situation. Feelings predominate over events. We feel a certain way and react to the world based on that feeling; it is rarely the other way around.

She felt empty. Enjoy the hunger! she reminded herself. Learn from it. Food can fill a craving, but you must enjoy the sensation of wanting to feel satisfied. Learn to want the want.

"What are you staring at?" Rachel was by her side once again, following her gaze to Abram.

"Nothing."

"Right." Rachel smirked.

Hours later—it was hard to keep track of time at this point—Zosia felt fuzzy. Her boundaries were collapsing, nebulous. *Stay awake!* she coaxed herself and pulled a shared wool blanket over her legs. The tired body was a cold body, too exhausted to keep its internal heater on.

One of the university's janitors approached the group, carrying a bucket. Was he going to yell at them to leave? To drench them? Was he planning on watering the winter grass? "Here," he said to her when she got up to meet him, offering her the bucket. "In case anyone needs a drink. Are you sure you're all alright?"

This generosity touched her. "We're fine," she said, but sensing how much he wanted to help, she took the bucket. "Thank you. We will keep it just in case." He wanted to give, she wanted to take. And yet.

She still needed to convince a journalist to write about Wanda.

Just then she saw Fanny. When had she arrived, and what was she wearing—an entire Russian circus bear? She was holding a camera and standing with Abram. They laughed, linked arms. Fanny said hello to the Bundist guards: Did she know them? It dawned on Zosia that she may have gone with Abram with meet them . . . Zosia felt faint. It was the hunger. The thirst. Then Fanny waved at her, and she waved back.

Fanny caught it in a click.

Zosia felt funny, not herself, and she did not like the idea of being captured unaware. She shielded her face, though of course it was too late, the moment already enshrined into permanence. Fanny just laughed, as if it was all a joke. *What a strange life that woman led,* Zosia thought, *documenting the world around her for posterity, constantly, as if it was normal.* It made it hard to be around her, Zosia realized. One did not have conventional interactions with a photographer; it was a peculiar relationship, the power imbalanced, a person always recording, never living, always outside, and maybe Zosia didn't need it, didn't want it.

That's when she began to hear chants—other chants. She turned—the green ribbons were gathering.

"Jews out, Jews out!" Zosia froze. It was one thing to know how others felt; it was another to hear them state it so blatantly, and to her face. She felt their hate like heat from a fire, and her eyes stung. It began then, the call in her mind, the squeal becoming a roar. *Please, please let us in.* She could taste the tears in her mouth, the words mingled with thick salt. *Please.*

We can't.

Zosia noted policemen, more than last time, and her heart raced. They were there to protect the peace, she told herself again, but she knew it wasn't true. Why did they stand with the counterprotestors? They were protecting them, not her, and from what?

And was that—Marek?

Zosia felt faint. She edged back into the crowd, found Mira.

"We keep going," Mira said. "Peaceful protests must be the bedrock of society."

So Zosia chanted, even louder. The others followed. She looked back to the green ribbons—they were contained, they were not moving, but yes, she was sure it was Marek, the same oily hair from the nightclub, the same stomach bulging from ill-fitting pants. What if he saw her? What if he said something? What would Mira say? She turned away . . . it was impossible. He was far away, he didn't care about her . . . He had Fanny's name; did he have her name? She didn't think so, but someone had her name. It was official somewhere, looking for Wanda, *Zosia Dror*, moving against the will of the movement.

Their own chants grew louder. Maybe the counterprotestors actually helped activate the Jewish students.

Chants, counter chants.

The dryness that had begun at her lips spread to her tongue.

She'd fasted on many Yom Kippurs, she consoled herself. This shouldn't be hard.

"Hey!" Someone approached her, a comrade she did not recognize. "Didn't I see you the other day?"

"I don't think so—"

"Yes, it was you. In Przemyśl! I saw you wandering in the center of town! I knew I recognized you from lectures. What were you doing in Przemyśl?" he shouted, getting even louder at the name of the town, declaring her treason in front of everyone.

"What?" was all Zosia could muster. Air felt thin, the walls were closing in. The sound grew in her ears, the images, the locked door, the knocking . . . *Please, let us in* . . . Zosia stood up, shaky. And then she heard it—"Hey!"

Then, "Get off me!"

Two green ribbons had approached a young comrade. One threw his book bag to the ground. "This isn't your country, *zhyd*," he said. "Why do you think you can sit in our good seats? Because you think you own everything?"

The Jewish student was shaking. "I am a rightful student at this university," he said. "And a Polish citizen. Like you."

"Not for long, *zhyd*," the other said, and they both laughed. "Citizenship will be saved for those with pure blood. Now, move to the left of the path!"

"That's not true," the Jewish student responded quietly. "That's not even the law they are proposing. It has nothing to do with blood."

"If you go into a classroom and sit where you like, I will personally carry you to the Jew bench," the antagonist hollered. "You and all your disloyal friends."

Without thinking, Zosia slipped the wooden stake from one side of their banner and wielded it at one of the men, as if about to stab him. "Get out of here, you idiots, or I will stick this up your ass until it comes out your nose. And I'll tell the police over there."

"Calm down, girl." He laughed. "You think the police will care? What a joke! They hate you as much as we do."

Zosia swung—

And struck him across the face.

Like thunder and lightning, the very same phenomenon that were experienced at different times, she heard the smack before she felt the impact.

And then she ran.

Please, let us in, please . . . The bellow was loud, shrill. *Please!*

Zosia ran, panting, pounding through the campus; leaves and grass, dry and cold from the winter, bitter and jagged, clipped at her ankles, wet her legs. *Please!* Out the gates, steps cascading into each other, no direction. Running. She was here, she was not here, as if she wasn't planted in her own paces, like she was floating . . . The scream . . . It all blended into one, the sound, the fear, the thumping of feet . . . she remembered:

They were running . . . she and Tateh . . . Mameh and Bella had been away, in a neighboring town, visiting for lunch, tea, away. Zosia was helping her father, in a different neighboring town, procuring supplies for the grocery. There hadn't been a mob like that in years. No one expected it, no one had smelled the bigotry brewing right under their noses. Suddenly, there were fifty of them, a hundred. Zosia heard voices, a chorus. At first, it was muffled, unclear, maybe a workers' protest, a union march, a strike. But the chants got louder, clearer. Then, the words.

Jews, out! Jews, out!

It was hard to tell which direction they were coming from, where they were heading. Disoriented, she and Tateh dropped their bags of grain and peas and ran to the nearest home to find shelter. The chants were getting louder, coming their way. At the little house, she could hear people inside. She knocked on the door. No one came. She heard them. *Please, please, let us in.* The chants were growing even louder but the only way out was back up the same path that led to the street with the rioters. She kept knocking loudly, now wildly . . . No one came. No one let them in. *Please!*

It flashed before her: the end of her life. The end of Tateh. They would beat him first, she was sure. She grabbed his hand and they sprinted through the backyard, crouched under a gate until they reached a back alley. Tateh was older, heavier; he could barely breathe. Gasping, they loped along back paths to her village, straight to the shop. Where else could they go? Truth was, she could smell it, even then, the fire, but she didn't want to, she couldn't afford to let her nose dither in distractions. Their hearts were exploding by the time they reached the grocery but even there they could hear the attackers. *What do they want from us?* Tateh cried. *We have next to nothing!*

Without rehearsing, without discussing, they immediately got to work; the instinct to defend themselves from this age-old siege was baked into their blood. Tateh began stacking boxes against the front door, which opened onto the town's main road. He was blocking it with crates of *kitnyiot*, wooden containers of wheat germ, paprika, dried corn. Zosia started to help him but he insisted she go up into the attic, insisted that she be on lookout. She climbed the ladder to the alcove area. There was a window there, and from this surveillance point, she could monitor the situation. At first, she couldn't make out anything at all, and it confused her. But suddenly— she saw it. From the window: the throng. A dozen, two dozen, she didn't know the numbers. The group moved as one. They were chanting, and carrying something, maybe flags or banners. She couldn't see. Because they were also carrying something else.

Fire. Torches lit with fire. They were lighting the buildings on fire. They were burning down her town, trying to extinguish her. Flames erupted in front of her as if they'd been shot up from a hose, with force, a solid flume. Orange, yellow, purple. She smelled it. It stung the atmosphere, as if the air itself were being toasted. That's when she saw them, headed up the pathway to the grocery. *Tateh!* she screamed above the roar. *Get away from the door!* He was trying to block a fire with flammable boxes, a protective layer that would only conduct the violence. The crates would combust. The thing meant to stop the fire would just fan its flames. His barrier was the wrong barrier: It catalyzed what it was meant to halt. They came up the path. *Tateh!* she screamed, mustering every ounce of energy. *Come upstairs!*

Go, Zoshaleh . . . run, out the back door. Go get help.

She listened to him.

She ran. She tried to find help.

The heat reflected off her face, her neck. She tried the shoemaker and the tailor and the neighbors, but no one was there. No one was there to help. She shouldn't have left him, she couldn't breathe. The other fires fizzled out, but theirs just grew . . . and then she heard it.

Her father's bloodcurdling scream, a primal howl; it pierced the universe, cracked a core. Her father, in the purest form of pain. She darted back. Inside, the air was dark, all smoke, thick with debris, destruction. She couldn't breathe but threw herself forward, trying to open her mouth long enough to call *Tatenyu!* She saw his outline in the front room, the burning boxes, and a sizzling flame, white hot, purple. The threshold was on fire; she could not cross. She coughed and coughed; the smell, charred skin, hair, eyes; she was soaked with sweat and then the darkness crept in from the edges, blurred sides like in a photograph, and then, it all went black.

CHAPTER 21

Fanny

It was almost perfect, but for the sun. Why were its rays so lazy today? The shade would spoil it all . . . In this composition, she had the university building in the back corner, a group of students and protestors in front, their mouths open in chants, and a professor on one end . . . why was he moving? Alright, she would reframe it . . . Yes, if she leaned down a bit lower, she could catch the wool blanket shared among six legs.

Every click had its cost. The paper, the film, the chemicals. All of it came down to złotys. Each exposure was precious. She could no longer click away freely.

It dawned on her: What if the check she'd written Wanda's landlord had not gone through like her attempted payment at the hardware store? Fanny lived in a house of cards, thin, slippery cards.

"Fanny." Someone touched her sleeve. She turned to see Abram and a tingle of pleasure ran through her. Even in her furs, she felt that his hand was strong, reassuring. "Are you taking good photos?"

"I wouldn't take them if I thought they were bad."

"What confidence," Abram said and smiled boyishly. "What's a good photo, anyway? One that accurately presents our world, showing us a new way to see it? Or one that shows us what our world might become?" His arm was still on hers. "You're so easy."

"Excuse me?"

"To be around, that's all I meant!"

She smiled at him. Despite the relative springtime warmth, Fanny had worn her newest furs—a leopard-skin coat and hat—ostensibly to protect her from hours of sitting outside. But it was more than that: Just as the camera covered her face like a mask at a masquerade ball, her furs were an armor. Helmet and breastplate.

Fanny did not feel "easy" or comfortable on campus in her new role. She hated not being the student she'd once been allowed to be. She hated that she had to avoid friends, peers, professors with whom she used to banter and chuckle without a second thought. She didn't want to be here. So, earlier, despite knowing she was running late, she'd stopped at Jabłkowski Brothers on the way to examine the display windows, drinking in the beaded gowns and ethereal fabrics. She'd caught her breath at the sight of a dress that was white and gauzy like an angel, with layers that could be handheld like wings. The flower pattern intensified as the fabric fell, ending in a puddle of floral design at the hem. Fanny had come to the department store with her mother just after her father had refused her participation in the Jewish Beauties of Poland pageant. Mamo had shopped with military vengeance, muttering that Fanny would always be "Miss Judea," but in a classier context than a contest. She'd used her credit like a weapon, and dresses upon dresses were piled up for her to try. The world was her caviar. Ghetto benches, quotas, depressions of any kind—not hers. When had she become the person beneath the headline?

A wave of anger beat through her. Mamo had spent all their money, yet she continued to disapprove of Fanny's attempts at independence. What was she supposed to do? Was marriage really her only option? Her wedding to Simon was supposed to take place in just over three months.

Now Fanny brought the Leica back to her eye and looked through the apparatus, making out a few reporters, counterprotestors, and—was that Marek, the sleazy police chief? Was he a green ribbon?

"Their group is growing," Abram said, leaning in close. "I hope you ate enough and won't become too hungry."

Mamo had said nothing more about Abram, about the hunger strike, or about her leaving school. Instead, Mamo had doubled-down focus on the wedding: shoes, hairstyles, RSVPs—the list was infinite. That was her mother's way: Ignore bad news; distance yourself from anything with a tinge of the difficult, of sadness, of grief, of politics, of reality—and, poof, it would go away. Until . . . it wouldn't. Until all hell broke loose. Simon had stopped by to say goodbye to Fanny and Mamo just before he left for America. Mamo had hugged him and cried, as if he were her own child. "I'm not hungry."

"At least we have protection here," Abram went on. "The Bundists were ready for this. They do a lot more than just running gymnastics teams and daycares."

Fanny nodded. Everything was frightening, and so nothing was frightening. She looked at the number: ten shots left on this roll. She *had* to make each picture count.

Fanny took a breath and thought about focusing on something "bigger than herself." Where was that reporter?

"Excuse me," she said to Abram. "I just saw someone I need to talk to." They locked eyes for a moment. They were nice eyes, dark like cherries.

"Hello," she said as she approached the reporter, aware that her fur was not unremarkable. "I'm Fanny Zelshinsky, a photographer, and I'd like to have a quick word."

"Honestly, I doubt they'll run photos with this story." He smiled at her. "I don't think they'll buy any prints. I wouldn't waste your film."

"Oh, interesting." This was a new idea. She'd never considered selling her photos to the papers. She could make money . . . "In that case, I have something else for you. I wondered if, seeing as you are interested in the work of the Jewish comrades, you may be interested in a story about one of their leading members. A very juicy story."

"Oh?"

"She was arrested."

"Oh?"

"For communist activity. She's being held out of the city, and offered a sham lawyer, a fake trial—"

He cut her off. "Sorry, Ms. Zelshinsky, I don't want to know. It's important, sure, but the truth is, there have been years of communist purges, and no one is too worried about young Jewish women activists right now. Everyone is concerned about Hitler's advances: Austria, Czechoslovakia, and these discussions with Poland. I'm only here today following the green ribbons and their attempts to bring Hitler's fascist policies to campus. It's horrifying."

"Yes, this is why we need to free her quickly. Look, I'm sure Wanda's story, I mean Professor Petro—"

"Petrovsky?" He finished for her. Then he leaned in close and lowered his voice to a whisper. "My sources tell me that the government plans to use Wanda as an example. They're going to punish her harshly, to the highest degree."

"What does that mean?"

"Sorry, but I can't say any more." The man offered a bittersweet smile and headed toward the green ribbon crowd.

No one would help. No one. She needed to talk to Zosia; they needed a plan—a new, miracle plan, that did not involve men who dragged them into closets or carried guns.

"Fanny!" She turned around to find Jakub, a fellow student from Wanda's class. "What are you doing here? Are you taking photos for the end-of-the-year exhibit? That's not a half-bad idea. I'm not sure Parisian gallerists will love Warsaw student activism, but then again, it might seem exotic."

Fanny took a breath. Less than three months until the class show. She'd lost hope. The chances of her being included in that exhibit had vanished. How she would ever show her work and her independence, she'd never know. "What photos are you showing?" she asked.

"Bicycles! I took several series—"

Fanny had no time for bicycles.

She scanned the area for her comrade-in-crime. A custodian delivered a pail of water to the group. He offered it to Zosia, who was about to refuse it but then, meeting his kind eyes, smiled and thanked him. Fanny clicked, capturing a moment of genuine kindness, of pure human connection. And then, suddenly, in her device, the image flipped as reality reversed: It *was* Marek, and right next to him, there was a green ribbon throwing a Jewish man's bag. *Click, click, click . . .*

And then, there was Zosia—and what in the world—there was blood gushing from the green ribbon's nose, pouring as if from an open faucet!

"Pathetic people," she heard among the gasps. "You make your women defend the men!"

Then Fanny watched as Zosia, her face bloodless, stood still in shock, and then, like a gazelle galloping into oblivion, she bolted.

Clutching her Leica, Fanny ran right after her. Across the campus green, through the path between the humanities buildings, and right out the university gates. She could make out that gray tattered coat fleeing around bends and across crosswalks, then through a street market, and into a residential square lined with courtyards.

Dammit, Fanny had lost her. "Zosia!" she called. Unsurprisingly, no answer.

Panting, she began to check them all, poking her head into one cobblestoned courtyard after another.

Why did everyone she needed disappear?

For a second, the idea came to Fanny that maybe Zosia had never existed at all. Maybe she'd made up this woman entirely, imagining her as a child does an imaginary friend. After all, their liaison made no sense in the real world. Maybe Fanny's mind had conjured this friend for her to talk to; a figment so she wouldn't have to search for Wanda all alone. Was Wanda also a figment, a symbol for part of herself that had gone missing? What were people to each other if not merely representations of snippets of themselves?

Fanny felt dizzy. She stopped, dropped her head down, and took long and deep inhales, focusing on the air that emerged from her lungs, that had exchanged molecules within her own organs. She caught her breath, and her balance, and looked up.

There she was.

At the end of a courtyard beyond a courtyard, in a cul-de-sac, stuck, with nowhere to run, an enormous brick wall in front of her, and a small Christian shrine to her side. Fanny saw Zosia's back, her shoulders pumping up and down, her head bent, as if in prayer next to the altar, as if in sorrow.

Fanny lifted her Leica and looked through the lens. It was a beautiful composition, the woman caught at the end, the last stop, that coat against the brick, a palimpsest of browns that would become an onion of grays, alongside the Virgin Mary. *The Last Woman of Warsaw.* But she did not click.

"Hey," she said quietly when she was only a few feet away, and again, when she stood right behind her. "Hey." Zosia turned her head quickly and scratched her face, but Fanny knew she was wiping tears. "Why are you here?"

"Why are you here?"

Zosia said nothing. Then, "I'm just hungry."

Silence. Pigeons cooed.

"I hit somebody," Zosia said. "I actually hurt him."

"He's fine. Besides, he deserved it."

"Did he? Does anyone deserve to be physically hurt? I don't understand myself anymore. Do I even care if he's hurt? Can a person run out of feelings?"

"It seems to me like you have a lot of feelings."

"Do I?"

"Maybe even more than you can handle."

"The movement teaches us to understand our feelings, to analyze them, to use them toward truth and self-determination." Then Zosia added, "Not to hit."

"Maybe," Fanny said. "Maybe you're still learning how to make sense of your emotions." She debated for a second and then she put her arm around Zosia's shoulders. Zosia flinched in surprise, but forfeited, and, after a moment, melted into her.

They stood like that for a while, both looking at the brick wall.

"I feel confused," Zosia said. "Which I suppose is a feeling. Dror molded me, and I want to give everything back to the movement. But"—she paused—"some comrades are leaving, claiming these ideals are too dreamy. And why won't they help Wanda? Even if she's a communist."

"I don't know," Fanny agreed, feeling proud that someone smart like Zosia would confide in her. She didn't say anything more, not yet.

"What does it mean to have allegiance to a group? Does it mean I need to stand by every idea and decision? How can I be a true comrade and doubt? This is a one hundred percent type of life. If I have doubts, well, then, that makes me, well, that makes *me* an imposter."

Fanny removed her arm from Zosia's shoulders. "Why do you want so badly to leave Poland?"

"It's not safe here." Zosia shook her head. "I want to live in a Jewish place where I don't feel constantly threatened and on the lookout for an attacker."

"But your family is here, I imagine," Fanny said, realizing she knew very little about this woman's life. "You've lived here your whole life, haven't you?"

"I knocked and knocked but no one let me in. Safety was possible, but then it wasn't."

"Huh?"

"You wouldn't understand."

Fanny bristled. "I am about to lose my home, and then be forcibly sent to raise fowl in the suburbs, so yes, I think I would understand."

"I'm so sorry," Zosia said. "I had no idea. Are you really being forced to move to the suburbs?"

Fanny shrugged.

"Our self-declared home and our identities are completely intertwined," Zosia went on. "Without a home, whether you live in it or not, who are you? If you don't know what your home is, or is supposed to be, you lose yourself."

"Could having no home be your home? Is nomadism, or wandering, an identity?"

"It sounds good," Zosia said, "but I don't think so."

"Do your parents also want to move to Palestine?" Fanny asked.

Zosia shook her head. "My parents don't understand me."

"We might be more alike than you think," Fanny said and held out her ringed finger. "My mother just wants me to marry money. She's running out of it, and fast, which is why I'm losing my home, so her all-consuming project is to wed me to złotys."

"I guess we both want to live lives our parents just don't understand."

"We're modern girls," Fanny agreed. "Thirties women of the world. Women of Warsaw. Hey, let's get out of here and go for a walk."

"I can't face the world right now,". Zosia said. "Do I need to apologize?"

"You cannot go to him. He'll beat you up." Fanny shook her head. "But you also can't stay here forever."

Fanny led and Zosia followed. They made their way out of the courtyard. As they turned onto the main road, Fanny noticed that Zosia was shivering. She stopped, took off her leopard skin, and placed it over Zosia's shoulders.

Zosia pushed it off. "I'm fine."

"No, you're cold," Fanny said. "Let me help you."

Fanny had never felt so mature, maternal, sturdy. She didn't feel cold at all. She straightened the coat collar so it rested right on Zosia's neck. "It looks good on you."

Zosia rolled her eyes, but—Fanny could tell—she liked wearing it. It fit.

Just then, Fanny realized that they were standing near a beauty shop, just like the one from Wanda's photo—maybe even the same shop. It was a store where Fanny had already re-created the same shot a few long weeks ago. "Stand here," she told Zosia and took out her Leica.

"Me? At a beauty store? I can't think of anyone less suited to be in a hairdresser photo shoot."

"It's perfect," Fanny said. She began to braid Zosia's hair into two long pleats. "This is the same background as one of Wanda's photos. Makeup, wigs: It's a place of transformation, magic, illusion."

"Hairdos are distractions." Zosia shook her head. "Why are you so interested in fashion?"

"Fashion is not merely surface," Fanny said as she tied her own hair ribbon into Zosia's locks. "Fashion creates who we are. We project ourselves through our outfits, but our outfits determine how we sit, stand, move, and how the world sees us, thus creating ourselves. Costumes create courage. Everything you put on your body says something."

"I don't care about clothes," Zosia replied.

"Indeed," Fanny agreed. "Your clothes say that."

"Very funny."

"Just because something is on the outermost layer," Fanny said, "it doesn't mean it's not *true*." She stepped back, and back again, bending down and over, trying to find the right angle from which to capture the scene: Wanda's angle, only a few degrees off. "I already took a picture here copying Wanda's, but it will be so different with you in it."

"Why do you keep taking the same photo, and a photo that's not even yours?"

"Every time we look at something we see it differently. It's how you frame it. Do we only see what we want to see? Do our emotions affect what we perceive? In twisting the perspective, I assert my own identity."

"Do you?"

As Fanny aimed her lens, she was suddenly unsure. Two clicks left of this roll. "It's all about the gray zones and gray tones," she added, trying to convince herself.

She looked again at Zosia and remembered: Wanda's photo had two women in it. So here was her angle, right? Woman—solo. *Click.*

"I think you should do what you want," Zosia said. "Not what Wanda wants or your mother wants. Make your own image. You're an adult, Fanny Zelshinsky. You need to see for yourself. It's your vision that counts."

Fanny's own image . . . but weren't you always just capturing the world around you? How could she divorce her own vision from the way others had taught her to see?

What *was* her own image?

"I think," Fanny said, "to rid your imposters, you need to be friendly. Get to know them, figure out who they are and what they want." Fanny paused. She had to tell her. "Wanda's being used as an example by the government," she revealed. "She's going to incur maximum punishment. A journalist told me."

Zosia's eyes went wide.

A peddler approached and startled them. "You look like such nice girls." Tears of age ran down her dried apricot cheeks. "Such nice friends. Want a bagel? On the house."

"We're on a hunger strike," Zosia said.

"It's not Yom Kippur," the peddler said. "Besides, it's only a bagel. You'll still be plenty hungry."

Fanny reached out and took a bagel from the woman's cart. Then so did Zosia.

Between their bites, they could hear the chants of the green ribbons growing louder and louder. The women looked at each other and nodded: They knew where they had to go.

THE BAR WAS IN THE OLDEST PART OF WARSAW, IN A MEDIEVAL square near the bright orange Royal Castle, the giant structure of empire since the 1600s. Its top peeked out triumphant over sloping rooftops.

"It was erected as a defensive structure," Zosia said, gesturing at the palace. "I learned this at school. It was meant to be a lookout point, with wide views of the water. The royals could watch for an enemy to approach."

Fanny had never heard that. They could give each other completely different tours of the same city.

The women skipped down a short stack of cement stairs into an old tavern.

"We're looking for Chlebook," Fanny said to the bartender, who didn't even waste a movement on showing them the way, waving his hand in the man's direction and wiping the bar with a rag at the same time.

Fanny watched impressed as Zosia approached with swagger. "*Cześć*. Vlad sent us. We need to talk."

Chlebook gestured to meet him outside.

By now the women were used to such things. They walked back up the stairs. "We don't have a gun," Zosia whispered, "but I have hands, and I'm not afraid to use them."

They waited around the corner. Chlebook appeared. "Walk with me."

The threesome wound silently through the medieval streets, passing a dark alleyway. "A famous gangster from the 1910s lived here," the guy finally said. Another type of tour.

"So?" Zosia asked.

"I think of it as our own Alley of Hell."

"Our what?"

"Up in medieval Stockholm the town needed an executioner. No one wanted the job, so they opened it up to criminals. Any prisoner on death row could become the town executioner. The way they got the job was by murdering the current executioner."

"Then he lived the rest of his wretched life waiting to be killed by the next?" Fanny asked.

Chlebook grunted.

"But why live if you are going to die at any second?" Zosia asked.

"Isn't that the case for all of us?"

Where the hell was he taking them, going on about death and leading them into darkness?

He stopped in the middle of a street. "So, what is it?"

"Here? You want us to tell you in the middle of the street?"

"Why not?"

"Wanda's been arrested," Fanny said. "Sixteen women, communists. They're in Przemyśl. They're going to do a fake trial, no real lawyer. Late this summer. She needs help. They're making her an example. She'll be trapped there forever."

"They won't allow a lawyer. I can bring someone, but they'll say no."

"We can at least try!" Zosia said. "Don't you know someone who can speak to someone about something, change the rule?"

"Yeah. For two thousand."

"What?" Fanny gasped. "That's the cost of over a hundred Luxtorpeda tickets."

"Or four thousand loaves of bread," Zosia added. "Or twenty months of a worker's salary."

"Fine, one thousand."

"What?" Fanny repeated. "That's absurd."

"What do you think? That people will do this for free? I have one guy who will wheel and deal with them down there. Find them someone they'd rather sacrifice than Wanda . . . there's always a trade to be had. Or blackmail works too."

"I thought you're all communists," Zosia said. "Why's it always about money?"

"Zosia," Fanny whispered and squeezed her hand. "You don't need to—"

"Precisely why we need a revolution," Chlebook said. "We need to get rid of the fucking fascists. I'm doing my part; I have half the city's landlords under my fat thumb."

"Do you believe in it all?" Zosia asked him as they were still standing in the middle of a road.

"Of course."

"Do you ever have doubts?"

"Sure," Chlebook said. "Everyone gets overwhelmed, everyone has hesitations. There is no such thing as belief without doubt. You have to sit inside your questions for a little bit; and then, roll off, stand up, and refocus. At the end of the day, as your Judaism teaches us, actions trump reflections. You can think whatever you want, really, as long as you act for good."

"Do *you* act for good?"

"I do what I can." He pulled the women to the side as a car passed.

"So, how will we get money?" Fanny interrupted this spontaneous philosophy seminar. "I have nothing."

"She has nothing," Zosia agreed.

Chlebook gestured at Fanny's camera.

Fanny panicked. "I can't sell it! I cannot!"

"I didn't say to sell it, relax. Use it to earn money. Take pictures, sell them. People love having their portraits taken in Theatre Square."

"It will take a lot of portraits to make a thousand złotys. The country won't exist by then!"

They all stood silent for a moment. Another car swooshed right past, nearly knocking them over.

"Think of a way," Chlebook finally said. "And don't come here again—these people are uncouth. When you have the cash, find me at Jozek's."

CHAPTER 22

Zosia

WAS THERE A SHADE OF BLACK DARKER THAN PITCH? ZOSIA wasn't sure, but it felt like this was the color of the sky, the color of the whole world, as she quietly walked down the stone path, careful not to tread in puddles.

Less than two hours earlier, she's tiptoed out of Dzielna and into the cold Warsaw pre-morning. She'd breathed a sigh of relief when she realized she had made it out the door without anyone noticing. After their rendezvous with Chlebook, her mind whirring with their lack of articles, their lack of funds, their lack of any leads, her lack of a visa, not to mention images of her gaunt, pallid former comrade in a jail yard that flashed through her mind, she'd come straight back and fallen into a deep sleep. Thankfully, no one had woken her, not even when they'd returned from the hunger strike. She could not possibly face Mira, Rachel, none of them. And she certainly could not face Abram.

When she herself stirred and checked her watch—four a.m.—she knew it was her chance to escape.

Now, she quietly opened the gate to the Grochów commune; it jammed in the frozen earth as if telling her *No, you don't belong*, but Zosia pushed until it jumped and, letting out a loud creak, opened for her. Had someone heard? Just her luck, she'd be mistaken for an intruder, get arrested, and find herself in jail . . . She imagined her jury: Mira, Rachel, all the top brass, even though they did not believe in brass. They'd shake their heads, knowingly, disapprovingly. *Not Zosia again; the comrade who held so much promise and let herself be swept astray by a woman in leopard and an imprisoned chain-smoking communist.*

She squeezed her hand so tightly that even her short nails dug into her palms. The memory of the man's bloody face rang fresh in her mind. The green ribbon movement was growing and growing.

She was failing herself, and Dror, and Wanda, who was in serious, horrible trouble. She had until summer to amass one thousand zloties. One thousand—it was an unheard-of number.

She could not run out on Wanda like she'd run out on her father.

Here, at Grochów, she was going to make up for her sins and do good. She'd cook those noodles to boiling and then some, and then drain the tainted water from the sieve.

"Morning," Sarah the comrade called to her. "Haven't seen you in a while."

Zosia jumped in shock. "Good morning. I hadn't realized you were up."

"The land sleeps like a cat," Sarah said, still hoeing. "A few hours here and there, but by five a.m., it's ready to be reaped."

"Sure is." *Here is a real worker,* Zosia thought, *not an imposter.*

"Did you bring back Zvi and Daniel?" Sarah asked.

"Who?"

"The comrades who went to the hunger strike. I assumed they stayed in Warsaw with you last night?"

"Yes, of course." Zosia heard herself lie again. No, no, she needed to be more truthful. Truth begot truth. "I mean, I'm not sure where they are right now. I wanted to come here very early, to get started. Since, as you say, I haven't been back in a while. The ghetto bench campaign has been very intense." Had Sarah heard about her attack? No, it wasn't possible.

"Sounds like it."

"I'm glad to see you, working, in pants."

"Well, I wouldn't work naked," Sarah said and laughed. "It's not that kind of commune! Even if we do promote the naked truth."

Zosia chuckled, unsure. She wasn't used to such a bold sense of humor. But then she realized: Here was a strong woman. Daring. Independent. She laughed harder.

Sarah looked at her as if she were mad.

"It's still early," Zosia said. "I'm going inside to prepare. See you for the seminar at eight."

"Eight? Good luck with that," she said, and then mumbled, "Sometimes too early and too late are the same thing."

Zosia nodded. Was she implying that the others wouldn't be ready? Was Sarah working so hard because she was an imposter and pretending extra-hard not to be? Zosia heard her conversation with Fanny play back in her mind: Was Zosia herself an imposter? What was an imposter?

She reminded herself that it wasn't a question of doubts or inner integrity; she had to find those who were *explicitly* trying to play the system.

At quite a bit past eight, the seminar did not start easy either. "Any news on Wanda?" a young man asked. "Is it true she left the movement and moved to Spain?"

Spain? Zosia shook her head. "No news, I'm afraid," was all she said. "Now, wake up, sleepy comrades! I am giving each of you five minutes to prepare a speech. I want you to come back ready to defend your position articulately and bravely: Herzl's Zionism versus Gordon's versus Katznelson's. Go!"

Two of the ten students jumped up. The other eight stared at her.

"You shouldn't even need five minutes! Your hearts and minds should already be embroiled in these positions. I changed my mind. Three minutes. Now go!"

The students slugged off to corners. Zosia scanned the young comrades: Their bodies and feelings and identities were all entangled in a giant soup of *friendship.* Not timed exams and cross-examinations and sieves. What in the world was she doing?

"Never mind," Zosia said. "I mean—I changed my mind. We can do that, we're allowed to do that." It was true: She could rethink things once in a while, reassess her values upon further research. A dancer, after all, needed to be strong *and* flexible to create elegant, powerful moves. Zosia gestured for the students to return to the center of the room. She thought about the moments she liked Mira the best: when she was unexpectedly honest. She thought about Abram, how he was shifting gears.

"Sometimes," Zosia said, "I don't know why I do all this. Is the movement everything? Does any of this resonate with you? If so, I'll go on. Feeling confused does not mean you are an infidel. In fact, it might be the most important part of belief."

"It does resonate," Sarah said.

Others nodded their heads. "Go on."

"I also feel confused," someone said. "One day I think our socialist Zionism is the absolute goal of my life. But the next day, I miss my sister."

"Me too," another comrade offered. "I miss my father's advice. Like, 'words should be weighed, not counted.' Or the little things: Don't eat cheese before bed."

"Missing something makes you realize all that you had," Zosia offered. *If you cannot be grateful for what you have received,* her father used to say, *then be thankful for what you have been spared.* "That memory, that sense of ownership, can never really be taken away."

The group sat quiet, but it was a good quiet, Zosia sensed.

"My aunt," Sarah finally said, "lost nearly everything because of the new laws that all business must shut on Sundays. She prints prayer books and Sundays were the main day of trade. But with these new restrictions she can't open to so many of her clients and customers, and it breaks my heart to see her suffer. Now she's ill, and her children don't earn enough to feed her, let alone themselves. This makes me want to protect our people. I remind myself, we all have an aunt, or a brother, or a grandfather like this, and we need to help our whole community."

"My mother is ill," another comrade said. "Sometimes I feel I must change the world so that the world can help her. But," she quickly added, "I also understand it's not just her. She represents misfortune, which so many experience in different ways."

Zosia nodded. "I look forward to talking more tomorrow." She breathed in relief. They were opening up. Did these answers about their doubt veer toward imposterism or did this mean they were particularly committed, their principles so grounded that they were able to be dubious? Did it even matter?

What mattered was, she was opening up too.

"Zosia!" She heard Mira's stern voice as she crept back into Dzielna the next evening. She had spent the previous night at Grochów and then, this morning, still unable to face her leaders, her movement, even herself, she'd found a lift by droshky to another small commune where she pretended she'd been sent to review the books but had spent most of the day raking the old leaves that had emerged when the snow melted.

"Come to my room," Mira said, stern, from across the hall. "Now."

Zosia didn't even drop her bag. Excuses, justifications, apologies—these things ran out like shampoo: suddenly, even though you saw it coming. She followed her leader, ten paces behind, like a subordinate wife. Here it was: the grand trial. She'd had a fit at a hunger strike, struck a human being, run off with Fanny, gone to Przemyśl against orders . . .

Her insides seized up, blood rushed away from her head, and, for a second, she felt sheer terror, as if her whole being were in free fall, which did *not* feel like freedom. Who would she be if she was kicked out of Dror? Where would she go?

She stopped, leaned against the wall, caught her breath, then walked into the room. Mira was standing, waiting, facing the door.

"Two imposters left Grochów today," she said.

"I'm sor—" Zosia started. "What?"

"We're happy about this. We're proud of you."

Proud? No. "I'm sorry," Zosia said. "I mean, I'm grateful that you are proud of my work, but I'm sorry about my behavior at the hunger strike. I shouldn't have started with the guy, picked up the stick, run away. As for Prz—"

"You hit a person," Mira said. "No matter who he is, or what he believes, that was not alright. Dror won't tolerate violent behavior unless it's for self-defense, as in Jewish law. Don't have doubts. Push them away, Zosia, and keep your eyes on work."

Zosia shook her head in shame and frustration. She opened her mouth to say something, but what? "By the way," Zosia finally said as she exited the threshold. "Do you know which two imposters left?"

"A young man, Mordechai, I think. And a young woman, Sarah."

"Sarah?" Zosia had been wrong. Now she felt terribly guilty. Because of her, these two youths would likely never get visas; they would never live a free Jewish life in Eretz. Then again, Zosia reassured herself, they were smart, honest, hardworking people. They would become leaders here, running Poland's Jewish community in the future. Poland of the 1940s and '50s would need these comrades; need them to provide ideas, and warmth, and support.

Back in her room, waiting for her: a third letter from her mother.

> *I finally got a note from you, Zosia, but it was so short. Why aren't you writing more? I worry. You didn't tell me anything, just that you are healthy. Listen, tayereh, my dearest, the store is more and more disorganized. Boxes are piling up. We need you to run things, to do the math. Remember the time you presented Tateh with a business plan? You were so young, but it made sense. Come home, my darling. And don't forget to light the candles for Passover.*

Zosia tossed the letter onto her cot and herself on top of the letter.

Yes, she recalled her business plan, how she had calculated and tabulated and determined how they could save at least five percent. She remembered how that night her father had anointed her, a child, into a position wasn't sure she wanted. He'd leaned over, his ice-gray scraggly beard tickling her ear, and placed his hand on hers. With warm cigarette breath, he'd told her: She was the daughter he trusted. She was the smart one, the reliable one. One day, she'd take over the grocery.

Alas, one day, it all changed.

She couldn't go back to Byten, not until she found a way out of all her messes, not to mention one thousand złotys.

She needed to help the woman who had picked her up and put her onstage when she'd been scared. If not Zosia, then who?

She closed her eyes and let her mind wander to her little sister's wedding. She envisioned the *bedecken*, the veiling ceremony that took place just before the *chuppah*. Berl, who wouldn't have seen Bella for twenty-four hours, would enter, dancing with his friends. Bella would be sitting on a throne-like chair in the middle of the room. Berl would approach and, ensuring she was herself, place the veil over her eyes. The point was to check, to make sure that she was indeed the correct bride. Apparently, this came from biblical times, when Jacob married Leah by mistake. Well, not by mistake—he had been tricked into it. He was supposed to marry her sister, the beautiful Rachel, but his father-in-law switched brides at the last second, fearful that the older, less pretty Leah would be left a spinster.

We can be so naïve, Zosia thought, dismissing the truths that rotted right under our noses.

Zosia forced herself to sit up. She grabbed her dip pen and a notebook but—

Instead of replying to her mother, or preparing for her next lecture, Zosia put on her coat and headed out the door.

CHAPTER 23

Fanny

FANNY STOOD BEHIND A PASTEL-PAINTED SCREEN AND SHIMmied into the brown pencil skirt that Natalia had picked for her. It had been a while since Fanny had been in the Fashion Café and it felt different. Frostier. Had the windows always let in such drafts? It was as if the cold blew right through the glass.

"Does it fit?" Nat asked from across the divide. They were in the small gallery near the office.

"Yes." It was the first time the women had been alone together since Nowak forced Fanny to the ghetto bench. On the one hand, what was Fanny even doing here? The whole country was brewing with trouble. On the other hand, there was her artistic career to consider. Why should she give up her world and her dreams because of bigots? She would fight! She had every right to participate in her own culture.

Also, she reminded herself, she was here for a reason. One thousand reasons.

"I really like the journalist look for you," Nat said. From her side of the screen, she passed Fanny a checkered blouse and a skinny brown belt with a golden clasp. "I love this buckle," she added, chipper. "The belt is a fine line that slices the body in half yet holds the entire outfit together."

"Or tears it apart," Fanny answered, "if it's not exactly right."

Fanny put on the clothes Nat had selected and stared in the mirror that had been placed on her side of the divide. She did not know how to act around this friend. Fanny felt ashamed that Nat had seen her as the victim of bigotry, but also angry that Nat had never said anything to defend her. She'd never even checked in on her afterwards. Just imagine what Nat would think of her if she knew Mamo was broke too.

"You look stunning!" Nat squealed as Fanny emerged from behind the screen. "Now, for my favorite part. Shoes." Natalia perused a collection of accessories that were littered across a shelf on the studio wall. "These!" She brought over a pair of black heels, high like the seafood towers at French brasseries. They looked heavy and not particularly comfortable. "I can't see any reporter running for a story wearing those."

"But they're so cute," Natalia cajoled. "Besides, they're for when you're writing the story down."

Fanny wasn't sure anyone needed high heels to write, but then again, she understood the sense of power one felt when tall, as if watching over the world. Mamo had taught her all about heels.

Natalia handed her the pair. "Look, I know you haven't been to class in a while, and I just wanted to say, well . . ."

"Yes?"

"You can borrow my notes," she offered, sheepish.

"Your notes?"

"Yes. Just today, we learned about how Descartes said that our own senses can deceive us."

"Our senses are not to be trusted?" Fanny stressed the last four words.

"For instance," Natalia said, extra bubbly, "Descartes had a dream. In his dream he was sitting by a fireplace, and he felt hot. He experienced heat, a real sensation, when there was no real fire. So, our senses don't really tell us what's in front of us. They tell us what we imagine. Or rather, our mind supersedes our physical experience."

"But it was a dream," Fanny said. "Clearly one must distinguish the experience of being asleep and being awake."

"I guess."

"Besides, is the opposite also true?" Fanny asked. "Do our senses take things in but our minds don't notice?"

"I'm sorry, I suppose I'm not explaining it well," Natalia mumbled. "I'll lend you my notes, really, anytime."

"No, thank you," Fanny declined, dangling the pair of heels in her right hand. Anger wasn't productive, but guilt could be. "But there is something you *can* do for me."

"Sure. What is it?"

"I love that you're staging your own fashion show here," Fanny said. "I'm inspired."

"Thank you, Fanny, that's very kind."

"I would like to have my own show here too."

"Fashion?"

"No, photography. The photos I took of the preparation for your show, and a few of my other fashion shots." Fanny announced her grand plan with confidence. If she couldn't participate in the university exhibit, she could try to do one here. And, while she was at it proving her independence, she could sell her work to make money to hire a lawyer for Wanda. "I'd like to show them before the summer."

"Now that's an interesting idea," Nat said. "I will definitely ask the committee."

"Ask?"

"I will suggest—"

"Suggest?"

"I will highly recommend it to the selection committee."

"Thank you," Fanny said. "It means a lot, and I'm counting on you."

"Of course."

"Tell me," Fanny said. "At these shows, they sell the artworks, right?"

"Yes, I suppose they do."

"How much does a photograph sell for?"

"I have no idea," Natalia said and laughed. "But I do know that one day, you and I will run the Polish art world!"

"We will," Fanny agreed, but suddenly that possibility felt far away.

Then Fanny slipped on the heels. Truth was, they fit perfectly.

THAT NIGHT, FANNY WAS ASSURED THAT MAMO WAS OUT FOR the evening and likely until morning—she was at the Pfefermans for an old-style Warsaw dinner party, where dinner was served at eleven, dancing began at one a.m., hunter's stew was dished up at two, and a hostess would be upset if anyone left before six.

Fanny sat in the privacy of her own room, her lifelong place of comfort which, she feared, would soon be up for sale. Fortunately, thanks to Zosia, the room was now a secret photography studio and for the past few hours, Fanny had been experimenting with a synchronblitzer flash, which resembled a folding metallic umbrella that spread light when she clicked a button. But illumination wasn't as easy as it seemed. The flash had to be positioned at exactly the right angle to both the object and the ambient light or else all that emerged was a burst of white, as if a bomb had gone off right in the middle of the picture, damaging the entire photo. Now she was looking through strings of negatives, thirty-six by thirty-six by thirty-six, trying to figure out which ones would be worth developing. She'd used cash to buy supplies earlier that week but Mamo's secret stash was dwindling, and fast. She couldn't develop them all—she had to make choices. And there was little room for error, especially at the Fashion Café . . . With the light of a lamp, she glanced through the tiny images: Jabłkowski's windows, reflections of her lipstick, seamstresses' needles . . .

Which of these tiny pictures told a story that deserved to be inverted, black becoming white, white becoming black, nothing into something into nothing. What image held truth, and perspective?

But more than that: What would *sell*? Could any of them make money?

Wanda would be used as an example, incur maximum punishment . . . the journalist's words echoed in her mind. Fanny gulped at the thought that she still hadn't found any help for Wanda—no lawyers, no press. The trial was in mere months. As was her wedding.

The thought had struck her: She could ask Simon for the money. She could say it was for a wedding surprise. But then, she would owe him. Would saving Wanda be worth that debt? Should she trade one capture for another?

Simon had arrived safely in New York. His mother had left a message.

Fanny got up from the floor, put the strands of negatives on her desk, and opened her closet door. She would start by developing one of the pictures from the police headquarters. She recalled being drawn to the rows of boots; each shoe had personality, tracing its wearer along with greater feelings, the satisfaction of having taken steps.

As Fanny dipped and dried, she thought back to Abram's question: Is a good photograph one that shows us our present or our future? Or maybe it shows us our past . . . She recalled his arm on her sleeve, the weight of it not just comforting but enticing. Exciting.

Then her conversation with Zosia ran through her mind: Do we only see what we're trained to see, or what we want to see, or maybe what we *don't* want to see? How do we divorce our vision from what others have taught us to look for, and from our own emotions and pasts? She'd noticed the way Zosia got awkward around Abram, then glanced at him behind his back; it seemed she was trying hard *not* to flirt. But that made sense. There couldn't be anything between them because they worked together—

Suddenly, she heard a thump. Had Mamo returned?

She opened her closet door and saw that the noise must have been caused not by Mamo but by the negatives she'd stacked on her desk, her "leaning tower of Leica." They'd slid off, bringing their lacquered storage boxes down with them. The pictures had fallen into a pile on top of each other, like a jagged torso, a person filled with disparate memories, cut up and joined together at the same time.

She felt shivers. Fanny grabbed her Leica and, trying not to think about cost, began to work. Images of her own fingers, knees, an elbow, bits of her body, zoning in on the tiniest joints and pores, defamiliarizing the parts that are so intimate we barely notice them, chopping herself up, rearranging her own parts like—

"What on earth is going on in here? *Co do cholery!*"

Fanny looked up. Mamo stood in the doorway, her face red with rage against her head-to-toe canary yellow outfit. "Fanny Zelshinsky, what is all this? Where were you?"

"Where were *you*?" Fanny gathered herself, tried to push her negatives away, but it was no use. "I thought you were at the Pfefermans."

"That was yesterday. What's wrong with you? I was at the Chopin Competition luncheon that I was hosting at Avigdor's house, which ran late for a very special reason. I thought you were coming. We were celebrating the prizewinning pianist Isaac Zak, the best in the world. He's short but was very handsome in his velvet tuxedo. Cultured, successful, rich. Exactly the kind of person you should know. You need to start a life, Fanny, establish your position in this world, enhance the Brodasz name with cultural cache; that's your job. Instead, I find you here, sitting on your floor like a child! Playing with scissors, with silly toys."

"These are not silly toys." Fanny took a deep breath. "This is my work. I am a working photographer."

"You are no such thing," Mamo roared.

Fanny struggled to her feet. "This is who I am."

"Enough!" Mamo threw her hands into the air.

That's when Fanny noticed the diamond, big like a walnut, resting heavy on Mamo's left hand.

"Avigdor." Mamo saw her notice. "We're engaged. That's why I'm late. If you'd been there today, as you were supposed to be, you may have said congratulations, as is done."

Fanny caught her breath. That would make him . . . her stepfather. Here she was, doing whatever she could in a desperate attempt to become independent, to avoid a marriage, and Mamo was throwing her towel in with slimy Avigdor? How shameful that Mamo would stoop that low, would sacrifice herself for money. "That creep? Congrats, Mamo."

"Watch your mouth. It's not what you think, Fanny." Her mother's painted lips went tight like the end of a salami.

"Oh sure—"

"Now clean this up." Mamo slammed the door, then called after her. "We have two weddings to work on tomorrow, urgently!"

This is who I am. She'd said it! Fanny felt alive and she shivered all over. She clicked on her arm one last time, recalling the pressure that Abram's hand had exerted. Firm, supportive, yet entirely different, electrifying. She realized she wanted to talk about her work, to tell someone about her ideas, about the images of her body, sliced and diced and yet still, somehow, constituting her. She wanted to tell *him.*

Fanny rushed to meet Abram on the corner of Ujazdowskie Avenue and Matejski Street, at the spot he'd chosen. He'd seemed rather surprised but also pleased to hear from her when she'd managed to get him on the phone at the pharmacy next door to Dror the day before. Now, Fanny was excited, nervous. She reapplied her lipstick.

What on earth was she doing?

She turned to find him smoking a cigarette. "One thirty-three," he said.

"Fashionably late."

"Let's go for a walk." Abram smiled.

"Sure." She smiled too, and her insides may have fluttered. *Date against type*, Natalia had once told her.

Fanny stepped into sync with his wide strides. They talked about the balmy spring weather, even though small talk was so unlike him, and she wondered if he was nervous too. The thought of him feeling awkward was strangely compelling. He always seemed so competent, so confident.

Where was he taking her? She'd heard there was a spring fair nearby. Maybe he'd surprise her—*ready for some amusement?*—and they'd spend the afternoon riding the Ferris wheel, living in fast, gratuitous danger, imagining how high they were (*As high as the Eiffel Tower! As high as a hot-air balloon!*). They'd play games and he'd win her a giant stuffed teddy bear.

"Have you ever read Maria Kuncewiczowa's *A Man's Face*?" she asked. "In that one, the woman shares her feelings first."

"I find her novels sentimental," he said.

"But she just won the Gold Laurel from the Polish Academy of Literature! Kuncewiczowa is very sympathetic to the Zionist cause, you know. She's going to visit the Jewish community in Palestine."

"Good luck to her. That's important work, if you can get it." He changed course and turned onto a small street, a quiet location. A romantic corner? He led her into the courtyard of a tenement building. It was empty, except for a few children who chased pigeons. "Here we are."

"Where are we?"

"A protest," he said. "Or rather, an action."

"An action?"

"The Bund's self-defense league has created a militia. We need to be able to defend ourselves as a Jewish nation within our home country. They are committed to working with the Poles and fighting the increasing numbers of fascists. Most Poles aren't fascist, of course, but they can fall for their lines, for their empty promises. We need to fight their lies at the root before it's too late."

Fanny's heart sank. This was not a date but his audition with an illegal militia. She scolded herself, embarrassed, as they approached the building. What had she been thinking—she was engaged, for crying out loud! "I don't see any protestors," Fanny said, making sure she remained even-keeled. "No pickets, no signs, no crowds."

"They're inside the second courtyard," he said. "Take out your camera." Ah, so she was just a camera to him. At least he continued to take her abilities seriously.

"What do you want me to capture?"

"Our activity." He stepped quickly now toward the building. "These Jewish workers are being thrown out of their homes by a landlord who wants to increase their rent suddenly and dramatically. We rely on our workers as a society and no one should be treated this way, let alone those who form the basis of our functioning. We are resisting and refusing this unethical eviction. Home is home."

She took her Leica out of its bag. She couldn't afford these shots, but he would never understand.

Inside the second courtyard, it was a different world. Furniture, linens, and dishes were all over the cobbled ground. Families were confused. Mothers were crying. Children ran around. Rows of young Bundists were picking up boxes and suitcases.

"The landlord's agents, bailiffs, and police threw them out, but we're moving them back in," Abram explained. "We have to work fast."

Fanny made her way closer to the action, camera in hand. She'd promised herself she'd only take a handful of perfect pictures, and yet she began to click on pots and pans, on children jumping on cots en plein air. Then she shot socialists, some with guns in their holsters, as they quickly passed crates and couches back upstairs.

Suddenly, a "Halt!" Everyone turned to look. The police had returned. "What are you doing?" There were a dozen of them, maybe more.

Fanny's heart raced.

The Bundists formed a chain and chanted, "Our home is home." Fanny made her way to the sidelines.

"Capture the police," Abram, close at her side, whispered. She tried not to notice that his skin smelled of tobacco and a heady mixture of spices. "Capture how they abuse the people. You of all people can do it."

She found a spot behind a door. She'd sell off her clothes to afford the shots!

Screams and threats, chants and arguments, but nothing more went on for well over fifteen minutes, after which it seemed the police appeared to lose interest. Were the cops really on the side of the landlord as Abram had insisted? Whose side were they on—no one's?

Click on a cap, on thick leather boots that ran all the way to the knee. She looked into the lens, following her view right up his body to his cuff links: M.

Fanny hid her face with her Leica and hid most of her body behind the door.

The afternoon sun casting a blanket of light over the group of workers. *Click.*

A policeman chewing tobacco. *Click.*

Marek holding a stick up to a protestor's face, yelling at her, red cheeks. *Cli—*

"You!"

Fanny finished her click. Then she put her Leica down.

"What are you doing here, Zelshinsky?"

"I'm sorry, Commander Broz," Fanny said, with a smile as flirtatious as she could muster. "I was just taking photos—of the fashion."

"The fashion?" He looked her up and down. His costume gave him clout, but her expensive outfit gave her innocence. He shook his head.

Fanny looked over to the woman he'd been yelling at. She was trembling, clearly relieved that his bayonet had been brought down by Fanny's intrusion. Her eyes were open wide, and tears began to stream down her cheeks. Fanny felt like she was looking in a mirror: She was this poor woman, one and the same. Unsure if they'd stay in their home, unsure of their position.

"If you ever take a photo of me again"—he was right next to her, whispering in her ear—"you will be sorry."

Fanny looked up. Abram was standing between a mother and another bayonet, strong and decisive.

"I'll destroy the photo if you help Wanda," Fanny whispered back, barely moving her lips.

"In your wildest dreams, dear. In your stupid wildest dreams," Marek said. Then he leaned right into her face and hissed, "Little Lenora is growing up . . . she finally understands that everything has a price."

Fanny was about to ask him what his price was when a smoke bomb went off, sending them all running.

"Are you alright? Can you breathe? I didn't mean for you to—" Abram had pulled her outside the tenement, onto the sidewalk.

"It's alright," Fanny said, though she was shaken. "I know him."

"You know him?" Abram chuckled. "Who are you, Fanny Zelshinsky?"

"Well, it's a long story—"

Suddenly, he reached for her, pulled her right into him, leaned down, and pressed his lips right onto hers, direct, firm. He pulled back, and they looked at each other in surprise.

She felt strange, flushed, a little dizzy.

"I'm so sorry," he said and pulled away. "You're engaged."

"Engagement," Fanny said, breathless, "is a bourgeois construct."

Abram laughed and kissed her again. "Come with me," he said.

CHAPTER 24

Zosia

Zosia froze.

Her insides stopped. All whirring, pumping, sensing halted.

She'd gone out at four a.m. and waited at the news stall for the day's papers, She'd found the correct broadsheet and picked it up, warm like fresh bread. She'd held it for a long moment in her arms, cradling it like a baby, and then, with trembling hands, she'd slowly, gingerly, opened the pages, skimming each one.

She'd expected it to be an emotional morning, a time of pride and fear, hope and fear, excitement and fear.

But not this.

Zosia blinked, trying to erase the sight.

Trying to focus.

The other night, she'd planned to write lesson plans, and then to write to her mother, intending to tell her that she was safe and well, and, once and for all, that she could not come home and work in the grocery when the idea struck: *She* could write. She'd gone to Wolf Shenkman and insisted, and he'd accepted the piece that she'd composed right in his office, impressed by her courage. Only after she'd left the building did it dawn on her that she should have used a pseudonym, Sholom Aleichem–style. Now she would have to face the consequences, but she believed in her actions, and so she could. She'd decided she needed to be at Dzielna that morning, so if and when people found out, she could explain, defend, share her side. She'd show Fanny later, as soon as she could. She'd tiptoed down the hall, back to her room.

Which is when she saw it.

Out of thin air. A slap in the face.

Outside Abram's door. The coat—unmistakable.

It was five a.m., her brain told her. It made no sense.

Neither did: An embrace, all passion and hands.

"Fanny?"

Don't run.

The hands stopped. Fanny turned around. "Zosia?"

Don't run, don't run, don't run.

But Zosia couldn't talk, couldn't reply, couldn't nod, couldn't deal head-on, defend, share her side. Her boundaries were not just porous, they were disintegrating.

Zosia hurled the newspaper to the floor and fled.

CHAPTER 25

Fanny

"ZOSIA, PLEASE!" FANNY CALLED. *I CAN EXPLAIN*, SHE WANTED to say. But what could she explain? Her ring was still on her finger. What on earth had she done?

Then again, she was tangled into him, his body peppery warm like a winter fire. She felt as if she were floating outside herself and, at the same time, entirely present in her flesh, stretching out her own organs. She smelled of him, of all of him, everywhere.

Fanny knew: There was no turning back.

His arm still lay on her back, in the same spot as that first night at the Dzigan show. It was his little shelf on her, a territory he'd immediately claimed.

"Zosia!" she called again. She gently pushed him off and headed down the hall after her friend. Fanny picked up *The Workers' Paper* from the ground. She scanned the headline, her eyes running over the article.

"What is it?" Abram asked.

"It's about Wanda. It's a short piece exposing that the talented, hardworking Wanda Petrovsky is being held in prison for months. Zosia must have gotten someone to write about it, to help get her released."

"You know Wanda?" His arm had found its way back around her, to its shelf.

"She was my mentor." She didn't say anything else, not yet.

"Of course." Abram paused. "I heard she was missing. Who wrote it?"

"Zosia must have gotten someone to do it." Fanny scanned again. "Oh my lord, it was her. Zosia wrote it."

"What?" Abram removed his arm from around her body, pinched the page from her hand, and read. "This is incredible. Absolutely incredible that she did this."

Fanny heard it in his voice: He was impressed. Truly impressed. Suddenly Fanny became aware of something that she already deep-down knew: Abram and Zosia shared something elemental, something Fanny could not access.

Of course she'd realized that Zosia had a work crush on him, but maybe it was more profound. Her friend truly fancied the man she'd just slept with.

And maybe he liked her too.

Fanny felt a terrible stomach pang, this time of guilt. "At the very least," Fanny said, trying to move on from this topic in her mind, "people will know about this miscarriage of justice. Maybe it can help raise funds for a lawyer."

"I hope so," Abram said.

"I'm going to find Zosia," Fanny said. She needed to get out of there. She didn't understand herself or her actions anymore. Also, she had things to do: only a few days left until the fashion show that would hopefully lead her to raising money, to *her* doing something useful. "See you . . . later."

It felt like she should say more. For a second, she considered inviting Abram to the show, but then she looked at him, still devouring the article. Perhaps having her secret socialist paramour who was loved by her best friend attend a high-class Polish fashion event wasn't the best idea.

"ARE YOU ALRIGHT, FANNY?" NATALIA ASKED, COMING UP from behind her.

Was she alright? For the past few days, Zosia had been missing; her comrades said she was at Grochów. She hadn't heard from

Abram and couldn't figure out if that was a good thing or a bad thing. Mamo had been forcing her to plan weddings even though she was a harlot. And there were no notable results from Zosia's article except a few gasps here at the Fashion Café where everyone loved a scandal. Fanny was going to lose her home, and without a show to call her own, Fanny had no independence or money.

But why wouldn't she be spending her time strutting on a runway? Fanny smiled. "I'm wonderful. Just nerves."

"Ten minutes until the Work show!" someone called out. Their "dressing room," which was really the large yellow room at the Fashion Café, bubbled with anxious hubbub.

Fanny noticed a tall woman whom she didn't recognize whisper in Natalia's ear.

Fanny reminded herself: She was doing this *for* Wanda. She'd show Nat her commitment, confirm her own photo show, then convince Nat to let her put it up as soon as possible so she could sell the works and get money to Chlebook for a gangster lawyer before the summer.

"Well, I hate to say it, but"—Nat looked back at her, made a funny face, and pointed at Fanny's torso—"you look, well, strange."

"Excuse me?"

"Turn to me. Turn again. Did you gain weight?"

"No."

"Lose weight?"

"No—"

"I don't know, Fanny. The outfit just doesn't fit your body anymore." Nat sighed. "It doesn't sit right on you. The belt, for one, is completely off."

Fanny straightened the accessory. What was she talking about? Had her night with Abram changed her physique such that everyone could see?

"It's packed out there," one of Fanny's fellow models announced.

"I think it looks fine," Fanny said. "I can take off the belt." She unclipped it and spun around.

"Still, no." Nat went on, scrutinizing her. The tall woman

whispered to her again. "Maybe it's best you continue in your role as photographer and stay backstage. I think that may be a more comfortable place for you, Fanny. Backstage."

Fanny couldn't breathe. "I need to use the restroom." It was one thing to be forced into ghetto benches at school where cold ideologies and mob mentality reigned, but Nat was supposed to be her friend, and this was supposed to be *her* world of beauty and dreams and hope. She headed to the hall, to where Wanda's photos hung. She needed to see them, to take in their wisdom and beauty. To remind herself, to inspire.

But the photos weren't there. The wall was empty.

Four stamps of Wanda's genius removed, eradicated, as if they'd never existed at all. The wall wasn't even dusty or sun-stained; there was not a single mark to indicate that something had inhabited that space, had shed such light from its boundaries. Nothing.

Fanny burned in fury. Wanda was being used as an example by one enemy and erased by the others.

She looked toward the Fashion Café's front door that she'd breezed in and out of so many times. She could run out, forget this whole thing, cross the threshold and flee forever. Or she could go back in, stay backstage, try to appease Natalia—maybe that would help her get her own photo show? She looked back to the bare patch of wall. Fanny felt it in her bones: She did not want to disappear.

She wished Zosia were here.

Back in the dressing room, the models were lined up for the runway.

Natalia approached Fanny. "Oh, there you are. Here's your camera." She shoved it into Fanny's hands. "So just capture behind-the-scenes."

Fanny took the camera, turned from her, and—stepped in line with her partner out on the runway. *Forward and front.*

Suddenly, in front of her: flash. She blinked, careful not to trip on a stone. Someone had taken a photo of her, *at* her.

For a split second, Fanny stopped.

Then she lifted her Leica and, as she strutted and pivoted for the walk back, she shot at the audience.

Fanny shot eyes and faces, hands and legs, dresses and suits, catching their glimpses and all their gasps. She took photos of the people seated at their round white tables watching, subverting subject and object, viewer and viewed, taking control with her camera. *Look at me now, but I'll be watching you forever.*

Click, click, click.

Shivers.

View from the Catwalk, she would call the series, she thought, as she made it back to the end of the runway and stepped off.

Natalia looked at her in shock.

Fanny smiled.

Afterwards, she was surrounded. "Genius," a writer told her. "Loved you," a fashionista said. "We were all so surprised!" Fanny smoked a cigarette and took it all in. She'd caused a fashion-world kerfuffle, and nothing was better than that. Even for Nat. Especially for Nat. She would have to let her show her work.

Then, a poet Fanny recognized put his arm around her shoulders. "Avant-garde, fascinating take." He called Nat over. "How lucky that you got this smart girl to show your beautifully curated looks."

"Thank you," Nat said, with a tight smile.

"I'm a photographer," Fanny said. "I will be showing my photos here very soon."

"Of course you're an artist," he said. "Will you include the ones you took today?"

Fanny nodded. "Backstage, onstage, offstage, the audience; I'll show myriad perspectives. But all from my own perspective. It will be universal *and* personal. Truth." She proudly quoted Wanda.

"I, for one, can't wait to see your show! I want to—"

Natalia interrupted him. "We're working on a show of Fanny's photos. We're all so excited. So much to do."

"Wonderful," he said. "I really—"

"In fact, I need to talk to Fanny about it, tout de suite," Nat said and gestured for Fanny to follow her.

Fanny breathed in relief. It was going to work. Now if only she could get her to agree to mount the show before summer . . .

Nat directed her to the table where, months earlier, they'd sat eating pierogis.

"Listen," Natalia said quietly. "I'm grateful for all your help. But let me just level with you here. Your show is not going to happen."

Fanny pulled back. "Why?"

"Well . . . There have been so many submissions, more than usual."

"Who else wants to show fashion photos?"

"It's not for me to say. There's a whole committee. We spend a lot of time, days sometimes, debating which pictures to include. And"—Nat paused—"there are politics."

"Politics? My photos are of seamstresses."

"*Personal* politics."

"What personal politics?"

"It's just that, I'm not sure how to say this."

"What?"

"People are talking about you. You've been spotted at protests and hunger strikes and tenements, and, we really are a *fine* art institution, not political art."

"What?"

"Fanny." Natalia looked her in the eyes for a long moment, drawn out like syrup. Then she turned to leave and called back, "Your people are losing their popularity. I'm sorry."

Fanny rounded her corner, running from one non-home to another. Her face was hot with tears, and she was sure she looked like a sad clown, a Pierrot with makeup dripping down her visage. Nat had rejected her, and for what? For being Jewish? For being political and Jewish? The Fashion Café, her happy place, was not her place at all. Had she been wrong to simply turn and walk out? For how long does one stay and fight those who turn on you for no reason?

"Wow, you look fancy."

Fanny jumped, startled. He was waiting on her staircase. "What are you doing here?" She quickly wiped her cheeks with both hands. She was still wearing the journalist costume from the fashion show, even the towering heels. Now she moved the belt to the side, her way.

It was one thing to be in his bed at night, another to be with him in broad daylight in front of Mamo's apartment! Her stomach quivered, or was it a knot? She quicky scanned the area to see if anyone was looking, and ascended, careful to keep her distance. Her feet rested on two different steps, her own body confused about its height.

"I have to talk to you," Abram said.

"Here? We can't . . ."

"It's not about us," he whispered. Then he frowned and shook his head. "Sadly, I'm sorry, but I don't think Wanda is going to be released." He reached into his satchel for a copy of *Gazeta Polska.* "This Polish paper is much more widely circulated than *The Workers' Paper.*"

Aware that others could see them here, together, Fanny skimmed the headlines: Hitler is moving forward, Europe is in fear, the Munich Pact . . . Germany will annex the Sudetenland, an analysis of Poland's tourism industry . . . In 1937, 194,000 tourists visited the Eastern Borderlands of Poland, with 66,000 of them visiting Vilna . . . So?

Her eyes dashed ahead. Then she gasped.

Another headline. "Wanda Petrovsky, Communist, Criminal." Wanda and the other fifteen radicals were a danger to decent Polish society and needed to be locked up for good. And hopefully they would be, at the end of the trial that would take place—in two weeks.

CHAPTER 26

Zosia

THE TIME HAS COME TO ESCALATE OUR PROTESTS. THE TELEgram had come to Grochów from Warsaw. There'd been an assassination attempt on Konrad Górski, one of the Catholic professors who'd helped circulate the anti-bench letter among international universities. If a student member of the Nationalist Party had tried to murder one of his own people for defending Jews' rights—what would they do to the Jews themselves?

Zosia had read the text and, not without hesitation, got on the first train back to the city. She'd spent the past few days at the suburban commune, avoiding Fanny and Abram, not to mention Mira and anyone else who may have read her article. She hoped to soothe herself with washing, laundry, and hoeing. Fortunately, the small newspaper to which she'd contributed had not made it to these parts, but the *Gazeta Polska* had. Zosia spent one evening at the local *kretchme,* escaping from her escape at the inn, drinking water at a bar that smelled like wet rag, and the article had caught her eye: Wanda's trial was in two weeks.

Sure, she'd thought to come back to Warsaw right away, but what more could she possibly do? Counterfeit one thousand zloties?! Her chances of getting a visa were deflating by the day. A niggling thought had sprouted in her consciousness: What if Abram was right? What if there was no more point to the homeland movement? She'd extinguished the notion quickly but could not deny it had occurred. On top of that, she had no claims on Abram, nor on Fanny, who'd lost her fortune and was tied into a marriage she didn't want. Who was she to interfere with their mutual attraction? It was embarrassing, really, that she had run off like that. Zosia *had* to control her emotions and throw herself into greater causes.

Now, an assassination attempt, a new protest, a telegram.

At the university, Zosia had walked quickly across the campus, scanning for green ribbons—in particular, the one she'd hit. Inside, she'd joined a group that included Fanny. "You're here!" Fanny nearly pounced on her. Despite herself, Zosia imagined her entwined with Abram and shuddered, but she forced herself to swallow her feelings and nod. She, Fanny, and a few comrades waited outside Nowak's lecture hall until they heard that the class was beginning. Zosia's heart raced, but she reassured herself that she could do this.

As soon as Professor Nowak began to talk, his voice hitting its stride as he eased into his lecture, Fanny looked at Zosia as if asking for permission, and Zosia nodded again. Then Fanny flung open the doors. She walked right to the Jewish bench. But she did not sit. She stood.

Zosia followed and stood. She felt all the eyes in the room fix themselves upon her. She allowed it. She kept her gaze up and her expression firm and absorbed their stares. Among the mahogany walls, Zosia felt alive.

Nowak stopped and looked at Fanny. Fanny stared right back.

Nowak kept talking. Fanny and Zosia kept standing, literally standing up to the bigots.

The other comrades joined them.

And that's when it happened. Zosia heard shuffling to her sides. She glanced over: Jewish students in the bench were getting up! One by one, they rose. Slow, steady, and composed, it was the most elegant protest she'd ever witnessed.

Zosia thought of all the other students across the university who were standing right now. All of them, defying, in pride, in principle, together.

Finally, Nowak caved. "What is going on here? You'll all be expelled!"

"We will not sit in the ghetto benches," Fanny responded. "We would rather stand."

The Jewish students calmly agreed, with "Hear, hear." Zosia chimed in, louder, "Hear, hear!" Zosia felt more pride than she had in a long time. It was so simple—standing. Straight, direct, quiet. Staying still made waves around them.

Then, one of the Christian students stood. She caught his eye and smiled. He nodded in return. Another one stood. And another . . .

"Look at the Jews here, disturbing our lecture, disturbing *your* learning," Nowak spat out, livid. "Ruining our country as usual. I can't teach this way." He threw his notes on the floor.

"That's too bad," Fanny said. "Because we will continue to stand until these ghetto benches are outlawed. We will stand up for ourselves. How dare you abuse your position of power to shame me in front of the entire class. How could you dehumanize me because I'm Jewish?"

The awkward honesty hung thick in the air.

"Class dismissed," Nowak frothed. "The administration will have to intervene. The police!" He grabbed his hat and stomped out of the room.

Click.

Suddenly, there was clapping. Zosia turned around and saw that two of her students from Grochów had also come. "Good work, Big Sister," one of them said.

But then—booing. Heckles and insults.

The mood turned in an instant.

"Jews, you ruined our lecture!"

"Get out of here!"

The rest of the Christian students stood up and now both sides began to taunt each other, approaching each other over the ghetto bench "line."

"You go!"

"No, you go!"

It was mayhem. Zosia's heart began to race. She started to hear the roar, itching and burning, her hands to her ears—

Fanny clasped her hand and dragged her through the bottleneck of students, out of the room and toward the staircase. "Take a breath," she told her. "We'll make it out."

Outside, the women ran to a quiet patch on the campus lawn. Gasping, Zosia had to stop and lean over to catch her breath.

"Who knew the university would become the site of all this," Fanny replied and sat down on the thick springtime grass. "At least, I finally took the picture I'd wanted to take for so long. *My* photograph."

Zosia nodded, then scanned the campus around them. No green ribbons, thankfully. At least, not yet. She wasn't sure how much to offer, nor whether to keep tying herself to Fanny, but then she blurted, "The trial is in two weeks."

"Believe me, I know. What on earth are we going to do?" Fanny said.

"I don't know. My article did nothing," Zosia said. "I feel so useless. All that risk for no reward."

"Don't feel useless! It was a bold and important article. I tried to tell you . . ."

Zosia didn't reply. She pretended to still be trying to catch her breath.

"It's been a hard few days, very hard," Fanny went on. "I was rejected . . . from the Fashion Café."

"Oh." Fanny's shoulders were uncharacteristically slumped. She sat down next to her.

"Natalia refused my exhibit because I'm political and Jewish. We've known each other for almost two years. She told me stories about boyfriends, intimate things. We shared notes, studied together for exams. We laughed at the stupid personal ads. She used to drink from my cup, Zosia." Fanny paused and shook her head. "She was in class today. She did not stand up. She didn't even look my way.

"Where in the world can I show my work if not there?" Fanny

continued, before Zosia could speak. "And if I can't get that show, I won't have a chance to prove my independence, to sell my work, and to make money for a lawyer to help Wanda. Where will we get the funds? We've come so far. We need to help her."

Zosia paused. Then she took Fanny's hand and gave it a squeeze, just as Fanny had done to her before. "Do it yourself."

"Do it myself?"

"Just like I had to write the article on my own," Zosia said. "We can't wait for others. No one is coming to save us. If Dror taught me anything, it's that. I did something, now you do something. *That* will show independence."

"What does doing it myself even mean? What does that look like?"

"What do you think?" Zosia was getting annoyed. "Put on your photo show yourself—ourselves—and we'll sell the work."

"What do you know about putting on an art show?"

"Dror may not have provided me with curatorial training, but the movement did teach me to organize. We just need a space."

Fanny shook her head. "I don't know."

"What do you mean you don't know?"

"We'll never make enough money to get a lawyer. We need a thousand złotys! And what if Chlebook can't find us anyone good? It's too hard, Zosia. I have nothing."

"And so, you have nothing to lose. Stop being so scared of your own creativity. Go right now and start developing. It's the only chance we have."

Fanny began to stand. She clutched her camera bag. "Listen—"

"Go!"

She sat back down. "Zosia, I really am sorry about Abram. I feel terrible."

"It's nothing."

"Well, it's not nothing. It's not something, but it's also not nothing."

"Do you love him?" Zosia blurted. She couldn't believe her own candor.

Fanny took a moment. "No," she said, and Zosia exhaled, just a little. "I just needed, well, I needed to do something radical, indelible."

"Why?"

"I'm not sure," Fanny said, clearly thinking as she was talking. "I suppose I needed a reason to destroy my engagement. If I could do something like this—have an affair, and with Simon's polar opposite—well then I knew I couldn't go back to Simon. I needed a tangible reason to call it off, even one of my own doing."

"Why?" Zosia repeated, recalling how Fanny had mentioned Mamo had pressured her into marrying złotys. "Why call it off now?"

"I don't want to get married," Fanny finally said—out loud and to herself. "At least not to Simon. I want to be with someone who knows me, who likes all of me. I don't want to have to hide my camera under my chair. Maybe I'm in love with photography."

"Maybe you need to fall in love with yourself," Zosia said.

"How very un-socialist of you!"

Zosia smiled. "You're sure you aren't in love with Abram? I've seen you two flirt like professionals."

Fanny shook her head. "He came over to my flat, he showed me the newspaper article about Wanda, and then he invited me on a date—he wanted to take me to a café for sardines."

"So?"

"So! Sardines? I realized in that moment that we are not suited for each other. What's next, Bund barbecues? I told him I'd get back to him with a time, but . . . I still haven't."

"Oh."

"But I think you should join him for sardines." Fanny put her arm around Zosia. "I know you like sardines, and I think you'd love to eat them together."

CHAPTER 27

Fanny

FANNY HAD ONE LAST IDEA.

A few days later, she ran up the stairs to the Museum Narodowe, the National Museum, the largest in Warsaw. This was one of Fanny's favorite spots in the city and normally she'd stop to photograph the slick modernist building, its grand rectangular columns and linked pavilions outlining a geometric courtyard. Fanny loved the entire Jerusalem Avenue, with its art nouveau homes, precious modern buildings, and the royal Park Na Książęcem. But today, there was no time.

"Mamo!" she called to her from across the courtyard. Mamo had received a special invitation to preview *Warsaw Yesterday, Today, Tomorrow*, a major exhibition about Warsaw's future. Mamo wore a mauve silken shawl that wrapped around her round frame like a clamshell.

"Look at this detailed mock-up of old Warsaw," Mamo said once they were inside the first of twenty-four white-walled galleries. A few workers lingered in the unfinished space, but otherwise it was silent.

Fanny examined the three-dimensional piece. It felt powerful to look at her city from this viewpoint, its problems reduced to inches of clay. "Mamo, I need to talk to you."

As usual, nothing more had been said since their altercation the other night.

As usual, Mamo was ignoring Fanny's feelings.

Mamo walked past display boards about the city's changing demographics, a photo montage about the metropolis' great transformation over the past two decades, and blueprint plans for future urban projects. "Look at this, Fan-Fan." It was a cross-sectional model of Krakowskie Przedmieście Street, depicting the underground placement of electric, telephone, and gas cables, and even an underground metro. Next to it was a photograph of the new Polish Radio building, which broadcasted one national and nine regional channels in six foreign languages. "Gorgeous," Mamo said. "All of it. The building, and especially the photograph. So elegant."

Fanny knew what Mamo was doing. "I know that you think this is *real* art, whereas what I do is just a stupid, tacky hobby."

"I never said that," Mamo replied. "Stop being so immature."

"You literally said I was a child playing with toys—"

"What do you want, Fanny? For me to go around town loudly exclaiming how much I adore your work? Now *that* would be tacky. I'm your mother. I try to be dignified, to give you space."

"Oh."

"Your drive is remarkable. I envy your ambition. Lord knows where you got it."

"You do?"

"Listen, Fanny. I just want the best for you. Is that such a crime? In this crazy world, I think that's quite gracious of me. I want for you safety, comfort, a place in society. A good partner. The best."

"Then we're in agreement. I need money," Fanny blurted. "I need to borrow from Avigdor."

"Borrow money?"

"You said he was rich."

"I never said he was rich," Mamo said. "What I said was: You don't know anything about him. Did you know he is spending the afternoon at the Montessori school where he used to fund all the education programs?"

Fanny stopped in her tracks. "Used to?"

"He has next to nothing. Lost it all in the Depression."

Fanny froze in shock. "What?"

"He thought *I* was the rich one!"

"But." Fanny gestured at the engagement ring.

"Family heirloom. We'll probably sell it."

"But, then, you're not even safe, not secure, no place in society. So why—"

"I don't want to be alone," Mamo replied. "And he's charming, and he likes art. We connected over a particular type of loss."

Fanny was dizzy. There really was nothing beneath her, no net. "What about his connections? He must still know people, have businesses, something that can help—"

"All he has left is a rotten canoe and a decaying tenement in the Jewish Quarter, and he's desperately trying to sell both . . . Speaking of which, I should let you know that we are strongly considering selling his home. We'll probably move to the countryside too, just like you."

"No, Mamo—"

"No what?" For once, Mamo stopped and looked at her. "I know what you're going to say and—"

"I can't. I can't marry Simon."

She'd said it to Mamo.

She couldn't believe it . . . she'd said it to Mamo!

Silence echoed through the gallery, ricocheting off the white walls. Mamo used her ringed hand to clasp Fanny's wrist. "You need to be careful. You're very smart and very talented. But also, very naïve. That's my fault."

At least for once, Mamo was taking the blame, even as what she said hurt.

"But don't make the biggest mistake of your life," Mamo went on. "In fact, I won't let you."

"Mamo, I'm a grown—"

"You have nothing, Fanny, you are a dependent. Your wedding is in less than three months. Now let's go to the dressmakers. If there's one thing that I know to be true, it's that you like a nice dress."

"No, I—"

"Yes."

The truth was, Mamo was right. Fanny was a dependent.

For now.

FANNY CLUTCHED THE KEY AS SHE WOUND AROUND THE streets of the Jewish Quarter, past the razor shop and galosh repair; crawling with beggars, it seemed even more desperate than when she'd last been here. Fanny handed a few złotys to a young, gaunt woman who sat by the gutter. She thought of the Chełm story her grandmother once told her: Everyone in town was terribly poor and they worried constantly. They decided that this was a waste of energy, so they hired a town worrier to do the worrying for them. But then they figured, if everyone was paying him, what did he have to worry about?

Fanny headed for the building off Chłodna Street. *Her* building. At least, for the next week.

It had only been twenty-four hours but Fanny loved this building—she loved *the having* of her own space. *A room of her own*, as the English novelist said. After the dress fitting, she'd gone straight to Avigdor and pleaded that he lend her space in his decaying tenement. As it turned out, the storefront had recently been abandoned by a family of tailors who could no longer make rent. "At least the space has windows!" he'd offered, surprisingly eager to help her. Of course, light was the last thing she needed for developing photos, but Fanny thanked him profusely and grabbed the keys.

In less than a week, Zosia and Fanny had cleared out old garments and fabric scraps, moved the sewing machine to the center of the room to function as a thematic centerpiece, painted the walls, set up a darkroom area in the back storeroom, advertised on posters at cafés, and handed out flyers. Finally, she'd show Mamo her real independence.

Zosia and Fanny had come together in defiance to help a cause greater than themselves. They'd told Chlebook they almost had the funds and that he should start lining up a lawyer. They'd also decided on pricing: 125 złotys per print. They needed to sell eight. Eight people needed to fall in love with her work . . . But before she could even think of that, she had to finish developing the photos. There was so much more to do. Only a few days until the trial—

"Hello, Fanny."

Fanny jumped ten feet. She pulled her coat tightly around her and positioned her key in her fist as if it were a weapon.

It was a police officer. He was young, younger than she was, and tall, and blond. "I need to talk to you, Fanny Zelshinsky."

"How do you know who I am?"

"We know everything about you."

"Who is *we*?"

"You put posters up all over the neighborhood about your upcoming show." He looked her right in the eyes. "You are giving away all your information."

"So what?" He was right: She'd been naïve, just as Mamo said.

"So, I'm here to tell you . . . well, to pass on a message."

"What message? From who?"

"My commanding officer."

"Let me guess . . . Broz?"

He nodded. "You cannot show photos of the police. If you do, you will be in serious trouble."

"It's not illegal," Fanny shot back.

"Actually, it is," the officer said. "You cannot share classified information, threaten public security, or promote anti-Polish ideals."

"I'm not sure that's true," she said. "Besides, isn't it illegal to harass civilians?"

"This is not harassing, this is a kind warning," he said. Then he added, under his breath, "Jews may not be civilians for long."

"For a burly policeman," she said, "you sure are worried about the power of a Jew girl."

Suddenly, she took a photo of him, a face shocked and unsure of himself, dislodged from his manliness.

Then, hiding her shaking, she turned and walked through the building's front door.

After that, Fanny did not leave the studio except for when she used the telephone at the pharmacy down the block and left a message for Mamo saying that she'd be working on her show and lying that she was staying with a friend. Abram had no idea where she was . . . which Fanny appreciated. *No distractions!* as Zosia always said. Fanny was developing, printing, choosing, hanging, cleaning.

Now, she scanned around her. The pictures were all up—the close-up of the skirt she'd shared with Wanda on that last day in class, a seamstress sewing the hem on a dress for Nat's show, the peasant's blouse, and of course, the shocked audience members at the fashion show. For a split second she'd thought about including the print of the police boots, each pair with their own demeanor, but the last thing she needed was trouble. She'd seen firsthand what had happened at Dzigan and Schumacher's show—how in an instant, a gala became gallows.

It was all looking good, so good, as if she'd been sharing work here forever, as if she and the room were one and the same; she'd implanted her vision on the walls, and the walls were creating a new version of Fanny. She already knew she'd do anything to keep the space; she'd do countryside portraits and Bund headshots and street art and whatever anyone needed . . .

Fanny looked at the time: three o'clock. She had two hours to get everything ready for the vernissage. She grabbed a few bags, put on her coat, and headed out. She couldn't afford caviar, of course, so had decided on vodka and candy, which she hoped would help create a festive feel and make people want to shop. As Mamo had taught her, one had to spend money to make money. They needed the cash tonight to pay for the lawyer for the trial—tomorrow.

At the confectioners, Fanny purchased krówka, cow candy, named for the brown bovine image on its yellow wrapper, a creamy caramel mix of milk, butter, and sugar, as well as Danusia candy bars with their chocolate-nut filling and deep blue wrappers. At the liquor store she batted her eyelashes and asked the stocker if he would carry the bottles home for her. He couldn't say no.

But when they arrived back at her door, he was the first one to gasp. Fanny, head in a million places, hadn't even noticed the graffiti on her door.

It was small but sharp. In deep black paint, it said "Zhidova," *Jew girl.*

She stopped breathing. She scanned down the hallways—no one.

"Don't worry about me," she said to the boy who was blushing.

"Can I clean it for you?" he asked.

For a second, she was about to say yes and point him to a pail. But she stopped herself. "No, thank you," she said. "It's the name of my show."

CHAPTER 28

Zosia

"My gut tells me you are in love with this one," Zosia said to a woman looking at one of Fanny's photos. The woman was as unfamiliar to her as the words emerging from her lips.

"Am I? It does remind me of something . . . something from my childhood, yet I'm not sure what."

It was an abstract photo of the edge of a perfume bottle—one could make out the Daj-Go brand name on the side, and Zosia wasn't sure what this had to do with anyone's childhood, but it didn't matter. "Yes, I really do sense that from you. The image completes you." Where had she even gotten this language? Zosia was trying to keep her head on straight. She had three hours now to sell, sell, sell. People, dozens of people, were here at the exhibition, looking at Fanny's art: Fashion Café regulars, students from the university and several of Fanny's friends from gymnasium. Though they were keeping their fundraising plans a secret, Zosia had not invited her Dror comrades, who not only had no money to spend on art but would have been rather shocked to see her acting as a wheeling-dealing gallerist. So far, no police.

Zosia thought of Wanda, their honorary absentee guest. Wanda *needed* them. "Would you like to speak directly with the photographer?" Zosia asked the woman and handed her a chocolate. "I'll give you special access." She gestured for Fanny to come over.

"What does this piece mean to you?" the woman asked.

Zosia hoped Fanny would say something intense, complicated, sales-forward. Instead, she said, "I'm a photographer, not a writer."

"It's so nice to be among all this art," the woman continued dreamily. "I have three shows to see tonight! Nineteen thirty-eight is shaping up to be a wonderful year."

"So, will you buy it?" Zosia blurted.

"Sure, I'll take it!" she replied. "And I'll also take that one." She pointed to a print of a dress in a department store window.

Two hundred and fifty złotys! In the first hour. In her entire life, Zosia had never imagined such sums. She felt strangely positive; this was going to work.

"How are you doing?" she asked Fanny.

"I'm dizzy—this whole show is wild! All my art, my friends from such different walks. I feel like I am both inside and outside the experience at the same time. It's like I have a fever."

"We're doing well," Zosia told her. "We've already sold two."

"Three! I sold that one of the Fashion Café audience to an upper-crust poet who's in the front row of the image."

Zosia ran over with tape and a pen and wrote SOLD beneath all three pieces.

"I'll take this one," someone called to them. Then, when he saw Zosia, he smiled. "Is this you? Are you the model?"

It was Zosia in front of the beauty parlor. She blushed.

Fanny gave the man a hug—a rich acquaintance, Zosia imagined. Zosia followed with the tape and kept a running log: 5 paintings, 625 złotys already!

"Fanny Zelshinsky, I'm the editor at *Polish Women's Voice*," a woman said to her friend.

"Want to buy a photo?" Zosia blurted. "I'm her manager."

"I'm not sure about that, but I may have some work for Fanny. Can you come by our office next week?"

"Sure, I'll do that," Fanny said.

"Listen." Zosia put her arm around this woman, directing her to a photo of a seamstress sewing a dress. "How about a photo for your office? This one is all about women's work."

Zosia saw: Abram had come in. He was wearing a dark cap and a long wool coat and his cheeks were flushed.

Zosia's heart fluttered, still.

He was carrying a box of chocolates from Wedel. She watched as he approached Fanny and they began speaking in hushed tones. Zosia tried not to stare, not to notice how their bodies inched closer together. She could not make out what they were saying. What if Fanny did love him and just didn't know it and he loved her and he—

Zosia turned to a new "client" to distract herself. "Please, look at this picture of a designer making art. It's art about art; very modern."

"As an old friend of Lenore's, I feel I should support Fanny. I'll take it."

"Really? Alright, wonderful." Seven hundred fifty złotys.

"Come here!" but Fanny was calling her over. She had no choice.

"I told him what we're doing here," Fanny whispered. "After all, he knew about the article. I hope you don't mind, Zosia. We need all the support we can get right now."

"No, of course, I mean, sure, of course." She still couldn't talk to Abram like a normal human.

Someone on the other side of the room summoned Fanny, and Zosia was left to stand with Abram.

"Seems like you're selling out—"

"You two make a perfect couple," she blurted like an idiot. "You're a match made in heaven. Entirely *bashert.* Opposites attract and all that."

"A couple?" Abram repeated.

"You want the same things, the same places," Zosia went on. "She's good for you."

"I don't think so." His brow wrinkled in confusion. "She broke up with me. Told me she wasn't interested last week."

"Oh!"

There was something in his eyes she couldn't read. She could feel his warm breath. He was close, too close.

"I'm so sorry," she went on. "I didn't know."

He shrugged.

"The heart wall is thick," Zosia said, consoling him, "but it's still a fragile organ."

"Thank you," he said, softly. Then he offered her the Wedel box; it was a wafer cake with hazelnut cream. "Fanny thought you might like this."

"Me?" She looked up at him but stopped at the sight behind: It was Lenore. She wore a tight mustard-yellow frock with poufy sleeves and an enormous bow at the neck, along with a small brown cap. To Zosia, she looked a little like a sausage with mustard.

Zosia politely excused herself and headed straight for Fanny's side.

"You came, Mamo." Her friend was clearly shocked.

"You left me a message and so I did."

Zosia grabbed Fanny's hand as they watched Mamo look at print after print. She said nothing. Then she turned to Fanny, a lone tear slaloming down her cheek.

"Beautifully composed," Mamo said, gesturing at the photo of the gilded mirror. "Deep and graceful."

"You like it?"

"I don't know what you'll do with your talent, or how it will help you," Mamo went on. "It will probably hinder your life. Complicate it, at least."

"Thanks?"

"But you do have it."

Fanny squeezed Zosia's hand, hard. "I'm independent, Mamo," she said. "See?"

"Fanny," Mamo said after a long pause. She turned toward the front door with the Jew graffiti, and Zosia and Fanny followed. "If you're crazy enough to throw away your marriage, then at least come with Avigdor and me. We're going to Hungary." Now her voice became a whisper. "There's too much political instability here, the upcoming elections, Hitler, extremism on every end, all of it. You can't handle it on your own. No one can. We've decided to relocate to a village outside Budapest where Avigdor has friends. There's room for you there. Or if that's so unappealing, then Avigdor has cousins in Liverpool. It's not the time to be naïve or contrarian. Sometimes, like at a party, it's wisest to leave a little before the end."

Zosia watched the women stare at each other. They were a mirror reflection: the same high cheekbones, the same fierce eyebrows, dark and perfectly curved.

"I'm independent, Mamo," Fanny repeated, even as her eyes filled with tears.

"Don't be stupid." Mamo shook her head and left the studio.

"She never left a party early," Fanny said to Zosia as they watched her ascend into her car.

But there was no time to brood. Both women watched in shock as their next guest arrived.

Marek.

The air lodged in Zosia's throat. He was accompanied by the young policeman. Both wore full uniforms.

Marek entered the room, and chatter became mutters became silence. He slowly walked the perimeter, examining each photo.

People started to slip out the door.

Marek threw his cigarette on the floor and stubbed it out with his boot.

He came and stood right in front of them.

Fanny squeezed her hand—tight.

"Well, well, well, it *is* just fashion," he said. "Good work, little girl."

Fanny said nothing.

Marek turned, coughed, and walked out.

Zosia would have collected herself and continued to sell, but . . . everyone had gone.

The room was empty.

There was nobody left.

Seven hundred fifty złotys. It just wasn't enough.

"Fucking police," Fanny said as they walked over to Dror.

"Mind your French."

"I'll speak French all I like. I fucking studied it. The trial is tomorrow. Tomorrow! It's in fourteen hours. What can we do?"

"We have to go," Zosia said. "We must show Wanda support and bring her home if she's acquitted, *ptu ptu ptu*. We must witness it firsthand, see the sham for ourselves, and record it, in words and images. We need to tell the whole country about this perversion of justice. And we must get our answers. We have to be on that five a.m. train."

At Dror, in her room, Zosia packed a few of her things into her beat-up bag in case they'd need to stay over in Przemyśl. Fanny paced in the tiny area near her bed until she was nearly knocked over by Rachel, who burst into the room.

"I have our mail," her roommate said and tossed Zosia a letter. Her mother. Zosia sighed. Perhaps if all her disappointments and failures came at once, they would each feel a bit less painful.

Please, dear. Help. Come home. We miss you. Please.

Zosia closed her eyes. How could her mother not understand that Zosia was meant to help not just her family but her people?

"Also," Rachel said, "Mira wants to talk to you."

"Mira? Now?"

Mira was standing in the doorway. "What are you doing?"

"Packing a few things for—"

"For Wanda's trial?" Mira asked.

Fanny and Rachel both stared, silent. *Honesty above all.* "Yes," Zosia said.

Mira pointed at the newspaper on Zosia's cot. "Did you write an article about Wanda, after I told you to stay out of it? Did you visit her in prison?"

"Not in this paper, but—yes."

Fanny made her way to Zosia's side.

"How did you get money to afford the train tickets to the trial?" Mira asked.

"I was selling work at an art show—"

Mira looked at her for a long moment and shook her head.

Zosia paused and fought back tears. It was all unraveling. "I understand," she muttered as Mira left the room. She understood nothing. She felt Fanny grab her hand and squeeze.

"Oh my God! Oh my God!" Rachel shrieked.

"For God's sakes," Fanny said. "What?"

"I got one."

"What?"

"Zosia," Rachel said, holding up a yellow paper. "I got a visa! I'm going to Eretz Israel!" She ran out of the room.

It was the first time Zosia actually saw someone get a visa.

Right in front of her, her fantasy was illuminated, brought to life like magic—but for someone else. She watched her own dreams crumple, hopeless. Zosia thought of Rachel and that first night, how she'd suggested that Wanda was going to help Zosia get a visa, how she'd seemed envious. Now it was Rachel who held it.

What *had* Wanda wanted to tell her? She would likely never know, never get a visa, never move on.

"Where will I go now?" Zosia looked at Fanny, blinking back tears. All she did was try, but everything was going wrong.

Fanny grabbed Zosia's suitcase, grabbed her hand, and told her, "*We're* heading to the station. We are not missing the first train out." Then she gave Zosia a hug. "Onward."

The women settled into their third-class seats. The bench felt uncomfortable, almost aggressive in its uncompromising firmness.

"Where will I go if I can't go back to Dror?" Zosia asked. "If I don't go back to Dror?"

"You can sleep on my studio floor."

"I'm poor but I'm not a rat."

"So go back to your family. Take time to figure things out. I'll come visit," Fanny said. "Who knows . . . once I break off my engagement, though don't ask me when or how, I might have to move in with your family too. Better than Budapest with Avigdor."

"I can't go back to my family," Zosia snapped.

"Why not?" Fanny asked.

A maelstrom of thoughts and excuses ran through Zosia's head—*the movement, the promised land, Jewish independence.* "My father was attacked in a pogrom," she blurted instead. "We all were, but he was the one who suffered the injury."

"What are you talking about?" Fanny asked. The train shook. "What happened?"

Without thinking, Zosia launched into her story. She told it all—the chants, the knocking, the way that no one came to the door, the way no one let them in. Then, the running, the boxes, the attic. The fire. The bloodcurdling scream that haunted her. She told the whole story of the pogrom—for the first time, words tumbling out, picking up speed like the vehicle upon which they rode. "The fire had caught him," Zosia told Fanny. "Burned up his whole face. Tateh is completely blind."

"Oh Zosia." Fanny placed her hand on top of Zosia's and Zosia felt its warmth.

They sat like that for a while.

"What I keep thinking—" Zosia felt dizzy.

"Go on." Her friend squeezed her hand, urging her. "I want to hear it all."

"What I keep thinking is that I listened to him." Zosia hung her head. "I ran and tried to find help."

"Of course you did."

"It was my fault. I know you'll say it wasn't, but it was. I ran away and it saved me, but it ruined my father's life."

Zosia was crying. The tears rolled off her like Ping-Pong balls.

Fanny put her arms around her, held her tight. "You did the right thing."

"A few weeks later, I went to my first Dror meeting. I found people who also understood the dangers of living in Poland and who had active responses to it. I understood: I had not defended my father, but now it was time for me to defend my people."

Zosia had soaked Fanny's lapel with her tears. She started to apologize, but Fanny reached into her handbag and passed her a silky handkerchief. Zosia hesitated for a moment—it was so luxurious—but then she took it. The women sat side by side and stared out the window, viewing tree trunk after tree trunk, as if they were passing through a forest of lines.

"Is that why you find it hard to get close to people?" Fanny asked after a while.

Zosia thought about Abram, Fanny, her lack of friends . . . Maybe it was true.

"By the way," Fanny asked, "what ever happened to the culprits?"

Zosia shook her head. "There were never any arrests. No accountability. No justice. The antisemites roam free. And, Fanny"—she paused—"they really hate us."

The women were silent. The train clicked forward.

"That's why," Zosia added, "we have to leave." She thought of Rachel's slip of paper, and for the first time it struck her: Leaving was not just a pipe dream or a theory or a romantic scheme, but a real possibility.

CHAPTER 29

Fanny

"ORDER IN MY COURT!" THE JUDGE BANGED HIS GAVEL.

Fanny's heart waltzed: They were here.

The courtroom was small, so much smaller than Fanny imagined in her head, and the number of women on trial was almost as big as the rest of the crowd, legal workers and witnesses included. At the front, a corpulent judge sat at an elevated desk; Fanny couldn't tell if he was nonplussed or simply exhausted. On one side of him, "the state." On the other, all sixteen women, young and rail thin, with matching circles under their eyes, dark ovals stretching down their faces. Then there were a few benches set up for the public, Fanny assumed. She'd looked around her at solemn, teary faces. Was Wanda's family here? Parents? Cousins? An activist lover? She had no idea. It struck her that she didn't really know Wanda at all . . . Fanny could barely see her from her spot in the room.

Fanny placed her hand on her camera bag. Zosia, next to her, had her pen in hand, ready to start writing. After her harrowing story, which Fanny was still absorbing, Zosia spent the rest of the train ride, and then the entire walk from the station, repeating: We must record every word. Everything.

Fanny had also been trying to absorb her mother's comments at her show. There it was—the praise and recognition she'd been waiting for for so long: Mamo liked her work. However, Mamo's burst of acceptance did not make her feel *that* happy. Perhaps Mamo's opinion was not worth as much as she'd imagined, Fanny mulled. Perhaps it didn't matter what Mamo thought of her, either good or bad. She didn't need to impress her mother. And the flipside: She didn't need to refuse something, or someone, just because Mamo pushed it on her.

Fanny had been told very explicitly that she could not take photographs, that she must keep her camera in her bag. It was a miracle they'd even been allowed inside—and one only granted because of Fanny's portraits of the police officer's wife, which she delivered in a package with a bow. If nothing else, Fanny knew a nice touch. He'd snuck them into the back row.

"Order in my court!"

"This is the trial of the state against sixteen women for treasonous activity," an officer announced.

The audience groaned.

"Order!"

Suddenly, Wanda stood, her chair, caught up in her cuffs, banging as she moved. The room gasped. "She's so skinny," Zosia whispered. "Even skinnier than last time." Fanny's stomach knotted at the sight of the woman, all jutting bones and sinking bags.

Wanda turned to the judge, looked him directly in the eyes, and simply said, "My honorable sir." This caused a new round of gasps and commotion, but the judge gestured at the officer who'd rushed over indicating that he should leave her be. "Please, sir," Wanda went on, "please, good honorable sir, may I say a few words?"

More gasps.

The judge shook his head.

"Please, sir, pl—"

"Fine. Let her speak."

The room was shocked into silence. Even the prosecutor looked surprised, but then he rolled his eyes. *Beautiful women always get their way,* Fanny could just imagine him thinking. *Now we all have to wait . . .* Fanny tried to silently slip out her Leica. They were surrounded by law enforcement, but what the hell. Zosia didn't stop her; she was already writing furiously. *Every word must be recorded.*

Wanda stood in front of the charged women. "Thank you, Your

Honor," she started. She faced the judge but also turned to the pews. "I would just like to say a few words on behalf of myself and my fellow accused. And those few words begin with"—and here she paused for effect—"Poland is great."

There were confused murmurs around the room, from Zosia too.

"Poland," Wanda went on, "is the world's most sophisticated nation."

"Hear, hear," someone called out.

"We are a nation that has fought for our independence time and time again, for hundreds of years. Nestled between the huge forces of Europe that can't stop trying to conquer us, we have risen to show that we will not be defeated. We are a diverse country, made up of many minorities—we are the first in the world to have a charter that protected religious freedoms, back in 1245—and yet, there is still something solid, something about us, something so very Polish in our hearts that keeps us going. Our Polishness, and perhaps here I mean something about our pride in our land, our inspiration from our heritage, our commitment to our passions, is a permanent fixture in our souls."

Fanny could feel the room warm up. She thought of Mamo's advice: *When you're bargaining, start by complimenting the merchandise, then ask for a reduction in price. Some people start by insulting the wares, but this never works. Everyone appreciates a compliment.* But where was Wanda going with this?

"I am so deeply proud to be a citizen of this country, the country with the world's greatest pianist, chemist, astronomer, and cabaret artists." Titters. "I am as proud a Pole as is possible to be. It is my honor to stand in front of you today in a Polish courtroom at a Polish courtroom proceeding. I am proud to be tried in front of each and every one of you as a Pole—a Pole who could never imagine engaging in any form of treason against this beautiful and complicated country."

Fanny felt herself choke up. She too felt this pride. She was Polish, born and bred, a prime citizen of this diverse and special country that, despite it all, bred countless political groups and impassioned parties, and its essence would never leave her. She could never flee to Hungary.

"I could go on about valuing all people, helping others, class equality," Wanda continued. "But I won't. What I want to talk about today is truth."

The audience hushed.

"What is *the truth* really? Is truth what we feel or what we think? When we tell ourselves to be guided by the truth, do we mean emotional truth or intellectual truth? Which truth is more true? Emotions may seem like the opposite of calculations, but wisdom emerges only when the two coalesce. The truth can be complicated, and ugly, and it's often not what we want it to be. But we must remember it and let it guide us."

Click.

A few people turned to look at Fanny, but the guards didn't notice.

"I am Polish," Wanda went on. "You are Polish, honorable sir. We are so busy dividing ourselves to define ourselves. Our identity is not found through difference but connection. Us versus them makes no sense when ultimately we all want the same things, even if we think we can get to them differently.

"We are stronger together. We must protect and fight for each other, not against each other. Until we understand that, nothing will ever change."

The entire room burst into applause. Fanny felt her heart balloon in her chest: They may not have been able to help Wanda, but . . . Wanda didn't need their help!

The judge banged his gavel. "Order in my court!"

The prosecution got up. None of the women being charged had accepted representation by the government lawyer so he had little work to do. The young women sat in forced silence as they were accused of treason. It took the arrogant prosecutor less than five minutes to make his pathetic case, that is, that communism is illegal and these women engaged in activity organized in conjunction with the Communist Party.

When he sat down, the judge announced that he didn't even need a break.

The room rumbled in anticipation.

The judge held his hands together in front of him and pronounced. "The women are found . . . guilty."

Fanny could not believe this.

"They will be sentenced to twelve years in prison."

Twelve years?

The room became noisy; the gavel was banged.

"We'll fight this, we'll appeal," Fanny said to Zosia and grabbed her hand, which was limp. Inside, Fanny too felt limp. She understood something: Her Poland, this beautiful Poland that Wanda went on and on about, was going extinct. How could this be happening? Something dislodged inside Fanny. It was one thing to lose her place in her classes—both academic and social—and another to deal with crooked police, but this was beyond all that. It was like something she'd known to rely upon her whole life—something bigger than her or family—was, well, poof. The world felt jagged, cold, lined with spikes. A cactus of an existence, no soft spots.

She was about to tell Zosia this, to share her existential shudder, to ask her what she thought, but her friend broke away and was barreling against the crowd toward the front of the room. Fanny followed.

"Wanda!" Zosia called.

"Zosia, Fanny, what are you doing here?" Wanda turned and said something to the guard who was leading her away. He shrugged and they stopped.

"What can we do to help you?" Fanny said. "We'll try Vlad and Chlebook again, and we'll try again to find a lawyer and we'll let people know that you are a good person."

Wanda looked right at them. "Thank you."

"Wanda, I know this might sound out of line, but do you know how I can get a visa?" Zosia pleaded. "What did you want to tell me, that first night I was in Warsaw, at the university?"

"I'm sorry," Wanda said. She spoke quietly. "It was about your family."

"My family?"

"I'm sorry, Zosia," she whispered. "I'm so sorry."

"For what?"

"It was my family home. That night of the pogrom. You and your father came."

Fanny watched the color seep from Zosia's face.

"The truth was, we heard you. But everyone was so scared, so shocked, we hid in the cellar. We couldn't risk opening the door. I've felt terrible, Zosia. I really have." Wanda shook her cuffed hands. "If anything, I am guilty of that—of prioritizing myself and my family."

"What?" Fanny couldn't believe this. Wanda, the woman they'd spent all this time trying to save, had been the one to shut Zosia out.

"I'm guilty of that," Wanda repeated as the guards took Wanda away. "Guilty of family."

"Are you alright?" Fanny leaned into her friend who was shaking violently. She tried to put her arms around her, but Zosia flinched and pulled away.

"I need to go." Zosia pressed the notebook with Wanda's words into Fanny's hands and ran out the door.

CHAPTER 30

Zosia

If riding into Grochów seemed like entering 1895, then Byten was like entering 1795. The "station" was a platform twenty minutes on foot from the main road, itself illuminated by a smattering of kerosene lamps. Before she knew it, Zosia found herself at the beginning of the town's main street. She was sure it was a twenty-minute walk, but she'd only been on the go for five. Did distance grow in one's memory? Or had the walk felt like twenty minutes in her youth because every minute back then was stretched out like sticky candy, every sensation registered, considered, absorbed? Every detail was noticed, the difference between train station and home a universe apart. But time sped up as she aged, as each second marked a lesser percentage of her overall existence.

Zosia was spiraling.

Breathe.

Linshom.

It was Wanda . . . she felt hot, her face burning. It was Wanda's fault they hadn't been rescued. It was Wanda who hadn't let her in. Wanda, for whom she'd risked everything. There'd been no political secret, no visa tip, just a meager apology for ruining their lives.

Knuckles rapping on hard wood, panting, sweating. Let us in, please, please!

Zosia was reeling with confusion. Wanda had spoken about the glories of Poland, just as Abram had done, and she was right, and he was right, and it was true, and Zosia was Polish, she'd felt it in the moment, despite all her longings to flee. Maybe certain elements could never be extracted from one's soul, she'd thought, and then it hit her again, how Rachel's papers had come, how she too might one day actually get up and go, go, go, how that was truly possible . . . but then . . . Wanda. Wanda was the culprit, the cheater, the reason. It was all down to Wanda.

Zosia had to see her family.

Zosia trudged through the bluish haze of the streetlights, past the synagogue and the bank. It was so terribly quiet: How had she spent most of her life in this silence? How loud the pogrom chants had appeared against this muzzled background. The damp ground wet her boots. Zosia's legs walked, but they felt alien, distinct from her mind. Everything felt detached. She was still in shock.

She tapped her pocket. *Only a person with money checks their wallet,* her mother used to say.

Her mother would be happy to see her. She tried to focus on that. She envisioned the scene: *It's been so long, my darling. I forgot what you looked like,* Mameh would say, gripping her wrists as if to make sure she stayed put. She'd look her over, tell her the big city had left a stamp on her. *Don't worry if there's not enough food,* Zosia would say. *Of course there's enough!* her mother would lie. Zosia would inhale the sweet, eggy smell of baking; she'd hear her sister and her friends scampering around. Bella would grab her arm, lead her to the wedding-dress-in-progress that she was sewing. Then, Zosia would trap her mother in the doorframe, fix her apron strings, and tell her: *You see, Mamenyu, I'm fine. You're fine. We're all fine. All those panicked letters were for nothing.*

Now, suddenly, close to home, she felt ravenous for her parents and Bella, desperate to see them. She had to tell them: Wanda did it. Zosia picked up the pace. She passed the town's shabby storefronts and decrepit wooden houses; she passed Byten's kosher bakery and noticed how the entire back wall lay crumbling in charred shambles; it hadn't been rebuilt since the pogrom. In fact, there was the town library, with, Zosia was shocked, shards of glass still piled in the yard. The tiny building where the tailor had once worked had been inflected with gaping injuries. All the small structures along her way were bruised with scorch marks. Zosia had changed so much, yet Byten had remained frozen in tragedy, unable to afford renovation, unable to afford life.

What if she never saw the town repaired? She was struck by the permanence of decay, of movement, of choice. A maelstrom of feelings. Zosia pounded down the road. Engulfed by fury like the fires, her fists were hot, her cheeks full.

It wasn't my fault!

It was Wanda, Wanda all along.

Now Zosia entered her front yard for the first time since she'd left for Warsaw. The gate creaked, as it always had, alerting the little wooden house that a guest was about to enter. From outside, she could smell the scent of what was once comfort and calm. For a second she flashed to that time years ago when the cholent had not cooked through. They'd panicked and Mameh had to call the Shabbos goy to bring it back to the baker's oven.

Zosia opened the door, walked into the kitchen as if a ghost in her own home.

Then, her mother. In the hall, facing the doorway, on the cooking warpath, in an apron. "Zosia?" She gasped.

"Mameh." Zosia was shocked at the sight of her, all bones and joints, angular and rake thin.

"Zosia." Her mother ran over and grabbed her so she couldn't breathe. Zosia hugged back, feeling her mother's spine protrude from her skin. The house was cold, so cold, and dark. Dampness had settled into moldy corners.

"It's been so long, my darling. I forgot what you looked like." She grabbed her wrists and pulled away to look at her. Zosia looked back: her near twin, except for the creases of experience, the indelible marks of caring for others. "Let me look at you . . . The way you wear your cap, wrap your coat. The boots, the bag, how you fasten your belt to the side—you've become a regular city girl. Warsaw has put her stamp on you."

"I suppose she has."

"Come," her mother said. Still clasping one wrist, she pulled Zosia with her to their bedroom.

In the darkness, Tateh.

Her father no longer went to work, to the shops, to synagogue. He stayed in his room, sitting in a chair, waiting to be cared for, fed, changed, waiting.

Mameh led her straight to him. He grunted from deep in his throat, acknowledging a presence. Zosia kneeled in front of him as if he were a king. She put her hand in his. His leathery fingers did not startle but trembled slightly, and then, they crowned in around hers, firm. He knew it was her, a palm reader. "My baby," he said. "How I've missed you. There is nothing so whole as a broken heart."

"I need to talk to you both," Zosia said as tears ran down her face. "I need to tell you something."

"Go ahead," her mother said and, as always, she began to comb her husband's hair. *Commitment*, Zosia thought, *gives your life meaning.*

She hesitated for a moment, then slipped her hand from her father's clasp and dug into her bag. From it, she removed a stack of złotys and put it in her father's hand.

"Oh, Zosia," her mother said. "We don't need all that, it's too much—"

"Shush," she said. "It's for the wedding." The art show money would not go to a crooked lawyer to help the woman who hurt her but to her family. "Besides, I need to tell you the truth. I found out who did it."

Zosia was about to form the words, but her mother looked at her quizzically, and she wondered: What was the point? The truth would not un-hurt them. What did it matter that it was Wanda had rejected their knocks and caused Tateh his vision? Zosia looked at her parents, vulnerable and soft with age. If places were reversed, she would have done the same thing. Her leader was a mere human.

"I'm sorry," Zosia said instead. It wasn't her fault, but still. "I'm so sorry." *I'm sorry for leaving you, for wanting so badly to leave Poland, for all the anguish I've caused, for all the pain we cause those we love, our families, our friends, our countries. I'm so very sorry.*

"For what?" her mother asked.

She stared at her father, took him all in . . . She'd been carting around mounds and mounds of guilt. But it wasn't her fault.

She stared at her mother, took her all in . . . For better and for worse, Poland was her country. Her family was her family. She missed them.

And yet. She still wanted to leave for a Jewish land. She did not want to stay here, with scorched buildings and murderous slogans. It was both things. To leave, and to love. A part of her had also frozen in the heat of the pogrom. But she had to let her feelings thaw; she had to hold and experience both the desire to abscond and the guilt and sadness over absconding. She had to live in the gray zones, black and white but also white and black, like Fanny's photos. She'd been running to a principle, but she'd also been running from pain. She'd been running toward, but also away. She didn't need to tell them the truth; she needed to feel it.

As for Wanda . . . She'd marred Zosia's life but had also given her a new one. Wanda was a threshold, offering the possibility of future. Wanda was just Wanda. In Hebrew, a healer.

A single tear trickled down Tateh's worn cheek. "My Zosheleh," he said. "You are a good person. We may have our differences, but I raised a good person."

"Thank you, Tateh," Zosia said. "Now where's my sister Bella? We need to plan a wedding!"

CHAPTER 31

Fanny

Back in Warsaw, Fanny ran. She clutched Zosia's notebook, confused about all of Wanda's words, anxiously wondering where her friend had gone after the awful revelation. Fanny was alone, and she felt it. The tectonic plates had shifted from under her. Her precious Poland, the land of soft *kolachki* cookies and rosy youth, had dissipated. All that was left were thin air, cracked glass, fine lines. Nothing was safe, and she could not look for salvation outside herself because, well, it simply didn't exist. No one was looking out for her, even if she was a Zelshinsky. She was not exempt from danger; *no one* was exempt. The only safety was inside.

By the time she reached Mamo's apartment, she was sweating. She wiped her brow with her kerchief, the very same one that had been drenched with Zosia's tears, noting the thinness of the fabric, the way it was made up mostly of holes, of nothing between the fibers. Just like her skin, all pores. "Mamo!" she called from the front door. "I need to—"

But she was shocked at the sight. The apartment had been transformed into what looked like a warehouse, all boxes and draped sheets. The grand deco armoire was gone; it had left a mark on the wall, tracing its own farewell.

"Fanny, how nice of you to come home," Mamo said, emerging in a robe. Then she exploded. "Where in the world have you been? I've been worried sick."

Fanny gestured at the unfamiliar surrounds. "Home?"

"I told you, I'm moving to Hungary. I'm selling whatever I can.

It's not easy to find Polish antique buyers these days, people with taste and money. It never was an easy combination but now—"

Fanny had no home, not for now. And still. "I can't marry him, Mamo." She put down the notebook and slipped the ring off her finger. It wouldn't save her. "I'm independent."

They both stared at the jewelry held up between them. Off one's finger, the ring was small and light, mostly just air.

"It is rather tacky," Mamo said. She knew she'd lost.

"I agree," Fanny said. "Please, give it back to Mrs. Brodasz."

Mamo shook her head. "A truly independent person would end their engagement by themselves, without their mother's help."

Fanny stared at Mamo in disbelief. But her anger melted quickly. Her mother was right. Fanny understood it: A person could be wrong about so much, and then, once in a while, entirely, completely correct. Fanny would indeed have to take care of this on her own.

But first, she had one other thing to do.

"I'll move in with Avigdor for a little while, and then we're leaving for Hungary," Mamo said as Fanny made for the door. "I hope you will use your independence wisely and choose to come with us."

"YES, YES, PUT THE TEXT THERE," FANNY TOLD ABRAM AS they feverishly took down the remaining fashion shots and began to put up a new show—all about Wanda, about politics, real politics. She was calling it *Hero/Villain.*

Abram was beginning to hang Wanda's words. He and Fanny had taken Zosia's notebook filled with the transcript of Wanda's speech, and they were printing copies of it—on Wanda's printing press, which they'd dug up and brought over, putting it in the place of the sewing machine. The press hummed enthusiastically, strengthening Fanny's determination.

What is the truth, really? Is truth what we feel, or what we think? she glimpsed on the page. Her conversation with Mamo had really brought home Wanda's speech: We were all complicated, layered, and confused. Fanny had been mulling it over all night: Wanda's actions had deeply hurt Zosia and her family, but it wasn't Wanda's fault that they'd been attacked by anti-Jewish thugs, and she'd taken responsibility and apologized. Even if Wanda had suspect partisan views, she had great agency. She was important, an example for a country. Fanny had to forget about the personal and focus on the political, on the greater good, just as Zosia had taught her. She needed this art show to tell the truth of what was happening in Poland, to help save her country. This was all so much bigger than any one person, just as any one person couldn't have so much sway over Fanny. Fanny didn't *need* Wanda, except as a subject: a subject who was a fighter, a rebel, and an inspiration, a hero and an enemy all rolled into one. Wanda's story taught and empowered. Wanda was brave.

Which pictures should she include? She looked at the one from the hunger strike with Zosia on the ground, in the middle.

Again, doubt niggled. Would this show hurt Zosia? Zosia had said they must tell the world the truth. But Fanny reminded herself: One must hold many truths at once, and then, keeping this in mind, one had to decide how to act. She wanted to act for truth.

This was certainly no university exhibition, and there would be no Parisian gallerists.

"Any word from Zosia?" Abram asked, coming up behind her.

Fanny shook her head, and her insides flipped in fear.

She flicked to the next picture: Marek, drooling on his desk.

"Put this one up next," she told Abram. Enough threats. Let the world see this dozing wildebeest for who he was.

"We must invite all the journalists," Abram said. "We're opening tomorrow?"

"Tonight," Fanny said. "There's no time to lose. We need to reverse the sentence as soon as possible."

The truth can be complicated, and ugly, Wanda's words went, *and it's often not what we want it to be. But we must remember it, and let it guide us.*

Then she picked up the next photo from the pile. It was the one that she'd taken on that forever-changing night when she and Zosia were waiting for Wanda in her office: the picture of the nighttime, looking onto blackness, a window into the abyss. Her self-portrait, she'd teased when Zosia had accused her of capturing nothing. Now, she decided to call it "Nothing." All oily physicality, it was dark, mysterious, ominous. It would be the centerpiece of the show.

People, dozens and dozens of them, were milling about. They'd invited journalists, movement members, activists, and Vlad.

"Twelve years?" he said to Fanny, and she was sure he was about to cry.

"We're going to get her out," Fanny told him and gave him a quick embrace. "We will."

"Can we?"

"We have to. I'm doing this show to tell the story."

"I'll write about Wanda," Vlad said. "I'll write about the trial, about all of this. We need to release Wanda now, before the next election, before Polish elections, chaotic as they are, don't even exist anymore. Before Europe collapses into war."

Groups gathered at each picture; they pointed, discussed, disagreed, and questioned.

"How did you get images inside the precinct?" a Bundist asked her. "Staged or real?"

"It's all real," Fanny said, "whether we like it or not." Fanny took in the room. This may have been the catalyst they needed. People were making plans. They'd write articles, speak to local political figures, and make sure Wanda and the women were released. So far, at least, the police hadn't returned. Maybe bravery was the answer. Maybe the fascist bullies could be stopped.

Fanny looked around at the crowd that had gathered. She hadn't invited Mamo. It didn't matter if her mother saw how independent she was, she'd realized. In fact, *that* was independence.

"Zosia!" Abram saw her first.

Fanny yelped in relief. "Are you okay?" She rushed over to her.

"Yes," Zosia said, and hugged her. "I'm fine, really."

Suddenly, Abram was right there, and Fanny watched as Zosia fell into him. He held her, tight, firm, as if he were holding her together.

"Is it alright if we share these photos of Wanda?" Fanny asked. "Considering what she did—"

Zosia nodded.

"What did she do?" Abram asked. Zosia began to tell him.

Just then Vlad approached Fanny from behind and tapped her shoulder. She followed him to a corner. "My friend just brought this." He pushed a newspaper toward her. "Did you see?"

Fanny took the pages from him and read aloud: A transit camp was being set up for German Jews who had Polish citizenship in Zbąszyń, on the border. The Polish Jews were being thrown out of Germany, but Poland did not want to take them back.

We need to help those in need . . . We cannot fear what's inside . . . We cannot fear. Wanda's speech echoed through her mind. Poland was on the brink, and Fanny had to act, to do her part. "I'm going."

"Photograph them," Vlad said and shook his head. "Photograph us all."

"REFUGEE," FANNY SAID ALOUD, TRYING THE WORD ON HER tongue.

She had taken an overnight train, yet she felt no fatigue.

Zosia had offered to come, Abram too. But Fanny had declined. She needed to do things on her own.

The transit camp had been set up in a flour mill and the enclosed surrounding area on the outskirts of Zbaszyn. A series of huts were fenced in by a single wire. Guards stood watch.

Fanny was ready to flirt and immediately pulled out papers. "I'm press," she said, about to claim she worked for *Polish Women's*

Voice. It had taken her numerous tries to get the correct press passes. Indeed, she hoped to sell these photos to papers in England and America, to tell the world this story.

The guard looked Fanny up and down with disdain. Fanny did not smile. She did not take out the Leica, not yet.

"Thirty minutes," he said. "Hurry up. And no commotion in there."

She entered. The camp was eerily quiet despite hosting thousands of refugees.

These Jews had Polish papers but had lived in Germany, some for decades, and some, for their entire lives, she thought as she watched a group of children kicking an old gray ball. Of course, Poland's new citizenship law, which stated that anyone who'd lived outside the country for more than five years was no longer a citizen, meant they were no longer Polish either. They were of nowhere now.

She grabbed snacks from her bag: chocolate, cookies . . . She should have brought more.

She took out the Leica and began. The kids playing football. *Click.* Young ones play-acting a schoolroom with a teddy bear. *Click.* The family eating slices of bread in front of a hut. *Click.* The father, wrapped in tefillin, saying morning prayers, swaying back and forth. *Click.*

And then a young woman, Fanny's age, wearing a French sweater and booties that Fanny had seen in a recent *Vogue.* This woman stood in a courtyard and simply stared at the sky. *Click. Click. Click.*

As Fanny knew only too well, money didn't always help. It could all be lost in an instant.

Where were these people in transit to? Were they safe?

The same questions for her too, she supposed.

She heard shouts in Polish, and it startled both the young women. The refugee turned and went inside.

Fanny kept her Leica by her side and discreetly snapped away at the guards who walked her way. They saw her, then pointed at their watches. *Your time is up.*

Fanny lowered her camera.

But she kept it out.

"Please, do you have a coat?" a teenage girl asked her. "We were barely allowed to bring anything with us from Germany."

Fanny took off her leopard skin. She placed it right on this girl's shoulders. The teenager began to cry.

The guard nodded at her. She had to go.

For now.

What would happen to these people, to these sudden prisoners of unfair laws? Would they be kept in this camp forever or sent across the world, to a country that they never chose and had no connection to? She needed to help them. She needed to stay in Poland—to work, plan, and fight. And with Zosia by her side, she could do anything!

She wrapped her scarf around her body, took a deep breath, put her Leica away, and headed out the gate.

That's when the guard grabbed her bag and smashed it to the ground.

Like at a wedding, the glass of the lens shattered all over her shoes.

PART 3

Warsaw, 1939

Two Polish Jewish women pose in their furniture shop.

CHAPTER 32

Zosia

THE SUN'S RAYS WERE HOT AND DIRECT, BURROWING RIGHT through the azure sky. Zosia smelled cut grass and dirt; the Passover dishes had been put away to hibernate for the year. The flu epidemic that had halted Warsaw to the ground that winter, sickening 130,000 people in the capital alone—the worst epidemic in years—was finally over. It was whole-scale spring, and it took her by surprise. She'd been so busy she'd barely been able to think about the next hour, let alone the next day, let alone the weather. But today's event was important.

Around her, people were digging ditches on the sides of the road. Civilians had volunteered to help the soldiers. The signs of impending war, the sense of unrest, was thick in the air. Varsovians were mentally getting ready for a potential repeat of the Great War, with men joining forces and considering where to run if needed. Back in the winter, the leaders of the Warsaw Jewish community had declared a month of mourning in response to a large-scale and organized two days of anti-Jewish riots all across Germany in which Nazis, SS troops, and ordinary civilians torched and vandalized more than one thousand synagogues, as well as Jewish homes, schools, hospitals, and cemeteries. Thirty thousand Jewish men were arrested and taken to camps. The police were told not to intervene. Fire companies stood by synagogues in flames with explicit instructions to let the buildings burn. An unfathomable ninety-one Jews were murdered. Zosia sighed and pushed aside the thought for now. How badly she wanted to be far away from all this, and yet there was so much work to do.

In the past months, Zosia had been busy at Dror. After apologizing for her dishonest behavior, she'd moved her few belongings back into Dzielna and threw herself into teaching and organizing; she finally became involved in the movement's large and impassioned theater group where she'd tried her hand at directing. She had realized that Dror's answers weren't always right, but they were the best answers she had for now. It hadn't been easy, but she'd found a way to merge her Dror family and her birth family: She'd gone back to Byten several times to help with the grocery and to attend Bella's wedding. She'd trained her new brother-in-law, Berl, to take over the store.

As always, she glanced at the headlines as she passed by newsstands. Her stomach turned as she read about Hitler's conquests and demands. A mutual help agreement between France and Poland had just been signed in Paris, weeks after Chamberlain promised that Britain would help Poland in case of an attack. Then there were the rallies hosted by the new far-right government here in Poland; the main opposition parties had boycotted the election and the Camp of National Unity won by a wide margin, unsurprisingly. If only she could write the news . . . right the news.

She wanted to leave Europe more than ever. And yet.

Now she was on her way to the Tarbut School. The movement had asked her to give a talk about her article, addressing the annual Warsaw gathering, a meeting for all the leftist Zionist groups held before comrades went off to summer retreats and camps. At first, she'd wanted to decline; she was still upset that this woman for whom she'd risked her own hopes had not risked it in return. Sure, the leader was flawed like we all were, but to understand was not the same as to forgive. However, she reminded herself, in these extreme times, politics were bigger than Wanda, bigger than Zosia, and Zosia decided to box her personal feelings and say yes. Frankly, Zosia deserved this honor.

Less than an hour later, she found herself in the auditorium about to go onstage. Summoning strength from her days on the kitchen stool, not to mention the stand-up campaign and her rollicking performance as Fanny's manager, she walked to the podium where she was introduced as "Zosia, our Mamaleh." Hundreds of faces looked up at her; it was her largest audience yet, filled with the intense students of Bialystok and the rebellious Vilnians. The Jews of Poland, she thought, may have a thousand different opinions, but ultimately they were a strong community. Her stomach fluttered and her breath caught in her throat, but she pushed on and told Wanda's story. After that, she talked about Masada, when the Jews, refusing to give in to their assimilators, chose the ultimate sacrifice and committed mass suicide. What did it mean to sacrifice oneself? Was it brave or self-defeating? Had they gone too far or were they the ultimate heroes?

A young woman raised her hand: "What do *you* think?"

Zosia cleared her throat. "I'm not sure." She could be scared and still be a leader. Brave people felt fear but moved forward regardless. "In the past, I may have declared them heroes. But now, I understand that the privilege to live is precious. Maybe Masada was too extreme. Couldn't they compromise? Then again, why should they have had to compromise?" *The gray zones.* "I am trying to hold ambivalence, to respect complication and nuance." Zosia noted the irony: She'd learned how to perform and also how to be honest, two opposites rolled into one. Maybe we were all imposters to some degree; after all, as part of a mutual society, imposter-ness might just be a healthy manifestation of collective doubt.

Then, as if mocking her celebration of complication: Abram. He was standing at the back of the hall. Her heart did a lutz, still.

After the applause, she made her way to him. "What are you doing here with us Zionists? Shouldn't you be at Bundist conferences now?"

"I'm learning from the best." He smiled.

She was going to leave, he was going to stay, she reminded herself. But that was all in the future . . . for now, she could be in the moment.

"Come, let's go for sardines," he said.

Zosia laughed. "I'd love to."

A WEEK LATER, ZOSIA LOOKED UP TO THE SKY. SHE WAS headed toward a huge event, one of the biggest of the season. Fanny had at first asked to meet her at the brand-new Kino Napoleon, a luxury cinema with a grand balcony and purple upholstered armchairs decorated with golden N's that served expensive coffees. *I don't drink expensive coffees,* Zosia had said. Fascism was in the air, and on the ground, yet the Warsaw arts scene was booming. Movies, theater, an explosion of music—it was almost as if the political tension catalyzed robust creative output. *Fine,* Fanny had said. *Even better, let's meet at the balloon competition.*

Zosia had some news.

Around the bend of the field, Zosia could already make out crowds. Ballooning was a matter of Polish pride, especially as everyone geared up for Poland to host the Gordon Bennett Cup in September. How would she find Fanny here?

Then, right above her: the first balloon. Red and orange. Rising into the sky like a flame. A lantern. A shingle of hope. *Click,* Zosia thought.

"Fanny!" She saw her, pointing her Leica. Fanny turned toward her. "Take the photo!" Zosia urged.

She did.

"Click," they both said, raising their eyebrows and looking at each other. It had become a joke.

Zosia helped Fanny with her work whenever she could. Fanny had stopped going to university; she would not sit in any Jew bench, she would never be allowed into the art show, and she could not for the life of her see the point in suffering for a degree in French. Fanny had placed her energies elsewhere and started her own photography business. Fanny's recording of the Jewish refugees at the camp had led to assignments for various newspapers. She'd been taking photographs of rallies, train accidents, new rail lines, and municipal elections. She'd also decided to do her own "work show." She'd learned that forty-five percent of the Jewish workforce in Poland were women, and she began to chronicle them in their workplaces, showing how labor created one's identity.

And then, there were the photos of scrawny, pale children. In the Jewish Quarter, she'd begun to document the youngsters selling soft drinks on the sidewalk outside the ice-cream store; the lines of mothers waiting at the social services office, begging to get their children into a summer camp program so they could eat regularly and breathe fresh air for a few weeks. Poland suffered; there was no end to the people who needed help, no end to the help they needed.

"Well," Zosia said. "This is quite something."

"I knew you'd love a race," Fanny answered.

"I'd love competitive ballooning?" Zosia raised an eyebrow. "I need to tell you something. Actually, two things. That's why I wanted—"

"What is it already?"

"Wanda might be released."

"Might?"

"Yes. Apparently, for good behavior. It's good, it's—"

"I wouldn't get my hopes up, but we can pray. She owes you a favor."

"She certainly does," Zosia said. "And you too."

"Did you know she's doing political work *from* prison," Fanny said. "She's fighting for the improvement of prisoners' conditions and for better relationships with the wardens. Hitler wants to conquer half the world, and she's advocating for workers' rights. What will happen to her in jail if war breaks out?"

"What will happen to any of us?" Zosia asked in a hushed tone.

"Mamo is harassing me to get out of Poland this summer, to meet them at Avigdor's Hungarian escape, but I refuse. Not everyone can just elope, sell off their art nouveau armoires, pick up, and leave. I need to stay and fight. For Wanda, for the refugees, for all Jews. I need to be here to take pictures and tell stories."

Zosia listened, proud of her friend for being so determined. But her own thoughts strayed to her date the other night with Abram. After her lecture, they'd gone to a small café and had talked about the future, about how they would weather the storms of these strange times. Would he ever consider moving to Eretz?

Oh Zosia, he'd shaken his head, *we'll never get papers, not now.*

One must hope! she'd countered. *Jewish self-determination is more important than ever.*

So be determined here, he'd said.

How? she'd wondered, and noted that he hadn't outright said no . . .

She'd smelled his cologne, a scent of excitement. He squeezed her hand. She tingled all over. He put his arms around her back and kissed her firm and hard on the lips. He tasted like cigarettes and sweat. His stubble rubbed her skin, all sandpaper and smoke. Though he'd pecked her good night before, this was new, a rare moment of passion, and it caught her off guard. He let her go, though he kept hold of one of her hands. She'd had to take a moment to catch her breath. Her feet fluttered in her shoes. She'd felt slanted off slope.

"Abram kissed me," Zosia blurted now. Fanny had told her many times that she approved of them, had even helped set them up, but still.

"It's about time." Fanny hugged Zosia. "Mazel tov to you! Maybe it will be a nice fall wedding?"

"Oh please." Zosia blushed. "We just kissed."

"But it's love," Fanny teased. "I can tell."

Maybe.

"Peas in a socialist pod," Fanny went on. "Just like me and Simon."

At that, both women burst out laughing. Fanny had spent weeks panicking about and dreading returning the ring to the Brodaszes. She'd finally plucked up the courage and, escorted by Zosia who waited around the corner, rang their doorbell. "Oh,"

Mrs. Brodasz had said, surprised and also confused, and she traded the ring for an envelope. "I'm so sorry." The letter had already been opened. Fanny slipped out its contents: a missive from Simon. He'd decided to stay in New York. *Contact me if you ever come over this way,* he'd written. "I guess that's a wrap." Fanny had laughed in relief. Mrs. Brodasz had never quite made sense of it all.

Perhaps he'd been right, Zosia wondered, to have stayed far away.

"September weddings are the best," Fanny said. "The best weather. Plus, the days between Yom Kippur and Sukkot are not just holy but super holy. Sunday, September 24, 1939. I'm already ordering the fish."

"Before you get too carried away, I need to tell you my second thing," Zosia said.

"I think we're on number eight or nine already."

"I was given a new role at Dror. I am now a national leader, alongside Mira. The chances of my getting a visa are higher. Much higher."

"What does that mean?"

"I will probably not be here by September twenty-fourth," she said. "I will most likely be on a ship well before that. Eretz Israel may not be a dream after all. It could be any minute now."

"Oh." Suddenly Fanny grabbed her and hugged her tight. "It will be alright," Fanny said. "We'll write letters, visit each other. We will reside in each of our memories, in our hearts."

Just then, like fireworks at a festival, a whole sky burst into color: Red, blue, green, and yellow stripes and checkers. Nineteen thirty-nine: the beginning of the rest of her life. The future.

The women of Warsaw craned their necks to see the balloons that floated above them, bobbing in the air, delving into the sky, and eventually disappearing from sight, forever.

"All emigration to Mandate Palestine has been postponed," comrade Yossi told her a few weeks later as she entered the workroom at Dzielna. He threw the paper on her desk. "*The New White Paper Approved.*" Jewish immigration to Palestine will be extremely limited. With the threat of looming war and a desire for stability in the region, the British were rolling back on their commitment to establishing a Jewish state. She'd been mentally making plans for visiting Byten to say farewell to family, as well as making plans for seminars to give once she reached Eretz. Of course, Zosia had known this could be coming—the greatest restriction on Jewish immigration yet. But somehow, a little naivete had crept under her skin these past months. She'd come to believe, against the odds, that maybe this time she would actually be gone.

"Postponed?" she asked. The air was warm with early summer. A tear careened down her right cheek. She let it drop into her collar before wiping her face. "Or canceled?"

"Postponed," he said. "I know it's hard, but you have to have faith."

It's alright. She'd been through this before, and if 1939 wasn't her year to leave, well then, 1940 would be. In the meantime, she had a full life here in Poland, where she was needed. She flashed to Abram. She had to have hope.

"On the plus side, Dror has selected you, Zosia, to be a delegate at the Twenty-first World Zionist Congress. You will be part of the global movement electing officials, deciding on annual policy, determining how funds will be allocated, and, of course, contributing to the main discussion this year: how to respond to this British White Paper."

"Me?"

"Yes," he said. "In August. I'll be there too. Turquoise lakes, charming architecture, fancy stores, and manicured lawns. Have you ever been to Geneva?"

"No, I haven't," Zosia said. She'd only ever left the country once before on a youth camp mission to Lithuania. "I may enjoy the scenery." Fanny had rubbed off on her . . . "I look forward to it."

"To Geneva!" He nodded his head, as if to say, *It will all work out.* "To Geneva."

CHAPTER 33

Fanny

August 25, 1939. This time of year was always strange to Fanny, how the air still sat heavy and warm, but the sun sunk earlier and earlier. Evenings were balmy, despite the dark that hinted at the fall to come.

On her way home, Fanny passed the bustling audience that waited outside the Warsaw Yiddish Art Theater's popular operetta *Shulamis*, before approaching the orange sellers on Smocza Street, as she'd been doing since moving into the neighborhood. She stopped to wish them a good evening but halted at the sight of their fruits: the oranges looked wrinkled and dry, and there were so few of them. Warsaw was changing, she felt it in that instant. The city, the whole country, was going forward and backward at the same time.

Outside her building, Fanny noticed a small leaf on the pavement in front of her. It was green, yet dead. This leaf had not gone through the normal stages of decline; it had fallen before its time. *Click.*

At last, she opened the front door to her building and headed to "the Jew door," as she and Zosia called it, and let herself into her home.

Home: a place to store one's secrets.

Inside, she placed her camera bag and keys on a small crate. A string of prints hung above her like a bunting. These were photos of a Bundist rally against the authoritarian government she'd taken a few days earlier: She'd shot the scene from the edge of the roof of a nearby building, sprawled across a brick like a sniper. She was lucky she hadn't fallen. She shuddered when she thought of the risk she'd taken, the precarious position that she'd literally put herself in, but reminded herself that she was working for a reason—she'd been pulsing on adrenaline, fueled by a sense of duty.

Fanny pushed away boxes of clothes with the side of her foot in her attempt to cross the room to her worktable. She owned so much stuff . . . What did one really need to start a new life? Her camera bag, a few pairs of underwear, a toothbrush . . . Then, from one open box, she pulled out the most gorgeous pink Angora cardigan, with shiny beige buttons. She brushed it to her face, soft like love. Could she help those in need and at the same time be taken by an exquisite jumper?

No, probably not. The world was falling apart, the Polish army was being mobilized; in Moscow, French, British, and Russian negotiations were ending—and she was flirting with organza? She threw the chemise into her rubbish bin.

At her worktable, the ticket stared her in the face.

Mamo had left for Avigdor's Hungarian home a few weeks earlier; prior to departing she'd bought a train ticket for Fanny. A ticket to England. *Lay low for a bit*, Mamo had told her, and handed her the slim envelope. *Please.* It had sat on Fanny's worktable.

"Look at me now, Mamo!" Fanny said to herself but out loud. "I'm an artist. I've done fine on my own without your schemes."

She took the ticket and threw it in the rubbish bin too.

It landed right on top of the sweater.

Fanny had to get to work.

Wanda had not been released as hoped, and Fanny was preparing for a second exhibition of photographs of Wanda's imprisonment, to be held at the Bund headquarters—a larger show than her previous mad-dash effort. Her hope was that more awareness might incite a retrial for all the women. Fanny had developed dozens of photos and needed to select the most compelling pictures. She pulled up her stool and began flicking through images: Which ones were immediately arresting and which revealed themselves over time, asking a viewer to look more deeply? There was her speech at the trial . . . oh, and the one of the jail door in Przemyśl, the visitors' entry that opened onto that small, winding street.

And then, falling from the pile, the one she'd shown at her own exhibit, from that very first night in the university when Wanda went missing, the "Nothing" she'd taken of the outside, the all-black shot that Zosia had told her was ridiculous. Fanny smiled to herself, thinking how far she had come since then. She stared at the photo some more, finding texture in the murkiness. Suddenly, something in the photo irked her. The bottom left corner. She saw the vague outlines of . . . *herself.* It was her reflection in the window, disappearing into the darkness.

Fanny grabbed her camera and took a photo of her own photo. As she pressed *click*, she felt shivers run through her. It was a Russian doll of photography . . . she saw herself seeing herself . . . Her shivers intensified until her whole body began pulsating and she sensed the foreboding in her own self-portrait. It was the same feeling she'd experienced at the trial, that she was perched on a fault line and the quake was imminent. Fanny understood the danger, just as Zosia had taught her. Zosia, who was now in Geneva for a conference . . . It dawned on Fanny: Surely, she wouldn't come back to Poland, not now. She'd always wanted to leave. She'd always known. She would find a way out.

Relationships depend on two people. Her father's words echoed in her mind. Suddenly, Fanny was eight years old again, and Papa came into the kitchen to kiss her goodbye before he left for work. She was eating English porridge, as Mamo had insisted Nanny serve her, rather than Polish sausage and eggs. *Goodbye, Papa,* she said, his sad smile implanting in her mind. He kissed her forehead. *Goodbye, sweetheart.*

Fanny looked at the ticket perched on top of the trash. No, she did not want her mother to save her . . . Then again, she had learned to stand up to Mamo, to be her own woman. Besides, not everything had to be about standing up to her mother. Why was she still so obsessed with rejecting Mamo? That in and of itself was what gave Mamo power over her.

At the end of the day, Fanny knew, we are of our parents . . . her mother was her.

You'll help more people from the outside, Zosia would tell her. *Leave, and tell the story.*

Fanny grabbed a few of her photos, her camera, and a toothbrush. From the rubbish bin, she picked up the pink sweater and with it, the England ticket. Then, she looked around her studio. Maybe, she thought, only once you really found your true home, could you leave it. Then she headed toward the train station. "Onward."

CHAPTER 34

Zosia

THE TRAIN RUMBLED INTO THE STATION. ZOSIA HAD MADE A decision—*the* decision—and now, as the sites went from a high-speed blur to in-focus city, she felt the weight of it. She felt calm.

Zosia also felt grateful. The train journey had taken twice as long as normal, two full days, with extended stops at every border crossing, *passports, documents,* barking dogs. Europe was on the fritz, off-kilter, faltering on the edge of the beam, locking down. She was lucky she'd made it.

Now that she approached her final destination, Zosia exhaled and thought back to her last hours in Geneva, to how she'd trotted out the hotel's front door, carrying her trusty bag, with her "nice" skirt and blouse (selected by Fanny), and, in the thin front pocket, the golden ticket. To Milan.

She had walked quickly, barely able to breathe, ingesting the notion that she was taking the risk, going to Palestine. Finally! *And you, loyal western winds / Carry my ship to the shore / As my heart, with eagle's wings / Has so longed for.*

Outside in Geneva, the golden sun had lit the treetops like halos. A universe of angels. How could the world be such a mess and yet be so beautiful? How could a crack run so deep and yet the surface brim with beauty? The lake shimmered, the roofs glistened, the dew sparkled.

Click, click, click, she'd thought. Fanny, she'd felt, was everywhere, all around her.

But. *She hadn't said goodbye.*

On those pristine Swiss sidewalks, she'd stopped in her tracks. What had she learned this past year? To trust her gut. To let herself feel her emotions. To make decisions based not on fear but on desire. She learned that running doesn't necessarily solve the problem. Horrors are everywhere but so is hope. Poland needed her. Her people needed her. She was a leader now; she had a responsibility to care for Poland's Jews, to defend them on the front lines. Then she thought of Bella's wedding, how her sister had clutched her clammy hand as they danced the hora in a woman's circle, around and around, step behind, step together, all hope and connection, circling into the sunset. Zosia needed both of them: her birth family and her chosen family. Fanny, Abram. Together they would weather the storms of these strange times. She hadn't said goodbye because she hadn't wanted to. She needed to move forward. To run *toward*. Zosia would stay and fight. And, maybe, just maybe, she would have a wedding, on one of those auspicious afternoons between the holiest days.

And so, Zosia had turned. She'd run back across the street, to the hotel, breaking a sweat, up the stairs, to the third floor, to her room. She hadn't locked the door, thank God, they hadn't cleaned it yet, thank God, thank God, and there it was.

Zosia had flung herself to the desk and grabbed it—the ticket back to Warsaw.

Now, the train jolted to a stop in the city that finally belonged to her. Golden Warsaw.

She couldn't wait to tell Fanny she was back. She would head straight to her studio . . . and maybe, just maybe, she'd stop in on the Bund on the way, see if Abram was there . . . Then, to Dzielna, to her room.

"Welcome home, Zosia," she said out loud as she grabbed her trusty old bag. She was changed, she was new, and she smiled, ready for all that was to come.

This is when she heard the radio announcement. *Nazis invade Poland: This Means War.*

EPILOGUE

Brooklyn, 2018

"Good evening. Thank you all so much for coming out in the rain. I know people have traveled here tonight from Manhattan, from Canada, and even from New Jersey. [Laughter] I so appreciate you all being here. Please enjoy the Sugarfina treats.

"As curators, we work in the realm between art and criticism, between creativity and context. It's hard to put all our thoughts into words since we live in the liminal space between objects and text; we balance on a thin line that connects verbal and visual media. Sometimes, the curator has an overarching thesis; at other times, we suggest at stories, encouraging you to find your own.

"As granddaughters, on the other hand, we live in a space between fact and fiction, or perhaps, heart and hand. Who are these figures we both know intimately and yet don't know at all? We have guttural knowledge of their touch, their palm imprinted on our cheek, their wrinkle lines scattered with toast crumbs, and yet we have so little sense of their youths, of their lives outside us, outside *our* existence. What of one's Bubbie (that's Yiddish for "grandmother") can we really understand? How can fragments narrate a past? How is ancestral memory formed?

"Tonight, please welcome me in opening this show about my grandmother, Fanny Zelshinsky Zucker. Or should I say, this show *by* my grandmother, the photographer, Fanny Zelshinsky Zucker. (Or perhaps, Fanny Zelshinsky . . . She wasn't married when she took these photos.) Today would have been her hundredth birthday. She had a strange love of birthdays, and on our last one together, just weeks before she died two years ago, she insisted on taking me to Le Bernardin and then the MoMA. She may have spent her life living in Queens, but she liked Midtown dining and museums, contemporary but classic. She liked things that were *good kvality.* [Laughter]

"During that final ladies' lunch, I had no idea that she would leave me so soon. I also had no idea about her oeuvre. Sure, she had mentioned that she had once liked to take pictures. She stored a couple in a cardboard box, from Poland, that she showed me once every few years, when I was in the mood to understand her, to see her, and even then, only when I begged. They were beautiful, certainly, and seemed somewhat random: a woman putting on lipstick in a mirror, reflections cascading off an ashtray, and a group of refugees. *Could these quick showings have influenced my entire career choice?* I have wondered more than once. Upon her death, I found in her closet more than just that box; there was a whole collection of her photographs, dozens of pictures of Poland in the years just before the war. I would like to take this opportunity to thank the former Castel Gallery in Paris, which, it seems, sent them to Zelshinsky in 1956.

"But I am getting ahead of myself. First let me tell you a bit about my Bubbie. Fanny Zelshinsky was born in Warsaw in 1918 to an affluent and assimilated Jewish family who worked in the *shmateh* business (that's textile industry, for you goys out there). [Laughter] Her mother's family had owned a large sugar refinery. She studied at gymnasium and began a degree at Warsaw University where she was accepted despite Jewish quotas. She never finished her degree, presumably because of the war, but we're not sure. Zelshinsky (I'll use a surname, to treat her as I would any other artist who was not my maternal grandmother who changed my diapers) began taking photographs as a teenager; she was particularly interested in fashion and photographed fashion shows at Warsaw's Fashion Café. (Warsaw fashion—or even cafés—who would have thought?) [Laughter] Bubbie always loved "a nice blouse" but who knew that she'd been a fashionista?

"Fanny fled Warsaw just days before the Nazis attacked. Bubbie crossed Europe pretending to be Christian—apparently, she spoke a fine Christian Polish and she was fluent in French. She ended up in Liverpool, and eventually came to the USA. She spoke so little of all this, keeping it locked tight under her baby oil–cleansed skin (which she swore by until the day she died) that it's hard for me to piece together her story. I only know anecdotes that don't add up to a full arc. Admittedly, it is very hard for me now to understand why I never asked her more. Instead, I have tried to piece together her biography through interviews, testimonies, hours of googling and searching archives, and chats with my own mother, who also knows remarkably little. I was also helped by fellow family historians, including one Nora Pomerantz, who I will introduce shortly. Perhaps due to her survivor's guilt, perhaps out of a desire to start fresh, Zelshinsky never talked about her photography or showed her work. Even to her family.

"Now, it's true, from time to time my grandfather asked her to show us her art, but she invariably brushed him off. My grandparents knew each other back in Poland too, before the war, but they re-met here in New York in 1947. My grandfather's story is remarkable, and one day, I will have to find a way to give him his own show, though he also did not speak about his life all that much. But, briefly, what I understand: He also grew up in Poland—I think outside Warsaw, and then in Warsaw—in a working-class family. My grandmother never let him forget that! As a teenager, he became a member of the Bund, a working-class, socialist, Diasporic Yiddish political group. [Cheers] I see we have some Bundists here tonight. You folk always show up . . . Thank you for coming . . . With them, Abram fought in the Warsaw Ghetto Uprising. He helped blow up an entrance to the ghetto so the Nazis were pushed out. He survived in hiding after that, somehow. He came to the USA on a ship and was involved in New York's Yiddish world, editing magazines. One day, at a concert, he happened to meet my grandmother. They were so shocked and delighted to find each other alive; they got married and had three children and eight grandchildren, including yours truly. Shout-out to my cousins Tamar and Anna for being here tonight! It's always been funny for me to think of my grandfather, Zaidy Abe Zucker—who watched daytime TV while snoring *and* awake, as having been a Nazi fighter. [Laughter]

"My grandfather became a plumber—a successful one at that—and Bubbie became a housewife. They settled in Queens. Fanny lived a quiet life. She cooked, she cleaned, she loved buying clothes at Filene's Basement and drinking sweet tea. She was an archetypal "Bubbie." She used to get so upset when someone talked down to her, implying that Eastern Europe was uncivilized. *Queens is so sophisticated?* she would ask. *I don't see a National Opera here.* New York, however, had welcomed her, had saved her, had given her a family and love. She lived it, she loved it. But, truthfully, I never saw her touch a camera, not even once. She never talked about her life in Warsaw.

"I investigated the Castel Gallery, which no longer exists, but it appears that the gallery miraculously received a shipment of photos from one Avigdor Radetsky from Hungary in the early years of the war. I believe they even showed Fanny's work at some point in the early 1950s. Mr. Radetsky was the second husband of Fanny's mother; I suppose that makes him my step-great-grandfather. Bubbie Fanny never talked about him either. It appears she left many of her photos in one of his buildings; Avigdor had been a wealthy man at one point. One of his workers managed to send them to the countryside estate in Hungary where he'd been living with my great-grandmother, Lenore. He'd then sent a few to a gallerist in Paris who had tracked down Fanny after the war. We're not exactly sure how many of Fanny's—I mean, Zelshinsky's—works survived nor how many more there were that didn't, but it's a miracle that we have what we have. Avigdor and my great-grandmother Lenore were murdered at Auschwitz in 1944.

"I have already said way too much. I'm glad we are standing here among Zelshinsky's thrilling, intense works and that you have been able to look at them while I've been talking. I hope their energy makes its way into your souls, as I know my Bubbie would have wanted. When I found the boxes of her works, it was shocking and overwhelming. There were so many: representational, abstract, political, fashion. But what I noticed when looking through them was a recurring motif. Two women—working, playing, creating, window-shopping. Why always two? Are these women mirrors of each other, or do they represent a split screen, a duality within the self, a what-if; the path not taken? Copies or opposites? Or both? In this show, which does not at all focus on the Holocaust but on *life* in Poland, I opened each of the three rooms with a large photo of two women that I felt set the tone. I invite you to fill in the blanks.

"But first! A few more words—and fascinating ones. I managed to track down one Dr. Nora Lipschitz. Nora is the granddaughter of the sister of the woman who introduced my parents—the matchmaker! Nora is a pediatrician who has spent a lot of time researching her family history. I came across her excellent website during my own research. I invited her here tonight, and we are so very fortunate that she agreed to come and speak. All the way from Toronto, please give a warm welcome to Dr. Nora Lipschitz."

"Thank you so much, Faith, for inviting me—what an honor. And thank you all for coming. I'm actually from Montreal, not Toronto, but you are forgiven! I know it's all the same to Americans, but trust me, you *don't* want a Toronto bagel . . . [Laughter]

"Alright, so, let me explain who I am. My grandmother, Bella Tarnovsky Lipschitz, was a young newlywed in the Polish town of Byten when war broke out. Her new husband—my grandfather, Berl—happened to have a brother in the east of the country, near Russia, and he convinced Bella to leave her parents and flee east. Her father had been injured in a pogrom not long before and Bella hadn't wanted to abandon them, but eventually she relented. Bella and Berl ended up in Russia and were forced to live in a Siberian labor camp through the duration of the war. But they survived. By the way, this is how two hundred thousand of the three hundred thousand Polish Jews who survived made it through the war, even though we never hear about this.

"My grandmother had an older sister, Zosia. Oh, how she adored this sister. Her sister was part of the Labor Zionist youth movement and had moved to Warsaw to become a leader. That's also where she met Abram. He was a Zionist, so I'm not sure about the Bundist connection, but we'll have to figure that out later, Faith. [Laughter]

"In Warsaw, my understanding is that Zosia had a mentor named Wanda Petrovsky. She became a communist and was arrested. Wanda also knew Fanny, presumably through photography (she was a photographer too, as well as a communist) and Faith and I imagine that's how they met, and then that's how Fanny met Abram, though the circumstances are not entirely clear.

"But let me tell you a little bit about both of these remarkable women, especially because they appear in several of the photographs on display here. Wanda was arrested in the late 1930s for organizing factory strikes around Poland; communism was illegal at that time. She was arrested along with fifteen other female organizers and they were tried in a sham trial and sentenced to twelve years in prison. (Legend has it that Wanda convinced the judge to let her speak at the trial, and her hour-long talk was so moving that two days later the prosecutor brought her roses!) When the Nazis attacked and occupied Poland in September 1939, many of the prison guards fled, and Wanda took advantage of the confusion to escape while also leading a group of female prisoners out with her. Wanda joined the anti-Nazi underground movement, working for both Jewish and Polish-communist resistance groups. She sabotaged a weapons factory by leaving windows open so all the pipes froze and exploded. She became pregnant and gave birth by herself in a basement hiding spot. The baby died soon after, and Wanda became very depressed, but she kept fighting, eventually with the Kraków underground where she helped procure weapons to blow up a Nazi Christmas party. She was eventually caught and imprisoned in a Gestapo political prison where she was brutally tortured and killed. [Long pause]

"As for my great-aunt Zosia . . . She was a leader in the leftist-Zionist youth underground in the Warsaw Ghetto. During the war, she felt that the Zionist Party, and all the "adult" political parties, were too complacent about Nazi occupation, afraid to rock the boat, so she helped lead the youth movements to plan a revolt. She ended up working as a weapons smuggler; apparently, she was an excellent performer and extremely good at dressing up and pretending to be an upper-middle-class Polish woman. In this disguise, Zosia smuggled explosives into the Warsaw Ghetto for the uprising, in which she fought. Zosia was killed in Mila 18. Most of what I know about her is from unpublished testimonies by her fellow movement members, held in the archives at Yad Vashem. I believe she was also connected with Abram in the ghetto, based on a testimony he once provided for the Grushstein Archives, which I recently shared with Faith. It sounds like they were in different fighting groups but the groups remained linked through the two of them, and they spent a lot of time together, intimately, during the war.

"Both women are Jewish heroes.

"I am so grateful that Faith reached out to me and shared photographs of these incredible women from before the war. I am so honored that their lives are evoked in this show. I speak tonight in honor of Zosia's and Wanda's memories. As Faith said, please, go around, look, learn, and fill in whatever details we cannot. May their memories be blessings and inspirations. As the Labor Zionists said, *Chazak v'amatz*. Be strong and brave. Thank you."

"Thank you so much, Nora, for your beautiful words. It strikes me that here we are again, two women, two granddaughters, our paths converging for a moment to carry on the past.

"Oy vey, I've talked a lot, I know. Don't worry! I will end my remarks once and for all by mentioning this photo that's hung right behind me. It's unusual. You can tell from the mark on the back of the print; it was developed in England, I imagine when Zelshinsky was in Liverpool. It seems entirely out of place, and it made no sense until I saw that Fanny had scribbled its title on the back: *The Last Picture: A Picture of a Picture of "Nothing" (1938), 1939.* It's a Russian doll of darkness. Funny and self-aware, my Bubbie in 1939. It's so hard to imagine her without her thick upper arms, soft like silk. *We are of our mothers,* Fanny used to tell me and feed me potatoes. *The reflections and repetitions never end.* I never really knew what she meant until I kept staring at this picture. I noticed at the bottom left—and you can all see it—a mushroom-shaped smudge. *What is it?* I kept asking myself as I looked and looked. A fingerprint? The shadow of a lurker? But then I realized I could see someone in it.

"It was a reflection: mine.

"In all these photos on display here today, the women come and go, fold into each other, just like the past and the future. Are we living out their dreams? Or their nightmares? [Laughter] Like photography in the greatest sense, we are all copies of one another, the generations, and we don't even know it. We inherit our ancestors' naivete, but also their enormous strength. We share their insecurities, yet thrive through their passions. We live with their same fears, and forge ahead with their chutzpah. We *feel* so original, but time does nothing if not repeat. I hope you enjoy the show, *The Last Woman of Warsaw.*"

Author's Note

ON HISTORY—

Research and Further Reading

In our contemporary minds, historical Warsaw conjures images of gray and death. In 1938, however, headlines referred to its "epidemic of lunacy." Varsovians were obsessed with entertainment, and why not? The city overflowed with theaters, vaudeville, cabaret, fashion shows, and nightclubs with revolving dance floors and colorful cocktails. Josephine Baker performed her banana-clad dance to adoring crowds. A 1938 blockbuster exhibition focused on the city's future: A metro was coming! Fashion magazines called the city "the Paris of the north." Long before Vegas, Warsaw was the capital of neons, its night skyline dotted with glittering cocktail glasses and chefs carrying platters of roasts. Much of this artistic production was Jewish.

In *The Last Woman of Warsaw*, I hope to showcase the art, culture, and politics of interwar Warsaw, and to do so from the perspective of young Jewish women. As a historian who was rigorously trained to footnote, endnote, and strive for accuracy *über alles*, I feel compelled to share that this book is indeed fiction! All the characters and settings, and many of the storylines, are inspired by my research into real people and events that took place throughout the 1930s. But in order to paint as rich a world as possible and present it cohesively, as well as for the sake of narrative, I have collapsed time and altered some place names.

The characters in this novel are fictional, but their stories are informed by hundreds of women I researched for *The Light of Days* and I drew from their extraordinary personal accounts and testimonies as well as historians' works about them. Zosia's character is inspired by figures including Zivia Lubetkin, Frumka Płotnicka, Chajka Klinger, Bela Hazan, Gusta Davidson, and Tosia Altman, who were all leaders in various socialist–Zionist youth movements. I've borrowed tales from all their memoirs and biographies. Bella Gutterman's biography of Zivia Lubetkin, *Fighting for Her People*, begins in Geneva, a scene that truly moved me. I am indebted to her for this opening idea and for several anecdotes she shares from Zivia's life in Byten and later.

Fanny's character was inspired by Tosia Altman, Niuta Teitelbaum, Lonka Kozibrodska, and Anna Heilman, all of whom were either graduates of Warsaw University or from more affluent families. Fanny was also inspired by the Jewish photographer (and later Partisan) Faye Schulman and by the artists featured in *The New Woman Behind the Camera*, a fascinating exhibition that I saw at the Met in 2021.

Wanda was inspired in part by Zofia Chomętowska, a Polish female photographer well-known in the 1930s, but mostly I drew on the life story of Mire Gola (sometimes referred to as Gola Mire), a Jewish poet and activist who was expelled from her Labor Zionist youth movement for being a communist. The trial here (even the story about the roses!) was based on Mire's arrest and court case, which had occurred in 1936. While only a very small number of Polish-Jews were communists, Jews did make up a large minority of the Polish party. Communist activity was illegal in Poland and many underground communists were arrested in the interwar period; the Polish party was officially dissolved in 1938. I also want to note that in the 1930s, in Poland's universities, numerous women held the title of associate professor rather than professor, but their roles were beginning to grow. Photography was a burgeoning artistic practice in Poland in the 1930s, and several universities and institutes had photography departments. Photography courses were more likely offered at Warsaw's Academy of Fine Arts than at the University of Warsaw.

Though people generally think of pre-war Polish Jewry as a backwater, shtetl-based religious community, the Jews of interwar Poland (who comprised approximately ten percent of the country's population) were a diverse populace, ranging from impoverished to wealthy, ultra-religious to completely assimilated. In the 1930s, Warsaw had the largest Jewish community in all of Europe, second only to New York, and Jews made up roughly thirty percent of its population. (For context, right now, New York City is about eleven percent Jewish.) Here, Jewish tradition met Europe's secular enlightenment, ritual met modernity. The tram driver announced the stops by the name of the local Yiddish play ("*Dybbuk!*"). The thriving and sophisticated Jewish arts and culture scene was seen in the city's cafés, tangos (or Yiddish *tangelehs*), jazz shows, art exhibits, comedy, poetry, dance competitions, Miss Judaea beauty pageants, and a proliferation of Jewish intellectual views, artistic visions, professorships, and political parties (for instance, Zionist, Bundist, religious, Folkist, assimilationist), which each tried to address where the Jewish future lay, whether the community was best served by embracing democracy or authoritarianism, and whether Jewish identity should be tied to religious observance or secular culture. The movements established networks of organizations across Poland, from publications, schools, and libraries to youth movements, which ran summer camps, theater troupes, orchestras, and sports leagues, and provided Jewish youth with a sense of purpose, identity, and belonging.

Over 3,000 Jewish publications were produced in the country; Warsaw had 180 Jewish newspapers and magazines, including women's magazines that focused on gender issues, and—between the Realists who explored transformations in the shtetl to the Idealist symbolist poets and the modernist, expressionist The Gang—just about as many warring literary circles. In the interwar years, professional and amateur Yiddish theater companies performed in more than 400 Polish cities and towns, showing original works and adaptations that drew upon the stage techniques of European avant-garde and classics. Several important troupes in Warsaw staged canonical Yiddish dramas alongside the works of Shakespeare, Molière, and Eugene O'Neill. "Kleynkunst" theaters specialized in satirical and musical revues and cabaret; *smonzes* were a whole genre that poked fun at assimilated Jews; sophisticated marionette shows abounded. Finally, Warsaw had more than fifty movie theaters, including the luxurious Kino Napoleon that served a curated coffee selection. From 1910 to 1940, 170 Yiddish films (feature-length and short) were produced worldwide, about half in Poland. The first Jewish films starring Jewish actors were made in Warsaw. That is, all until 1939. The Nazis murdered ninety percent of Poland's Jews and, along with them, this creative culture.

The interwar period was also a progressive era for women. Jewish women were educated, emancipated, and employed. Polish women had the vote in 1918 (before most Western countries); education was mandatory for boys and girls through eighth grade; women were admitted to university (the majority were Jewish). Jewish women worked and comprised nearly half the Jewish labor force, even though their earnings were not equal to men's. Related, they married in their late twenties and early thirties and had fewer children. Jewish women were poets, novelists, journalists, shopkeepers, lawyers, and dentists. Polish culture celebrated female athletics and they played sports. Even their clothes favored comfort and movement. Young Jewish women, some of the first not to be match-made and pursuing love relationships, were learning to make their way in the modern world, fueled by neat haircuts, fitted blazers, and shorter skirts. (*"One could see the whole shoe!"* a satirist wrote at the time.) These women were ready to soar—figuratively and literally.

One hundred thousand young Jews were members of the youth movements in the 1930s; these organizations had great influence on day-to-day life and shaped Jewish culture in many small towns. Dror was one of the left-wing Zionist movements, but here I've combined elements of a few different groups to create a fictional version of Dror. (In reality, Dror was more a working-class group, and less strict about alcohol and sex, at least formally. As I've mentioned, Poland hosted dozens of Jewish political groups and their attendant youth movements; I've simplified party platforms and politics.) "Imposters" looking for visas to Mandate Palestine was an issue for the movement, but earlier in the 1930s, when more visas were available. (I have imagined how this issue was resolved.) To simplify: Visas for Jews had spiked in availability after the Balfour Declaration and the British commitment to creating a Jewish homeland in Palestine, but since the swell of German emigration from 1935, and the Arab Revolts that began in 1936, the allotted number had decreased and they'd become much, much harder to obtain. Group morale amongst the Labor Zionist movement was in crisis as the hope of emigration dwindled.

In describing Warsaw, a city that was mostly quite poor but also housed the wealthy, I was inspired by historical accounts. The descriptions of Warsaw—the castle, parks, bridges, boating club, cafés, cabarets, streets, museum exhibition, fashion shows, Josephine Baker's concert, theaters, movies, restaurants, upscale apartments, downscale apartments, shops, synagogues, and nightclubs—are all based on nonfiction accounts, though I did adapt dates and geography. (Hot-air ballooning was a popular event in Poland, but the race here is fictional.) The Fashion Café (which was actually called The Art and Fashion Café) was established in a former orangery. The street scenes, venues, political rallies, and parties are all based on historical accounts. Jabłkowski Brothers was known as Warsaw's Harrods.

Comedy-duo Dzigan and Schumacher had a cabaret theater in Warsaw, and their show *The Last Jew in Poland* was indeed censured by the police (though this occurred in 1939). The duo also played a "stunt" on a café owner pretending to be religious Jews (though this occurred at the Institute of Propaganda, Ziemiańska's rival café). Their dialogue is taken from historical accounts. Fat Jozek's existed, but it closed in 1932 after Josek dropped dead of a heart attack in the middle of the club. The personal ads that Natalia reads out loud were actually published at the time! Divorce was rare, and it wasn't always easy to find a rabbi who would grant a *get*, but it certainly happened, and Mamo and Papa's separation was inspired by a true story.

As mentioned, the Jews of Poland were multilingual, flipping between Polish, Yiddish, Hebrew, and for some, even German, Russian, and French. For ease of reading, I did not generally indicate which language the characters were speaking, but Fanny would have spoken Polish; Zosia and Abram would likely have talked to each other in Yiddish; within Dror the comrades likely used Yiddish and some Hebrew.

As for Poland's politics: After more than a century of occupation that ended with World War I, Poland was newly independent and filled with promise and the republic was negotiating its identity: The left aimed to celebrate its long-standing ethnic diversity; the right-leaning parties hoped for "purebred" nationalism. The country was a quasi-democracy—elections were held, but they were often chaotic and manipulated. When Jozef Piłsudski, Poland's authoritarian leader who was generally trusted by the Jewish community, died in 1935, he left a power vacuum and a state of political instability. An extreme nationalist and right-wing party, which wanted Jews out of Poland and whose platform was based in antisemitic slogans and values, many inspired by Nazi ideology, began to gain more power.

The anti-Jewish legislation mentioned in the novel—limiting professions, business deals, days of trade, and kosher ritual slaughter—occurred in the 1930s, as did campaigns that tried to fight them. Jewish quotas in education were not outright laws but were often practiced in Polish universities and in particular in "professional fields" like science, medicine, and engineering. Indeed, Jews were not allowed to dissect Christian cadavers and many young Jews left Poland to study. It was rare for a Jewish professor to maintain a university post due to quotas. Though I didn't address this in this in this novel, universities were temporarily shut down because of violent anti-Jewish riots; several Jewish students were attacked with razors and some were murdered. The Ghetto Benches were first instituted in Lodz in 1935 and were made official government policy in Warsaw in the fall of 1937; I fictionalized the date by a few months. The account of the Catholic-Polish professors who stood up against this ruling is based on a true story, as was the assassination attempt. The anti–Ghetto Bench campaign that I describe in this novel was fictionalized, but it was based on stories I read of campaign activity in Vilna. Around the country, Jewish students stood. The White Paper and immigration restrictions and the Polish elections and political platforms are based on real events. A violent pogrom in 1936 surprised the Jewish community, which hadn't been viciously attacked in years and hadn't realized how much antisemitism festered in the local population; this was my inspiration for the pogrom that hurt Tateh and traumatized Zosia's family (it did not occur in Byten). The citizenship law I refer to in the novel (that one lost citizenship if they lived outside the country for five years) passed in March 1938. The transit camp for expelled German Jews was established in the fall of 1938; 17,000 Jews with Polish citizenship were arrested in their homes and deported from Germany. The number of Jewish deaths released by German officials after Kristallnacht was ninety-one, but more recent scholarship suggests that hundreds of Jews were killed; many died of injuries in the weeks that followed the pogrom.

Despite all that, the year 1938 was considered by many to be a hopeful time. The economy finally seemed to be recovering from the disastrous Depression, and there were actually fewer anti-Jewish incidents than in previous years. Indeed, Poland's Jews had spent ten centuries finding their place in a country where they were "othered," but also were tolerated, emancipated, and thrived. They saw themselves as postwar, not pre-war, and they were producing reams of creative work during these changing times in which their position in the new republic was being negotiated. Jews were also navigating their own identity, defining their notions of selfhood, home, and future in an increasingly hostile Europe, often debating the best course of action when your country doesn't want you anymore. Jews lived in a moment of cultural flourishing and growing feminism alongside a tremendous spike in hate. I hope this book sheds light on the inner lives of the Jews who were murdered, presenting them not as victims of genocide but as relatable, modern people with passions and politics.

Further Reading

My research into this book began in 2007 when I accidentally came across the Yiddish book *Freuen in di Ghettos,* which led to my book *The Light of Days.* In my eighteen years of study on women and the Holocaust in Poland, I have read, listened to, and watched hundreds of testimonies by and about Jewish underground members, which also address their lives before the war. For those interested in reading more: My sources included books, articles, essays, testimonies, memoirs, novels, film footage, and photographs. Please see the extended bibliography included in *The Light of Days* for many relevant materials. Additional sources that were particularly enlightening about the 1930s period include: *The Jews of Poland Between Two World Wars,* edited by Yisrael Gutman, Ezra Mendelsohn, Jehuda Reinharz, and Chrone Shmeruk (1989); the exhibit at POLIN museum in Warsaw (and its catalog essay about the interwar period by Samuel Kassow); and *Image Before My Eyes* (1981) by Lucjan Dbroszycki and Barbara Kirshenblatt-Gimblett, a photography book and companion documentary (directed by Josh Waletsky). *Warsaw: The Cabaret Years* by Ron Nowicki (1992), and www.culture.pl are critical sources about the period's art and culture. *Poland's Threatening Other: The Image of the Jew from 1880 to the Present* by Joanna Beata Michlic and *Shtetl* by Eva Hoffman are illuminating, as is *Palestine 1936* by Oren Kessler. Dalia Ofer and Lenore J. Weitzman's *Women in the Holocaust* (in particular, "Part 1: Before the War") and *The Shalvi/Hyman Encyclopedia of Jewish Women* are main sources about Jewish women of the time. *The YIVO*

Encyclopedia of Jews in Eastern Europe provided significant historical context. Roman Vishniac's photography is an important record; additionally, I have drawn on photographs from the US Holocaust Memorial Museum, the Ghetto Fighters' House, and Poland's National Digital Archives collection (in particular, of fashion shows), as well as numerous in-person interviews and conversations with Michael Katz (who is the subject of *On Bonifratrow Street: How a Boy from Lwów Escaped the Nazis* by Mia Swart). I scoured for additional sources and a selection includes: *New Yorker* cartoonist Ken Krimstein's *When I Grow Up*, in which he illustrated excerpts from Jewish teenagers' essays from the time (and which has its own helpful recommended reading list); the *Forward*'s Zoom seminar about what pre-war Polish Jews ate for breakfast; and *Three Minutes: A Lengthening*, a documentary based on three minutes of family film from 1938 narrated by Helena Bonham Carter. I even tried a few recipes from the recently translated *Vilna Vegetarian Cookbook* by Fania Lewando. (I can't say that my children loved the savory-ish Passover cheesecake, but it was certainly "interesting.")

As for fiction . . . an astonishing amount of noteworthy Jewish literature was created in Poland in the interwar years. The vast majority of novels, short stories, and plays have not been translated into English; neither has most Polish feminist literature from the time. For those interested in reading more: One can find English translations of the works of the Singer siblings, novels by Maria Kuncewiczowa, Chana Blanksztejn's experimental short story collection *Fear*, which came out a few years ago, and a collection of Ephraim Kaganovski's stories, *Jewish Warsaw Between the Wars*, translated by Bracha Weingrod. *Sons and Daughters*, Chaim Grade's epic fictional reflection on the period written in the 1960s and 1970s, was recently translated into English by Rose Waldman. Anthologies like *A Treasury of Yiddish Stories*, edited by Irving Howe and Eliezer Greenberg, originally published in 1954, are indeed treasures. There is almost no contemporary fiction about this period but for the Polish novelist Szczepan Twardoch's vivid book *The King of Warsaw*, which was translated into English in 2020.

All four of my grandparents spent their young adulthoods in interwar Warsaw. In the late 1920s, when my paternal grandmother's family was trying to leave for Canada due to antisemitism, my Bubbe Annie threatened a visa officer with a knife, claiming she'd commit suicide in his office if he didn't sign the papers. In 1940, my maternal Bubbie Zelda stood in Nazi-occupied Warsaw's ration lines, where she understood the sheer depth of the Nazi threat and decided to flee, ultimately surviving the Holocaust in a Siberian gulag. Years later, when my grandparents first visited New York, they were impressed by the glitz but remarked, *"It's no Warsaw!"*

Interwar Poland was a locus of complicated identity struggles, with tensions between tradition and modernity and new notions of what it means to have a home and to be a people. I hope this novel helps to memorialize Warsaw's golden age of creativity, and the Jewish art and culture that, along with six million lives, was also decimated in the Holocaust. I hope to shed light on the agent and dynamic role of Jewish women in Poland before the Holocaust. It is crucial that we understand what a vibrant and sophisticated place Warsaw was, because only then we can understand that "they" are like "us," and what happened to their spirited, cosmopolitan world can so easily happen to ours.

Acknowledgments

It takes a metropolis . . . This novel would not exist without the support and inspiration of so many individuals. With bottomless thanks:

To my editor, Maya Ziv, for gallantly holding my clammy hand; for spending your weekends in interwar Warsaw; and for your mammoth wisdom, grace, and patience. Our *shidduch*, urged on by my mother's spirit, was for me *bashert*. To my agent, Alia Hanna Habib, for once again artfully fostering a project from its moment of inception (it was on a call with you in May 2021 that I spontaneously came up with this story . . . and here we are!). Thank you, both, for your above-and-beyond fervor and dedication, and time.

To the Hadassah-Brandeis Institute, for granting me the indispensable *Ilse Hertha Strauss Rothschild Research Award on Women, Gender and the Holocaust*, and for once again making a publication possible. To Antony Polonsky for your continued encouragement.

To Justina Vasquez, Nicole Jarvis, Lauren Morrow, Sarah Thegeby, Amanda Walker, Stephanie Cooper, John Parsley, Melissa Solis, Erica Rose, Erin Byrne, Lorie Pagnozzi, William Ruoto, Sarah Oberrender, Muriel Jorgensen, and the rest of the dream team at Dutton, for your diligence, sensitivity and savvy. To Rebecca Gardner, Will Roberts, Gabe Sherman, and the entire crew at Gernert, for always having my (aching) back. To Sophie Pugh-Sellers, for your clever suggestions.

To my forever readers, Leigh Abramson, Nicole Bokat, and Sarah Mlynowski, for offering invaluable insights on very early and very late drafts, and for nudging me along in between.

To the long list of knowledgeable individuals who helped me research *The Light of Days*. This "prequel" emerged from those years of work and I remain deeply grateful for your generosity. To my mentors and writing teachers over the decades, for sharing your sagacity.

To my wonderful, compassionate readers, for your smart questions which motivated so many of the ideas in this book.

To Zelda, Billie, and Bram, for your tolerance. What a nightmare to have an author for a mother! I promise, as soon as this book is done, I will make that salmon again. I totally love you.

To Jon, for everything (and especially, for years of ordering salmon).

To salmon, for fueling us all. (Don't worry, tuna, you too.)

To my late mom, who may have left me during an early draft but continued to give me notes in my head (as she always warned me she would . . .). This novel is, of course, for you.

Credits

All three photos in this book were taken in Warsaw from 1937 to 1939. The photo illustrating the Part 1 cover page, "Two young Polish girls look at a beauty parlor storefront in Warsaw" by Julien Bryan, is from the United States Holocaust Memorial Museum, Julien Bryen Archive, Collections No. 2003.214. The photo illustrating the Part 2 title page, "Pokaz mody w kawiarni Sztuka i Moda przy ulicy Królewskiej 11 w Warszawie" is from Poland's National Digital Archives, Reference No. 3/1/0/11/12591. The photo illustrating the Part 3 title page, "Two Polish Jewish women pose in their furniture shop," is from the United States Holocaust Memorial Museum, courtesy of Hank Federman, Collections No. 2005.392.

"You can be what you want, a Zionist, a Bundist, who cares? But Leibke, the time will come when even the most religious Jews will have to learn the Tango and the Charleston!" is from "Come, Dance, Leibke," a well-known song by the then famous Mordkhe Gebirtig (who was murdered in the Holocaust). This translation is from Samuel D. Kassow, "Oyf der yiddisher gas, On the Jewish Street, 1918–1939," *POLIN: 1,000-Year History of Polish Jews*, Museum Catalog, edited by Barbara Kirshenblatt-Gimblett, 2017, p. 228.

The Sea Song's (*Yam Lid*) Hebrew verse was originally written around 1100. Chaim Nachman Bialik translated it to Yiddish and adapted it. The music was published in 1917. This translation is my own.

The Almond Tree Is Blooming was written by Israel Dushman; the music was written in 1933. This translation is courtesy of www.hebrewsongs.com (https://www.hebrewsongs.com/?song=hashkediyahporachat).

Bal u Starego Joska (*A Ball at Old Josek's*) was written in 1934 and became well-known. This translation is my own.

"Love Forgives You Everything" was sung by the famous Hanka Ordonowna and written for the movie *Spy in a Mask,* which came out in 1933. This translation is from Culture.Pl. (https://culture.pl/en/article/10-quotes-from-classic-polish-love-songs).

About the Author

Judy Batalion is the author of several books of award-winning nonfiction, most recently *The Light of Days.* Judy's work has appeared in *The New York Times, The Washington Post, Vogue,* the *Forward, Salon,* the *Jerusalem Post,* and many other publications.

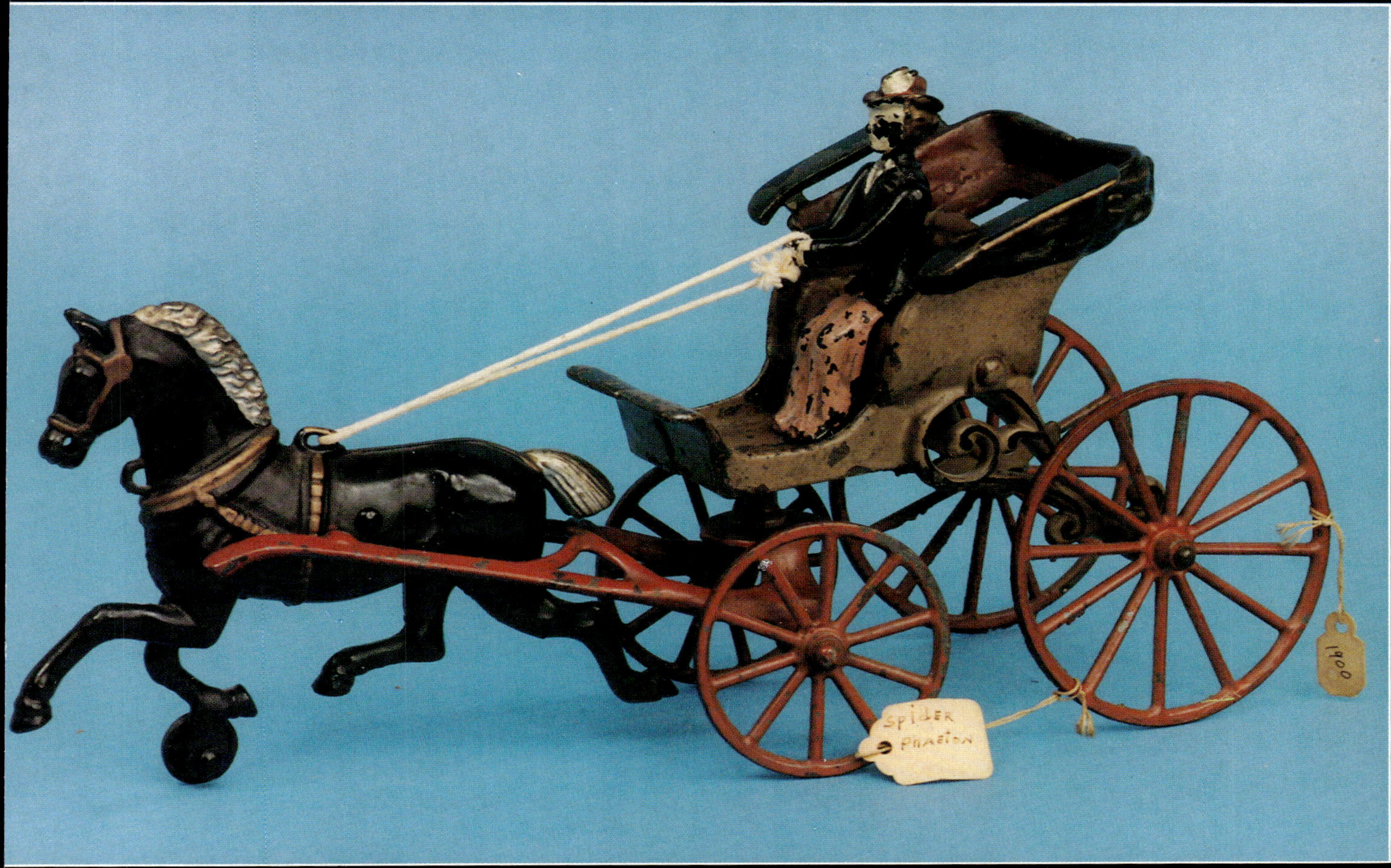

77 Lower Valley Road, Atglen, PA 19310